THE MYSTERIOUS BENEDICT SOCIETY

AND THE RIDDLE OF AGES

WRITTEN BY TRENTON LEE STEWART

ILLUSTRATIONS BY MANU MONTOYA

Megan Tingley Books
LITTLE, BROWN AND COMPANY
New York   Boston

Copyright © 2019 by Trenton Lee Stewart
Illustrations copyright © 2019 by Manuela Montoya Escobar
Text in excerpt from *The Secret Keepers* copyright © 2016 by Trenton Lee Stewart
Illustrations in excerpt from *The Secret Keepers* © 2016 by Diana Sudyka

Cover art copyright © 2019 by Manuela Montoya Escobar
Cover design by David Caplan
Cover copyright © 2019 by Hachette Book Group, Inc.

Hachette Book Group supports the right to free expression and the value of copyright. The purpose of copyright is to encourage writers and artists to produce the creative works that enrich our culture.

The scanning, uploading, and distribution of this book without permission is a theft of the author's intellectual property. If you would like permission to use material from the book (other than for review purposes), please contact permissions@hbgusa. com. Thank you for your support of the author's rights.

Little, Brown and Company
Hachette Book Group
1290 Avenue of the Americas, New York, NY 10104
Visit us at LBYR.com

Originally published in hardcover and ebook by Little, Brown and Company in September 2019
First Trade Paperback Edition: August 2020

Little, Brown and Company is a division of Hachette Book Group, Inc. The Little, Brown name and logo are trademarks of Hachette Book Group, Inc.

The publisher is not responsible for websites (or their content) that are not owned by the publisher.

The Library of Congress has cataloged the hardcover edition as follows:
Names: Stewart, Trenton Lee, author. | Montoya, Manu, illustrator.
Title: The mysterious Benedict Society and the riddle of ages /
by Trenton Lee Stewart ; illustrated by Manu Montoya.
Description: First edition. | New York ; Boston : Little, Brown and Company, 2019. |
"Megan Tingley Books." | Summary: "With the Ten Men on the
loose and a telepathic enemy tracking them, Kate, Reynie, Sticky,
and Constance must join with a new Society member to keep their world safe."
—Provided by publisher.
Identifiers: LCCN 2019009426| ISBN 9780316452649 (hardcover) |
ISBN 9780316452632 (ebook)
Subjects: | CYAC: Adventure and adventurers—Fiction. | Friendship—
Fiction. | Schools—Fiction. | Science fiction.
Classification: LCC PZ7.S8513 Mym 2019 | DDC [Fic]—dc23
LC record available at https://lccn.loc.gov/2019009426

ISBNs: 978-0-316-45262-5 (pbk), 978-0-316-45263-2 (ebook)

Printed in the United States of America

LSC-C

Printing 4, 2021

For Maren
—T.L.S.

Contents

In a city called Stonetown, on a quiet street of spacious old houses and gracious old trees, a young man named Reynie Muldoon Perumal was contemplating a door. The door, currently closed, belonged to his study on the third floor of one of those houses—in this case a gray-stoned edifice half-covered in ivy, with a magnificent elm tree in its courtyard and, surrounding the courtyard, an old iron fence quite over-grown with roses. From his study window Reynie might easily have been looking out upon that tree or those flowers, or he might have lifted his gaze to the sky, which on this fine spring morning was a lovely shade of cobalt blue. Instead, he sat at his desk in an attitude of attention, staring at the door, wondering who in the world could be standing on the other side.

For a stranger to be lurking in the hallway should have been impossible, given the fact of locked doors, security codes, and a trustworthy guard. Yet Reynie's ears had detected an unfamiliar tread. His ears were not particularly sharp; indeed, his hearing, like almost everything else about him, was perfectly average: He had average brown eyes and hair, an average fair complexion, an average tendency to sing in the shower, and so on. But when it came to noticing things — noticing things, understanding things, and figuring things out — "average" could hardly describe him.

He had been aware, for the last thirty seconds or so, of something different in the house. Preoccupied as he'd been with urgent matters, however, Reynie had given the signs little thought. The shriek and clang of the courtyard gate had raised no suspicions, for not a minute earlier he had spied Captain Plugg, the diligent guard, leaving through that gate to make one of her rounds about the neighborhood. Hearing the sounds again after he'd turned from the window, Reynie had simply assumed the guard forgot something, or was struck by a need for the bathroom. The sudden draft in his study, which always accompanied the opening of the front door downstairs, he had naturally attributed to the return of Captain Plugg as well. He had wondered, vaguely, at the absence of her heavy footsteps below, but his mind had quickly conjured an image of that powerfully built woman taking a seat near the entrance to remove something from her boot.

Too quickly, Reynie realized, when he heard that unfamiliar tread in the hallway. And now he sat staring at the door with a great intensity of focus.

A knock sounded—a light, tentative tapping—and in an instant Reynie's apprehension left him. There were people in Stonetown right now who would very much like to hurt him, but this, he could tell, was not one of them.

"Come in?" said Reynie, his tone inquisitive. There was no reply. He glanced at his watch, then at the clock on the wall, and then at the two-way radio that sat—silent, for the moment—on his cluttered desk. "Come in!" he called, more forcefully.

The doorknob rattled. Slowly turned. And at last the door swung open, revealing—as Reynie had by this point already deduced—a child. It seemed the most unlikely of developments, but the fact remained: The stranger was, of all things, a little boy.

"Well, hello," Reynie said to the boy, who stood grinning shyly with a hand on the doorknob, swinging the door back and forth. The boy's hair, very fine and black, was in a frightfully tangled state. His skin, of a light olive tone, was smudged here and there with a dark, oily substance, and stuck to various places on his shirt and trousers (both quite filthy) was the fur of at least two kinds of animal. But the boy's large eyes, so dark brown as to be almost black, were shining with excitement.

"I'm Tai," said the boy, still swinging the door back and forth. "I'm five."

Reynie feigned confusion. "Wait, which is it? Are you Tai or are you five?"

The boy giggled. "Both!" he said, letting go of the doorknob and approaching Reynie's desk in a rush. He drew up short, resting his hands on the edge of the desk and his chin on the back of his hands. "My *name* is Tai Li, and I'm *five* years *old*." He said this without lifting his chin from his hands, and thus with some difficulty.

"Oh!" Reynie exclaimed, with another glance at his watch. "I think I understand now. Well, Tai, my name is—"

"Reynie Muldoon!" the boy interrupted, with a delighted laugh. "I know who you are! I have a name that starts with *M*, too! My middle name does. I'm not going to tell you what it is, though. You have to guess."

"It isn't Muldoon?" Reynie asked, quickly moving the radio, which Tai had noticed and reached for.

"No!" said Tai, laughing again.

"Tell you what," Reynie said. "I'll make more guesses later. And I'll let you touch the radio later, too, okay? Right now it's important that we don't touch it. Right now we're expecting to hear from a friend—"

Tai gasped. "Is it Kate Wetherall? The Great Kate Weather Machine? Who always carries around a red bucket full of tools?"

Reynie raised an eyebrow. "Well...she used to, anyway. These days she's more of a utility-belt-and-secret-pockets kind of weather machine." A wistful expression crossed his face at this, like the shadow of a swiftly moving cloud. Reynie fixed the little boy with a curious gaze. "You seem to know an awful lot about us, Tai."

"You saved the world!" Tai whispered excitedly, as if he'd been bursting to let Reynie in on this secret but knew he wasn't supposed to.

"Oh, I wouldn't say the *whole* world," said Reynie with a

skeptical look. "And I assume you're talking not just about me, but—"

"All of you!" Tai whispered. "The four of you! And Mr. Benedict, and Rhonda, and Number Two, and Milligan..." Here the little boy frowned and consulted his fingers, counting off names in a whisper. He interrupted himself to scratch furiously at an itch on his arm, then began again.

"Hold that thought, Tai," said Reynie, and raising his voice, he said, "Intercom. Sticky's office."

A beep sounded from a speaker on the wall near the door, and Tai whirled to look. The speaker hung at an imperfect angle, with plaster peeling away all around it, and was speckled with ancient paint. It would not appear to be a functioning speaker. Nonetheless, its green indicator light flickered to life, and after a brief initial crackling sound, a young man's voice rang out.

"What's the word?" said the voice, quite loudly and brusquely.

Tai gave a little jump. He glanced at Reynie, then gawked at the speaker again.

"No word yet," Reynie replied. He cleared his throat. "But, say, George. Were you aware that a five-year-old boy named Tai Li has entered the house, evidently by himself, and is now standing here in my study with me?"

There was a pause. Another crackle. Then: "Huh."

"Right?" said Reynie, as if they had just discussed the matter at length.

"The timing is not exactly what one would wish."

"I'm guessing the timing has everything to do with it."

Tai turned to Reynie with huge eyes. "Is that Sticky

Washington?" he whispered. "Who's read everything and knows everything and never forgets anything? But gets ner—"

"That's him, all right," Reynie interrupted. "Although lately he prefers his given name, George. And by the way, Tai, he can hear you even if you're whispering."

Reynie wouldn't have thought the little boy's eyes could get any wider, but wider they got, and two small hands flew up to cover his mouth. They were very dirty hands, too. Reynie supposed now wasn't the moment to discuss hygiene.

"Hello, Tai," said the voice through the speaker. "I look forward to meeting you."

Tai made as if to clap his hands, then seemed to think better of it. He ran over to stand directly beneath the speaker. "Hi!" he shouted, gazing up at it. He stood on his tiptoes, trying to reach it with an outstretched finger.

Reynie leaped up from his desk. "Let's not touch the speaker, either, okay, Tai? It might fall off. Let me find something you *can* touch, how about?"

The speaker crackled. "So, Reynie, would you say this matter needs immediate attention, or—?"

"No, I've got it. Just keeping you in the loop."

"Roger that. Intercom off."

"Intercom off," echoed Reynie, and the green indicator light turned red.

"It turned red!" Tai declared. "So that means it's off!"

"Right you are," said Reynie, casting about for something to give the little boy.

Tai, seeing what he was up to, also looked around. The study in general was rather less cluttered and unruly than the desk, with less to offer his curious eye. Overstuffed bookshelves stood against every wall; an overstuffed chair stood in one corner; and behind the desk sat an antique chest covered with tidy stacks of papers, which Reynie now hastily began to clear away.

One particular stack of papers, however—a thick bunch of envelopes—seemed to catch in Reynie's hands. Each envelope was addressed from one of the world's most prestigious universities. Most were still sealed, but the few letters that Reynie *had* read said almost exactly the same thing: *Delighted to inform you…would be among the youngest ever to attend this university in its long, illustrious history…naturally covering your tuition and room and board, along with a generous stipend for expenses…an extremely rare honor…if you will please reply as soon as…*

The envelopes all bore postmarks from months ago. Reynie had yet to reply. He looked at the stack in his hands for a long moment, as he had done many times in recent weeks, before finally setting it aside.

Meanwhile, as this clearing away of papers seemed to be taking a minute, Tai turned and spotted, on the back of the door through which he had just entered, a large map of the greater Stonetown area. Concentrated in the center of the map, in the heart of Stonetown itself, were thirteen pushpins. Tai counted them out loud—twice to be sure.

Reynie, without looking, knew full well what Tai was counting, and as he felt beneath the lid of the locked chest for its two secret catches, he prepared himself for the inevitable question. Under normal circumstances, it would hardly seem wise to inform a young child that those pushpins represented thirteen of the most dangerous men in the world; that those men, just as the location of the pushpins suggested, were now gathered right here in Stonetown; and that Reynie's sole purpose at present was to deal with them—which meant that the child, simply by being associated with Reynie, might be in great peril.

Tai's presence in Reynie's study was a clear indicator that these were decidedly *not* normal circumstances, however. Perhaps, given time, Reynie would sort out an appropriate answer. For now, he opted for distraction.

"...thirteen," Tai said, finishing his recount and turning to ask the question.

"Do you know what a baker's dozen is, Tai?" Reynie asked before the boy could open his mouth.

Tai knitted his brow, thinking. He scratched his chest and then, holding his palms out in a very adultlike fashion, announced, "Well, you know, a dozen is twelve. I know that."

Reynie couldn't help smiling. He tapped his nose and pointed at Tai. "That's right. And if you add just one more, some people call that a baker's dozen."

Tai thought about this, making a great show of knitting his brow again. Then a look of understanding came into his eyes, and he laughed. "You told me that because I was counting the pins! Because there's thirteen!"

"Right again!" Reynie declared. He did not explain that "the Baker's Dozen" was the rather pleasant term that he and his friends used for some extremely *un*pleasant men, eleven of whom had just escaped from a supposedly escape-proof prison in Brig City. Nor did he explain that the breakout had been engineered by the remaining two men (who had never been captured in the first place) with the assistance of a mysterious figure whose identity was yet unknown.

Reynie said none of these troubling things. Instead he opened the antique chest and said, "Have you ever seen a kaleidoscope?"

By way of reply, Tai dashed toward Reynie, stumbled over evidently nothing at all, recovered his balance, and arrived at Reynie's side with face alight and hands outstretched. "Can I hold it?" he said, bouncing up and down on his toes. "Can I *look* through it?"

"Be very careful," Reynie said, placing the large kaleidoscope in the boy's hands. "It's heavier than you think." He felt Tai's small hands dutifully tighten their grip; only then did he let go.

Tai studied the kaleidoscope reverently before putting it to his eye (his other eye remained wide open) and directing it at Reynie's midsection. "Wow," he breathed. "This was on a submarine?"

Reynie blinked. "You're thinking of a periscope. This is a kaleidoscope. It has colors! Try pointing it at the light."

Without lowering the kaleidoscope, Tai turned his whole body around and craned his head upward. "Oh, that's even better!"

"Isn't it, though? Try closing your other eye."

Tai tried ever so hard but couldn't quite manage it. "I'm still learning to wink," he said, half squinting in a way that gave him an air of great seriousness. He kept staring through the kaleidoscope, moving it slightly back and forth, and uttering quiet expressions of delight.

Reynie felt an urge to tousle the little boy's hair. He resisted, however, because of the tangles, and was instead about to pat Tai on the shoulder when the radio on his desk gave an extremely loud squawk. So sudden and so loud was the noise, in fact, that Tai dropped the kaleidoscope. Or rather, he did not drop the kaleidoscope so much as fling it up and away from him, and only by diving forward with hands outstretched and landing painfully on his belly did Reynie manage to catch it. For a moment he remained in that position, emitting an involuntary moan of both pain and relief.

"Hooray!" Tai cheered. "You caught it!" He tumbled down onto the floor next to Reynie and lay with his face a few inches away. "I'm sorry I dropped it, though," he whispered, and again Reynie noticed how the little boy's dark eyes shone. He also noticed how badly Tai needed to brush his teeth.

"That's okay," Reynie whispered back. "I know you were trying to be careful."

The radio squawked again. Reynie hauled himself to his feet. Tai followed suit, and together the two of them stood looking at the radio. "Sometimes it takes a second or two," Reynie whispered. He opened a drawer in his desk, took a peppermint from a tin, and handed it to Tai. "Don't run or jump while you have that in your mouth, okay?"

Tai nodded happily, slipped the peppermint into his mouth, and went back to staring at the radio, which rewarded him with yet another squawk. This one was followed by the sound of a young woman's voice.

"Secret password!" said the young woman. "Are you there?"

Reynie adjusted a knob on the radio, pressed a button, and replied, "Roger that." To Tai he explained: "'Secret password' is our secret password. It's just a joke."

Tai giggled.

"Confirming all clear?" came the young woman's voice.

"Copy that. Confirming now." Reynie released the button and hailed Sticky's office on the intercom. "We have her!" he called. "How's the frequency?"

"Checking," came the reply. And then: "All clear!"

"All clear," Reynie said into the radio.

"Well, great!" said the young woman. "What's the word?"

"Both major airports and all private airports compromised. Still awaiting word from Grand Central."

"I got the word from Grand Central myself. Also compromised."

"No, no, no," Reynie muttered. Then, remembering Tai, who was following everything with riveted attention, he glanced down and explained, "I'm just a bit frustrated, Tai. Everything's going to be fine."

"Oh, good!" Tai said brightly. He made a loud sucking sound on the peppermint, which seemed to fill his whole mouth.

After a long pause, during which Reynie made various private calculations, the radio squawked again, and the young woman's voice returned. This time she sounded as if she was shouting in a windstorm. "Stand by for ETA!"

"That means 'estimated time of arrival,'" Reynie said to Tai, who nodded agreeably, though without evident signs of comprehension. "We're not exactly sure where she is right now," Reynie went on, "but my guess is that by tonight or tomorrow morning—wait. Why did it sound so windy?"

"I wondered that, too!" Tai said.

"Oh boy," Reynie whispered, just as the radio sounded again.

"ETA three minutes," shouted the young woman. "Give or take thirty seconds. Going silent now. Will update you shortly." The radio went quiet.

"Did you get all that, George?" Reynie said, as if into the air.

"I got it. Do you think it means what I think it means?"

"I don't think it can mean anything else, do you?"

A long sigh issued from the intercom speaker. "At least we won't have to wait long to see how this turns out."

Tai tapped Reynie on the elbow. "Why don't you just ask her what it means?"

"Good question," Reynie said. "Did you hear her say she was 'going silent'? That means I couldn't get through to her even if I tried. We just have to—"

The radio squawked. "Hi again!" shouted the young woman. She rattled off a string of data. "ETA two minutes. Meet me on the roof?"

"Roger that," Reynie replied, shaking his head.

"What were those numbers and things?" Tai asked.

"Coordinates and altitude," came the voice from the intercom, followed by another sigh.

"Here," Reynie said, removing the kaleidoscope lens and ushering Tai to the window. "See? It's actually a spyglass— probably the best in the world." He handed the instrument to the astonished boy and showed him where to aim it.

"She's coming from the *sky*?" Tai exclaimed.

"Evidently," Reynie murmured. He put a hand on Tai's

shoulder. "And that, my friend, pretty well sums up what you need to know about Kate Wetherall."

Reynie returned to his desk, amused to hear the little boy repeating him in a whisper ("pretty well sums up...") but also troubled by something he had yet to lay a mental finger on. He began flipping rapidly through various piles of paper and folders on his desk. What was he forgetting, he wondered, and why did it matter?

"Is she going to land way over there?" asked Tai, for Reynie had directed his aim to the northeast.

The intercom speaker, with a crackle, explained that a projectile possesses both vertical and horizontal velocities, to which Tai responded by asking if those were real words.

"She'll be coming in at an angle," Reynie muttered. "And quite fast."

Tai, meanwhile, had lowered the spyglass, which had grown heavy. When his thin arms had recovered, he raised it again and gasped. Far away, against the backdrop of blue sky, he could see a figure falling.

"I see her!" he squealed, and started jumping up and down.

"Good job," Reynie said distractedly. He glanced over his shoulder. "Hey, what did I say about jumping? Also, *please* be careful with that spyglass — it's actually Kate's."

Tai had already stopped jumping, anyway, in order to hold the spyglass steady. The distant figure was now coming into focus: a young woman in a black flight suit, plummeting at a steep angle, arms tight against her sides. Yellow hair streamed like flames from the back of her visored helmet, which was fire-engine red.

"There's a dot following her," Tai said. "Oh! It's a bird! There's a bird following her! It's diving just like she is!"

"Stooping," said the intercom speaker.

"Stooping?"

"That bird is her peregrine falcon, Madge. When falcons dive like that, it's called stooping. ETA one minute, Reynie. Shall we head up there or not? I'm thinking it might be better not to watch."

Reynie snapped to attention, realizing what had made him uneasy. "Stick—I mean, *George!*" he cried, fanning the pages of a bulky day planner. He found the page he wanted and jabbed his finger on an entry that read "Experiment 37-B: Effects of Decreasing Atmospheric Pressure, etc."

"What is it?" the intercom speaker asked. "More trouble?"

"Well, on the night of the evacuation, you were scheduled to run your chemical experiments on the rooftop patio, but then everything went haywire. I don't suppose you cleared—"

The answer to his unfinished question was the banging open of a distant door, followed by footsteps charging down a hallway.

Reynie flew to the window. An elderly neighbor had emerged to work in her flower bed, and a mail carrier was whistling down the sidewalk, depositing letters in mailboxes. The street was out of the question. It would have been a risky option, anyway.

He jumped back to the radio. "Hey, can you slow down at all?"

"Copy that," came the reply. "Only a little, though."

"She *was* doing *this*," said Tai from his place at the

window. He clapped his hands to his sides, narrowly avoiding striking the spyglass on the windowsill. "But now she's doing *this*!" He threw out his arms and legs as if to do jumping jacks.

Reynie was already hurrying from the study. "That's great! Please be careful! I have to go to the roof now!"

"Wait for me!" Tai exclaimed, racing after him.

Reynie ran pell-mell down the hallway, turning the corner just in time to see a large square section of the floor settling into place. He ran over to stand on it. "Sticky's already up there," he said as Tai caught up. "Hang on—this is a shortcut." He stomped the floor four times, then grabbed Tai by the shoulders to steady him.

A trapdoor in the ceiling fell open, and suddenly, with a terrific rattling sound, they were racing upward. Tai, thrilled, shouted something Reynie couldn't make out. They passed through the trapdoor and kept going, up and up, through a gloomy attic filled with seemingly infinite contraptions and oddments scattered in all directions, through yet another trapdoor in the attic ceiling, and at last into fresh air.

"We're on the roof!" Tai exclaimed.

"Yep!" Reynie cried, leaping to an open instrument panel nearby. He threw a lever to secure the platform, then spun to face Tai. "Promise me you'll stay right there!"

Tai looked utterly amazed to be asked. "I promise!" he said in a reverent tone, and clutched the spyglass to his chest.

The rooftop patio, a flat expanse situated between two of the house's gables, was about half the size of a tennis court. Kate would have had little room for error under even the best of circumstances—and these were hardly those. Wind gusted fiercely from what seemed like every direction, sending scraps of paper dancing in the air like a wild mob of butterflies. Even worse, Reynie realized, those scraps were labels that had come loose from innumerable stoppered beakers arrayed on folding tables all across the patio. Every single one of those beakers, he knew, contained a different substance or mixture of substances, some of them quite dangerous.

Reynie glanced at the sky to the northeast. His eyes detected what might have been a tiny insect hovering a few inches above him, but he knew it was actually a far-off Kate. She hadn't even pulled her parachute yet. He glanced at Tai to make sure he was staying put. Yes, the boy was rooted to his spot, safely out of Kate's line of approach, and staring past Reynie with an expression of excited fascination.

That expression was more than warranted, Reynie knew, for moving frantically among the tables, snatching up beakers and placing them into a wicker basket, was George "Sticky" Washington. The young man looked exactly as the young boy watching had expected him to look: naturally slender and muscular (this was easy to determine, as Sticky wore a tank top, shorts, and flip-flops), with light brown skin and a well-shaped, perfectly bald head. Tai had also expected Sticky to be wearing unusually stylish new spectacles, and sure enough he was. So stylish were the spectacles, in fact, and so well did they suit the young man's features that under different circumstances Tai would have thought him an altogether dashing figure. Under the current circumstances, however, Sticky looked slightly ridiculous: His face was awash in panic and self-reproach, his feet shuffled awkwardly in their flimsy sandals, and his basket was beginning to overflow with beakers—as if he were an overgrown, desperate child on some bizarre variety of Easter egg hunt.

"There's no time to clear all of them!" Sticky shouted as he worked. "I'm just getting the lethal ones!"

"The *lethal* ones?" echoed Reynie. (He'd been thinking "dangerous," which seemed more than sufficient.) He glanced at the beakers on the nearest table; only a few still had their labels. Two days of rain and now this wind had done their damage. "What can I do?"

"I set it all up like a chessboard!" Sticky yelled, shoving a stopper into a beaker. "Eight tables, eight beakers per table—"

"Got it!" Reynie cried, seeing the pattern. Each table represented a row on the chessboard, each beaker a space. "So, which ones?"

Without looking up from his work, Sticky shouted chess notation instructions: "A2, D4, and C5! I've got the rest!"

"A2, D4, and C5!" Reynie repeated, already hustling to grab A2, a stoppered beaker in the first spot on the second row. It contained a liquid of an alarming vermilion color, which Reynie tried not to think about as he scrambled around to the fourth table. D4 contained a colorless liquid that looked like water but moved like sludge when Reynie picked up the beaker. He shuddered. Fortunately, this one was stoppered, too. He ducked under the table and came up next to C5, an open beaker full of what looked to be harmless black pebbles. "Uh, should there be a stopper for C5?"

"Oh, yes! Believe me, you don't want *those* to spill! Use the one from C6! It's fine!" Sticky shuffled past with his precariously full basket. "This is all of them!" he panted, his eyes swiveling skyward. He gave a yelp and doubled his pace. "Reynie! Here she is!"

Reynie, still shoving the stopper into the last beaker, didn't even have time to look up before he heard Kate's voice from shockingly close by.

"Get down, boys, I'm coming in hot!"

Reynie, clutching the beakers, dropped onto his back.

In the next instant his vision was filled with Kate Wetherall, a parachute, a glimpse of sky, a falcon with wings widespread— and then the rooftop seemed to explode. Kate's boots, having cleared the first four tables, caught the fifth and sixth in quick succession. Two rows of beakers shattered in a fraction of a second; the air was suddenly filled with glass, powder, liquid, and Kate—and still she continued, crashing through the seventh and eighth tables, her parachute, dragging behind her, gathering wreckage. And still she crashed, right across the end of the rooftop patio, through the low railing, and out of sight. Her parachute, full of debris, dragged after her to the broken railing, where it caught and held.

Reynie sat up. He glanced at Sticky, who was crouching with the basket in his arms and his jaw hanging slack, and then at Tai, whose eyes seemed too huge for his head. Reynie peered back across the rooftop patio. A purplish haze, not exactly smoke, shifted this way and that in the contradictory breezes. For a moment, the three of them stared at the parachute in shocked silence.

And then they found themselves staring at two gloved hands, which had appeared from beyond the patio edge, clutching at the parachute silk. The hands were followed by a fire-engine-red helmet, and finally a figure in a black flight suit. Boots crunched on broken glass, gloved hands went up to remove the visored helmet, and there stood Kate Wetherall, grinning.

"Hi, boys," she said, brushing glass and splinters from her broad shoulders. She gestured at Tai. "Who's this little guy?"

Reynie and Sticky, neither recovered enough to speak yet, exchanged a look.

Tai, on the other hand, was bouncing up and down. "I'm Tai!" he squeaked excitedly. "Reynie let me hold your spyglass!"

"I see that," said Kate, leveling an accusing look at Reynie before bursting into a laugh and striding forward to greet him.

Reynie, who had long ago learned that Kate's greetings could be painfully enthusiastic, was quick to show her the beakers. "We're holding dangerous chemicals, Kate!" he said, climbing unsteadily to his feet.

"Why would you be doing that?" Kate asked, laughing again. "You boys need to be more careful!" She gave him a peck on the cheek, then swooped over to Sticky (who flinched) to do the same.

At the sight of Tai raising his own cheek expectantly, Kate put on a dubious look. "Let's get you a bath first, mister. Have you seen your face?"

With a worried expression, Tai shook his head.

Kate pretended to be shocked. "What? Never? You've never seen your own face?"

At this Tai giggled, and with a quick "Fine, one kiss for the dust bunny," Kate swooped in on him, too.

After Reynie and Sticky had very carefully put down

their burdens, the three friends stood regarding one another. Despite having grown at different rates, they had all arrived—perhaps only temporarily, but still much to their amusement—at precisely the same height. Thus, Reynie's and Sticky's brown eyes were at the same level as Kate's familiar ocean blues, but that was not the reason they communicated so much, and so easily, without speaking. The three of them had been through more together as children than most people experience in a lifetime, and they had been best friends for years. So it was that everything they had been through, not just over the years but also in the last few days, everything that remained to be done, everything still at risk—these things and more passed among them without a word.

"Boy, am I hungry," Kate said, breaking the silence. She reached up to retie her ponytail; a sprinkle of debris fell from her hair and was carried off by the wind. "Are we under imminent attack, or is there time for a sandwich?"

"We don't think they're making a move today," Reynie said. "They're holed up in different parts of the city, awaiting some sort of message—most likely instructions from Mr. Curtain, though we don't know how they're going to manage that. It's not like he'll be granted permission to make a quick phone call to his former henchmen."

"I should say not. And Mr. Benedict?"

"He's safe at the moment as long as he stays put."

"Super," said Kate. "How about we have some lunch and catch up, then? I especially want to know how *you*"—this she said to Tai, who stood in the middle of their little circle, gazing up at their faces—"came to be *here*."

"I want to know the same thing," said Sticky. "By the way, Tai, it's nice to meet you in person. I'm...um, *George*," he said with some hesitation (for, like his friends, Sticky still thought of himself as Sticky, despite his recent declaration to the contrary). He extended his hand, and Tai, beaming, shook it so energetically with his free hand that his other one almost dropped the spyglass.

"How *did* you come to be here, anyway?" Kate pressed Tai, kneeling to be on eye level with him (and reaching, ever so subtly, to take hold of the spyglass).

Tai shrugged and scratched his chest. "She told me how. She told me all about you, and she gave me directions, and she kept me company the whole time!" Lowering his voice secretively, he added, "Even though I couldn't *see* her!"

Kate raised an eyebrow. "Even though..."

"Oh boy," Sticky muttered.

"I wondered," said Reynie, nodding. "I mean, I figured."

"That's right!" called a strident voice from behind them. "*I* told him. *I* brought him here. If not for *me*, he'd be in hot water right now. But I guess you're all having your happy reunion on the roof without me? You don't even send the platform back down — you make me take the stairs?"

By this point everyone had turned toward the stairwell doorway, in the frame of which stood — with arms crossed and eyes flashing — a very angry-looking girl.

"Hi, Constance," sighed Kate.

And just like that, the Society was reconvened.

A KIND OF HISTORY

OR THE NATURE

OF THE MESS

As many things seemed to do, the appearance of Constance Contraire—prodigious telepath, reluctant genius, accomplished composer of rude poetry—drew a gasp from Tai Li. In this case, the little boy was surprised by the way she looked. Over the last two days, as she had mentally guided him on his journey to Stonetown, Constance had kept him entertained by recounting the adventures of the Society. But in those tales, she had been very young—even younger than he was himself—and although he knew that years had passed since the dark days of the Society's first mission, Tai's only mental image of Constance was of the girl she'd portrayed herself to be back then: small, blond-haired, blue-eyed, and rather on the round side. Thus, the girl who appeared in the stairwell doorway looked nothing like the girl he'd been imagining. Tai had no doubt it was Constance, however — her crankiness was unmistakable — and he flew to her with an excited squeak.

"Good grief, you're filthy," Constance muttered as he flung his arms around her, but nonetheless she gave him a good long squeeze.

The current version of Constance was, to Tai, a fascinating hodgepodge of features: the bright blue eyes of her earlier years had changed, as young children's blue eyes often do, and were now an indeterminate mixture of blue, green, and gray. Like-wise had her wispy blond hair darkened into a light shade of brown, another common change, but in Constance's case she had promptly begun to dye it extremely *un*common colors — it was currently a shoulder-length mop of scarlet. She was much taller than Tai, though much shorter than her friends, and much to his delight she was wearing a very baggy green plaid suit, which was quite familiar to him from her stories.

"You're wearing one of Mr. Benedict's old suits!" he exclaimed, running around her to admire the outfit from all sides. "The kind you said he used to wear to keep him calm!"

"Yes, well," Constance said, holding out her hand to stop his circling, which was making her dizzy. "I've been in seri-ous need of some calming lately. Number Two altered the size for me — as much as possible, anyway."

Tai could picture Number Two, that brusque young woman with her yellowish complexion, her affinity for yellow clothing, and her eraser-red hair. And he knew that, like Constance, Number Two was one of Mr. Benedict's adopted daughters and that, like everyone else who'd been drawn into Mr. Benedict's circle, she was uniquely talented. But he hadn't realized that she knew how to use a sewing machine, and upon discovering this now, he gasped.

Constance rolled her eyes. "Really?"

"Is it working?" asked Tai, evidently immune to sarcasm. "Is the suit keeping you calm?"

"Don't I seem calm to you?"

Tai frowned. "Maybe you should get a hat, too."

"Maybe I should."

During this exchange, the three older members of the Society were trading glances and shaking their heads. It seemed as though everything in the world were happening at once.

"I don't see how we're ever going to get caught up," Kate said. "Stick—sorry, George. Do we need to take care of this mess right now? Will the chemicals eat through the roof or anything?"

"It can wait," Sticky said. "Reynie and I should just secure the dangerous ones. The rest...Okay, why are you looking at me like that, Kate?"

Kate put on an innocent expression. "Like what? Oh, sorry, it's just that—I know I haven't been away that long, but I'd already forgotten about your new spectacles. You look so stylish! To be honest, it's kind of distracting."

"Oh, please," Sticky said, grimacing. "Can we please not do this again?" He gave Reynie a warning look, but it did no good.

"She's right," said Reynie with a serious air. He tilted his head to one side, then to the other. "They're so perfect on you. Something about the symmetry, I think. It's like you're a magazine advertisement."

"I can't *help* it!" Sticky said, feeling, as usual, a flustering combination of embarrassment and pleasure. Ever since he'd reverted to his bald, bespectacled look (abandoning the contact lenses and varying hairstyles of recent years), his friends had been unable to resist teasing him for being suddenly, noticeably handsome. Even now, they were sneaking amused glances at each other—or pretending to sneak glances, at any rate, for Sticky's benefit, and after a moment he said, "You know I can see you doing that."

In the next moment the three of them were laughing. Even before the crisis of the last couple of days, there had been significant tension and no small degree of sadness among the three friends, the result of developing plans— Reynie's, Sticky's, and Kate's alike—that had put a strain on their long-established, easy way with one another. This shared laughter came as a great relief to all of them. For the moment, it almost felt as if nothing had changed.

"Is this not an *emergency*?" Constance snapped from the stairwell, and their laughter fell away. "Do we even have a *plan*?"

"Of course we do!" Kate replied cheerfully. "We're going to find a way to stop the Baker's Dozen from breaking out Mr. Curtain!"

"Without, you know, getting hurt by them in the process," Sticky put in.

"Definitely," said Reynie. "That's definitely an important part of the plan."

Constance stared. "And that's it?"

"Well, we need to sort out the details," Kate admitted, "which we can do over lunch!"

It was decided that Kate would hustle down to the kitchen while Sticky and Reynie carried the chemicals to the basement lab (or the "Blab," as Kate insisted on calling it, though the term had yet to catch on). Constance, grudgingly accepting a forehead kiss from Kate, also grudgingly agreed to help Tai wash his hands.

"After we eat," Kate informed Tai, "you'll be taking a bath. Maybe two baths."

"Okay!" Tai cried, as if nothing sounded more wonderful than two baths. He pointed at Kate's parachute, snagged on the broken railing and fluttering in the breeze. "But don't you need to put your thing away?"

"I'll do that after lunch, too," Kate said with a wink. "Maybe *we'll* all clean up while *you're* cleaning up."

Tai giggled, then grew serious again. "But what if someone sees it?"

With a raised eyebrow, Kate looked at Constance.

"He knows we're keeping a low profile," Constance said.

"It's supposed to just look like Captain Plugg is staying here," Tai said. "That's what Constance told me."

Kate plucked at his chin. "That's right. You're very smart to be so careful. Don't worry; nobody can see up here to this patio. We made sure of that long ago."

"Great," said Tai, beaming from the compliment. "Can we go down the same way I came up? That was fun!"

"For *you*," Constance grumbled.

"You two go ahead," said Kate, gesturing at the platform,

where Sticky and Reynie were now waiting with their beakers. "I'll take the stairs."

Approximately two seconds later, already on the third floor, Kate could hear the rattling of the platform machinery kicking into gear. With a quick window peek to verify that her falcon, Madge, had settled onto a favorite branch in the elm tree, Kate slid down the stairway banister (polished smooth from countless previous slides) and landed at a run. Above her the platform was just settling into place, and as she disappeared down the long hallway, Kate heard Tai asking if they could do it again.

The dining room, situated on the second floor of Mr. Benedict's house, had never been tidy. Like all the other rooms in the house, its walls were lined with cluttered bookshelves, and in order to sit at the long table, or in any other available chair, one usually had to move a newspaper or book. Yet the room's present state of disarray was such that Kate, on her way into the kitchen, felt compelled to stop and take it all in. The magnitude of the mess was remarkable, for sure, but what froze Kate in her tracks, and caught at her heart, was the *nature* of the mess: the multitude of dirty dishes on the table, the forgotten reading glasses on an open newspaper, the abandoned needlework in the corner easy chair—all signs of a happy, busy day, suddenly and alarmingly interrupted.

Given what she'd been told and what she saw before her now, Kate's mind had no trouble conjuring the scene. Most of their community of family and friends would have been in this room when news of the breakout reached them, for though Sticky and his parents lived in the house across the street, and the Perumal family (Reynie and his mother and grandmother) had their own quarters downstairs, as a general practice everyone converged here to take their midday meal together. Moocho Brazos, the former circus strongman and much-admired cook, always prepared something delicious (he had rooms in the basement, as did Kate and her father, Milligan), and the wonderful aromas emanating from the kitchen signaled the approach of hubbub and laughter as surely as any clock could. So it had been for years now.

And yet change had been in the air lately, as unmistakable as the scent of Moocho's baked apple pies, though not as sweet. "Bittersweet" was the word for it. Reynie had joked some time ago that perhaps they should acquire a taste for the bittersweet. But it was not a taste easily acquired. When Rhonda Kazembe had moved out, for instance, everyone was happy for her: She'd married a charming physicist and seemed delighted about the development. The couple were moving to a different city, where they both had excellent job opportunities at laboratories; they had plans to start a family. It was all good news, and Rhonda remained in close touch. Nonetheless, her departure had prompted many a tear, and her absence was still felt.

And that had been just the beginning. There was much more in the works. It wasn't long after Rhonda's departure that Reynie had begun to receive those extraordinary university invitations, and then, even as they were all trying to make sense of this new development, Sticky had been offered something even *more* remarkable: a chance to direct—not just work at, but *run*—the most important chemistry lab in the country. The position would be open in the fall. If

Sticky took it, he would be, not surprisingly, the youngest person ever to have held it. He would make history.

Kate's own aspiration, meanwhile, was by its nature *not* the sort of thing to make headlines. Her success could never be measured by fame, for her plan was to become—like her father before her—a secret agent. Not just any secret agent, either, but a top special agent in Milligan's own agency. She was already well on her way.

All these new possibilities, so pleasing to contemplate on their own, had sent everyone's minds spinning, for every possibility came at a cost. Even a single departure spelled the end of the Society as they had known it, and each of its members felt a kind of horror at the prospect of being the first to open the door—the one responsible for ending what they had.

But all consideration of what might be coming next had been rudely interrupted two days earlier, when bad news arrived in this very room. The impossible had happened. The infamous villains known as the Ten Men (so called for their reputation of having ten ways to hurt you) had been broken out of the Citadel in Brig City. Kate and Milligan, who had been away on an intelligence-gathering mission, got the word first: *Thirteen Ten Men, current whereabouts unknown, but certainly headed for Stonetown.*

"That's a bad baker's dozen," Kate had muttered grimly, and thus was the moniker born.

She'd known at once who was behind the breakout. The fact that several top agents in the Stonetown area had been ambushed in recent months, sending every one of them to a high-security hospital, was the reason she and Milligan had gone to do their sleuthing in the first place. Those ambushes had been executed by the last two uncaptured Ten Men, the notoriously elusive Katz brothers. (The brothers' gift for always smelling a trap, and always avoiding it, had led to their being nicknamed—by Kate, of course—the Scaredy Katz.) It was the Scaredy Katz, naturally, who had just freed the other Ten Men.

But how? The brothers had never engaged in risky confrontations before. Instead they'd been known to be secretively looking for someone—they had been at it for years—but exactly *whom* had remained a mystery.

After the ambushes started, that mystery was what Kate and Milligan had gone to investigate. They had just hit upon a kind of answer, too, when they learned of the Scaredy Katz's mystifyingly successful breakout operation at the Citadel. The agent reporting to Milligan could relay only a single, tantalizing clue: Some guards swore they had counted fourteen figures fleeing the site. *Fourteen*, not thirteen. (The rest of the guards had all been unconscious and could not confirm.)

"Regardless," Kate had said to Milligan, "if they're headed to Stonetown, we know what they're planning to do."

"I'd have to agree with you there, Katie-Cat," her father had replied. They hadn't even needed to say it out loud.

The Ten Men's plan, no doubt, would be to infiltrate Stonetown's brand-new, maximum-security facility and break out its only current prisoner: the most dangerous genius in history, their former employer, Ledroptha Curtain. With Mr. Curtain free again, the threat of the Baker's Dozen would be magnified exponentially. Their unique talent for violence paired with his terrible brilliance had once almost changed the world.

Almost. That word pertained only thanks to the Society, and therefore the Baker's Dozen probably also had revenge in mind. They were Ten Men, after all. They wouldn't have taken kindly to the role Mr. Benedict and his associates played in their capture.

What troubled Kate and Milligan most, however, was that the Ten Men knew about Constance. A telepath—especially one who hated them—might well endanger their future schemes. The Baker's Dozen would surely make it a priority to eliminate any such threat.

Milligan had radioed Mr. Benedict's house.

"It's happened," he'd said to Number Two. "Less than an hour ago. Waste no time."

And just like that, the meal was over. Life as they had known it was over, and whether it would ever be the same again—or even close—would depend on what happened next.

Kate took one last look around at the mess, at the evidence of the life they'd been living. Then she moved on to the kitchen. It was not at all her style to leave dirty dishes on the table. But these she would leave just a little bit longer.

A few minutes later, on Kate's suggestion, the Society members and young Tai Li carried their sandwiches down the hall to the sitting room, where the untidiness was more typical and therefore less depressing. On the contrary, the familiarity of the room was a comfort. The piano in the corner, the grandfather clock, and the giant globe, now long outdated, sat exactly where they had on the first day the Society members set foot inside this room, the very same day they had met one another. The books on the crowded bookshelves were the same books; the same paintings hung on the walls. One painting was of an observatory, the other of a boy on a bluff. Both featured starry skies—and both, Mr. Benedict had told them, were the work of a childhood friend. The sitting room was a kind of history itself, a history of new friendships and lasting ones alike.

Tai Li admired everything, exclaiming at the piano, spinning the globe, pointing up at the paintings, which fortunately were out of reach of his fingers. "I can see the Big Dipper in that one!" he declared. "It's the consultation in the sky above the boy!"

"Well, it's Orion," Sticky corrected gently, "but you're right that it's a *constellation*, whereas the Big Dipper, strictly speaking, is what we call an asterism, which—"

"I can see Orion!" Tai cried, looking over his shoulder at Constance for approval.

"Nice work," Constance mumbled wearily as she settled onto the rug.

The others joined her. They were all hungry, and for a minute or so there was scant talking and a great deal of chewing. The sandwiches were variously loaded with vegetables, cheeses, lunch meats, and condiments—each according to the taste of the person for whom Kate had assembled it (for Tai she'd taken a successful gamble on peanut butter and jelly)—and after noting the others' differing compliments and expressions of thanks, Tai realized that something extraordinary seemed to have occurred in the time it had taken him to wash his hands.

"Kake," he said (meaning to say "Kate," but with a mouthful of peanut butter), "were these sankwiches already make?"

"No, and thank goodness," Kate replied. "The kitchen was a nightmare. I wouldn't have eaten anything prepared in there, not until I'd gotten the place cleaned up first." (At this Tai's eyes grew huge, and he swiveled them around to see if anyone else was astonished that Kate had done so much so quickly. No one seemed to be.)

"How in the world did it get that bad?" Kate pressed, likewise looking around at the others. "I know things have been crazy since the evacuation, but that doesn't account for what I just saw in there. Do you realize there was a *spoon* stuck to the *outside* of the refrigerator? The outside!"

Reynie and Sticky glanced at Constance, then glanced away again and shrugged. Now was not the time to engage in a blame battle. The truth was they hadn't even seen Constance the last two days—she'd been holed up in her room, and they'd been too busy dealing with the present crisis to try and draw her out. The mounting mess in the kitchen, evidence of her nighttime raids, had actually been a source of reassurance. Yes, it *was* annoying to find globs of jelly in the silverware drawer, empty ice-cream cartons in the cupboard, and the floor so mysteriously sticky it almost pulled one's shoes off. But at least they knew Constance was alive and eating.

"Never mind," said Kate, who could guess the answer easily enough. "Let's get up to speed. I have things to tell you, but I want to hear more about how it all went down here when the news hit. And of course we need to hear about *this*." Kate waved her sandwich in the direction of Constance and Tai, who were sitting next to each other on the floor. (They were all on the floor, in fact, for it was the Society's long-established custom to begin serious discussions at ground level, and seated in a circle.)

"Let the boys go first," Constance said. "I want to finish eating...." She seemed to be about to say something else, then checked herself and shot a warning look at Tai, who nonetheless burst into a grin.

"You were going to say a rhyme!" he exclaimed. "Something to do with liverwurst! Is that what's on your sandwich? And—oh!" Tai looked at Sticky and Reynie and clapped a hand over his mouth. "I'd better not say the last part."

"Oh no," Sticky said. "The insulting poems are back?"

Constance shrugged. "He thinks they're funny."

The apparent return of Constance's rude versifying, a habit she seemed to have broken long ago, was dispiriting to the others. But in silent accord they let the matter drop, for Constance too often took protests as encouragement.

"I know you were in the middle of lunch when Milligan radioed," said Kate, getting the conversation back on track. "Tell me what happened."

"It was such an odd moment," said Sticky. "There were three different conversations going on, as usual. Then Number Two charged in with the news. She said, 'It's evacuation plan A!'—and every single person in the room looked at the clock."

"Mr. Benedict had different emergency plans for packing up and leaving," Reynie explained to Tai, "depending on how much time we had."

"Oh!" Tai said, nodding. He took a bite of his sandwich.

"Number Two saved most of the details about the breakout until we were all ready to go," Sticky went on. "And honestly,

I never would have guessed that could happen so quickly and so calmly. My parents, the Perumals, Moocho—no one hesitated. Everyone put down what was in their hands. Then for about twenty seconds everyone went around hugging everybody else, and then we all hurried to our rooms to pack."

Kate was shaking her head. "I wish I could have seen it. So strange! After all these peaceful years, and then—" She snapped her fingers. "Everybody out. Actually, I guess I'm glad I wasn't here. I suppose there was a fair amount of crying."

"There were a few tears," Reynie said. "Quiet tears, though. Nobody broke down."

Sticky opened his mouth to interject something, thought better of it, and disguised his original intention by cramming the last of his sandwich into his mouth. He chewed with impressive focus, resisting the urge to glance at Constance— who technically, perhaps, had not broken *down*, but who certainly had broken *things*.

(Reynie, too, avoided mention of Constance's tantrums. Discussing the evacuation without upsetting Constance all over again was going to be tricky enough, for she had grown quite furious with Reynie and Sticky that day, and was very likely furious with them still. It seemed only wise to proceed with special caution as they continued their account.)

Trunks and suitcases had been packed and loaded into taxicabs. A stream of farewells were made to Captain Plugg, who promised to do her utmost to safeguard their homes. (It was understood that if any Ten Men entered the picture, however, the guard's orders were to prioritize her own safety.) Curious neighbors waved as the caravan of taxicabs drove away down the street. Mr. Benedict's strange little community was well liked throughout the neighborhood, but not at all understood. It was widely assumed that this mass departure by taxicab simply signaled the beginning of some kind of weird vacation.

The taxis, driven by Milligan's most trusted sentries, had proceeded directly to Stonetown Harbor, where the evacuees expected to wait for the arrival of the MV *Shortcut II*—the world's fastest cargo ship, piloted by old friends Captain Noland and his energetic first mate, Joe "Cannonball" Shooter. As it happened, though, there was no waiting to be done: Against all probability, the ship had already arrived, and in a great whirl of activity, crew members were dispatched, dockworkers were employed, and the families and all their luggage were aboard in a matter of minutes. Everyone, that is, except Mr. Benedict, who instead of joining the others was heading straight to the high-security facility where Mr. Curtain was imprisoned.

(It was this fact, announced before the caravan's departure, that had been the reason for Constance's tantrums.)

"You're sure it's the best thing, Nicholas?" Captain Noland had asked as the two lifelong friends—the brisk, trim, gray-haired ship captain and the disheveled, gentle, white-haired genius—shook hands on the dock. "There's no one else who can implement these emergency security measures?"

"I'm afraid not, Phil," Mr. Benedict replied. "Don't worry, though. I'll be as safe in that facility as anywhere in the world. Until this unfortunate situation is resolved, I'll remain there and keep my brother company."

"I sometimes forget Curtain is your twin," said Captain

Noland, shaking his head. "It's hard to imagine anyone more different from you. I do earnestly hope you succeed in keeping him locked up. In the meantime, I promise to keep your people safe and comfortable."

"You have my word, too, Mr. Benedict!" cried Cannonball Shooter, striding up to join them. "I've laid in the best possible provisions, and plenty of them. We're all completely up to speed on communication protocol. There's not a Ten Man alive who could find us in the middle of that big, beautiful ocean! And even if they did, they couldn't catch us, ha ha!"

"I have no doubt, Joe," said Mr. Benedict, warmly shaking his hand. "I'm indebted to you both."

"Oh, Nicholas, as for that," said Captain Noland, "you know very well that the debt runs in the opposite direction."

It was at this point, as Mr. Benedict took his leave, and Constance, Reynie, and Sticky looked down from the ship's deck, that Constance had said in a tight, desperate voice, "Captain Noland is afraid he'll never see Nicholas again!"

The young men understood at once that Constance, intentionally or not, had read Captain Noland's thoughts. This would have been clear enough even if she hadn't referred to Mr. Benedict as "Nicholas" instead of "Dad," which was what she'd called him since the day of her adoption. After years of training to avoid accidentally reading others' minds, Constance still couldn't help it sometimes. Her friends and family members had likewise learned how to keep their most private thoughts better guarded when Constance was in the room. But at a time like this, an untrained mind in high emotion would always pull at Constance's mental attention like a powerful magnet.

"He may be afraid of that," Sticky had said quickly, putting a hand on Constance's shoulder, "but that doesn't make it true, right? You know that. It's going to be okay."

Reynie, for his part, had felt his own mental gears suddenly cranking at high velocity. Because of those years of training, it had been quite a while since he'd witnessed Constance reading another person's mind. Now that he had, he felt some kind of answer emerging, but what was the question?

As Mr. Benedict waved goodbye to them, and Sticky did his best to comfort Constance, Reynie concentrated. He needed to figure something out, and he needed to do it right away, he could tell. Yet there was so much commotion as Cannonball whisked Mr. Benedict away on a motorized cart, and dockworkers and crew members swarmed the gangway, and Captain Noland shouted his announcement that they would be launching as soon as the ship had finished refueling, that Reynie had felt the need to steal away by himself. He'd gone below, letting himself into the captain's quarters (which they had been urged to treat like their own home), and was sitting at the captain's desk when suddenly it all came clear to him:

The truth behind the Ten Men's breakout. The explanation for the mysterious success of the Scaredy Katz's ambushes. The importance of the fourteenth figure. Everything fit together at once.

Leaping from his chair, Reynie started for the door, then checked himself. There was no way he could catch up with Mr. Benedict now, even if he were allowed off the ship, which he would not be. Yet Mr. Benedict would need help, he felt sure of it; and here in this moment, when everything mattered the most, Reynie couldn't just sit by and hope for the best.

And so he had formed his plan.

BRIGHT SIGNALS AND DARK PLACES

Wait, you're telling me the Ten Men have a telepath? Like Constance?"

Kate spoke from behind her sandwich. She had just been about to take another bite, but now she lowered her hand. "Why, that explains so much! The successful ambushes, the secret codes and hidden keys the Scaredy Katz would have had to get their hands on—oh! And you think it's the fourteenth figure!"

"It certainly made sense to me," Reynie said. "I only wish I'd thought of it sooner. All this time we've been assuming

Constance was the only one, but why shouldn't there be others?"

"Right," Kate said, still turning the idea over. "And, good grief, if they have someone like that—"

"It changes everything," Sticky finished. "Which is why we had to get off that ship."

At this, with a wary glance at Constance (who returned his look with an unreadable expression), Reynie went on to explain that just before the MV *Shortcut II* set sail again, two young sailors in ill-fitting uniforms, their caps pulled low (and one of them with very stylish spectacles hidden away in his pocket), had hurried off the ship, down the bustling gangway, and onto the docks again. (Their notes of explanation and apology, left behind on the captain's desk, would be read later—too late for them to be stopped.) Moving with purpose, carrying a crate between them, they drew no notice. Soon they had blended in among the crowds of sailors, stevedores, and other workers on the busy docks.

The two had walked briskly, keeping their heads down, with Reynie in the lead, calling out occasional directions and warnings to Sticky, whose too-distinctive spectacles had to remain hidden away for the present. At length the young men were out of view of the MV *Shortcut II*, obscured by the shadows of other docked ships. When they heard their own ship's horn signaling its departure, in silent agreement they set down the crate, taking a moment to rest—and also to steady themselves. It was such a large ship, and there was so much confusion, they felt sure that their absence would go unnoticed until Constance and their families were well on their way toward the safety of the high seas. Their daring maneuver had succeeded; their reward was a mutual pang of sadness and guilt.

Still, they had reason to be hopeful. Their cover was perfect. They had clearly been seen boarding the ship—there were witnesses aplenty—but no one had recognized them as they disembarked. The Ten Men would track them as far as the harbor and confirm their departure, and that would be the end of it. The Baker's Dozen would have no idea that two of the Society's members were still in Stonetown, working in secret to thwart their plans.

"I hate you both," came a voice from inside the crate.

Reynie and Sticky jumped. They stared at each other, each watching his friend's expression change from one of surprise to one of profound dread. The only thing worse than leaving Constance behind was discovering that they'd actually failed to do so.

"I thought you said it was empty," Sticky moaned.

"It *was!*" Reynie said.

The voice from inside the crate said, "Were you keeping an eye on it while you changed into your ridiculous costumes? Were you thinking you could betray your supposed friend without her even noticing?"

Reynie and Sticky didn't relate the details of this conversation to Kate. It was enough to say that they had intended to leave Constance on the ship for her own safety—since, after all, they knew that the Ten Men might be particularly interested in tracking her down—but that she'd insisted on coming with them. And that of course they had apologized, repeatedly and profusely, for having left her out of the original plan.

Constance said not a word during all of this, only kept her face blank and nibbled at her half-eaten sandwich as if no longer hungry. Eventually she handed it to Tai, who had finished his own sandwich and begun eyeing hers. He took a bite, screwed up his face, and tried to give it back. But Constance just wrapped her arms around her knees, and though she didn't speak, Tai whispered, "If you say so," and crawled over the rug to hand the sandwich to Kate.

"She says you'll eat it," he declared.

"And she's right," said Kate, happily taking it from him. To Sticky and Reynie she said, "So, what happened next?"

"We split up for a bit," Sticky said. "Reynie went to find a phone booth to call Mr. Benedict at the facility—we didn't dare call from the house, because there'd be a record of it. Too risky. So Constance and I waited—"

"I waited in the crate," Constance said, glowering at Sticky.

"Right, because she didn't have a disguise. So Reynie went to make the phone call and grab disguises from our stash at the Monk Building—"

"In the crate," Constance repeated, still glowering. "I had to wait. In the *crate*."

"For crying out loud, Constance," Kate interjected. "You're the one who got into the crate in the first place, right? What were they supposed to do?"

Sticky and Reynie winced, and Kate realized her mistake. Too late. Constance's face turned almost as red as her scarlet-dyed hair. Her eyes narrowed, and, directing them at Kate, she began to recite, spitting out her words:

"To wait in a crate is quite horrible, *Kate.*
I find your reminder deplorable, *Kate.*
You suppose that I chose it for any old reason?
You have to think fast
when your friends commit treason."

Tai let out a delighted laugh. "Wow!" he cried, clapping. "That was good, Constance!"

The older three pursed their lips, took deep breaths, and moved on without further comment on the matter of the crate. Reynie told Kate that he had managed to get through to Mr. Benedict, who expressed dismay, but not exactly surprise, when he learned that the three of them had abandoned ship. Nor was he surprised when Reynie shared his idea about the telepath.

"It occurred to me, too, my dear boy," Mr. Benedict had said on the phone, "and I intended to discuss it with you this very evening. I've spent the last several days trying to persuade the new warden at the Citadel to take immediate precautions, but despite my credentials and connection to the case, he was skeptical. He's one of those dubious bureaucrats who even now mistrust the idea that the Whisperer ever existed. He could believe that the Ten Men and my brother were dangerous criminals, he informed me, without subscribing to fanciful notions of mind-control machines and psychic abilities. 'Our thoughts are our own, Benedict,' he said to me this morning, 'and you'll never convince me otherwise.' So I urged him to take special care of the very small number of thoughts he seemed to possess—I'm afraid in my frustration I grew a tad snide—and was in the process of persuading the relevant committees to override his authority when the breakout occurred."

"So my warning to Mr. Benedict was unnecessary," Reynie told Kate, having paraphrased Mr. Benedict's report. "I should have predicted that. But I still knew he needed our help, and I told him so. He doesn't want us putting ourselves at risk, of course. And of course I argued with him. I explained that George and I were absolutely resolved to help him however we could—that we were going to try, no matter what—and so the best thing would be for him to *help* us help him. He knew I had him cornered with that, and there was no time to argue. Obviously, the most critical thing from his perspective was that we keep Constance safe."

"Obviously," Kate agreed. There was the briefest pause as the older three traded glances, prepared for Constance to react in some surprising, unpleasant way, but Constance only rested her chin on her knees and said nothing.

In the end, she had been compelled to wait in the crate for almost an hour. By the time the three of them left the docks—two sailors and a surly, undersized stevedore, all of them in dark sunglasses and caps—the Katz brothers were already on their way to the harbor.

Kate hurriedly swallowed her last mouthful of liverwurst. "Wait, what? The Scaredy Katz were already in Stonetown? Milligan knew they'd be sent ahead as scouts, but that was fast even for them. They must have flown!"

"They did," Sticky said. "A private plane. And we narrowly avoided them. They'd already been by the house and had a little interview with Captain Plugg—the three of them standing in the courtyard, pretending to be so nice and civil—until they were satisfied she really was the only person here. Naturally, she lied about where we'd gone, but they knew she was lying. They sniffed out our trail soon enough and made straight for the harbor."

"How did you get back in here without the neighbors seeing you?" Kate asked.

"I'd already called Captain Plugg from the phone booth," Reynie explained. "I told her where we'd be hiding out, and she came and got us on her motorcycle. She had to make two trips."

Kate frowned. "That still doesn't explain—"

"Duffel bags," Sticky said. "She smuggled us into the house in duffel bags."

Kate slapped her thighs and laughed. "She's so strong! And you must have been so uncomfortable! I love it."

Tai was leaning toward Constance and trying to whisper, but everyone heard him say, "Oh, those are good rhymes! What's a 'kerfuffle'?"

"Never mind," Constance muttered.

Kate's expression turned thoughtful. "Listen, though, how did you know the Katz brothers came by private plane? Not even Milligan's agents knew that—no one reported it."

Reynie shrugged. "It was Constance. Somehow she knew." Turning to Constance, he said, "I've wanted to ask you about it ever since, but you've been in your room this whole time, and Sticky and I have been trying to keep up with everything. Now we're all here, though. Including our new friend"—this with a wink at Tai, who giggled—"so can you fill us in?"

There was a long silence. Then Constance heaved an equally long sigh. And then she said, "She's been in my head.

The Listener. That's how I think of her, anyway. Ever since the harbor, she's been in my head, trying to find us." Constance tilted her head toward Tai. "And trying to find *him*."

ᴧ:ᴗ

The others, dumbfounded, stared at the little boy, and at Constance, and at one another.

"It's true!" Tai said, flopping forward onto his belly. Idly fiddling with a stray thread in the rug, he went on in a rapid-fire stream: "I was at the orphanage and I started hearing her and she started asking me where I was, and then Constance interrupted even louder and said nope don't answer that, kid, and asked me what my name is, and I told her Tai M. Li and asked her to guess what the *M* stands for, and Constance said not right now, she wanted me to come here so you could all take care of me, and I needed to hurry because the Scaredy Katz were coming to find me and they are not nice *at all*."

"Tai," Constance interjected when the boy took a breath, "would you go to the kitchen and bring back some cookies? There's a tin in the pantry, hidden behind a big jar of pickled onions."

"Yes! I! Will!" Tai exclaimed, leaping up. He dashed from the sitting room, and they could hear his tiny feet pattering in the wrong direction, stopping, then pattering in the direction of the kitchen.

"I've been trying to keep it from being scary," Constance said in a weary voice. "He knows they're bad guys, but he thinks he's safe as long as I'm talking to him—as long as he's with us."

"Well, this is…astonishing news," said Sticky, running a hand over his scalp. "You realize that, right, Constance? What in the world is going on? What have you been dealing with?"

"It started when I was still in the crate," Constance said. "While we were waiting for Reynie. I could just suddenly *feel* her looking for me. It took me a few minutes to figure out what was happening. I could hear what she was thinking—or at least what she was concentrating on the most, which was me. Trying to find me. Because McCracken told her to."

At this mention of the most fearsome of all the Ten Men, the other three stiffened. *McCracken*. It was a name none of them ever wished to hear.

"Oh, Constance," Reynie said. "I'm so sorry."

"Me too," Sticky said. "I can't even imagine."

Kate moved across the rug and sat next to Constance. She didn't say anything or even look directly at her, only sat down beside her. Kate sometimes forgot the lessons that years with Constance had taught her, but sometimes, like now, she remembered.

Constance gave a slight nod that could have meant anything but that probably was an expression of appreciation. She bit at one of her fingernails, which she'd already bitten quite short, and with a small sigh she went on.

"It had never occurred to me to try to look for anyone like, you know—me," she said. "Someone with an especially bright signal. That's not a perfect way of explaining it, but it's close enough for now. But McCracken knew I was out here, and he told her to try it. The moment she started concentrating, I sensed it. Then she zeroed in on me, and I had to think fast. I was going to do what you all learned to do as a defensive measure—you know, think hard about random things that don't matter. But before I could even get started, I heard her thinking, *She's in a dark place.* Which I was. I was in the crate. That's when I realized how hard it was going to be."

Pattering footsteps approached, and Tai rambled into the room, already eating a cookie. He went around with the tin, handing cookies out to everyone, then settled into Reynie's lap. Reynie, surprised, patted the boy's thin shoulders. He scarcely seemed to have any weight at all.

"I'm explaining things to them," Constance said to Tai, who nodded, chewing happily. "Anyway, as Tai here knows, the reality of the place you're in has a huge amount of substance. Your surroundings make such an impression on your consciousness, you don't have to concentrate for them to stand out in your mind. That includes the people who are with you. Do you see what I'm saying?"

"So *that's* why you didn't mention this to us back at the harbor," said Reynie, suddenly understanding. "When you barely spoke to us, we just thought you were"—he almost said "sulking" but instantly corrected himself—"angry. But you were trying to keep thoughts of us out of your head. I assume that's why you've been holed up in your room, too. Or one reason, anyway."

Constance tapped her nose and pointed at him. "With the lights off, yes. Also, I just needed no distractions. What I did with part of my mind was concentrate on real memories of places we've been—here in this house for starters, but also the Institute, the *Shortcut*, the castle in Portugal, the abandoned village, the prison, every place I could remember vividly. I moved from scene to scene to keep the Listener confused. She couldn't tell what was happening now and what had happened in the past. She still can't, by the way— I'm still doing it. I throw a lot of other mental garbage at her, too, the way you all learned to do. But ever since I got out of the crate, I think of that darkness more often than anything else. Her best guess is that I'm still in some dark place, but she doesn't know where."

"Unbelievable," Kate murmured as Sticky and Reynie shook their heads in amazed agreement. "You were doing all that at the same time you were leading Tai here? I don't see how in the world you've done it, Constance."

"It hasn't been easy," Constance said, and indeed it was plain to her friends just how exhausted she really was. Her face was drawn, her eyes dark, her voice raspy. "But I had to do it, because the Listener found him, too. She *was* just looking for *me*, but then he turned up as well. Once I sensed *that*, I also sensed *him*."

"I have a bright signal!" Tai exclaimed, sending a puff of cookie dust from his mouth.

Constance looked around at the others. "It's like the three of us are on our own special frequency. Tai has the ability, but he doesn't know how to use it yet. He can't do anything on purpose. Sometimes he hears people's thoughts. A lot of the time he doesn't. It's a good thing you've all had practice warding me off. I rarely hear thoughts by accident anymore, but we can't say the same for Tai."

"Good to know," Sticky said. "Listen, though, Constance, I trust you, but can you help me out here before I panic? If Tai can't control his thoughts the way you do, and the, uh, this *Listener* is looking for him, and he's with *us*... You see where I'm going with this?"

"I do!" said Tai, climbing out of Reynie's lap and dropping into Sticky's. "I'm a candle, and Constance is the sun!" He popped the lid off the cookie tin and took out another cookie, then put the lid back on. For some reason he was doing this every time, even though it seemed clear that he intended to eat every remaining cookie.

Sticky, taken aback by the arrival of Tai in his lap, made awkward patting motions around the little boy's head without actually touching him, and then lowered his hands to his sides. "Hey there," he said. "What do you mean, you're a candle?"

Reynie spoke up. "It's the relative brightness of your signals, isn't it, Constance? You think she can't pick up on Tai's signal if he's with you, because yours is so bright? Something like that?"

Constance shrugged. "Something like that. And I don't just *think* it; I *know* it. She's confused. She thinks he's gone farther away—out of range, basically. Which makes it easier for me, since now I don't have to constantly tell him what to think about, and barrage her with false leads, and keep my own whereabouts secret—"

"And keep me company!" Tai leaped out of Sticky's lap and ran to sit in Kate's, evidently committed to giving everyone the honor. "And tell me stories! And tell me how to get here!"

"How exactly *did* you get here?" Kate asked, playfully swatting his hand away from the cookie tin, which he was trying to open again. He laughed and leaned back against her, tilting his head so that he was looking at her face upside down. When he looked back down again, she had a cookie in her hand, and the tin was nowhere to be seen.

"Hey!" he squealed, laughing harder. Kate produced the tin from behind her back and handed him the cookie. Tai took a bite and said, "I got some money from the headmaster's money drawer and got on a bus, and that took me to the train station, where I asked a lot of people which platform was for the train to Chicago, and when they asked me where my mom was, I said in the bathroom—even though *that* wasn't true, because I don't even *have* a mom *or* a dad— and then I went out and snuck onto a train to Stonetown. It was fun!" He transferred the cookie from one hand to the other, then used his free hand to scratch vigorously at the opposite arm.

"Constance told you how to do all that?" Kate asked.

Tai nodded. "She said it would confuse the Scaredy Katz, and it did! I just needed a good place to hide, and I found a *great* place—in a train car full of sheep! They were so nice! I petted every single one of them, and they didn't even bother me when I fell asleep! I think they gave me fleas, though," Tai added quietly, almost to himself. "But that's not their fault."

"Ooookaaay," Kate said, immediately lifting Tai from her lap.

A look of dismay appeared on every face in the room, accompanied by a spontaneous universal itching.

Reynie, already scratching at his ankles, said, "Next time, Tai, anything to do with fleas is probably something you should mention right away."

"Roger that!" Tai said, shaking the empty cookie tin to hear if it rattled. "That's what you say to each other when you understand something."

In short order Tai was whisked away for a bath, and Sticky (furiously scratching at his chest) hurried down to the basement lab to whip up an effective flea shampoo, which he quickly distributed to the others. After a hasty round of showers and wardrobe changes, with the morning's clothing being fumigated in an impromptu disinfectant chamber, the Society members took turns wishing sweet dreams to a now squeaky-clean—and abundantly yawning—Tai Li. The little boy was put down for a nap, without even a murmur of resistance, in an old pair of Constance's pajamas.

Kate, as usual the first one ready, cleared the dining room table (she'd left the dishes unattended long enough— half an hour was an eternity to Kate) and made a pot of tea. By the time the others joined her, she had set out cups and saucers, honey, sugar, and milk, and was peering through the window blinds.

"What are you looking at?" Sticky asked as he dropped into a chair.

"Just checking on Madge," Kate replied. In an admiring tone she said, "She's getting to be an old bird, but she's still in fine form, isn't she? I mean, *look* at her."

"What's she doing?" asked Reynie, already spooning honey into his tea.

"Eating a rat," Kate said in the same admiring tone. "Just sitting on that branch like a queen, eating a rat."

Both Reynie and Sticky made polite noises, but neither joined Kate at the window.

Constance, meanwhile, seemed scarcely to be listening. She had filled her own cup half-full of sugar, over which she now dribbled a modest amount of tea. She was wearing yet another old green plaid suit of Mr. Benedict's, one that Number Two had yet to alter, and it fairly swallowed her. She had rolled the jacket sleeves up over her elbows and the pants over her knees. Beneath the jacket she wore her favorite top—an oversized, faded pink T-shirt, emblazoned in large black letters with the word "NO."

Sticky and Reynie, for their part, had both thrown on whatever semi-clean shorts and T-shirts were closest at hand, and Kate was in what had become for her a daily uniform: loose-fitting trousers and shirt, a canvas jacket, lightweight boots—all equipped with secret pockets—and a utility belt of her own design, one that was noticeable only when Kate reached for something tucked away in her jacket's inner pockets or for a tool from the belt itself.

Before Kate stepped away from the window, she made a subtle, thorough five-second review of her tools, patting every pocket and every item on her utility belt to ensure all was in place: her penlight, her mini-telescope, her Swiss Army knife, and her coiled rope, among several other things. On the intelligence-gathering mission with Milligan, she had, like her father, carried a tranquilizer dart gun, hers concealed beneath her jacket. She hadn't needed it, though, and at present it was locked safely away in her room. She thought of Milligan now, wondering if he was worried about her, wondering if he was angry. He hadn't exactly given her the okay to skydive from the plane.

Only take necessary risks, Katie-Cat, her father was always telling her. *You'll find that there's more than enough of those without taking unnecessary ones.*

Kate was convinced that getting here as quickly as possible had counted as a necessary risk. Milligan surely would have agreed with her decision, too, if she had discussed it with him before climbing out of the plane. Which, upon reflection, she probably ought to have done. She *had* shouted her intentions and blown him a kiss as she left him in the cockpit, but once she was outside, clinging to the wing strut, Milligan really hadn't had much say in the matter.

When would she see him again? Kate felt a sudden pang. Surely it wouldn't be long, she thought. Surely. But it was impossible to say when.

Reynie, meanwhile, having watched Kate make her quick inventory of tools, was thinking about the thousands of times he had seen her do the same thing with her bucket. She hadn't used the bucket in a year, though. He knew that Kate wanted to be a field agent, as her father had been (Milligan, before giving up dangerous operations to become agency director, had once been the best of them all), and Reynie had to admit that carrying around a red bucket does tend to make a person conspicuous. That hadn't mattered to Kate when she was a young kid. But now—well, now *what*?

It was a question they were all asking themselves. And they were all short of answers. But Reynie knew one thing for sure: He missed Kate's bucket.

"Captain Plugg's coming to check on us," Constance announced when Kate moved to join them at the table. "You might as well meet her at the door. She'll be excited to see you."

Sure enough, Captain Plugg's heavy tread was soon heard on the stairs, and moments later Kate was greeting her with open arms and a mischievous grin.

"I *thought* I heard you up here," declared Captain Plugg, a stocky, gray-eyed woman with an unusually large, square head—over which she now playfully lifted Kate as she might have done a toddler. "No one else pounds the floorboards the way you do. Your footsteps are like jackhammers. But how did you get here without my knowing?"

"Put me down and I'll tell you," Kate said, laughing.

Captain Plugg listened to Kate's account of her rooftop arrival with a look of barely concealed distress (understandable in one whose main job had long been to keep Kate and the others safe), then grew sheepish when Kate said she'd heard that the guard had faced down the Scaredy Katz in the courtyard.

"Oh, as for that," said Captain Plugg with an embarrassed wave, "those two don't like to fight, not if there's a chance they'll get their noses bloodied. You can see it on their faces. Anyway, they had no reason to try to get into the house once they were satisfied it was empty. They know Mr. Benedict would never leave behind anything that might be valuable to them."

"But listen, I need to ask you about something," Captain Plugg said. She announced that one of Milligan's secret sentries—there were always several posted in the area—had seen a small child enter the neighborhood, moving in the direction of Mr. Benedict's house. Captain Plugg wondered if perhaps—

"Yes, he's here," Constance interrupted. "He's sleeping in my room."

Once again the look of distress appeared on Captain Plugg's face, and this time she didn't try to hide it. Instinctively turning to Reynie for explanation and reassurance (and thus missing Sticky's twitch of irritation), the guard was soon filled in. She could hardly be at peace with the situation—complications seemed to be mounting by the minute—but she was satisfied that they were doing what was necessary for the little boy's protection.

"I'll inform the sentries in person," Captain Plugg said. "I assume it would be best not to mention him on our radios."

"I think you're right," said Reynie, for she'd been looking at him when she spoke. But even after Captain Plugg had gone downstairs and they'd heard her motorcycle roar to life, Reynie could feel Sticky's annoyance hanging in the air.

I didn't ask *her to ask me,* Reynie wanted to say, but there was no point. They'd been through this before. Reynie's ability to analyze problems—and people—had been established long ago, and as a result (unless Mr. Benedict was in the room), it was on his judgment that everyone tended to rely.

Even when you're wrong, Sticky had pointed out more than once. *Even when any of the rest of us could answer just as well as you.*

Reynie couldn't argue with that. Sticky was right. But was it his fault? True, Sticky never said he *blamed* Reynie; he was just annoyed. Nor did Reynie blame Sticky for *being* annoyed. But it did still *annoy* him when Sticky was annoyed, and his own annoyance annoyed Sticky even more....

No, it was better to say nothing and move on.

Kate, meanwhile, had dropped into a chair and was pouring herself some tea. "Well," she said, "is no one going to ask me what I found out on my mission with Milligan?" She said this while looking around the table rather than at her teacup; even so, she stopped pouring just as the tea reached the brim. "It might be important, you know."

Sticky, already irritated, rolled his eyes. "Please forgive us, Kate," he said in a stiff voice. "What did you find out on your mission with Milligan?"

"I'm glad you asked!" Kate said brightly. "We hit about a dozen dead ends, in four different cities, but we finally figured out what the Scaredy Katz were looking for. Or, I should say, *who* they were looking for. It was—"

"Actually, you *should* say *whom* they were looking for," Sticky observed. "Or 'for whom they were looking.'"

Now it was Kate's turn to roll her eyes. "*Fine*, Stick— George, I mean—we finally figured out for *whom* the Scaredy Katz were looking. After all these years, Milligan and I got to the bottom of it! And guess what? It was—"

"The telepath," Reynie interrupted. "I mean, that's obvious, right?" He glanced at Constance and Sticky, who both nodded.

"For crying out loud!" Kate exclaimed, throwing up her hands. "Do I not even get to tell my story?"

"Sorry," Reynie said, though in truth everyone except Kate was now in a better mood. "Please go on."

"*Thank* you," Kate replied curtly. And then, in her usual spirited tone (for she couldn't hold a grudge more than a second if she tried), she continued: "I actually wasn't going to say the telepath. You're right, though; it *is* obvious now that you mention it. What I was going to say was that the Scaredy Katz were looking for a Helper!"

"Wait," Sticky said. "You mean a *Helper* Helper? From the Institute?"

Kate tapped her nose and pointed at him.

Her listeners suddenly understood much more than Kate had said aloud. When the Society members had gone on their mission to the Institute on Nomansan Island, enrolling as students while operating as spies for Mr. Benedict, they discovered that the laborers there—the infinitely sad and subservient Helpers—had suffered the same fate Milligan had: They'd been brainswept by Mr. Curtain's Whisperer, all memory of their true lives hidden away from them.

Unlike Milligan, whose secret-agent training had helped him to escape immediately after he'd been brainswept, the unfortunate Helpers had been given new identities and convinced that everything was as it should be—that all was well as long as they did Mr. Curtain's bidding. Their presence at the Institute had been the unsettling, unhappy background to the children's secret investigations. And in the aftermath of their mission, using the Whisperer to return the Helpers' memories had been Mr. Benedict's first priority. It had been a daunting, exhausting job, but it had met with complete success—or so they had thought, until now.

"So one of them got away? Like Milligan?" Reynie asked.

"It turns out that Milligan was the *reason* she got away," Kate replied. "That day he escaped—overcoming his guards, running from the school, diving into the bay from the island cliffs—he set off every alarm. The Ten Men—or, you know, the Recruiters, as they were called back then—"

"We *know*!" Constance snapped. "Get on with it!"

"The Recruiters," continued Kate, unaffected, "were

shouting all kinds of orders, sounding all the alarms, getting Executives and Helpers involved. They broke out the boats, they opened the bridge gate, they tried to form an unbreakable perimeter on the mainland shore—they made use of every single body they could muster. Well, it did them no good. Milligan escaped, as you know—"

Constance made a hissing sound.

"—and in the process, a lot of the Helpers got confused and wandered away. They went off looking for this person they were being told to stop. In the commotion, most of them made it a fair distance before they were missed. So then the efforts had to be directed toward catching *them*. Eventually they were rounded up—all except one."

Sticky whistled. "So she's been out there all these years, not knowing her real identity?"

"Right. And she moved from city to city, keeping a very low profile, because she sensed that someone was trying to find her, and it scared her. That's what Milligan and I think, anyway. We think Mr. Curtain put the Scaredy Katz on her trail, and they've been playing a game of—well, of cats and mouse—all this time, until recently. They finally tracked her down."

"And they've either forced her or somehow persuaded her to help them," Reynie said. "That's why she was so important to Mr. Curtain. He must have known she was a telepath. In fact, I'm sure that's why he brainswept the poor woman in the first place—he perceived her as a threat to his plans."

Constance made another hissing sound.

"Yes, yes, we *know* you already know all this, Constance," Kate said. "We're just trying—"

But the sound Constance was making was not a hiss of exasperation. Rather, she was shushing them, for she had sensed that the radio was about to squawk. And now it did. Reynie, who had carried it down from his study, snatched it up and set it on the table.

The next squawk was followed by the familiar voice of a sentry named Clarion, who rattled off a code phrase. Once Reynie had given the appropriate response, Clarion said, "This is a high alert, my friends. Be advised that two well-dressed businessmen have entered the neighborhood in a rented luxury vehicle. The one in the passenger seat is extremely large, and his description seems to match—wait, Captain Plugg has just walked into the room; she's telling me something...."

Garbled sounds followed, and when Clarion spoke again, his voice was in a higher pitch: "Yes, she saw him, and she says there's no doubt about it! A pair of Ten Men are headed your way, and one of them is McCracken!"

THE BENEFITS
OF EMPTINESS

I repeat with all urgency," Clarion was barking into the radio, "it's McCracken! It's McCracken! And look, my orders are not to engage with Ten Men, but you're in danger—"

Reynie cut him off with the press of a button. "No, thank you, Clarion, but under no circumstances engage any Ten Men! You won't be able to stop them, and you'd pay a heavy price for trying. Please tell Captain Plugg to stay with you for now. Tell her that's our best chance. Over and out."

Kate was already whistling for Madge, dashing from the dining room and headed to the roof, for McCracken had good reason to recognize the falcon, which had once spoiled his plans in style. Most people wouldn't notice a particular bird tucked away in the branches of the giant elm tree. McCracken would.

"What do you think, Reynie?" Sticky asked. "Fight or flight? And by fight, I mean hide."

Reynie was up and pacing. He thought of Tai napping in Constance's room. He considered what they risked if they fled, what they risked if they stayed. Everything depended on what happened in the next few moments. So why did his mind keep returning to the ship, when he and Sticky were putting on the sailor uniforms and Constance, unbeknownst to them, was sneaking into the crate?

"I know what you're thinking," Constance said, startling him. "And, yes, I can do this." She was already rising from the table and walking to the window that overlooked the courtyard. "I just need a good reason to give him."

Reynie jumped to her side. "Captain Plugg wouldn't have left the house unprotected if there was anything or anyone of value inside, right? There's your good reason."

Constance eyed him. "That's why you told her not to come back."

"Well, that and the fact that there's nothing she could do, anyway, except get hurt."

On every side of Mr. Benedict's house, certain specially designed windows had been installed. They appeared to be normal windows, but in fact they were impossible to see through from the outside—they always looked as if the light were just at the wrong angle—while from the inside they remained perfectly transparent. Their design had been one of the Society's educational projects. On this side of the house, the two lookout windows were in Reynie's study and here in the dining room. Constance took her place at the window, therefore, with no danger of being spotted, and her view of the courtyard and front gate was clear. Nonetheless, her skin prickled and her breathing was shallow, as if she were about to face down a charging bull—as if a single misstep would be the end of her.

Sticky came and looked over her shoulder. "There," he whispered, pointing. A small black limousine, polished and iridescent as a raven's wing, had just eased around the corner and onto their street.

"I see it," Constance said. "Now don't say anything else. Your breath is bad."

Sticky started to protest, then thought better of it. Now was not the time. He did, however, make a mental note to brush his teeth as soon as possible, assuming he got out of this situation with his teeth intact.

Kate crept into the dining room, having gotten Madge safely within the house, and stole over to stand with Reynie and Sticky. They could all see past Constance easily enough, and all watched in tense silence as the car pulled up to the curb. It seemed to tilt slightly toward them, as if its passenger-side tires were very low—indeed, almost flat. Then the front passenger-side door opened, and the explanation for the tilt became apparent.

The well-dressed man who stepped from the vehicle was enormous. Even had he not been wearing such an expertly tailored suit, even had his brown hair not been so perfectly coiffed, even if a large silver watch had gleamed on only one wrist rather than on both — even then there could have been no mistaking the imposing figure of McCracken.

With a word to the driver, who remained in the car, the most feared of all Ten Men approached the courtyard gate, absently straightening his tie. His eyes roamed the windows of the house. They glanced up into the elm tree, then back at the house. McCracken rested one hand on top of the gate — it might have been the gate to a children's play area in a library, so small and insubstantial did it seem before him — and stood there as if considering.

"He saw Captain Plugg on her motorcycle," Constance breathed. "He knows she isn't here." She glanced nervously at Reynie, just the quickest flick of her eyes, but he saw it and leaned in close to her ear.

"He certainly doubts that she would leave us here unprotected," Reynie murmured. "And, after all, the Katz brothers reported that we weren't here. Witnesses saw us get on that ship."

Constance nodded. She squinted in concentration. "Yes," she whispered. "He felt the need to check for himself, but would she really leave us here unprotected? This really is a waste of his time."

"Such a waste of his time," Reynie murmured. "It really is."

Constance stared and stared.

McCracken removed his hand from the gate. Still he remained there on the sidewalk, studying the house.

The Society members collectively held their breath. It had been years since they were this close to any Ten Man, much less the worst of them all. McCracken's shock-watches glinted in the sun. His dangerously scented handkerchief peeked from his suit coat's breast pocket. His elegant necktie might have been a serpent. The man positively radiated menace.

McCracken crossed his massive arms, evidently deep in thought. Then, at long last, he glanced up at the clear sky, smiled to himself, and returned to the limousine. The vehicle, once more listing to the passenger side, eased from the curb and cruised away.

"You did it!" Kate whispered, grabbing Constance by the shoulders and giving her a little shake of congratulations. Sticky and Reynie echoed the whispered cheer, but Constance pushed away from them and walked unsteadily to her chair at the table. Her eyes shone with tears, and she looked very pale and downcast.

"Did that make you feel sick?" Sticky asked, for influencing others' minds had used to take a terrible toll on Constance. When she gave a slight nod in response to his question, Sticky hurried from the room, returning a few minutes later with a beaker of orange liquid. "Try this," he urged. "Don't worry, I added way too much sugar."

Constance dutifully sipped from the beaker, her breathing growing deeper and steadier.

At length she was ready to talk. After insisting that they not prompt her with questions (the others obliged her by locking their lips with invisible keys), Constance began to relate what they all had been present for but only she had observed.

"Before McCracken decided against opening the gate," Constance said, "he was wishing he had the Listener with him. He figured she could tell him if anyone was here or not.

Which, you know, she probably could. But he doesn't like moving her around town, because he feels it's too risky. She's as precious as gold to him. In fact, he was anxious to get back to her and make sure she was being well guarded. He'd left her with Crawlings, and you know how he feels about Crawlings not using proper caution."

The others nodded and kept quiet.

"So I played that up, too," Constance went on. "I turned up the volume on his anxiety, and that sealed it. He decided to get moving. But then—you all saw him just stand there for a while? Well, he was thinking about *me*. How he wished I'd been here, because he wants to use me if he ever gets a chance."

The others exchanged grim looks as Constance shuddered and went on: "He was thinking—so casually, the way you might think about what to have for breakfast—that if he can't make me do what he wants, he'll just get rid of me. It wasn't like he was thinking about a person at all! I'm just a potential weapon—like something he keeps in his briefcase—and if I don't work for him, he'll throw me away, as simple as that, just as he would anything else that's useless to him. Like a piece of trash. It was horrible."

The others' expressions now ranged from deep sympathy to fury, but Constance had looked down at the table purposely to avoid seeing them.

"So," Constance said, "there was that. But I'm not the only person McCracken has his eyes on. He and the others are making long-term plans. Right now they're awaiting word from Mr. Curtain, but if they don't hear something soon, they may move on. They each have a long list of people they intend to seek revenge against—just to get started—and there's an even longer list of people who stand between McCracken and the power he seeks. Did you see him smile? He was thinking about those lists. He was amusing himself with visions of overflowing hospitals and long lines at the morgue. Not just in Stonetown, either—all over the world."

Constance shivered again. "They weren't just dark fantasies," she said. "They were plans."

The Society remained at the dining room table for some time, urgently discussing the situation. It had occurred to Reynie that the Listener might have sensed Constance reading McCracken's thoughts. If so, and if she reported it to McCracken, their location would be betrayed after all. Fortunately, this had also occurred to Constance, and even as she'd been dealing with everything else, she'd thwarted that possibility by cycling through various memories of McCracken.

"Like showing a horror film," Constance said, "except all of it was true. The Listener doesn't know whether to believe any of it—she knows I might be trying to trick her. But the point is, I gave her too much to process. She's already moved on. She's just back to listening again."

It was a little unsettling for Reynie to think of Constance privately developing and employing such tactics. But it wasn't only Constance. Until recently, there had never been an occasion when each member of the Society operated so independently of all the others. For the past two days, while Kate was off completing her mission with Milligan, Reynie had been wedded to the radio: communicating in code with Milligan's remaining local sentries and agents, tracking the arrival at Stonetown of the Baker's Dozen, and exchanging coded messages with the MV *Shortcut II* (whose passengers, dismayed by the disappearing act Reynie had orchestrated, were equally grateful to hear that he and his friends were safe).

Sticky, meanwhile, had been glued to his specialized computer station, monitoring the radio waves (among other invisible signals) to ensure that Reynie's communications were not themselves being monitored, and to pick up—as he had done three or four times—private chatter among the Ten Men, whose conversations skittered across frequencies like water bugs on the surface of a pond and were impossible to keep up with for long. On such occasions Sticky would engage the intercom and recite to Reynie what he'd overheard, and Reynie, for his part, had kept Sticky up to speed on all his coded communications. For two whole days the young men, working on the same floor of the same house, had seldom laid eyes on each other—and never on the presumably sulking Constance, who in fact had been hidden away dealing with her own secret missions.

The experience had been unsettling for all of them, not only for Reynie, and despite what had just happened with McCracken, there was also an unmistakable sense of relief in the air. They had come through the ordeal of the Ten Man's visit successfully. The Society was, for the moment, all together again.

Constance was still on the subject of the Listener. "What Kate was telling us about her before *he* showed up was actually good news," she said, "and it couldn't have come at a better time. It boosted my confidence when I was muddying the picture for her about McCracken."

"That's great!" Kate said. "But how so?"

"Until then," Constance explained, "I'd been thinking that she was stronger than I am." She tapped her head. "Up here, I mean. Sure, I'd been able to put her off, but it took a lot of work, and whenever *I* tried to get a better look at *her*, I had no luck at all. She didn't even seem to be trying—she just projected an emptiness that I couldn't penetrate. But do you see? I couldn't get at what was hidden because *she* can't get at it, either! She has no idea who she is! She hardly knows what she's doing!"

"That *is* good news," Reynie said, nodding. "The best news since all of this started."

Kate looked back and forth between Reynie and Constance. "Once again, I'm delighted to hear it," she said. "But can you explain why? I mean, is there some sort of 'battle of the telepaths' scheduled that I'm unaware of?"

"There's been one all along," Reynie said. "When I spoke with Mr. Benedict, he told me that Constance should only reach out to him if we knew she could do it safely. We had no idea of the telepath's whereabouts or identity, no idea of the extent of her abilities. What if she eavesdropped on our plans? The Ten Men would know everything. But if Constance feels confident that she can keep the line clear, so to speak..."

"I can at least make it incredibly hard for her," Constance said. "It's scary, and it makes me nervous, but that much I think I can do. And I can keep our location secret, no matter what. I'm sure of that now."

"So you can get in touch with Mr. Benedict," Sticky said. "That's what you're saying? We can make our next move?"

Constance tapped her nose and pointed. "He can tell us what to do!"

"Yes!" said Kate and Sticky at the same time. They traded amused glances and crossed their eyes, for long ago this had become the settled response among the Society members to such occurrences, which were hardly uncommon.

"Dad will have something in mind," Constance was saying. "He'll have a plan A, a plan B—all the way down to plan Z. You know he will." She spoke insistently, as if to convince herself of the truth of her words.

"Of course he will," Kate agreed, "and I hope it calls for some serious hurrying. I'm getting antsy with all this sitting around."

Sticky looked at her askance. "You literally dropped out of the sky before lunch, Kate. Do try to be patient."

Reynie, who had risen from his chair, stopped and turned toward the table when he realized that the others had fallen silent. They were all looking at him expectantly, for whenever something set Reynie to pacing, a new mystery, problem, or revelation was surely on its way to being announced.

"A couple of things," Reynie said. "First of all, Constance, you gave me a mental nudge back in the captain's quarters, didn't you? Like you just did with McCracken? Now I know why I was thinking of it earlier. I haven't quite been able to accept that I didn't notice you sneaking into that crate. I distinctly remember feeling preoccupied with my shoelaces—I kept thinking they might be untied. I checked them three times."

Constance screwed up her face, as if she were about to have to eat something disgusting. "Yes," she admitted after a pause. "I gave you those shoelace notions. I also helped you to believe that the crate was still empty, just heavier than it looked. And...I'm sorry. I was desperate not to be left behind, and you're way too observant not to have noticed otherwise."

"Did you convince *me* of something, too?" asked Sticky, prepared to be indignant.

Constance shook her head. "No need."

At this, Sticky truly did become indignant, but for an entirely different reason.

"I forgive you," Reynie said. "What's more important to me is how you felt afterward. You didn't seem to feel horribly sick. And you seem to have recovered pretty well from what happened just now."

"No, it wasn't terrible either time," Constance said. "I got a headache and felt a little nauseated, but that's all. Maybe because I was trying to be careful—I didn't try to convince you of anything you wouldn't ever think of yourself. Like you said, it was just a nudge. And that's how we went about it with McCracken, too." She considered a moment. "You're wondering if the consequences are less severe because I'm older, aren't you? It's possible, I guess. I haven't tried that kind of stunt in a long time."

"Oh, brother," said Sticky when he saw what they were getting at. "You're thinking the Listener might figure out how to change people's minds. If she develops her abilities, and she doesn't suffer very much as a result, she could do almost anything, couldn't she?"

"It's not an encouraging thought," Reynie said. "Right now

she's just getting a handle on her abilities. Who knows if she was even aware of her gift before the Ten Men caught up with her? Whatever she knew in her old life—the Whisperer hid it from her. But now she's actively using the gift, cultivating it. For all we know, she might improve very quickly."

"That's all the more reason to reach out to Mr. Benedict right away," said Kate, "while Constance still feels like she's got the upper hand."

"True," said Reynie, "except that brings me to my second thought. Constance, when was the last time you slept?"

Constance explained that she'd only been allowing herself short naps—and only when Tai was sleeping. She had the impression that the Listener was equally exhausted but also equally vigilant, and only slept when Constance did.

"That's what I figured," Reynie said. "She's constantly on alert, waiting for you to reveal something useful. So why don't we be as smart as possible? Let's wait until the Listener is asleep."

Kate groaned. "Why do you have to make so much sense? I hate it when the smart move is to wait."

"I think we can speed the process along," Reynie assured her. "Constance, at this point you could probably fall asleep at the drop of a hat, right?"

"No hat required," Constance replied. "I could fall asleep right here in this chair. Just say the word."

"Great. Here's my idea," said Reynie. He went on to detail his plan, which they all thought a good one, and in less than a minute Constance was curled up in an easy chair in the corner, her hands tucked under her cheek, her scarlet hair falling across her face.

"Don't watch me," she mumbled. "I hate it when..." Her breathing deepened, and she was out.

The others sat quietly at the dining table, exchanging significant glances. They would very much like to speak privately while Constance was asleep, but they dared not even whisper. It was crucial that she stay asleep. They would give her ten minutes. If the Listener was in a similar state, she would surely be asleep by then herself, desperately taking advantage of Constance's nap.

I wonder what Constance's dreams might reveal, Reynie thought. He had no idea if the Listener could pick up on a dream, bright signal or no. But dream information wouldn't be considered reliable. He hoped not, at any rate. It was hard to imagine how these telepathic mechanisms worked. Constance spoke of bright signals, which made them seem visual, but she had often referred to some people's thoughts as being *louder* than others'. And they were distinctive, she said: Mr. Benedict's thoughts sounded like Mr. Benedict's voice in her mind, while Reynie's thoughts sounded like Reynie's voice, and so on.

These things were naturally fascinating to Reynie, though he knew that for Constance they had been a burden. She was in possession of such genius, by all rights she should know more than the rest of them put together. And yet she'd spent these last years, under Mr. Benedict's supervision and care, almost entirely focused on simply learning how *not* to read others' minds. It was of critical importance, Mr. Benedict had said, in order for Constance to have a happy life. So it was that Constance remained exhaustingly childish and cranky much of the time, though in many ways her mind was more sophisticated than that of anyone they knew, including Mr. Benedict.

There had been a couple of peaceful years, not long after Mr. Curtain and most of the Ten Men had been captured, when Constance seemed relaxed, contented, and generally cheerful, not unlike young Tai Li. Reynie and the others could scarcely believe their luck. But as time passed, as Constance grew, she had once again taken a turn for the peevish. She was not yet a teenager, not even what some people called a *tween*ager, but had become, as Kate put it, a *mean*-ager.

"It will all balance out in the end," Mr. Benedict had said more than once, and Reynie certainly hoped this was true. He believed in Constance, believed she would come out all right. But only if they succeeded in their dangerous task at hand.

"It's time," Kate said without glancing at the clock, and of course she was right. Ten minutes had passed.

"Here we go," Sticky said.

The three rose and went to the chair where Constance slept. She was not exactly snoring, but rather making spouting sounds like those of a breaching whale, and with each breath the scarlet curtain of hair over her face fluttered. The older three all hesitated, looking at one another with small smiles—it was so much easier to feel their love for Constance when she was sleeping—before giving over to the dread of waking her up.

"You boys are cowards," Kate said at last. She shook Constance awake.

"It's not an *apple*, it's a *monkey*!" Constance cried, sitting bolt upright. She pushed the hair out of her face and looked around with wild eyes.

"Easy, Connie girl," said Kate in a soothing tone. "You're absolutely right. Also, you were dreaming."

After she'd groaned miserably for a minute or two and Reynie had brought her a glass of water, Constance came more fully awake. She sipped the water, smacked her lips, and frowned in concentration.

"She's asleep," Constance announced briskly, suddenly all business. "Now's the time. I'm going to reach out to him." She closed her eyes.

The others watched her face attentively. No matter how many times they had seen her project her thoughts, they never stopped being amazed. Even more mystifying was the idea of Constance *receiving* a person's thoughts from so far away. But, then, they were not just any person's thoughts. They were Mr. Benedict's, and when Mr. Benedict concentrated, Constance had often said, his thoughts were louder than a trumpeting elephant.

"He hears me," Constance breathed, her eyes still closed. "He's there with Mr. Curtain and…S.Q. is there, too."

The others nodded without speaking, not wishing to disturb her concentration. They knew that S.Q. Pedalian, a kind young man improbably loyal to Mr. Curtain yet also a friend to them, was allowed to visit Mr. Curtain in his security suite. Other than Mr. Benedict, he was the only person who ever did.

"Hush!" Constance hissed, though no one had spoken. They all held their breath. Her frown deepened. She nodded as if to indicate that she understood what was being said to her, as if someone else was in the room with them. "He's going to let us help him," she murmured, scowling with concentration. "He's—okay, here it comes...."

A moment of tense silence passed. And then in a halting, uncertain tone, Constance began to recite:

> *"Where one who stands defies the name,*
> *Dare hunt the hunter in his frame*
> *And strike the clenches from their floor*
> *And—* GET OUT!"

These last two words Constance uttered in something between a snarl and a shriek. The others flinched, glancing around in alarm, but the only intruder in the room was impossible to see. Constance swatted furiously at the air as if being swarmed by hornets. "The stupid—she woke up! He *woke* her up! McCracken did! Oh, I hate him, I hate him, I *hate* him!"

To her extreme irritation, Constance was unsure how much the Listener had heard of Mr. Benedict's message. Perhaps none of it, perhaps all of it. The moment she'd sensed the Listener eavesdropping, she'd begun blasting images and jumbles of words in her mind, at the same time warning Mr. Benedict to say no more.

"I don't think I needed to warn him, though." Constance spoke without looking at her friends, still gathered around her easy chair. "I think he noticed her listening as soon as I did."

"He was obviously being careful from the beginning,"

Reynie said. "He was communicating in a way that wouldn't reveal where we are or what his plan might be."

"It was just like the old days at the Institute, wasn't it?" Kate said. "He was being cryptic—giving us clues he thinks only we can figure out. But, um, Constance, I don't suppose you heard the whole last line, did you? Did Mr. Benedict finish it before he went quiet?"

Constance glanced at her sidewise and shrugged uneasily. "I *kind* of heard it."

Sticky clapped a hand to the top of his head. "What do you mean by 'kind of'? You do realize that we need—"

Constance flew out of the chair, grabbed Sticky's shirt in her fists, and pulled him forward until his face was inches from her own. Punctuating her words with tugs on his shirt, she hissed: "I was. And am. A little. *Busy.* George."

There was a freighted silence. Then Sticky, very quietly and smoothly, said, "I'm sorry I expressed frustration, Constance. I realize you're under a great deal of pressure, and I in no way mean to suggest that you're to blame for the challenging circumstances in which we find ourselves. Furthermore, I appreciate your calling me by my given name, knowing as you do that I've been trying to make strides in that direction."

Constance blinked. She had actually called him George out of an angry reflex (for Sticky used to dislike his given name), but she decided not to reveal this fact. Instead she groaned, released his shirt, and flopped back into the chair. "It's weird now that you're good-looking," she muttered wearily. "You can say pretty much anything and it makes me want to believe you."

Reynie and Kate murmured their agreement. Sticky bit his lip.

"Anyway," Constance said, "I think I got the gist of the last part. Something about going through a door made out of clay—the kind that the French use."

"A French door?" Kate pressed. "Is that what he meant?"

"I guess?" Constance said. "What's a French door?"

For a moment no one spoke. The others were still sometimes amazed by the things Constance didn't know. Only a month ago, for instance, she'd accidentally revealed that she didn't know what the circulatory system was—she seemed to think it was a method of drawing perfect circles and had insisted Kate teach it to her.

Reynie turned to Sticky. "Care to do the honors?"

"Sure," Sticky said, clearing his throat. "Do you think we're talking about American French doors or British French doors? Because when the British refer to French doors, they typically mean casement windows that extend to floor level and open onto a garden or balcony or the like. They're also often called French *windows*, which really makes better sense, don't you think? In this country, though, Constance, the term 'French doors' typically suggests two adjoining doors that have glass panes from top to bottom and that open in the middle. So they're very similar architectural features in some ways, but not identical."

Constance was staring bleakly at him. "But neither of them is made of clay?"

Sticky shook his head.

Constance closed her eyes. "I give up."

"Sticky," Reynie ventured, "can you think of any doors

that *are* made of clay? Some kinds of masonry ovens, maybe? Kilns?"

Sticky confirmed that, indeed, several types of masonry ovens—also known as brick ovens, stone ovens, or even *cloam* ovens (though that term was used exclusively in the English counties of Devon and Cornwall)—

Kate cut in. "They all have doors made out of clay?"

"Not necessarily," Sticky said. "But sometimes."

"Not helpful yet," Kate said, casting a look at Reynie. "Or is it?"

Reynie shook his head. "Not yet. We'll get there, though. We should start at—"

Here, however, Reynie's words were interrupted by the appearance of Tai Li, who pattered sleepily into the room. His hair was newly tangled from the pillow, and his arms were wrapped around a fire-engine red bucket.

"Well, hello, young man," Kate said. "What have you got there?"

Tai grinned. "Your bucket! It still has stuff in it! I don't know how to open it, though," he said, setting the bucket on the floor and kneeling beside it. "Does it have secret catches, too? Like the chest in Reynie's study? That's where I found it."

"Yes, indeed," said Kate, and with a skeptical look at Reynie, who shook his head in silent reply, she went over to demonstrate how to open the bucket's flip-top. "So Reynie showed you the secret catches on his chest?"

Tai shrugged and pulled a horseshoe magnet from a pouch inside the bucket. "He just said it when he was getting out your spyglass. I had to press so hard it hurt my fingers! Does this stick to metal?" As he spoke, he moved the magnet toward the side of the bucket. With a sharp clang, the ends of the magnet snapped fast to the bucket. Tai laughed and tried to pull the magnet away again, but he only succeeded in dragging the bucket across the floor.

"Tai," Reynie said, "I don't remember telling you about the catches. Did I say that out loud, or did I say it in my head?"

The little boy, having dragged the bucket all the way over to the dining table, paused in his efforts to consider. "Oh! Yes, it was in your head." He sat on his bottom, pressed his bare feet against the side of the bucket, and yanked on the magnet with both hands. When it came free, he tumbled backward with a delighted squeal. Then he righted himself and immediately stuck the magnet to the bucket again.

The others in the room were exchanging troubled looks.

Sticky turned to Reynie. "Were you concentrating especially hard on the catches?" he asked in a low tone.

"I barely even thought about them," Reynie said. "If anything, I was concentrating more on everything *else*."

"It happens that way sometimes," Constance said. "You all remember how it used to be with me."

"So we're going to have to be on our guard whenever he's in the room," Sticky muttered. "Just like we do with you — or used to do, I mean."

Kate made a face. "Ugh, I hate doing that. It hurts my brain."

Constance fixed her with a look. "You do remember that I'm doing the same thing right now, don't you? Every single second? Complain some more, Kate."

"You're right, you're right," Kate said quickly. "Sorry. It's not a problem."

"One problem we do have, though," Reynie said, frowning, "is that in order to figure out Mr. Benedict's message, we need to concentrate. But if Constance concentrates—"

"Oh!" Sticky gasped. "Right! The Listener might hear whatever she's thinking. Did that occur to you, Constance, or...?" He trailed off, for Constance was looking at them each in turn, her face a mask of resentment, and tears suddenly standing in her eyes.

"I get it," she said quietly. She glanced across the room to where Tai was still entertaining himself with Kate's magnet. "You can't risk having me around. Okay, that's fine."

"Just a second, Constance," Reynie said. "That's not necessarily—"

"Tai!" Constance called in a tremulous voice. "If you need me, I'll be in my room." She wiped at her eyes with a rumpled sleeve of the suit jacket, cast one last bitter look at Reynie, and stalked out.

They all looked glumly after her.

"That went well," Sticky muttered.

Across the room, Tai made a whimpering sound and climbed to his feet. His face was puzzled. "Is Constance okay? It felt like she was sad, and now she isn't answering my thoughts. Can we ask her to come back?"

Reynie forced himself to turn from the door. "She's okay!" he called, trying to sound carefree. "Don't worry— she'll be back soon!" To the others, more quietly, he said, "We need to keep in mind that anything Tai 'overhears' might end up in Constance's head as well. They might not be able to help it."

"Right," Sticky said. "So we're trying to protect multiple

layers of secrets. Maybe we should ask Captain Plugg to look after him?"

"I don't want to go down there!" Tai cried, running over to them with big eyes. "I don't know her!"

"You didn't know us, either, until a little while ago, squirt," Kate said. "Captain Plugg is great."

"I don't want—!"

"It's fine, it's fine," Reynie said quickly. "She isn't back yet, anyway. I haven't heard her motorcycle. We'll introduce you to her later, Tai. Right now why don't you go back and play with the magnet? Everything's fine."

Tai hesitated. "And Constance is fine, too?" His eyes roamed their faces, which all instantly adopted reassuring expressions.

"Constance is going to be just great," Reynie said, which wasn't exactly what Tai had asked him, but the boy seemed satisfied. With a look of relief, he gave Reynie a hug and wandered back to the bucket by the table.

The older three all took deep breaths, then turned and huddled together.

"Okay," Kate said softly, "you were going to say we should start at the beginning, Reynie. So let's do that. What does he mean, 'Where one who stands defies the name'? What name? And who is the one standing?"

"He might not have meant a specific person," Sticky suggested. "By 'one,' he might have meant 'anyone.' You know, any person."

"That's true," Kate agreed. "So if any random person— or, I guess we don't know for sure, so it might also be a specific person—but anyway, if some person, whoever Mr. Benedict means, makes some kind of defiant stand…" She shook her head. "I don't know. What are you thinking, Reynie?"

"Big feet!"

This last came from Tai, who trotted back over to them with Kate's bucket. He was using the magnet, currently stuck to the side of the bucket, as a second handle.

"Excuse me?" Kate said.

"Reynie's thinking about big feet!"

Everyone looked at Reynie, who sighed. "I was thinking about S.Q.," he said. "I mean, that's one of the random things I was thinking about to keep a certain someone from hearing my deeper thoughts. I guess the big feet stood out to him."

"He uses big words, but his name is only two letters," Tai said. He had opened the bucket and was rummaging around in it. "That's pretty funny. And we like him, right? Even though he used to help Mr. Curtain do bad things, he didn't really mean to, and he's a good guy. Right?"

"That's right," Kate said. She reached into the bucket and took out two or three things that, upon further reflection, might not be suitable for a five-year-old boy to play with. She shoved them into her pocket. "S.Q. is our friend. He comes here for dinner all the time. One day, when all of this is over, you can meet him!"

"And see his big feet?" Tai asked hopefully.

"Unless he forgets to bring them," Kate teased. "Now, listen," she said, with a furtive wink at Sticky and Reynie, "I need to take a break to clear my head. You want to come with me and see my tranquilizer gun?"

"Oh, yes!" Tai squeaked. "Can I hold it?"

"Nope," Kate replied.

"Okay!" Tai cried, as if even more excited now. He scooped up Kate's bucket and ran toward the door.

"Maybe you two will solve it quickly if you don't have to run interference with the little one," Kate whispered. "It's worth a shot, right? I'll keep him occupied until Captain Plugg gets back."

She joined Tai at the door and whispered something to him. He giggled, and together they turned and bowed, then backpedaled until they were out of sight.

"Well, that's a relief," Sticky said.

"Definitely," Reynie affirmed.

They were both still looking at the doorway, and neither of them actually felt relieved. Not counting intercom communications from opposite ends of the house, the two hadn't worked alone together to solve a problem in ages. When Reynie had suggested the plan to sneak off the ship, Sticky had simply agreed to it. When the dangerous chemicals on the rooftop had needed urgent attention, it was Sticky's chess-notation instructions that made it possible—Reynie had only followed them. So when, Reynie wondered, was the last time they had sat across from each other to figure something out? He wasn't sure. Sticky would remember, of course, and it occurred to Reynie that asking him would be a way to break the sudden tension.

"Hey," he said, turning toward Sticky, "when did—"

"I guess—" said Sticky at the same moment. "Sorry, you go first."

"No, you go ahead," Reynie said. If Sticky had an idea, Reynie was determined to let him speak first. "What were you thinking?"

Sticky, who had only been going to suggest that they sit down, suddenly felt self-conscious. What if Reynie had already figured out Mr. Benedict's message? That wouldn't be unlike him. The last thing Sticky wanted was to say he was ready to get started, only to discover that Reynie had already finished. *That shouldn't matter*, he chastised himself. *The important thing is that we make progress.*

What Sticky said out loud, when he sensed Reynie waiting uncomfortably for a response, was this: "I was just going to say that I guess you've probably already figured it out. Have you?"

"Mr. Benedict's message?" Reynie said, caught off guard. How could he possibly have concentrated enough to figure that out yet? "Uh, no. I just..." He was about to suggest that they sit down and get started, but then he worried about seeming bossy. He didn't *think* it would seem bossy—it was a natural suggestion, given their history of sitting down together to work things out—but lately he'd had a hard time gauging his friend's feelings, and he didn't want to mess this up.

"You just what?" Sticky prompted. It wasn't like Reynie to hesitate so much, and Sticky's mind was racing, trying to figure out what the problem was.

Reynie realized he wasn't looking Sticky in the eye. That was no good, he thought. *First things first. Look your friend in the eye.* And so he raised his gaze to meet Sticky's—but then hesitated again, unsure what to say.

Sticky, disconcerted, cleared his throat and made a pretense of glancing at the clock. It occurred to him that Reynie was hesitating to speak because he didn't like what he was about to say. And what would that be? Sticky felt a wave of embarrassment wash over him. *He thinks I'm a distraction, too!*

"You know what?" Sticky said quickly, rubbing his scalp. "I should go up and deal with the mess on the roof. Why don't you work on this, I'll do that, and we'll get back together in a little bit?"

"I'll help you!" Reynie cried, taken aback. What had he done to offend Sticky? "We can talk while we're cleaning!"

"No, that's okay," Sticky said, already moving for the door. "Honestly, you'll probably get to the answers faster this way. Just—let me know if you need anything. I'll be back down soon. It won't take long."

Reynie opened his mouth to protest, but it was too late. Sticky was gone. Reynie closed his mouth. And then his eyes. He stood there alone in the dining room. How in the world was he supposed to concentrate when one of his best friends was upset with him?

They were supposed to have been prepared for a day like this, yet now that it had arrived, it was not going the way Reynie had imagined it would. Not at all.

MELANCHOLY MUSINGS
—AND—
RUEFUL RUMINATIONS

Down on the first floor, in Kate's room, Tai Li was jumping on the bed, something he had never been allowed to do in the orphanage. It was an especially springy bed with an especially sturdy frame, and with every jump, Tai thought he might be able to reach the ceiling with his outstretched fingers.

"You're not even close," Kate said from where she sat at her desk. "You realize that, right?"

"How close," said Tai, bouncing breathlessly, "am I getting?"

Kate watched him a moment. "Nine inches," she said, returning to her work. Arrayed on the desk before her were two dozen darts, ampoules of tranquilizer serum, and what resembled a very large water pistol. One by one, Kate was inspecting the ampoules, snapping them into their corresponding darts, then slipping the darts inside her jacket.

"Aren't you," Tai panted, "going to put the darts...into the gun?"

"With you in the room? No."

"How many...can you...put in there?"

"Six at a time," Kate said, then added under her breath, "I wish it were thirteen."

"Me too!" Tai said. "One for each...of the bad men."

Kate looked up, her mouth drawn tight. She had never liked it when Constance read her thoughts, and she did not like it any better when this little boy did. Even though, she had to admit, Tai Li was infinitely more agreeable as a little boy than Constance had been as a little girl. Anyway, he certainly wasn't doing it on purpose, and so she said nothing.

"What's the matter?" Tai asked, having either seen or sensed Kate's annoyance. "Do you want me to stop jumping on the bed?"

"What? No, have at it," Kate said, returning to her work. "You're really good at it."

"But what...if I break...the bed?" Tai panted, having been cautioned about such a disaster in the past.

Kate shrugged. "I'll fix it."

"But what...if I...fall off?"

"I'll catch you," Kate said.

"But you're way over there! And you're...sitting down!"

Kate shrugged again. "I'd still catch you, bouncy boy."

The rumble of a motorcycle sounded outside. Kate listened long enough to be sure it was Captain Plugg returning (Kate was thoroughly familiar with the guard's throttle patterns as she navigated the squeaky courtyard gate and then around to the back of the house). Satisfied, Kate held up one of the ampoules. "Did Constance tell you about these?"

Tai climbed down from the bed and went over to the desk. "They knock you out."

Kate snapped her fingers. "Just like that," she said, and as Tai tried in vain to snap his own fingers, she went on. "Rhonda Kazembe invented this particular formula. You know about Rhonda, right?"

"She's Constance's sister!"

"That's right, she and Number Two were Mr. Benedict's assistants, and he ended up adopting both of them, just like Constance. Well, among other things, Rhonda is an expert chemist, and she came up with this stuff so that Milligan could avoid hurting bad guys any worse than he had to. It was Sticky who whipped up this particular batch. Evidently, there's nothing he can't do these days."

Tai asked if he could hold one of the ampoules, and Kate gave him one. He held it up to the light, admiring the amber-colored liquid inside it. "Is it like duskwort?"

Kate raised her eyebrows. "What do you know about duskwort?"

"Constance told me that you went on a big adventure to find some, but there wasn't any left, only a plant called thwartwort"—Tai pronounced this word with some difficulty—"which doesn't do anything except glow in the dark. But *then* she said that for one of your projects you and Milligan went on an exposition—"

"Expedition."

"—expedition, and you hung from ropes on the side of a cliff for two whole days, and you found some duskwort! And you brought it home, but then it turned into dust, and it was the last in the world!"

"Let's have that back, mister," Kate said, for Tai was gesturing excitedly with the ampoule. He handed it over. "That's all true. It was Reynie's idea. He and Sticky— George—dug through scads of books, and based on what we already knew about duskwort, and what George already knew about climate, geography, botany, and I don't know what else, they narrowed the possibilities down to a few locations around the North Sea. Then they showed me what they'd figured out, I took it straight to Milligan, and a month later I was a hundred feet above the ground, sur- rounded by screaming cliff swallows, scouring jagged rocks for duskwort in a freezing rain. It was amazing!"

"And now it's all gone?"

"Yep. It's fragile stuff," Kate said. "I mean, it was. And George is now the only person in the world who ever saw it under a microscope. Not even Mr. Benedict got a chance— he wanted George to get the first crack at it."

"Wow," Tai breathed. "What did Constance do in the project?"

"Constance declared herself official project chronicler. She wrote a poem about it."

"That's how I know about it! She told me the poem!"

Kate snorted. "I'm sure she did. Well, I have to admit, it

wasn't a bad poem. There were some tricky rhymes. It was a little insulting, and I don't see why she had to make the entire last stanza about the importance of the poet in such endeavors, but we're all used to that sort of thing. It's funny if you take the right angle on it."

"I loved it!" Tai said, laughing. Then he grew serious. "Aren't you going to miss doing projects together?"

Kate narrowed her eyes. "So you've heard things are changing around here, have you?" She sighed. "Of course I'll miss our projects. That platform you like riding on so much? Well, the roof was leaking and there were rotten boards in the attic, and it was all going to have to be repaired anyway. So Mr. Benedict suggested we could use a little hands-on experience in hydraulics and construction. The boys and I built that platform ourselves!"

"And did Constance write a poem about it?" Tai asked hopefully.

"She did."

Tai giggled. "Tell me the other projects!"

"Honestly, there're too many to tell you all of them right now, but we put in the intercom system ourselves, and some special trick windows, and we used Mr. Curtain's technology to build a little machine that I nicknamed the Husher—a noise-cancellation device that makes everything around it perfectly silent. You can imagine the pranks we played on one another with that...."

"Constance says it was just you who played the pranks! Until everybody begged you to stop scaring them."

Kate frowned and considered this. "Huh. That might actually be true."

She had finished her dart preparations now and was double-checking that everything was in its proper place. She had a feeling that she was going to need to use the tranquilizer gun in the near future, and it was a nervous thought, even for her.

And yet, Kate realized, the nervous feeling was actually a relief, because it took her mind off the other feeling, the one prompted by Tai's question.

Aren't you going to miss doing projects together?

The melancholy feeling.

Kate much preferred the nervous one.

Tai was edging around the desk to get closer to the empty tranquilizer gun. Kate slid it out of reach. Tai began edging around the desk in the other direction.

"Are you as good as Milligan with that?" he asked.

"These days I'm even better," Kate said matter-of-factly. Then, upon a moment's reflection, she added, "I don't know if he realizes that, though. I used to be amazed at how fast and accurate Milligan was with his."

"But you aren't anymore?"

"Well, like I said, I'm faster and more accurate than he is now, and it doesn't seem quite the thing, you know, to be amazed at one's own abilities."

Tai's face took on a crafty expression. "I'll bet you really aren't as good as Milligan is."

Kate gave him a look. "I know what you're trying to do."

"Show me, Kate! *Please!*"

Kate took a deep breath. Not because she didn't want to give Tai a demonstration—she already felt as though she would do anything for this little boy—but because she knew her instinct was to make choices that others found rather less than careful. She wanted to be sure of her choice now.

"Okay, get down here behind the desk," Kate said. Tai eagerly complied. "Now peek over the top of it and look at that spot above the door—do you see it? Where there's a hole in the plaster about the size of a nickel? Good. Now get back down behind the desk again. We're going to be on the extra-safe side, you and me."

"Okay!" Tai exclaimed. He covered his ears.

"You don't need to do that. It's pretty quiet. Now look," Kate said, showing him a dart. She removed its ampoule of serum. "See that? Now I won't waste serum on a poor old wall that never hurt anybody."

"Right!" Tai said, grinning. He still had his hands over his ears, but Kate wasn't going to insist.

"So now I just load the dart like this," Kate said, showing him. "And then—" She moved so quickly that Tai uttered a startled squeak and fell backward. When he recovered his balance a moment later, the tranquilizer gun was resting on the desk, and Kate was regarding Tai with crossed arms. "And that's how I do it!"

"Did you shoot the dart?" asked Tai.

"What do you mean, did I shoot the dart? You saw me!"

Tai slowly stood up and gaped at the tiny hole in the plaster above the door. It seemed to have bloomed feathers. He gasped.

Kate smiled. Her own eyes went up to the ceiling, above which, she presumed, Reynie and Sticky were busy solving the message from Mr. Benedict. *You should be up there*, she thought. And then: *Or no, actually, you need to get used to this. It's good. It's all fine.*

"What's the matter?"

Kate lowered her gaze and discovered Tai looking up at her with an expression of concern. She put on a frown. "Are you kidding me? Nothing's the matter! Didn't you see that shot?"

Tai cocked his head uncertainly. "But now you're thinking about S.Q.'s big feet! Like Reynie did when he was trying to keep me from hearing his thoughts."

"Good grief," Kate said, shaking her head. "Can't a person think about somebody's big feet sometimes?" She made as if to tickle Tai, who giggled and leaped away. She took a deep breath and said, "I do believe that bed needs more jumping on. Can you help it out?"

"Yes, I can!" Tai cried happily, and for the moment, at least, Kate was out of danger of crying.

∿∶∾

In her room on the third floor, Constance lay in bed, her shoes still on, glaring at the ceiling. She could feel the Listener's presence, a palpable attentiveness, but she deflected the intrusions easily enough. The Listener was a person, too, after all, and Constance knew she was equally exhausted. Not to mention conflicted: Constance could sense the uncertainty in that invisible gaze. The Listener was understandably confused. And Constance knew she shouldn't be angry at this woman who had been brainswept, who was being deceived or compelled to buzz Constance's brain like this.

But Constance Contraire was very angry indeed.

She was angry at this mental attack, angry at Sticky and Reynie for their attempt to abandon her on the ship, angry at the way they and Kate confided in one another in ways they didn't do with her, angry at being left out just now, angry at being left behind in the future. Constance squeezed her eyes closed. She felt tears trickle from the corners. The tears made her angry, too.

She knew the older three were keeping secrets from her. They still treated her like a little kid. Although now that she thought about it, the way they treated Tai, who actually *was* a little kid, seemed far nicer than the way they were with her. Worse, she couldn't pretend that this wasn't partly her own fault. She was maddening to deal with—she'd been maddening to deal with even when she was cute little Tai Li's age—and this made her angry, too.

> *Why does Tai have to be cute as a button*
> *When I was a whiner, a snoot, and a glutton?*

Now Constance was angry for coming up with that poem. She hadn't even meant to.

Her mind skipped back to its previous track. Yes, she knew that the older three kept secrets from her, and secrets were infuriating. But Constance would never try to sneak a look at them. She had learned the hard way, years ago, that it was much better not to do so. For she had perceived one day, only by eavesdropping on Reynie's thoughts, that she was getting on his nerves. He was thoroughly annoyed with her and trying hard to hide it. To Constance, this was a crushing revelation.

For although she very often *tried* to get on the others' nerves (she could hardly have explained why), to discover that she could be annoying even when she *wasn't* trying was nothing short of horrible. It had taken her a long time to recover from that feeling. Without realizing it, Reynie had helped her get better by being his usual kind and patient self—and Constance did know that he loved her, and that everyone else loved her, too—and after a while she came to realize that she'd simply learned an important lesson: She needed to judge her friends and family by their actions, not by their thoughts, for thoughts are fleeting and temperamental, the reflection of a moment, and are very often confused and misleading. Thoughts formed into spoken words are a different matter, and actual deeds another matter still.

From then on, Constance had been extremely motivated to learn to avoid accidentally reading others' minds. She didn't want to feel that particular hurt again. And now, trying to calm down, she reminded herself that it was okay to have secrets sometimes. After all, isn't every unspoken thought a secret? And didn't she have some secrets herself?

But that proved an unhelpful line of thinking, for what Constance considered to be her greatest secret was the fact that, despite her best efforts, she hadn't been able to keep from knowing something, which was this: At one time or another in the last few years, every one of the older members of the Society had developed a temporary crush on one of the others. The extra intensity of feeling had unavoidably drawn Constance's mental attention. She had been very annoyed. But it was also true that in every case, the Society members had kept their crushes a secret, fearing that to reveal them would somehow risk damaging the Society as a whole. Thus, for a while, anyway, they had all made private sacrifices out of loyalty to the group. That kind of dedication seemed to be fading now. Which made Constance angry.

And what made her angrier still was the fact that *she* never *revealed* those secret crushes—not even during the worst arguments, when Constance had desperately wanted to lash out and hurt her friends. How embarrassing it would have been for them! But time and again she had resisted using this powerful weapon, and she viewed this as the greatest sacrifice of all, greater than any the others had made. And the fact that she had made a great sacrifice for their sakes and none of them knew it made Constance angry. It made her furious.

Constance opened her eyes. She wiped away the tears. She glared at the ceiling. She might not attack her friends, not really, but she definitely wanted to attack something. And there was the Listener, still present, still confused, trying to get inside Constance's head to figure out where she was, what her plans were, what she knew.

It's time to turn the tables, Constance thought, narrowing her eyes.

Sticky was on the rooftop patio, sprinkling black powder over a bubbling red puddle, which caused the liquid to swell and firm up. The resulting mass looked like lasagna. Sticky used a gigantic spatula to scrape it up and drop it into a metal container. He selected a different powder from his kit and went in search of a different puddle.

This was something he could do almost without thinking: His knowledge of chemicals and their complex interactions was unsurpassed. Sticky had already absorbed almost everything ever published about chemistry. This fact, combined with his own compelling experiments, as well as his unequaled ability to keep up with new research being reported in scientific journals (he read several each morning, in several languages), had marked him as an obvious candidate for directing chemical research in a laboratory. Whether or not he ran a distinguished lab, though, George "Sticky" Washington was already a famous name in the world of science.

So why did he feel like such a kid?

But there it was, the truth: Sticky still felt like a kid. He still thought of himself as "Sticky," despite his efforts to return to his given name. He still liked it better when the others accidentally called him that, too. It felt more natural. When they called him George, he felt as if they didn't know him, as if they were speaking to someone else. Yet he clearly had one foot in the adult world, and it seemed only right that he bring his other foot along—that he make the second step. But he didn't want to. Except that he did. Or did he?

Sticky Washington knew everything, evidently, except what he wanted.

He took out a spray bottle and squirted it onto what resembled a pile of gray ash in the corner of the rooftop patio. The ash made a squeaky, sputtering sound like that of a deflating balloon, turned into white smoke, and drifted away on the breeze. Sticky made a calculation in his head. He was tallying up the quantity and price of the chemicals his mistake had cost him. Yes, there had been an emergency, but if Sticky had thought to clear everything away sooner, there would have been no dangerous near miss up here with Kate, and no lost materials. Instead it was Reynie who had thought of it, just in time.

Sticky clenched his teeth. He didn't blame his friend for being such a nimble thinker. Nor was Reynie the kind of person who gloated. Quite the opposite, in fact. Still, what must it be like to be the first person everyone looked to for answers? The one who was always figuring out the last piece of the puzzle? Sticky couldn't help thinking it might be nice, though he knew it would also come with a lot of pressure.

Even so, if Reynie hadn't started thinking about leaving, Sticky might never have considered it himself. Certainly he wouldn't have sent letters of inquiry to prestigious laboratories. Not yet, anyway. But Reynie was inclined to go, or so it seemed to Sticky. Someone like Reynie could do anything, so who could blame him for not wanting to stay here with his childhood friends, working on projects, never really meeting anybody, never really testing his wings? No, Sticky didn't blame him. But then, why did he feel so abandoned?

Because you're still a kid, Sticky thought, rolling his eyes. *You're supposed to be so mature, but your friend talks about leaving and you start crying on the inside. You've barely been able to make eye contact with him for weeks.*

Sticky put away the spray bottle and powder canisters and took up a large push broom. He felt his eyes burning. Had he used the wrong neutralizer? He knew that he hadn't. He took a deep breath, let it out slowly, and began sweeping broken glass into tiny glittering piles.

It had been bad enough knowing that Kate wanted to go. But then, she was Kate. The world wasn't big enough for Kate Wetherall. She was always coming and going, wasn't she? That's what Sticky had focused on—the idea that Kate would always come back. But had he been deluding himself? Had he just been scared to look straight at the truth? So many things Sticky didn't know. But one thing he did: If he went away to direct a laboratory, he wouldn't be left behind here, feeling abandoned.

Sticky heard the stairwell door rattle and open. He turned to see Reynie in the doorway, panting and red-faced.

"We have *got* to fix that platform recall mechanism," Reynie said, wiping his brow.

"Sorry, I didn't expect you or I would have sent it back down."

"No, I know, it's fine," Reynie said, coming over. He surveyed the patio. "I see you've already got most of it, but I can help you with the tables. I guess we should let Kate deal with the parachute herself, huh?"

"Yeah, she'll have a system." Sticky looked at Reynie sidelong. "So, did you get it figured out?"

Reynie scratched his head. "To be honest with you? I can't seem to think straight. It's—I think it's unsettling me to have us all scattered around the house. At a time like this...I don't know." He shrugged. "I'm just not used to it."

Sticky nodded. His eyes were stinging again. "We probably all feel that way," he said in a slightly strained voice. "So, okay, then, if you're really that keen on helping, maybe we can discuss Mr. Benedict's riddle while we get this all cleared up?"

"Sounds like a plan," said Reynie gratefully. He took a step toward the nearest mangled table, then stopped. He turned to Sticky. "The way you had everything set up like a chessboard," he said. "Why did you do that? You don't need help remembering where things are."

Of course Reynie would think of that, Sticky thought, and he smiled. "It was in case you came up here," he admitted. "In case you were interested. I thought it would be easier if we could stand in one spot and I could use chess notation to point out whichever chemical I was speaking about at the moment." He paused. "But let me guess—you already figured as much."

"I just figured you had a reason," Reynie said. "It seemed like too much of a coincidence."

"Right," Sticky said. "Well…" He tapped his nose and pointed.

Reynie chuckled. "For the record," he said, "I was."

"You were what?"

"Going to come up here. Because I *was* interested. Still am, in fact. When all of this is over, will you catch me up?"

"Deal," Sticky said.

They jokingly shook hands, each feeling a small but welcome sense of relief, and together they set to cleaning up what remained of the patio mess. But they had hardly begun when Constance came panting out of the stairwell. Their mouths opened simultaneously, each ready to apologize for not sending the platform down—anything to keep Constance from going on a rage—but she gave them no opportunity.

"S.Q.'s in trouble!" she gasped. "We have to help him!" She doubled over, resting her hands on her knees, trying to get her breath.

Reynie bent forward, trying to see her face. "What do you mean? S.Q.? What could—?"

Constance looked up, and the fear was plain in her eyes. She had only to say the next word to send Reynie and Sticky running for the platform.

McCracken.

"I listened in on the Listener," Constance was shouting as the platform descended, "and this time I heard something! McCracken was trying to get her to locate S.Q., but it doesn't work that way. She tried, but she couldn't find him." She paused for breath.

"He doesn't have a bright signal," Sticky said.

Constance shook her head. They were passing through the attic, which grew suddenly dim as the trapdoor closed above them, shutting out the sunlight. "But McCracken and some others are going anyway. They still think they can catch him. It's all very confusing, but the Listener sensed the menace in McCracken's mind—it scared her, and that's why I think I could hear things as well as I did. Or see things. I could see what she saw as they were leaving. It seems really bad!"

"So S.Q.'s not with Mr. Benedict and Mr. Curtain anymore?" Reynie asked.

"No, he's somewhere in town—he left a message for McCracken in some secret location. Something in it made McCracken decide to go after him!"

The platform settled into place on the third floor just as Kate came bounding up from below. She was carrying Tai Li piggyback, the way she used to do with Constance, and was taking the stairs three at a time. "What's going on?" she said as they all came together. "Tai says you're scared about something, Constance!"

"McCracken's going after S.Q.," Reynie said quickly. To Constance he said, "Can you warn S.Q.? Send him a message?"

"I've already tried," Constance said with a frustrated shake of her head. "I don't know how to explain it, but if I don't know where he is, I can't…can't *aim*, I guess. And even if he heard me, I don't think he'd realize it was me. He's not like you, Reynie—I don't think he'd figure it out. Not in time, anyway."

"How much time do we have?" Kate asked.

"Minutes? Half an hour? I'm not sure. But not long."

Reynie and Sticky glanced at each other and took off running in different directions. Sticky was headed to his computer station, Reynie to the two-way radio, which he kicked himself now for having left on the second floor. He really *was* off his game. He descended the stairs as fast as he could and flew down the hallway. "Intercom! Sticky's office!" he cried as he ran into the dining room.

"All clear!" Sticky's voice blared just as Reynie reached the radio.

He spat out a string of code words followed by the bulletin: *S.Q. Pedalian in danger. If you see him, warn him to take cover immediately.* Reynie released the button he'd been pressing and stared helplessly at the radio. What were the odds that one of the handful of agents and sentries scattered about the very large city of Stonetown would just happen to spot S.Q.? Very slim. Too slim. He rubbed at his forehead, trying to work up some sort of answer.

And a sort of answer came to him.

"Sticky!" he yelled (in his urgency it didn't even occur to him to say "George"). "Have everyone meet me in my study!" Reynie ran toward the door, stopped, ran back for the radio, and headed upstairs. By the time he came puffing into his study, the others were waiting there. They stood around his desk looking at him expectantly, no one wasting time by asking questions. Tai, wide-eyed, sat in Reynie's desk chair with both hands over his mouth. Evidently he'd been counseled to keep quiet.

Reynie closed the door and gestured at the map of Stonetown. "Constance," he said, "you saw what the Listener saw, right? What can you tell us? Any detail might help us figure out where McCracken thinks S.Q. is!" He held up the radio. "We could send word! An agent might be able to get to him before McCracken does!"

All eyes turned to Constance, who purely out of habit

opened her mouth to protest, then collected herself and said, "I'll do my best! It's so hard to do all this at once"— she whirled her hands about—"but okay, yes, I'll try!" The whirling motions had loosened the pushed-up sleeves of the green plaid suit jacket, which slipped down now and covered her hands. She didn't bother to push them up again but crossed her arms and squeezed her eyes closed, looking as if she were in a straitjacket. Suddenly her face relaxed. Something had occurred to her.

"In fact," Constance said, "I can do better than that! I can show you. Everybody clear your mind."

No one hesitated even for a second. All eyes in the room closed.

What happened next was different for each person, but they all felt equally strange, and they all saw and heard the same thing. It was like having someone else's daydream. And what happened in the daydream was this:

McCracken sat in a vast, gloomy space—almost certainly a warehouse—holding a mostly eaten apple in one hand and a letter in the other. He was perched, minus his suit jacket, on the hood of a small limousine. An open briefcase rested beside him. His expensive shiny black shoes were visible on the concrete floor in front of him, and his wide feet, in handsomely patterned stockings, were braced on the car's chrome bumper. He was staring intently at the letter, chewing.

Standing nearby, evidently having just delivered the letter, was a familiar figure: a bald white head, a leering face with a single eyebrow, a deceptively spindly-looking body in an elegant suit. Crawlings. He was gulping air, doubled over with one hand braced on a knee, and his face was red from exertion.

"Do step back, dear fellow," McCracken said, without taking his eyes from the letter. "Your gasps agitate me."

As Crawlings shuffled backward a step, another Ten Man entered the scene—a red-cheeked, blocky blond man in a royal-blue suit—and took up a position beside him. Then, bizarrely, he seemed to do it again, as if the scene were starting over—but, no, it was actually a duplicate of the first man. They were identical twins. The Katz brothers. They stood in patient silence, watching McCracken finish the letter and slip it into his pocket. His face thoughtful, he took a last bite of his apple, then flung the core high into the air. On its way down, the apple core jerked sideways, its trajectory violently altered. When it hit the ground, both ends of a pencil could be seen protruding from it.

McCracken closed his briefcase and slid off the car, which jounced from the shedding of his tremendous weight. With quick, graceful movements, he slipped on his shoes, then walked over to a card table, which previously had been out of view. In strange contrast to the gloomy warehouse, the table bore a bowl of fresh fruit and a vase of cut flowers. McCracken took his suit jacket from the back of a folding chair and returned to huddle with the other Ten Men.

In a low tone, scarcely audible, McCracken asked something about a precise location. Crawlings shook his head noncommittally, uttering a sentence whose only intelligible word was "fair."

"Close enough," McCracken said, retrieving his briefcase

from the hood of the car. He gestured at the Katz brothers, and, leaving Crawlings behind, the three men walked swiftly to a door, passing through it into late-afternoon sunshine and slamming it behind them. The door, failing to catch properly, swung open again to reveal all three men simultaneously fitting expensive sunglasses over squinting eyes. A Katz brother reached back to close the door more securely. Then they were gone.

All of this occurred in the space of a minute. Precious little had happened, yet from the moment McCracken had speared the apple core with a razor-sharp pencil, the daydream had taken on an unmistakable feeling of threat. Instead of an apple, S.Q. was McCracken's target now. What he intended to do with their friend once he found him was impossible to tell. But what was very clear indeed was that McCracken would get what he wanted from S.Q., whatever it took.

"There, there, deary," Crawlings purred, looking directly at the daydreamers. "Don't look so troubled. Everything is as it should be."

Every eye in the room popped open.

Sticky, who stood closest to Tai, saw the little boy's anxious expression and reached to take his hand. Tai gratefully held on to it. "Constance," Sticky said, "why didn't we see McCracken asking the Listener to locate S.Q.?"

"I left that part out," Constance said. "It was a full minute of darkness, just her with her eyes closed, searching in vain as the others waited."

"So weird," Kate murmured.

"Okay," Reynie said, stepping to the map. "Their starting

point was a warehouse. Sticky—sorry, George—zoning regulations only allow warehouses in certain neighborhoods of Stonetown, right?"

"Right!" Sticky said. He gave Tai's hand an excited squeeze. "Some small-scale ones are allowed in almost every nonresidential area, but—how big do you think that building is, Kate?"

Kate considered for the briefest moment, then rattled off dimensions so precise it sounded as though she were reading them from a blueprint.

"Okay, that settles it," Sticky said. "Only four neighborhoods are zoned for a warehouse of that size." He quickly named them: the old meatpacking district, which was bisected by the train yards at the far north fringe of the city; the textile district, which began about twenty city blocks due west; the cannery district, in the southeast; and of course, considerably closer to them, the dockyards near Stonetown Harbor.

Reynie looked to Kate, intending to ask for a marker, but she was already handing him one. He circled the areas on the map. (Each circle also happened to encompass a few pushpins; Reynie, based on information he'd been given by agents and sentries, had already made some shrewd guesses about where the Ten Men might be holing up.)

"Okay," he said quickly, "we're looking for an area either within one of these circles or immediately to the west of them."

"Why does it have to be to the west?" Tai piped up.

"The sun," replied everyone else at the same time. The effect was startling, and Tai gasped. The others glanced at one another, but without the traditional amused expressions or crossing of eyes.

"It's late afternoon," Kate explained to Tai, "so the sun is low in the west. And did you see them all squinting when they put their sunglasses on? They were facing west when they set out."

"And we're looking for something close by the warehouse," Reynie said, "because they left on foot. They didn't even *think* about taking the car. And Crawlings was breathing hard, remember? He probably ran there with that letter, but it wouldn't have been from very far away. If it were, he would have used some other form of transportation."

"Wow!" Tai exclaimed. He let go of Sticky's hand to clap excitedly. "This is fun!"

The others exchanged furtive glances. No one was going to try to convince Tai otherwise. They were already doing their best to keep their anxieties managed for his sake.

"Crawlings said the word 'fair,' right?" Reynie said. He drew an arrow with his marker. "Fair Avenue runs just to the west of the cannery district, so that's one possibility. There's almost nothing going on around there—that could be a good reason to choose it as the place to leave the letter."

"There's also that miniature golf course called Fairway Fun," Constance suggested. "Isn't it near the textile district? We went there with S.Q. once, remember? He was always accidentally kicking my golf balls into the hazards."

"That doesn't make any sense," Sticky said.

Constance turned on him with blazing eyes, but Reynie quickly spoke up.

"It was worth mentioning, Constance," he said, tapping the map with his marker, "but look—Fairway Fun's to the *east* of the textile district."

Sticky had actually meant that the name "Fairway Fun" made no sense, given that miniature golf courses contained no fairways, only putting greens. But time was of the essence, and he let the misunderstanding pass, not least because a new idea had occurred to him: "There was a street fair scheduled for today! I read it in the newspaper. They were blocking off Second and Chance Streets downtown—that's just west of the dockyards!"

"Yes!" Reynie drew an arrow on the map. "If the streets are blocked off, that's another reason they wouldn't take the car."

"Uh-oh," Kate said, shaking her head. "Guys? This just got harder. Do you remember where S.Q. *lives*? Fairhaven Apartments!"

"Oh no, she's right!" Sticky groaned. "His rent's really cheap because the apartments are so close to the train yards. I remember trying to make a joke about it!"

There was an awkward beat of silence as Sticky's friends remembered his extraordinarily unamusing attempt at wordplay—something about S.Q. getting such a "fair *deal*" at "Fair*haven*." Even good-natured S.Q. had struggled to chuckle politely.

"Yes," Constance said dryly. "We remember that, too."

"So maybe Crawlings had a reason to think that S.Q. was walking home," Kate suggested. "And he told McCracken where S.Q. lives!"

"It seems more likely than hanging out at a street fair at a time like this," Sticky observed.

"The meatpacking district is so far away, though," said Kate, frowning. "Reynie, where are all the agents stationed right now?"

Reynie quickly made several marks on the map.

Kate's frown deepened. "This is bad! Look, nobody is even the least bit close to *any* of those neighborhoods!"

"That's no coincidence," Constance said with a dark look. "The Katz brothers are famous for avoiding agents, right? There's a reason nobody's ever managed to trap them."

Kate hurried forward and tapped the map with her finger. "Look, *we* are as close to all four of those neighborhoods as any one of Milligan's agents is. If I take Captain Plugg's motorcycle, I can get there faster than any of them could. I'll find S.Q. and warn him myself!"

Sticky winced. "Kate, at this time of day, average travel time is close to an hour for any of those neighborhoods except the dockyards. You could make it down to the street fair pretty quickly, maybe, but only if you got lucky with traffic. I know you're a lot faster than average, but—"

"I could at least *try!*" Kate snapped in exasperation. "I just need to know where to go!"

"You should ask Reynie, then!"

It was Tai who said this. He was bouncing in his seat with an expression of happy excitement. He pointed his finger repeatedly at Reynie, who stood at the map with his lips pressed tight.

"Ask Reynie! He knows!"

A QUEST TO RESCUE

S.Q.

AND A SECOND CHANCE ENCOUNTER

Reynie had reasons for not speaking up sooner, the main one being that the answer hadn't occurred to him until just before Tai made his announcement. Stonetown was a large city, and Mr. Benedict's community of family and friends was comfortably squashed together in two houses in a single neighborhood. Ever since the Society had come together here, *here* was where they spent almost all their time. Reynie knew a great deal about Stonetown, of course: He could name all the neighborhoods; he knew the history, the geography, the architectural trends. But he was really only personally familiar with a few neighborhoods. His home, his life, was in this house, with these friends.

In short, with a few exceptions, Reynie didn't know how long it took to get places. Unlike Sticky, who had absorbed extensive knowledge of local traffic patterns simply by reading and remembering everything—even the most boring things—Reynie hadn't realized it would take so long to reach those far-flung neighborhoods. Once he did, he knew that McCracken's warehouse was in the dockyards.

Hadn't Constance said earlier that McCracken woke the Listener up himself? That had been scarcely half an hour since he'd stood at their courtyard gate. And only a few minutes ago he'd already been settled in at the warehouse long enough to have removed his shoes and suit jacket, long enough to have eaten most of an apple. He'd gotten comfortable. Nor was it the least bit likely that McCracken would have sat on the hood of that car if he'd been in the warehouse for only a few minutes. After an hour's drive across town, the car's engine would still be extremely hot, its hood better suited for cooking on than for sitting on. The engine had had time to cool, though, and so McCracken had been there awhile already. All the clues were there. The dockyards were the only place close enough to make sense.

But just because Reynie knew where to find the warehouse didn't mean he thought Kate should fly to S.Q.'s rescue—not without all the facts available. What if they'd overlooked something? What if she were seen by one of the Ten Men? They'd know she was in town! Worse yet: What if she were actually *confronted* by the Ten Men? What if she had to face McCracken?

All of this and more had been racing through Reynie's brain. Now, with everyone staring at him, Reynie felt even more pressure. He needed time. Yet there wasn't time.

"I think..." Reynie faltered. "Listen—"

"The dockyards!" Tai squealed, unable to contain himself any longer. "He thinks Crawlings saw S.Q. at the street fair!"

And with that, Kate was off.

The sound of Tai's gasp was lost in the greater commotion of gasping, jumping, and other startled responses to Kate's sudden explosive movement. (Sticky made a kind of yelp with his mouth closed, for example, and Constance passed gas.) These sounds, too, made less of an impression than did the series of thumps in the house, which the older three knew to be from Kate's boots hitting the stairway landings as she descended, banister to banister, all the way to the bottom floor.

Reynie looked at the intercom speaker. He opened his mouth, then closed it again. There was no point trying to stop her now, not unless he was convinced Kate was doing the wrong thing—in which case she might listen to him. He wasn't convinced, though. He was afraid for her; he had concerns about the risks; but his own notions of risk were very different from Kate's, and now was no time for argument.

"Let it go, Reynie," Constance said quietly.

Reynie turned to her. She looked so exhausted. She also looked annoyed, but that was nothing unusual. And in fact he could tell she was trying *not* to look annoyed, for his sake. Which *was* unusual.

"You can't do anything about it," Constance said, "so

stop worrying like that. I'm trying not to know what you're thinking and feeling, but I'm not exactly at the top of my game, okay?"

"Okay," Reynie said, quickly composing his thoughts. "Of course. And thanks."

Constance rolled her eyes.

Sticky and Tai, meanwhile, had gone to the window, for Sticky knew that Kate would appear much sooner than one would expect, and he guessed correctly that Tai would like to see her go. Sure enough, in mere moments they heard the sound of Captain Plugg's motorcycle firing up, and just as Reynie and Constance arrived at the window, the motorcycle streaked into view from around the corner of the house. To everyone's surprise, Captain Plugg herself appeared to be riding it. They all recognized her helmet, uniform, and stocky build.

"I don't understand," Sticky said. "How is it that—?"

But even as he spoke, the motorcycle came to the courtyard gate and slowed not quite to a stop, and the person they had assumed to be Captain Plugg kicked the gate handle open with one boot, drove through the gate, kicked the gate closed behind her, and screeched off down the street with the cycle's front wheel in the air.

"So that would be Kate," Constance said, and they all nodded.

Ripping down a back alley, Kate considered how long it had been since McCracken and the Scaredy Katz set out to find S.Q. Ten minutes? Fifteen? It depended on how much time had passed between the actual event and Constance's panicky announcement. And she was still a few minutes away herself.

Oh, S.Q., Kate thought, *please get on a bus. Go somewhere unexpected. Don't be poking around the street fair.*

Ahead of her a delivery van blocked the alley. On one side of it, the driver stood handing boxes through a doorway. On the other side was just enough space between the van and alley wall for Kate to squeeze through with an inch to spare. She took the gap at top speed, and over the roar of the motor she heard the driver shouting in alarm, followed by the sound of a box being dropped.

"Sorry," Kate muttered, rocketing from the alley, across an empty street, and into another alley. She was avoiding traffic, making good time. She had already ditched the Captain Plugg disguise—the uniform padded with a couple of hidden pillows—as it was creating too much wind resistance. But she'd gotten well clear of the neighborhood first. If any neighbors had seen her go, Kate might have given them a new impression of Captain Plugg's skills, but she'd given them no reason to think anyone else was staying in Mr. Benedict's house.

Now she was approaching Second and Chance Streets, and from behind the tinted visor of Captain Plugg's oversized helmet, Kate kept her eyes peeled for Ten Men, for S.Q., for anything that might tip her off to their location. She was surprised to discover a great many people leaving the area in a hurry. They were in the streets and the alleys alike, and Kate was forced to slow down and proceed more carefully. Parents ushered along children with faces painted and balloons tightly clutched; couples held hands and exchanged nervous glances; random individuals pressed forward with shopping bags and arms full of knickknacks—all moving in the opposite direction of Kate. Everyone looked agitated—some annoyed, some frightened, some confused. This did not seem good.

And now Kate heard something in the distance ahead: A man was shouting into a megaphone, but she couldn't make out what he was saying. Slowing to a crawl, she called out to a frazzled-looking woman carrying a basket of handcrafted candles.

"They say it's a gas leak!" the woman explained, hurrying past. "They're evacuating the area!"

Kate considered this information for half a second. Then she rolled on. This was entirely too coincidental a development. She thought it very unlikely that there was actually a gas leak in the area. What *was* in the area might well prove to be just as dangerous, though, and she rode now with every muscle tensed, studying every face and figure she passed.

There were a few businessmen in the crowd, but Kate dismissed them with a glance. Now, at the tail end of the evacuation, she was mainly seeing street vendors, the folks who had been most reluctant to abandon their booths, who had stayed behind longer than anyone else, either locking things up or gathering as much of their precious wares as they could carry. She saw a flower vendor carrying an impossible quantity of flowers—he looked like a human vase—followed by a caricaturist stumbling along with an easel and rolled-up canvases. She passed a jangling, glittering jewelry maker wearing all her own jewelry. Kate passed an organ-grinder with a monkey, a limping clown with his red wig askew, a one-man band struggling under the weight of his own instruments. No Ten Men, though, and no S.Q.

The crowd had thinned now. Kate passed a few final stragglers as she headed directly toward the sound of the megaphone, turning onto Second Street just as the man wielding the megaphone was rounding the corner at a trot. He was a sweaty, nervous-looking fellow in a blue T-shirt that said "STAFF" on the front of it. He started at the sight of Kate and tried waving her back.

"You can't be here, miss," he said. "There's a—"

Kate stopped the motorcycle. "Who told you there's a gas leak?"

"Guy from the city?" the man said, hurrying on. "I don't know. He gave me the megaphone and told me to get everybody out. Listen, I've tried to be a good citizen here, but I need to look after myself, too, you know. I can't be responsible—"

"Absolutely," Kate said. "Well done, citizen! I'll take it from here!" She revved the throttle and proceeded down Y Street, veering around two food trucks that blocked the way.

There was no one in sight. Empty stalls lined the street on both sides. Paper plates, napkins, and other assorted trash drifted and skittered along the ground in a warm breeze that smelled of fried dough. The buildings framing the street showed no signs of life. This place had gone from street fair to ghost town in a matter of minutes, Kate thought. But why?

At the end of the block, Kate turned onto Chance Street, similarly desolate and abandoned. Her keen eyes scanned every doorway and window, traveled along the rooftops and fire escapes. She passed an empty hot dog stand, an empty balloon stand, an empty bookstall. She skirted a huge industrial trash bin with a wary eye, but there was no one behind it. She was beginning to think that perhaps there truly was a gas leak, that there was nothing for her to do here after all—no S.Q. to warn, no Ten Men to avoid—when she spied, farther down the street, a lone figure sitting at a table.

Kate stopped the motorcycle. The table was draped with a low-hanging black tablecloth, on the front of which, in glittery silver letters, were the words MADAME CANARD'S PALM READING! FORTUNE-TELLING! ADVICE! The figure wore a black shawl and sat hunched, her face concealed partly by the shawl and partly by the locks of unruly black hair that dangled from it. Her black-gloved hands she held before her, trembling—from fear? some affliction?—at the edge of the tabletop.

Kate narrowed her eyes. Something was *definitely* not right. The fortune-teller had not even glanced in her direction. Could she not hear the rumbling motorcycle? Was she too frightened to move? That seemed more likely.

Even more likely, Kate thought, was that this was some kind of trap.

She could just turn around and leave. Right now. Maybe the woman knew about S.Q., or maybe she needed help, or maybe both. But if this was a trap, then the last thing Kate should do...

Kate didn't even finish the thought. Her heart beating fast, everything in her on high alert, she crept forward on the motorcycle, studying the area around the fortune-teller as she approached. She noted the manhole cover in the street, the ice-cream truck blocking the way not far beyond it, the fire hydrant at the corner. Nothing seemed amiss except for the figure, who still did not look up.

"Hello? Excuse me?" said Kate as she drew near. No response. Kate shut off the engine, put the kickstand down, and slid off the motorcycle.

The gloved hands on the table continued to tremble violently, making faint tapping sounds against the tablecloth. Kate removed Captain Plugg's helmet, which was so large that it kept slipping forward and obscuring part of her vision. She glanced around again, saw no one. She took a step toward the table. *Tap-tap-tap* went the trembling fingers, so faintly as to be barely audible.

And yet familiar, Kate thought. The tapping was familiar.

Sometimes the fingers seemed to linger on the table; sometimes they touched it for the merest instant; sometimes they trembled without touching the table at all.

Morse code. It was Morse code.

Kate froze, holding her breath, and watched the fingers carefully.

Go. Trap. Go. Trap. Go. Trap.

"Can I help you, ma'am?" Kate said rather too loudly. She shifted the helmet, tucking it under her left arm while her right hand slipped casually inside her jacket. Her heart was hammering so loudly in her ears that she could scarcely hear her own words. If this was indeed a trap, what was her best move? Probably to pretend she didn't realize it was a trap.

"I don't wish to disturb you," she said, a little more naturally this time. "But evidently there's a gas leak. You should really come with me."

No. Go. Trap.

"Well, okay, suit yourself," Kate said with a sigh. She spoke soothingly, as if to a child. "I'll leave you alone, but I'm going to let the police know you're still here, okay? They'll come and help you. I'm sure they'll be here soon." She took a step backward toward the motorcycle.

"I wouldn't waste my breath, deary," said a familiar deep voice. "If the biddy knows how to speak, she's given no sign of it."

Kate whirled to see McCracken filling the doorway of the ice-cream truck. In one of his massive hands he held an ice-cream cone. Evidently, he had served himself. He seemed in no hurry to prevent Kate from fleeing, and in her peripheral vision Kate saw the reason: the Katz brothers had appeared at the intersection of Second and Chance. Whichever direction she chose, she would have to get past a Ten Man.

Kate stood where she was, trying to decide the best course of action. McCracken was taking his time with the ice-cream cone, and the Scaredy Katz were approaching slowly and cautiously, their eyes constantly on the lookout. She had less than a minute before she would be too tightly hemmed in to choose.

"I believe you've grown," McCracken said, stepping casually from the ice-cream truck, which seemed to grow itself— sitting higher on its axles than it had when McCracken was inside. "You seem larger than I remember. I suppose that happens with children."

"You've grown, too," Kate said. "I suppose that happens with prisoners."

McCracken chuckled. "Only those who take advantage

of the exercise equipment and the—how shall I put it?—the extra *time* available to them. Oh, dear Kate, I've had *so much* extra time these last years, a luxury I owe to you and your father. How can I repay you? Would you care for some of my ice cream?"

"What flavor is it?" Kate asked. She was watching the Katz brothers out of the corner of her eye. Neither of them was carrying a briefcase. And where was McCracken's?

As if in answer to that unspoken question, McCracken reached back through the ice-cream truck doorway and slid his briefcase into view. In answer to her spoken one, he said, "Rocky road. It seemed rather symbolic. I haven't had ice cream in a long time, my little chickadee. Now, how does that saying go? I scream, you scream, we all scream for ice cream?"

"Don't tell me," said Kate, "you're about to make a dumb joke about me screaming. You can save your breath."

McCracken looked perturbed.

The Katz brothers had gradually widened the distance between each other, the better to cover more area. Kate might be able to blast between them on the motorcycle—*if* she were already on the motorcycle. *If* the motor were already running. Yet here she stood. And she knew how fast McCracken was with the briefcase. Also, she realized, jumping onto the motorcycle was precisely what he expected her to do.

And so Kate made her decision. She waited.

McCracken, regaining his equanimity, tossed aside the remainder of the ice-cream cone. If he was puzzled by her lingering, he didn't show it. Perhaps she'd made the wrong decision.

"I came here," McCracken said, licking his fingers, "because I had reason to think that fine young man S.Q. Pedalian was in the area. I hoped to ask him some questions. I don't suppose you've seen him? Perhaps you had plans to join him at the street fair?"

The Katz brothers had drawn within a dozen paces. Kate could smell their expensive, spicy cologne. If the breeze had been blowing from the opposite direction, she thought ruefully, she would have known that McCracken was close by.

"You have ice cream on your cheek," Kate said to McCracken, resisting an urge to point. She kept her hands exactly where they were, and she stood very still. "Maybe you should use your handkerchief to clean it off."

"Or better still, blow my nose with it!" McCracken said with a roll of his eyes. "I know you'd love to see me knock myself out with my own handkerchief, sugarplum, but today just isn't your day. Now then, you didn't answer my question."

"I haven't seen S.Q.," Kate said. "But if I do, I'll be sure to—"

"Now!" shouted one of the Katz brothers, lunging toward Kate.

Instantly his lunge—accompanied by a whispery *swit! swit!*—became a plunge. For a moment he appeared to be trying to run on his knees. Then he twisted and collapsed onto his back, revealing the two feathered darts (neatly pinning his handkerchief in the breast pocket of his suit) that Kate had fired from her tranquilizer gun.

The other Katz brother had skittered sideways the moment his brother stumbled, and he proved to be so fast that Kate saw her third dart miss him by a good eight inches.

At the same time, Kate saw McCracken reaching into his briefcase, and she crouched behind the motorcycle for cover. She could hear the rapid-fire footsteps of the Katz brother as he raced to take cover himself—behind the ice-cream truck, from the sound of it. The fortune-teller, too, had dropped out of view behind her table. Everyone was hiding except for McCracken.

"Bravo, Kate!" boomed the Ten Man. "It hadn't occurred to me that *you* would be in the dart game now! My, how things change. Just like your father, eh? I believe you may even be a little faster than he was. He was always just a touch too slow to have success with me, you know—and I imagine he's even slower now."

As he spoke, McCracken made no effort to move away. He stood precisely where he'd been standing, and the confidence that this must have required was unnerving. He had seen Kate use the tranquilizer gun—he knew how fast she was, how true her aim—and yet there he stood, speaking in the most carefree tone.

"Felix!" McCracken called. "Why not join us? It's only a dart gun, old fellow!"

Kate heard the Katz brother reply from behind the ice-cream truck. "I have an aversion to darts, my dear!" he called with a laugh. "And it's easier for you, you know—you've borrowed my briefcase!"

"Very true," McCracken said. "He has a point, Kate. Our supplies are limited at present. Why, Garrotte—you remember Garrotte, I'm sure—Garrotte had to borrow a briefcase as well, and Sharpe was compelled to acquire one from a businessman we encountered on the street. It's of a sad quality, however, and they've had to share supplies between the two of them. Ah, here they are now!"

Kate felt goose bumps run up her arms. She peeked over the top of the motorcycle. Sure enough, walking toward them from the intersection beyond the ice-cream truck were two of the most dangerous Ten Men alive. She recognized the bespectacled Sharpe and the bearded, bat-faced Garrotte instantly. She had spent far too much time in their company, had hoped never to see them again in her life. Yet here they were. Impeccably dressed, of course.

"*Now* won't you come out and play, Kate?" McCracken called when he had greeted his associates. "It's a veritable party! And I know you have three darts left in your gun—a present for each of us, yes?"

Kate wiped her brow with her sleeve and took a deep breath. She had wasted a dart on the first Katz brother—one would have been sufficient—but she'd been overexcited. She needed to be steady now if ever she had been.

"Do join us, Kate!" came Sharpe's familiar voice. "We've missed you!"

"Yes, it's been ever so long!" echoed Garrotte. "We haven't had fun in years, not really. And that's all thanks to *you*!"

"I'm afraid she's a party pooper, gentlemen," McCracken said. "Simply isn't in the mood today. Very well, my dear! We'll bring the party to you! You'll notice I'm not offering you a chance to surrender. No, you had best use your darts wisely, for we do mean you harm. Did you hear me clearly, Kate? We mean you harm."

McCracken was enjoying himself. Toying with her. He was looking forward to a fight he knew they'd win.

"Shall we, gentlemen?"

Footsteps approached.

Kate took another deep breath. *You can do this*, she told herself. *With a little help.*

"Hey, fortune-teller lady!" she sang out. "If you have any tricks up your sleeve, now would be the time!"

The fortune-teller did indeed have tricks in store.

The cloth that had been draping the table flew upward like a theater curtain, and the table overturned. When the cloth fell aside, it revealed not a hunched woman in a shawl but a tall man with dirty-blond hair and ocean-blue eyes that matched Kate's exactly. What Kate had suspected turned out to be the case: The fortune-teller was her own father.

"Let fly, Kate!" Milligan said. "I've got you covered!"

Indeed, Milligan had been firing his tranquilizer gun from the moment he appeared—*swit! swit! swit! swit!*—and the Ten Men had scattered left and right.

Thwack! Thwack! went the sounds of briefcases deflecting darts.

"Not fair!" snarled Garrotte when the handle on his briefcase broke loose. It was Kate's dart that caught his shoulder as he struggled to regain his grip. "Most unfair! Such shoddy materials!" This last he uttered as he sank to his knees, then to his side, and closed his eyes.

Kate was already on the move. She didn't dare mount the motorcycle—she'd be too exposed—but with Captain Plugg's helmet back on her head, she began pushing the motorcycle along, crouching behind it for cover. Sharpe and

McCracken were concentrating on Milligan, who was using the overturned table for his own cover, but when Kate fired a dart at McCracken (which McCracken narrowly dodged), the two men spun in unison and flung pencils in her direction. Sharpe's ricocheted off a handlebar. McCracken's glanced off her helmet with a cracking sound that made her ears ring. Kate kept moving, and the men were compelled to refocus their attention on Milligan, who had just shoved more darts into his tranquilizer gun.

Kate headed for the ice-cream truck. Felix Katz had been hiding behind it, but perhaps he would run at the sight of her, knowing she had a tranquilizer gun. She only wanted half a minute to reload in relative safety. She was down to one dart in the gun.

Katz was not behind the ice-cream truck. Kate stooped to check beneath it. No Katz. In the near distance she could see the feet of McCracken and Sharpe moving left and right in a sort of lethal dance—they were avoiding Milligan's attacks, looking for an opportunity to charge him. But once Kate had reloaded, she could draw a bead on them from behind the truck. They would be caught in the cross fire between her and Milligan. Kate let the motorcycle rest on its kickstand and reached inside her jacket for more darts.

No sooner had she done so, however, than Kate felt the tranquilizer gun yanked from her other hand. With a cry she grabbed at it, but it had already flown upward, out of reach. Her eyes followed it as it sailed onto the top of the ice-cream truck, where Katz stood leering at her from above. He had unfastened his necktie and whipped it down to snatch Kate's weapon away. And now he dropped lightly onto the other side of the motorcycle, keeping it between him and Kate still wary, even with his newfound advantage.

They stood facing each other, only a few paces separating them.

"So sorry," the Ten Man said. "Were you hoping to reload your gun in peace? You should have known I'd be waiting for a moment like that."

"You know what's funny?" Kate said. "It still had a dart in it. You could have used it against me. But you thought it was empty, so you left it up there."

Katz twitched. "Ah, well," he said frowning, "I still have my weapons, and you have none. This conversation is at an end."

Shaking his wrists to expose two large silver watches from beneath his suit cuffs, Katz thrust both hands toward Kate as if trying to shove her from a distance. The shock-watches emitted their familiar electrical whine, the wires shot forth from each of them, and Kate—from Felix Katz's perspective—disappeared.

In fact, Kate had timed her backbend perfectly. She remained poised like that, her body a graceful arch, one hand pressing against the ground behind her head, until the electrical wires—having missed their target—recoiled into the watches. Reversing her original motion, Kate snapped back up into a standing position just as Katz was springing over the motorcycle with a snarl. She saw his eyes widen mid-leap when he saw the dart in her hand.

"No!" he cried simply.

"Yep!" Kate replied as she made her throw. Then she nimbly stepped aside, for Katz's momentum carried him lurching forward several paces before he collapsed onto the pavement, unconscious. "You didn't really think that one through, Felix," she said, turning back toward the motorcycle.

And there stood McCracken.

He seemed to have appeared out of nowhere, boiling up into view like black smoke from a fire. And indeed, menace radiated off him like heat. The look on his face was one Kate had never seen before, and it made her shudder. Gone was his usual easy smile. McCracken was taking her seriously now. And he was angry.

"You are being very *bad*!" McCracken roared.

Kate wanted to run, but she dared not turn her back on him. She tried to ready herself for whatever attack he threw at her—but she was not prepared for what he actually *did* throw at her, which was the motorcycle. She ducked beneath it, but one of the tires struck her helmet an indirect blow and knocked it clean from her head. She stumbled, trying to get her legs beneath her.

At the same time, on the other side of the ice-cream truck, Sharpe's voice rang out: "Watch your feet, lovey!"

McCracken, who had been about to pounce on Kate, instead leaped straight up into the air. A dart shot out from beneath the ice-cream truck, passing beneath McCracken's feet and skittering across the pavement beyond.

The motorcycle had surprised Kate, but what happened next shocked her. The instant McCracken's feet hit the ground, he slammed his shoulder against the side of the ice-cream truck, like a man trying to break down a door. His feet drove like sledgehammers against the pavement, his arms thrust out and up—and the ice-cream truck flipped over onto its side.

The next few moments were a chaos of motion as Kate shot forward and snatched up McCracken's briefcase (he'd put it down to throw the motorcycle); McCracken spun around looking for it; and Milligan, his legs trapped beneath the overturned ice-cream truck and his tranquilizer gun nowhere to be seen, shouted a warning to Kate—Sharpe was swooping in on her from the side.

Kate, spying her own tranquilizer gun on the ground, made an instant calculation: She wouldn't have time to pick it up before Sharpe was upon her. He had the better angle. But she could get close. And so she ran, and two heartbeats later Sharpe had her in a bear hug from behind, pinning her arms to her sides. The tranquilizer gun lay inches from her feet. So close.

"There, there, chicky," Sharpe said. "No more toys for you."

McCracken appeared, stepping up onto the side of the overturned truck so that he looked triumphantly down upon them all. "Don't let her go anywhere with my briefcase, Sharpe—there's a good fellow. And keep close tabs on your own." (He needn't have warned Sharpe, who was clutching the handle of his own briefcase so tightly that his knuckles were white.) Looking down at Milligan, McCracken said, "You've grown rusty, old sport. Still, that was fun."

Milligan, visible only from the waist up, had laced his fingers together behind his head. "Who's to say it's over?" he said calmly. "You all right, Kate?"

"I'm fine!" Kate growled, struggling in Sharpe's grip. She shifted her feet to the left, then to the right.

"She won't be for long, Milligan, I assure you," McCracken said. "Honestly, I'm beyond annoyed at the trouble you've caused us. I suppose after these years of being locked up, I've quite lost my patience. I believe some punishment is in order."

"You realize you're threatening my daughter," Milligan said.

McCracken chuckled. He put his hands on his hips. "Oh, I'm quite aware of what I'm doing. And if you think—"

"Excuse me for a moment," Milligan interrupted, then called, "What are you waiting for, Kate?"

Kate grunted, still shifting her weight about. "Just getting... the right... *angle!*"

With that, Kate kicked the tranquilizer gun. It had been important to hit it just so—not only to aim it but to avoid damaging it. It was really more of a sideways sweep than a kick, and she executed it perfectly, sending the gun skittering lightly across the pavement into Milligan's waiting hand. She heard Sharpe gasp with realization as she bent forward, lifting his feet off the ground, and turned so that his back was facing Milligan. She heard the familiar and most welcome *swit!* as the last dart in her gun found its home. Then Sharpe released his grip with a sigh and slumped to the ground, a feathered dart protruding from his rump.

Kate turned to see Milligan now aiming the tranquilizer gun at McCracken, who had, for once, been caught flat-footed. He stood on the ice-cream truck in a half crouch, arms outstretched in opposite directions, with absolutely no good place to go.

"I'm not the only rusty one," Milligan observed.

Kate, who knew that the gun was empty, did her best to appear calm. She tried, in fact, to look as though the game were won. It seemed to work. McCracken, glancing at her face and then back at Milligan, made no move.

"Well," the Ten Man said with a shrug of his massive shoulders, "let's get on with it."

"First I want to show you something," said Milligan, and with the gun still leveled at McCracken, he reached inside his jacket (a canvas jacket much like Kate's), produced a feathered dart, and shoved it into the tranquilizer gun.

McCracken's shoulders drooped now. "You can't be serious. It was empty?"

"Quite," Milligan said, reaching into his jacket again. He loaded another dart into the gun, then a third, then a fourth.

"Come now," McCracken chided. "Must I wait until—?"

"This will sting a little," Milligan said.

A dart bloomed in McCracken's left shoulder. Flinching, he uttered an angry growl. Then a look of uncertainty came onto his face. "I'm still standing," he observed.

Kate felt her mouth go dry.

A moment passed. Then another. The corners of McCracken's mouth twitched upward. He took a step forward, as if to jump down from the ice-cream truck, but Milligan pointed the tranquilizer gun directly at his nose.

"You wouldn't shoot me in the face," McCracken said, hesitating. "That's not your style."

"You're right," Milligan said, and fired a dart at the Ten Man's leg.

"That *hurts!*" McCracken snarled furiously. He yanked the darts from his leg and shoulder and drew both his arms back to throw them. "If your serum isn't strong enough—"

"Oh, those darts didn't have any serum," Milligan said. "I just wanted you to feel them."

Feathers appeared in McCracken's other shoulder. The Ten Man let loose a howl of rage, flung the darts down at his feet like a child throwing a tantrum, and collapsed onto the ice-cream truck with a tremendous bang.

Kate flew to Milligan's side.

"How badly are you hurt?" she asked, grabbing his hand and kissing his cheek. "Are your legs broken?"

"Only very lightly, I think," Milligan said, smiling. He brushed a stray lock of hair out of his daughter's eyes. In the distance, they could hear sirens approaching. "You were really amazing, Katie-Cat. When did you know it was me?"

"Who else could it be?" Kate said. "I don't know anyone else who could pull off that trembling-hand Morse code trick. But how did you happen to be here?" She was stretching out on the ground beside her father now, resting her head in the crook of his arm. "I thought there were spies in every airport in Stonetown."

"Oh, there are," Milligan said. "And when the one I encountered wakes up, I'm sure he'll make his report right away. None of that matters now. I just wasn't about to leave you here in the city without me. I heard Reynie's bulletin on the radio, and I knew where S.Q. was supposed to leave messages—in fact, I was already on my way here to see what I could discover about that when Reynie put out the word."

Kate looked at her father sidewise. "So it was you who got S.Q. safely away, wasn't it? You're the 'guy from the city' who raised the alarm about a gas leak."

"Yes, I found him right away, told him he was in danger,

and sent him off in disguise. You didn't happen to see a limping clown, did you?"

"I did!"

Milligan grinned. "What better way to disguise those big feet than clown shoes, right? He found them very uncomfortable, though. The original clown had smaller feet. And we had no time to remove that poor fellow's face paint, so I sent *him* off with a great load of flowers to hide behind."

"I saw him, too!" Kate laughed. Then she grew serious. She reached over and swatted Milligan on the chest. "I can't believe you shot those extra darts at McCracken just to hurt him! That's not the way you taught me! I mean, I enjoyed it, but still!"

"Give me a pass on this one, Katie," Milligan said. "He threatened my daughter."

Kate gave him a reproachful look. But then she smiled and leaned back again. "There's more to it than that, isn't there?"

Milligan chuckled. "The first two had broken ampoules. What was I supposed to do, let him know?"

The sirens were growing louder. Kate knew that some of Milligan's agents would be arriving with the emergency professionals. Soon he would have medical attention, and the unconscious Ten Men would be taken into custody. The full significance of it all had hardly begun to sink in, she knew. For the moment, she let herself rest there, snuggled up against her injured father.

The two of them gazed upward, watching clouds move across the blue sky.

Milligan cleared his throat. "Kate," he said quietly, "I

hope you know how proud of you I am. You're already as skilled as many of my agents—and even more skilled than some. And I want you to be happy. You get to choose what to do with your own life. It's just..." He faltered.

"You just want to protect me," Kate said, nodding. "I know. It's okay, Dad."

Milligan nodded, too. Kate heard him sniff, felt him wipe his eyes with his other arm. She kept her own eyes on the clouds.

"That one reminds me of Mr. Benedict," Kate said after a moment. She pointed. "See the profile with the lumpy nose?"

"You're right," Milligan said with a little laugh. "And look at that one—it's like a valentine."

Kate squinted. "A valentine drawn by a kid, maybe. But I see it."

Milligan gave her a squeeze. And for some time they lay there, a man trapped beneath an ice-cream truck, his legs lightly broken, and his daughter with an aching head, the two of them surrounded by unconscious men in elegant suits. The sirens grew louder and louder.

They both felt remarkably content.

THE IMPORTANCE OF LOLLIPOPS AND ICE CREAM

In the moments after Kate Wetherall, disguised as Captain Plugg, faded from view on the motorcycle, the remaining Society members were at a loss. It was difficult to think of anything other than what might happen to S.Q., or Kate, or both—and yet there was a little boy in their midst, and they all felt the need to protect him from worry. So they tried very hard to compose themselves and clear their minds of anxious thoughts as they awaited word.

"Do you, um, want to go and check our clothes in the fumigator?" Sticky asked Tai.

"No, thanks," Tai said, opening the drawer in Reynie's desk that contained the peppermints. He took out the tin and looked at Reynie.

"One," Reynie said.

"Do you have to be an orphan to be like me and Constance?" Tai asked as he fished out a peppermint. "Where you can hear people talking in their heads? Constance says she doesn't know."

The older three felt themselves relax a little. From Tai's point of view, the Mysterious Benedict Society had saved the world, and he naturally assumed that they would be able to take care of the current situation as well, no matter what might be involved. In short, he wasn't worried. As long as they kept relatively calm, it seemed he would be fine.

"We talked about the orphan angle on his way here," Constance said, rolling up her suit sleeves again. "We can't know about the Listener—she doesn't know herself—but Tai and I are the only telepaths in the region, as far as we can tell, and we've both been orphans all our lives."

"Could be a coincidence," Reynie said. "But if so, it's a really interesting one." He looked at Sticky, who rubbed his scalp thoughtfully.

"We do know," Sticky began slowly, "that certain kinds of stress—and the presence or absence of certain factors in one's environment—cause different kinds of chemical reactions in the formation of the developing brain...."

Tai took the peppermint out of his mouth. "What does that mean?" he asked brightly, then popped the peppermint back in.

"It means it's possible," Reynie said. "But hard to say."

Tai removed the peppermint again. "Do you know there's a country with my name in it?" he asked, changing the subject for no apparent reason.

"Do you mean Taiwan?" asked Sticky.

Tai, who had been returning the peppermint to his mouth, froze in mid-motion. "Yes!" he whispered, awestruck. His face lit up. "Do you want to see it on the globe? I can show you!"

Why, of course, the others assured him, they would be delighted to see Taiwan on the globe. And so, exchanging glances that betrayed mixed emotions, the older three followed Tai downstairs to the sitting room, where he carefully turned the massive globe with both hands.

Sticky and Reynie watched expectantly, knowing exactly when the globe would stop spinning, and Constance, who had always avoided studying geography, pretended to do the same.

"Here!" Tai proclaimed at last, jabbing his finger on the globe. "I told you!"

"You certainly did," Reynie acknowledged genially. He had brought the two-way radio with him, and he looked around now for a good place to put it. His nerves were so on edge, he felt sure that if it squawked while under his arm, he would drop it with a yelp.

"My grandparents used to live there," Tai observed. "It seems strange. My finger covers the whole word." He lifted his finger from the globe, drew his eye close to the point he'd been covering, then put his finger back and shook his head.

Constance was peeking over his shoulder to get a fix on the country's location. She was annoyed to discover how far off her own guess would have been. "How do you know where your grandparents were from?"

Tai shrugged. "I heard the headmaster thinking it once. I guess someone must have told him."

"Do you know anything about your parents?" Reynie asked. He set the radio next to a stack of books on the piano.

The little boy was spinning the globe again, rather fast this time, evidently just to watch it spin. "I think they got something bad in the mail," he said uncertainly. "That's what the headmaster thought."

"Tai, I think your parents were scientists!" Sticky exclaimed, to everyone's surprise.

"Oh, yeah!" Tai said. He looked admiringly over his shoulder at Sticky. "The headmaster thought that, too! You really do know everything! But how did you know about my *parents*? That seems weird."

Reynie and Constance wondered the same thing.

Sticky explained that he had read about them in newspapers and science journals. "They were well-known scientists," he said, "a brilliant married couple working together on major projects. It came out after they—well, after the Emergency—that they had secretly been working on an invention that could track people from far away by tracing their unique chemical signatures. Basically, a sophisticated, long-distance bloodhound. Once it 'smelled'—analyzed, you know—something that had belonged to someone, it would be able to locate that person almost anywhere. There's been plenty of debate about whether their invention could have worked if they'd lived long enough to finish it. They had some good ideas, though, and were clearly determined to try."

"Why would they do that?" asked Tai, who had stopped spinning the globe and turned to look at Sticky. He didn't seem upset, only curious. This was not especially surprising to Constance or Reynie, who had always been orphans themselves. But Sticky felt a bit disconcerted talking about Tai's parents, afraid of upsetting him.

"They, uh, your parents, I mean—I mean, I don't know *why*, but—"

Constance cut in. "During the Emergency the Whisperer was telling everybody 'the missing aren't missing, they're only departed.' Just—up *here*, you know," she said, tapping her forehead. "So people were confused. But lots of people were actually disappearing, thanks to Mr. Curtain and his thugs, and *some* people, anyway, were noticing—"

"People like us," Sticky interjected. "People with an unusually strong love of truth."

"Which means that *some* people," Constance continued, with an annoyed look at Sticky, "really wanted to know where their loved ones were. Your parents were probably trying to help people like that. I think they were heroes, Tai."

"Really?" Tai ran over and grabbed Constance's hands, which, much to her surprise, caused tears to spring into her eyes.

"I mean," she said in a choked voice, "I think so?"

"Yay!" Tai said, and hugged her.

Sticky and Reynie, meanwhile, surreptitiously wiped at their own eyes.

"Wow, you're all feeling the exact same way!" Tai exclaimed. "It's weird!"

"Oh boy," Reynie murmured, and then in a louder voice

he said, "George, what was this business about getting something bad in the mail, though?"

Sticky shook his head. "Just a tragic accident. They ordered some chemicals for their experiments, and one of them arrived mislabeled. In many cases it wouldn't have mattered. But they were doing really unusual work, and they ended up mixing some things that...put them to sleep. And they...didn't wake up."

Sticky grimaced as he said this, and Reynie and Constance each held their breath, all wondering how Tai would respond to this account.

"It's okay, everybody," Tai said with a very grown-up-sounding sigh. "I never even knew them. Anyway, *you're* my family now!"

At this, three backs straightened, three pairs of eyes widened, and three brains started racing. This was turning out to be a most complicated day.

✦

Despite the day's challenges, dinner was something of a celebratory affair. Captain Plugg, admirably brushing off the news of her damaged motorcycle, had made a rather less-than-successful squash casserole, which everyone—even young Tai, and in fact even Constance—was pretending to enjoy. (The kind guard had also brought up three tubs of ice cream for dessert, the knowledge of which somewhat softened the blow of dinner.) And here sat Kate, regaling them with her account of the Street Fair Melee (which was what she had termed her encounter with the Ten Men), relatively unharmed and indeed almost giddy. Milligan was safe and receiving proper care in the secret Security Hospital. McCracken and several of his cronies were already back in custody. Nobody had expected this turn of events, but all things considered, the day seemed to have gone rather well.

"He threw an *ice-cream truck* at Milligan?" Tai asked, not for the first time. He was enthralled by the story.

"Technically, he only *threw* the motorcycle at me," Kate said laughing, "and *pushed* the ice-cream truck onto Milligan. Who, in his defense, was at the same time fending off Sharpe and trying to keep McCracken from getting to me. Plus, you know, he's out of practice — otherwise, I'm sure, he would have avoided the ice-cream-truck attack."

Reynie chuckled a little absently. He was pleased with the good news, of course, but there were still plenty of Ten Men out there (more than a baker's half dozen, he thought), and the situation was still thoroughly precarious. He'd never stopped thinking about the message that Mr. Benedict had sent (*where one who stands defies the name, where one who stands defies...*), but at the same time he'd never been able to fully concentrate on it. The message was important; there could be no doubt. Yet Reynie's brain felt pulled in a hundred different directions. His only consolation was that the Ten Men seemed to be in a holding pattern. Both sides were in a waiting game whose rules had yet to become clear.

Constance, meanwhile, was slipping a forkful of goopy casserole onto Sticky's plate. It was the third such forkful, and Sticky (who was just as distracted as Reynie) had yet to notice. He just kept glancing down at his plate with concealed dismay, continuing to eat what was in front of him.

"Anyway," Kate was saying, "once Milligan was sure that

McCracken and company were properly dealt with, he sent every available agent to find that warehouse where Crawlings and the Listener were holed up. They weren't crack agents, but five of them against one Ten Man made for decent odds, and this might be the best chance to get the Listener away from them—which could very well turn this whole thing around, you know. And sure enough, they found the warehouse—"

"But it was empty," Constance interrupted. "We know."

"Oh...you do?" Kate looked disappointed.

Sticky jerked a thumb at Constance. "She knew the moment the Listener sensed the agents nearby. The Listener was focusing all of her attention on them. Constance actually tried to distract her, but she failed."

Constance gave him a withering look. "Really? You couldn't find a better way to put that?"

Sticky grimaced. "Sorry. I mean, it just didn't work." He looked down at his plate (where, to his distress, his serving of squash casserole seemed only to have grown).

Kate sighed. "Just once I'd like to report something you didn't already know."

"We didn't know about the ice-cream truck!" Tai said, waving his fork in the air and sending a glop of casserole onto the table near Reynie's plate.

"Thanks, sport!" Kate said, ruffling Tai's hair and grinning.

Reynie forked the glop onto his plate and covered it with a napkin. To Kate and Captain Plugg he said, "Constance has tried to guess where the Listener is now, but the Listener seems to have learned from Constance—she knows how to muddy the waters."

"I think they're in another warehouse," Constance said. "But she might be pulling one over on me. If I concentrate right now, for instance, I can see—what? No! *No!*" Constance flung her fork onto the table and covered her eyes. "No!"

The others were instantly gathered around her as she rocked in her chair.

"What's the matter, Connie girl?" Kate asked, touching her lightly on the arm. "What's happening?"

"She's not just with Crawlings anymore," Constance said. "There are other Ten Men with them. Crawlings has told her what to do. They know where McCracken and the others are being transferred to.... They're already there... and she's... she's just read the mind of a guard at the security gate.... She's giving Crawlings the code! No! Stop it!"

Reynie leaped to the radio, intending to send out a warning, but it squawked just as he reached it. Everyone stared at the radio as it squawked again, followed by an agent's voice: "Mayday! Transfer compromised! I repeat—"

But the agent did not repeat anything. The radio went silent. Everyone looked back at Constance, who was shaking her head furiously. She lowered her hands, her eyes shining with tears. "That man," she said. "I *hate*... that man."

"McCracken," Tai whispered, and his own eyes filled with tears. He began to tremble. "He's... he's hurting people! He's hurting *lots* of people!"

Even before Tai finished speaking, Kate had scooped him up. He buried his face in her neck and cried. "Shh," she whispered. "Shh, it's okay. They're going to be okay."

Constance was wiping her eyes, though she looked even more upset now. "Sorry! I'm so sorry, Tai! I was—I guess I was concentrating on it so much. Too much. Listen, he's not hurting anyone anymore. He's going away with Crawlings and the others. The agents…Kate's right, they're going to be okay."

Sticky had put his hand on Constance's shoulder. "It's true, Tai. They'll go to the hospital where Milligan is. They'll get better there. They'll…they'll probably get lollipops, if you want to know the truth."

His friends all winced. This seemed like much too obvious a ploy to make the little boy feel better.

And yet, after a moment, Tai straightened and wiped at his own eyes. "Will they, really?"

Sticky cleared his throat. "Well, certainly, if they ask for them. If they want lollipops, they will be given lollipops. No doubt about it."

Tai nodded. Whether he actually believed this or simply *wanted* to believe it seemed to make no difference. His anxious eyes grew less troubled, and he rested his head on Kate's shoulder.

"Speaking of treats," Reynie said, "I believe it's time for dessert. How would that be?"

Tai nodded again, and everyone sprang into action. Grave looks passed among them in the kitchen, but in the dining room with Tai, as bowls were set out and the ice cream was scooped, all minds focused very diligently on the ice cream.

"You call it the Blab?" Tai asked with a giggle.

"Well, Kate does," Sticky replied as they descended the

stairs. "And she calls the noise-cancellation device the Husher—get it? Because it hushes you."

"I get it," Tai said. "And you keep it in the Blab. That's why we're going down there first."

"You catch on quick," Sticky said.

The little boy had agreed to accompany Sticky to the rooftop patio for the last bit of cleanup. The idea of using the platform again would have been tempting enough, but promises of working in complete silence ("You won't even be able to hear *yourself*") had made the opportunity irresistible.

There was just enough daylight left for them to do the job. No need for lights, then, and the Husher would ensure that they couldn't be heard from the street. Sticky poked his head into Reynie's study on the way to the roof. Sticky nodded, the others nodded back, and he withdrew.

At first Reynie thought that Sticky and Tai had taken the stairs, for there was none of the platform's telltale rattling and clanking down the hall. But then his mind registered several small details—a subtle change in air pressure, among other things—and he knew they had taken the platform with the Husher already engaged.

"We need to be ready," Reynie said.

"I *am* ready," Constance said, though what she really looked ready for was an exhausted collapse into bed.

Kate, holding Madge on one glove-protected hand and stroking her feathers soothingly, felt no need to say that she was *always* ready. Although she did think it.

Down in the courtyard, Captain Plugg was pretending to pull up weeds. Or rather, she actually *was* pulling up weeds, but not at any great pace. Pulling weeds was her excuse to be in the courtyard when the Ten Men arrived—the better to casually greet them at the gate and avoid their coming to the door.

And the Ten Men *would* arrive. Of this there could be no doubt. McCracken knew Kate was in town now, so of course he would send someone to check Mr. Benedict's house. Perhaps he would even come again himself.

"He's got to be nursing a whopping headache from the tranquilizer serum, though," Kate said quietly, picking up the conversation where they'd left off a minute before, "and he probably thinks I wouldn't risk coming here, anyway. I doubt he'll waste his precious time. Though you're right, Reynie—I'm sure he'll send someone, just to be absolutely certain. And if he sends Crawlings with the Listener..."

This was their greatest concern, that the Listener would be dispatched to the premises. If that happened, their chances of avoiding detection would suddenly grow dismal.

"He doesn't like moving her around the city, though," Reynie pointed out. "He prefers to keep her hidden away. I don't think he'll risk sending her here, not when he thinks you probably aren't here anyway."

They all nodded, all hoping this was true, all fearing it wasn't.

Their answer came soon enough. Twilight was settling in, the light growing dim and bluish, with the occasional firefly blinking here and there over the courtyard, when the radio squawked. A sentry informed them that a familiar luxury car was heading into the neighborhood. It wasn't bright enough outside to determine who was in the vehicle, however. Reynie thanked the sentry and shut off the radio, whose squawks were so loud they might be heard from the courtyard. He also turned off the overhead light. His fingers were slippery on the switches, he discovered; his hands were damp with perspiration.

Reynie went to join Kate at the window. Constance, for her part, remained seated at the desk.

Captain Plugg had pulled the last of the weeds and was raking them into a basket when the car glided up to the curb. The car doors opened simultaneously. Out of them, to everyone's relief, stepped the Scaredy Katz. Each man was holding his head in precisely the same way; each had precisely the same pained expression. They approached the gate.

Captain Plugg went to meet them. She carried the rake in such a way that suggested she would rake the both of them into oblivion if necessary.

Reynie whispered, "They drew the short straws, I guess."

"No," Kate whispered, "I'll bet McCracken's punishing them for getting taken down by little old me."

"Shut," Constance whispered, "*up.*"

She was scowling with concentration, her eyes closed, her fingertips pressed to her temples. She had told them that the Listener, her concentration noticeably deteriorated, was every bit as exhausted as Constance herself was. But Constance was still throwing as much mental garbage at her as she could possibly muster. For the Listener surely knew that the Katz brothers were coming here, and if she perceived that Constance was aware of their presence now, then the jig was up—the Listener would know that Constance was hiding out in Mr. Benedict's house.

That was why Constance avoided looking out the window. She was concentrating on real and imagined scenes, anything other than what was happening right now. And yet at the same time she was reserving a fraction of her attention—a quiet corner—for the present moment. Just in case.

The Katz brothers were arguing with Captain Plugg, who had raised her voice. She was speaking so loudly, in fact, that the Ten Men were wincing—not from fear, but rather because the loud noise worsened their headaches. Nonetheless, they kept glancing at the house, methodically checking all the windows. One of the men, Reynie noticed, had placed his hand atop the fence near the gate, among the roses growing there. He leaned forward to snap angrily at Captain Plugg, who snapped back and rattled her rake at him, and then he jerked his hand away, evidently having pricked himself on a thorn. His brother, meanwhile, made as if to push through the gate, and as Captain Plugg shifted sideways to block his entry, the first man placed his hand on top of the fence again, more carefully this time. He seemed to have no more words for the guard, however, and at length he and his brother retreated with mocking bows, got into their car, and drove away.

"They're gone," Reynie told Constance.

Constance made no reply except to lower her head to the desk with a soft groan.

There was a tap at the door. Reynie opened it to find Sticky and Tai in the hallway. He gestured them into the study and turned on the light. Constance groaned again and did not look up. Kate told Sticky and Tai what had happened.

"The question is whether they actually believed Captain

Plugg," Kate said. "Maybe they just *want* her to think they believe her. Maybe they're planning on coming back."

"I think there's a way we can find out," Reynie said. "One of them kept putting his hand on top of the fence, even though he got pricked by a rose thorn. Why would he do that? My guess is he was hiding some kind of sensor there."

"I'm on it," Sticky said, heading for the computer station in his office. Presently his voice came over the intercom: "You were right, Reynie. I've found a signal from a camera. Getting a fix on what it's transmitting." There was a pause. "Okay, he's good. The angle's perfect. I can tell it's tiny and probably impossible to see among the roses, but it has a clear shot of the front door. I'm actually looking at Captain Plugg right now. She's coming inside."

They could all hear the sound of the front door closing below.

"No surprise, there's a second signal," Sticky's voice reported. "And...yep. They've placed one covering the back door, too."

"Roger that!" Tai shouted. Kate and Reynie flinched, Constance groaned, and Tai looked around, beaming.

"Nice job," Kate said.

"The good news," Reynie said when Sticky rejoined them, "is that they clearly *don't* think Kate's here. They've hidden the cameras in case she shows up."

Tai tugged on Reynie's sleeve. "Is the bad news that they'll know if we leave? Because they can see the doors?"

Reynie tapped his nose and pointed at Tai, who tapped his own nose and pointed back.

The sound of Captain Plugg's heavy tread on the stairs

announced her approach. She entered the study, looking cautiously pleased. "I wondered why it was so easy to persuade them to leave," she said after they had told her about the cameras. "Honestly, they didn't seem to be trying very hard. They just kept saying that they needed to come inside and talk with me in private, and I kept telling them to dream on. I could see that they were studying the house, of course, but more than anything they seemed preoccupied with their headaches. They looked like they just wanted to go to bed."

"They *did* just want to go to bed," Constance growled, at last looking up with her bloodshot eyes. "And they *were* preoccupied by their headaches. I made sure of that. And now *I* just want to go to bed, and I'm preoccupied with *my* headache."

"Constance nudged them!" Tai cried in delight. "And it gave *her* a headache, too!"

Reynie squeezed Tai's shoulder and said very softly, "You're right. I guess we should use our quiet voices for her, shouldn't we?"

Tai nodded, tapping his nose.

"The Listener fell asleep," Constance muttered. "Right in the middle of everything, I could feel her just sort of vanish. I'm sure she couldn't help it. Anyway, with her out of the picture, I decided not to take any chances. I immediately focused on the Scaredy Katz, and, yeah, I nudged them."

"But you couldn't even see them," Kate said (using her quiet voice). "I know they were close by, but don't you normally have to see people or hear them talking to do your thing?"

"I felt too exhausted to get up," Constance said, "so I just sort of piggybacked on what you and Reynie were seeing.

You were both concentrating very hard. I know that's against the rules, but give me a break, will you?"

"Break granted," Reynie affirmed. "And with thanks. Now you need to get yourself to bed, Constance. If the Listener's asleep, this is your opportunity, right?"

"You don't have to tell me twice," Constance said, dragging herself to her feet. "And you should come with me, Tai. If you wake up in the night, you have to wake me up right away, understand? No being awake without me."

"Roger that," Tai said very quietly. He glanced around for approving looks. Everybody gave him one.

Everybody also yawned. The mere thought of sleep had reminded them how exhausted they were, and it was quickly agreed that they would all go to bed, too. With the Listener desperately needing her sleep, it seemed unlikely that the Baker's Dozen would be making a move tonight. Nonetheless, Captain Plugg would monitor her radio until one of the Society members rose in the early morning, and then the guard would turn in.

"Let's hope for good rest," Reynie said. "Something tells me tomorrow's going to be a long day."

"Aren't all days the same length?" asked Tai.

"Not tomorrow, kid," Kate said, giving him a wink. "Tomorrow we save the world. That always takes longer."

A THOUSAND
HIDDEN FOOTSTEPS

The day, which would indeed be a long one—among the longest in Reynie's life—began early, before the sun had risen. Reynie woke to a cacophony of bird noises outside, not the usual predawn birdsong but a clamor he recognized from years of sharing a residence with a peregrine falcon. Her Majesty the Queen had just stooped upon a bird she intended as breakfast, and all the other birds in the area were putting up a ruckus of protest and alarm. No doubt many were shocked to discover that such a thing could happen.

Reynie, for his part, sat up in bed with a strange awareness of misplaced anxiety. How many mornings had he awakened recently with a feeling of dread, worried that he might be about to make a bad decision, that something valuable was in the process of being broken, and that he was partly responsible for the breaking? That same feeling settled upon him this morning in his first groggy moments of consciousness. Then he remembered the more urgent threat, the extremely dangerous one, and came fully awake with a jolt. He climbed out of bed at once.

It is remarkable what a good night of sleep can do, however. Reynie had been too tired to realize how tired he truly was. In particular, he'd been unaware of how much his weariness had been affecting his thinking. He had gone to sleep trying, without luck, both to deduce the meaning of Mr. Benedict's message and to identify something he felt he had overlooked, something that nagged at him in a way that important things always did. He had tugged at that mental knot for only a few minutes before succumbing to sleep. Now, though, as he hurriedly changed out of his pajamas, Reynie was struck by how clearheaded he felt.

He was nervous, and his mind was busy, but he felt *ready*. After checking in with the faithful Captain Plugg (who had nothing to report and went gratefully to bed still wearing her uniform), Reynie went upstairs to the kitchen. The house was quiet and mostly dark, and Reynie moved as silently as any person could do in an old building with so many creaking floorboards, for he had long since learned where all of them were, and he could avoid the worst ones. Although — he reminded himself as he walked into the dark kitchen — there was actually a new creaking board near the pantry, a recent discovery that had made a greater impression on him than one might expect.

Even houses change, Reynie had thought, and it had caused an odd flutter in his stomach. Weren't houses supposed to represent stability? Sure, the Society had changed a lot of things about Mr. Benedict's house on purpose, but some things, Reynie realized, they had changed simply by being there. A thousand footsteps on that particular board, and now it creaked.

Every member of the Society, too, bore a thousand hidden footsteps: effects of a different kind, many impossible to have predicted.

Reynie flipped on the kitchen light—and stifled a scream. Kate stood at the pantry, one leg raised behind her as if she were in the middle of a hopscotch game. She stood that way, Reynie realized, precisely to avoid stepping on that creaking board.

"Sorry to scare you," said Kate, turning from the pantry with a canister of oatmeal. (She looked far more amused than sorry, Reynie noted without surprise.) "Sometimes I just prefer the darkness."

"I know you do," Reynie said, putting the kettle on for tea.

"Are you trying to suggest that you know me well, Reynard Muldoon?"

"It's possible I've picked up a thing or two," Reynie said.

They smiled at each other and set about making breakfast in the way they had done many times before. Reynie handled the tea and toast, and Kate—like a hummingbird zipping from flower to flower—moved about the kitchen handling everything else. They spoke little, only inquired about each other's sleep (good on both counts) and confirmed that nothing terrible had happened in the night. Then the bread popped out of the toaster, and Reynie realized what he'd been trying to think of.

"Hey," he said as Kate handed him the platter he'd just been about to reach for, "McCracken and the others lost their weapons, right? Milligan's agents took their shock-watches and briefcases and so on."

"Of course," Kate answered, turning back to the stove. "Believe me, they put as much distance as possible between the Ten Men and their toys. And that's something, anyway, since evidently McCracken was already feeling the pinch — too many of their weapons confiscated, and not many replacements handy. At the Street Fair Melee, you know, none of them had laser pointers. Which was a lucky stroke for Milligan and me. But they still have a fair amount of hardware at their disposal."

"Right," Reynie said. "And for now they'll just redistribute what they have. But that's not what I was getting at. My question is, McCracken was probably thoroughly searched, wasn't he?"

Kate spun around. "That letter!"

Reynie nodded. "McCracken put it into his pocket."

"I'm sure they found it. Someone must have it."

"Seems like we ought to have a copy of it."

"Seems like, indeed," Kate agreed. "Why don't you jump on the radio? I can take over what you're doing here."

"Are you sure?" Reynie asked, and Kate's laughter followed after him as he hurried back into the dining room, where he'd left the radio.

Reynie had just radioed his request to the appropriate agent when Sticky, Constance, and Tai came in, all of them still in their pajamas, all yawning.

"We ran into George in the hallway," Tai announced in a sleep-raspy voice. "He was confused!"

Sticky was rubbing his face, trying to come more awake. "When I woke up in Mr. Benedict's bed, I thought I was back in my bedroom across the street, but everything had been moved around. I was completely discombobulated."

"And he was walking funny!" Tai declared.

"He appeared to be prancing," Constance mumbled. Her scarlet hair had fallen across her face. She pushed it sleepily aside.

"I'd been dreaming there were scorpions on the floor," Sticky said. "I think it's easy enough to guess why. Anyway, I see you've both been up awhile. Are those poached eggs, Kate? You're the absolute best."

"I know," said Kate, who had just swooped in from the kitchen. "Now, guess what? Reynie ordered up a copy of the letter McCracken was reading yesterday."

Sticky was pulling out a chair. He froze, looking at Kate and Reynie. "How did I not think of that?"

"None of us did," Reynie said. "We were all exhausted, and we kind of had a lot to deal with. I only remembered it this morning. Now we're just waiting."

Anxiously they all sat down to the breakfast Kate had prepared—a pot of oatmeal; toast, butter, and marmalade in abundance; eggs cooked three different ways; a pitcher of milk; and a variety of juices. They ate in uncharacteristic silence, waiting and thinking. Even young Tai, eating breakfast with the Mysterious Benedict Society for the first time, found nothing to say. He was excited, but he also kept drifting off into sleepy early-morning stares.

Half an hour later one of the morning papers arrived. This was not unusual. Several newspapers were delivered to Mr. Benedict's house every morning and evening, most of them tossed from the sidewalk and landing some distance from the door. Today, however, this particular newspaper was carried all the way to the house, where it was propped against the front door. The gate squeaked and clanged again; the delivery person went whistling away into the gloom.

The front door opened a crack, the paper fell into an unseen hand, and the door closed.

"I have it," said Reynie, walking into the dining room. He had already unrolled the newspaper and was flipping to the sports section—where, according to his instructions, the photocopied letter had been secreted away. He unfolded it: two sheets of unlined paper, filled front and back with handwriting so familiar it caused a shiver in Reynie, who remembered the first time he had read it. They'd been at the Institute, determined but scared, and the owner of that handwriting was a brilliant and seemingly unstoppable madman.

"It's from Curtain," Reynie announced, "and it's in code."

Kate, who had been doing handstand push-ups to clear her mind, paused in her exercise and regarded Reynie upside down.

"A familiar one?" she asked, dropping to her feet. A year or so after Mr. Curtain's capture, the Society had been given select copies of his confiscated letters—coded exchanges between him and his Ten Men—and had figured out how to decipher them. It had been one of their projects.

"I recognize it," Reynie said, nodding. "Where's Sticky?"

"He went to the bathroom!" Tai said. "He has to use the bathroom just like everybody else does!"

Everyone looked at Tai, considering this pronouncement without comment. Then Reynie sat at the table with paper and pencil that Kate had produced from a drawer, and for several minutes he scribbled away furiously, pausing from time to time to flex his cramped hand.

"So what does it say?" Kate asked as soon as he'd finished.

"You'd better read it for yourself," Reynie said, handing her the pages. With an apologetic look, he turned to Constance. "You know I hate to say it, but—"

"I get it, I get it," Constance snapped. "There's some reason I shouldn't read it, because of the Listener. Who's awake and back at it, by the way. Fine. Whatever. I believe I'll have another cup of tea. Will someone pass me the sugar?"

"Doesn't the Listener already know what's in the letter?" asked Tai, who took up the sugar bowl, carefully cradling it in both hands, and passed it to Constance.

"Maybe," Reynie said. "My concern isn't the letter so much as what Constance might think about it. The less she knows about some things, the better. Just in case."

"Just in case," Tai repeated, nodding. He noticed how much sugar Constance was spooning into her cup of tea. "Oh, I didn't know you could do that! Can I have some for my tea, too, please?" He extended his hands toward Constance in the same cradle formation, eager to receive the sugar bowl.

Constance eyed him askance and continued with her spooning. He was going to have to wait.

Kate finished reading the letter just as Sticky hurried back into the room, and with a significant look at Reynie, she passed it to him. "From Curtain," she said. "As expected."

True to form, Sticky read and memorized the pages at a glance. The letter read as follows:

Salutations, Gentlemen,

Allow me to congratulate you on your recently improved circumstances!

Now to cut to the chase, for I have but the briefest opportunity to write you. My tiresome brother, Benedict, has informed me that all security and maintenance personnel are being evacuated from the premises, and he alone will be allowed to remain behind as a visitor with extraordinary security clearances. He insists that he has no fear of your infiltration, for he believes the facility to be completely impregnable — believes, in fact, that for this reason he is safest where he is, "keeping me company" in my locked suite, rather than risking to move about the city, where he knows you have gathered in force. He has, however, negotiated a single exception: My devoted young follower, S.Q. Pedalian, has been given permission to procure a few supplies in the city and bring them to Benedict, who anticipates a potentially lengthy stay here until this "situation" is resolved. Yet I am told that S.Q.'s errand must be completed before sunset, when the last guard is under strict orders to activate the final locks, after which there shall be no entry into the facility whatsoever. (Such is the hope of my captors, at least. Naturally, I intend for you to spoil their plans.)

Time is short, therefore. This letter shall be delivered in a sealed envelope, with my signature across the seal, and deposited into our secret Vault. May it find its way quickly into your hands.

Gentlemen, you will not be surprised to learn that my plan is a brilliant one. Indeed, given your particular talents and tools, you're unlikely to find it even remotely challenging to accomplish. I am laying the groundwork myself — paving your path, if you will. Allow me to explain. This shall require a bit of background.

For some years now, my brother, Benedict, has been developing a brain serum that would help the young telepath Constance Contraire to better control her abilities. During his frequent visits to me, we've discussed his research and experiments in full detail — indeed, in the guise of civility, I have myself contributed the most important ideas, and although he has thus far been hesitant to test the serum on his adopted daughter (in fact won't even mention it to her, for fear of raising hopes that might eventually be dashed), I have no doubt that it will do precisely what Benedict intended. Who knows more about the complex workings of the brain than I? No one in the world. (My brother runs, perhaps, a distant second.)

Gentlemen, if you have indeed found the person we long sought (and I believe you have, as there's no other explanation for your newfound freedom), this brain serum will enable us to rapidly cultivate her gifts; she will soon be capable of previously unimaginable feats. Under my direction, she will change the minds of key figures in government. We former Institutionalists will be seen as misunderstood heroes, and our enemies will be seen as deceitful traitors. Imagine it: No security code, no password, no secret weapon or treasure in the world will be hidden from us. All will be ours for the taking. _You_ will be rich and powerful, and _I_, at long last, will be in control: I will set all crooked matters straight. It will not have been the most direct path to the destiny I once foresaw, but there is always more than one path, my friends. Some take longer to travel but are more certain in their destination. Soon we shall look back upon these recent days of curtailed freedom as a necessary step in a long process. The strongest tea must be allowed to steep.

Yes, we shall use the serum to boost the telepath's abilities, and we shall treat her very well, offer her every comfort, until we have achieved our aims. But I have still more secrets. Though Benedict, with his limited focus, seems not to have considered the wider possibilities, to me it is abundantly clear that the serum will elevate _anyone_'s mental abilities — will open new doorways in the brain. The effect on my brother or myself would be minimal, I'm afraid, for (to express this in a way you can understand) the vast majority of the doors in our brains are already open. In other words, it would simply be impossible for either of us to become very much more intelligent than we already are. But on the _average_ mind the effects would be extraordinary. Imagine suddenly being three or four times as smart as you were before you drank the serum. Yes, imagine being a spontaneous genius! Perhaps even one as brilliant as I, although I confess that possibility seems unlikely in the extreme. Nonetheless, I thrill at the notion of my top lieutenants being intellectual giants like myself. We would truly have no boundaries!

But how, you may ask, are we to acquire this serum? Allow me to explain the next part of my plan — which is, as I've mentioned, a brilliant one. Knowing as I do the precise chemical composition of the brain serum, and being (as you know) a gifted chemist, I've secretly developed the formula for a pleasant poison whose chemical compounds would be precisely counteracted by those in the serum. In other words, _the brain serum is the antidote to the poison_.

Over the last year, in accordance with my secret instructions (likewise delivered in sealed, signed envelopes), S.Q. has met with a network of black-market chemists, each of whom participated in one, and only one, part of the process of formulating the poison — thus, no single one of them knows the "complete recipe," if you will. S.Q. himself knows nothing of my overall plan, having been given to understand that I am simply helping former acquaintances with their personal, private research. Today, however, among the supplies he's being dispatched to obtain will be a famously delicious variety of tea, prepared by the last link in my chain of chemists, and awaiting pickup at a charming little tea shop not far from the location of the Vault.

Perhaps you begin to see how my plan is developing. S.Q. will deliver this poisoned tea that my unwitting brother and I shall drink together — yes, I shall have to drink it as well, for Benedict is the one who shall have to prepare it, and I'm afraid he is far too observant and clever not to notice any sleight of hand on my part. Afterward, I shall alert him to what we have consumed. He will understand as well as I what the effects of the poison will be: a day or two of increasing drowsiness, accompanied by a general sense of well-being — I told you it was a "pleasant" poison — concluding with a deep, unending sleep. You see how I put my fate in your hands. I am satisfied with any outcome, however. If I cannot join you in freedom, I am content to leave the world of the waking. Either way, I shall have my escape.

But Benedict, naturally, will wish to avoid letting the curtain fall so abruptly on his own life's production. Therefore, I will urge him to seek assistance. He will be unable to leave the facility, however, for he will be locked inside the so-called visitors area of my security suite. And so he will be compelled to communicate telepathically with young Contraire. (You'll recall that it was by this means that Benedict infiltrated our headquarters on our last fateful day of freedom.) Now, one of Benedict's associates, the young Mr. Washington, knows the precise formula of the brain serum and has ready access to the necessary chemicals. He will no doubt promptly formulate a quantity of serum and attempt, with the help of Benedict's other young minions, to deliver this antidote to my brother. (And I suppose to me as well, lest they all be accused of allowing my demise when they could have prevented it.) Despite this facility's supposedly impenetrable nature, those four are resourceful enough (as you have all seen for yourselves), and my brother knows the facility well enough, that I'm confident they will make their way in.

What they won't know until too late is that you will be following them. That's correct, gentlemen, you have only to follow them, applying pressure from behind to speed them along, and using the example of their own progress through the various layers of security whenever you find it expedient. Certainly you are supremely skilled when it comes to _hurting_ your way into and out of places, but in this case it may be helpful, even necessary, to adopt some of the young intruders' own methods of infiltrating the facility, for they may well be informed by Benedict himself. Even more important, however, is that their presence here will be critical in breaching the last (and truly impregnable) barrier into my suite — my foolish brother will open doors for them that he would not open for anyone else, not even to save himself. (I repeat, at least one or two members of his beloved foursome <u>must be present</u> when you arrive at the final security door; otherwise, I fear, your efforts will have been in vain.)

And now you see why my plan is brilliant! In one fell swoop we shall secure both the brain serum and our freedom, and together we shall make our escape into our new life! (Much to the horror, I might add, of Benedict and his lackeys, who will be compelled to see it all unfold, miserably aware that they have played key roles in our escape.)

I anticipate a final question: How exactly are we to make this escape? Even with the use of signal disruption to disable the facility's alarm systems, we cannot simply retrace your footsteps. Never fear! You'll understand my basis for saying that I know far more about my present environs than anyone would ever guess. This is a relevant fact for more than a few reasons. First, as it happens, I — and I alone — know the whereabouts of a secret cache of weapons: weapons of my own design, ones you have used with such gusto throughout your careers. Your current supply must be precious low, limited to the emergency store that the Katz brothers will have raided prior to your liberation. Those should prove sufficient to help you make your way to me. Then you shall have a fresh abundance at your disposal. What's more (and, oh, it is so very much more!), there is yet another weapon here, one with which you are unfamiliar. It has always remained hidden. Not a soul in the world has ever known of its existence; indeed, few would have even thought it possible. The same might have been said of my Whisperer, of course — even *you* doubted its abilities until I had demonstrated them. But although the Whisperer failed, in the end, to change the world forever, I have another secret means of doing so. I require only a little help from you. Come and see, gentlemen! Prepare to be amazed.

Finally, as for our exit, rest easy. You have only to reach me. Once you have done so, you may confidently place *your* fate in *my* hands. I have considered every angle, every potential obstacle, and I am triumphant in my conviction. Only reach me, gentlemen, and everything will go precisely according to my plan!

I look forward to reestablishing our acquaintance soon. I hope this letter finds you in good health, etc.

Cordially,

L. Curtain

PS. Should it interest you, I composed this entire letter in a mere eleven minutes, and as you can see, there is not a single strikeout or misspelling. Remarkable!

As remarkable as it may have been to compose such a letter in eleven minutes, even more remarkable, to the average observer, would be to see Sticky Washington read the same letter in a matter of seconds. His friends were hardly average observers, however, and were so used to seeing his prodigious abilities in action that they registered not the faintest surprise when Sticky reached the end of the letter almost as soon as it had been handed to him. His expression was now the same as Reynie's and Kate's, for all of them were silently thinking about the letter. Sticky, for his part, was essentially reading it again—looking at a perfect image of it in his mind—which led to a surprising announcement from Tai.

"I can see the letter in George's mind!" he declared. "I can read it!"

Sticky's eyes widened, and for a moment his expression turned guilty, as if he had shared the letter with the little boy on purpose. Then he looked concerned. They all did.

"You can read, Tai?" Reynie asked.

Tai's chin was raised, his eyes turned upward and slightly to the side. He had the expression of a person trying to remember something. He nodded slowly in response to Reynie's question and continued in the same attitude, presumably still looking at the letter in his mind's eye.

"Um," Constance said, "this is probably not good, correct?"

The others all opened their mouths, then closed them again, trying to think of what to say or do. This was not a problem they had foreseen. Several moments passed in a confused silence, until Tai interrupted it.

"What does 'salutations' mean?" he asked, and then he giggled. "Why did you all just sigh at the same time? Why do you all look like that?"

It was true they all looked extremely relieved, and none more so than Sticky, who had done nothing wrong, of course, yet couldn't shake the feeling that he had single-handedly caused a potentially dangerous problem. Reynie was right: There were things in that letter that Constance shouldn't know, and if Constance shouldn't know them, a five-year-old boy with unpredictable telepathic abilities certainly shouldn't know them, either.

"I'm going to take a break to clear my head," Sticky said, and quickly left the room.

"Hey, sport," Kate said to Tai, "where's my bucket? Don't tell me you left it in Constance's room with no one to guard it."

Tai's mouth fell open. "But I did," he whispered. "I'll go get it!" He ran out.

As soon as he was gone, Reynie said to Constance, "Mr. Benedict needs our help. The situation is dangerous, no question about it, but I want you to see—no, I *need* you to see—how confident I am that Mr. Benedict is going to be okay. Don't dig too deeply, all right? But take a good look at my certainty."

"Mine, too," Kate said.

Constance rolled her eyes. "You're *always* certain, Kate. That does me no good." She looked at Reynie. "Obviously, you've just made me really worried about what's going on with Dad."

"I know," Reynie said. "I'm sorry."

Constance was staring intently at him. "It's okay, I get it. And your confidence helps. I do see it, and it helps. So what *can* I know?"

"I'm assuming you haven't reached out to him since yesterday, right?" Reynie asked.

"With Miss Nosy Pants eavesdropping? Of course not."

"You're going to need to now," Kate said. "He probably

has a message for us. Don't worry about the Listener getting it, too. It can't be helped."

"Now, as in *right* now?" Constance asked. "Right this second? Just sitting here at the dining table? You two are making me so nervous."

"Right this second," Kate confirmed, and Reynie signaled his agreement.

"Wow, okay, then. Here we go." Constance took a deep breath and closed her eyes. "First I'm letting him know that we're safe," she murmured. "That's right, Listener Lady, no thanks to you. Okay, here he is! He's safe, too. He's still with Uncle Horrible," she said, using her favorite nickname for Mr. Curtain. "S.Q. isn't there, but I guess he brought them something? Tea. Mr. Curtain drank some tea — I don't know why this is important. Dad's showing me the container it came in. Fancy stuff, I guess. Uh-oh. Okay. He's imagining a skull and crossbones. Do you think he means poison? The tea was poisoned?"

"Yes," Reynie said softly. "That's what he means."

"Wow, okay," Constance murmured again. She was silent a moment. "He knows that the Listener is eavesdropping, I can tell. He's being very careful about what he tries to communicate."

"Tell him about the letter," Reynie said. "That will make it easier for him. Tell him Mr. Curtain sent a secret letter to McCracken, and we've got a copy of it. We know everything about his situation."

Constance did as Reynie suggested, and after a pause she said, "He understands."

"Tell him that Sticky can make the serum."

Constance opened one eye. "What serum? Is it for saving Uncle Horrible? Right, sorry, never mind. No questions. Okay, I'll tell him." She closed the eye. Another pause. She frowned. "He says he's sorry. He doesn't want us to take the risk. He *really* doesn't—I can tell. Especially not me, of course." She shrugged, her eyes still closed. "I don't know what he's talking about, but of course he doesn't want us to take any risks."

Reynie was chewing on his lip. Kate was watching him. "If you're going to think of something clever," she muttered, "seems like now would be a good time."

"Okay," Reynie said. "Constance, tell him not to worry. Tell him we aren't going to take any risks. We'll figure out some other way to help him."

Constance opened one eye again. "He isn't going to believe that, you know. I don't know how I'm supposed to make him believe it when I know it isn't true myself."

"It doesn't matter whether he believes it or not," Reynie said. "He isn't the only person who can hear your thoughts."

"Oh, *her*?" Constance shook her head skeptically. "I doubt she'll believe it, either, Reynie. Even if she does, McCracken won't, and you know she'll tell McCracken."

"Can you please just try? It's not your fault if it doesn't work. Just try."

Constance sighed. "Okay, Mr. Mastermind, I'll tell him we aren't going to take any risks." She concentrated awhile with her eyes closed. "No, I don't think he believes me," she murmured. "He just repeated that he wants us to be safe. He's keeping something from me, but maybe it's just because he doesn't want the Listener to know."

Constance gasped. Her eyes popped open. "He drank the tea, too, didn't he?" Her face was suddenly awash in horror. "This isn't just about Mr. Curtain — it's about *him*!"

Reynie jumped from his chair and went to Constance, who looked up at him with brimming eyes. He placed his hands on her cheeks, holding her face steady. "Look at me," he said. "Do you remember my confidence that Mr. Benedict is going to be fine? How often have you seen me be so confident and then be wrong?"

"Never?" Constance whispered, staring back at him. "Or almost never, anyway." She squeezed her eyes closed, trying not to cry, but tears trickled down her cheeks regardless, wetting Reynie's fingers. "I'm — I'm trying not to dig too deeply. I want to know what's making you so confident, but I know... I know..."

"He's so confident because we're *better* than they are," Kate said firmly.

Despite herself, Constance gave a little snort. She smirked. "Yes, we are," she mumbled, her eyes still closed.

"Is that enough to help?" Reynie asked. "Can you just trust us that everything will be okay?"

Constance nodded. "Fine," she muttered. "I hate it, but fine. Now get your hands off my face."

When Tai Li trotted back into the room carrying Kate's bucket, he saw Constance wiping her eyes with her pajama sleeves, Kate at the dining room table loading a plate with toast and eggs, and Reynie walking back and forth with his hands clasped behind him.

"This is weird!" Tai exclaimed. "What's everyone doing?"

"Constance is recovering from a bit of a shock," Kate said. "Reynie is thinking about Mr. Benedict's message from yesterday, and I'm eating a second breakfast. Because what good is a dining table if no one is dining?"

"That's true!" Tai exclaimed. He made a beeline for the sugar bowl.

Reynie stopped pacing. He had already felt himself on the verge of something, and now Kate had given him precisely the push he needed.

"Okay, listen," he said to no one in particular. "Mr. Benedict was giving us instructions yesterday, and the very first line focused on a place—the place where we're supposed to hunt the hunter. Now, I don't think he'd send us out on some wild-goose chase in the city, not with the Baker's Dozen in town."

"True enough," Kate said. "Go on." Sensing that her second breakfast was about to be interrupted, she made a sandwich of her eggs and toast and took a huge bite.

"Wow, you chew so fast, Kate!" Tai said.

"You think we're supposed to look somewhere here," Constance said to Reynie. "In this house."

"He couldn't come out and say that, of course, not if there was any chance the Listener would overhear. He wanted to make it completely confusing for her but easy for us. And it should have been easy! Think about it—what name is being defied by one who stands?"

"I *have* thought about it," Kate said between bites. "Does it depend on who's doing the standing? Or is it the hunter?"

Kate's mention of the hunter was the last piece of the puzzle for Reynie. "I know who the hunter is," he said excitedly, "but it isn't his name that's being defied by one who stands. It isn't a *person's* name at all!"

Kate was rising from the table, sandwich in hand. "Can you stop talking and maybe — ?"

"Right!" Reynie said. "I'll show you. Let's go!"

Key
QUESTIONS

The sitting room!" Kate declared as they hurried down the hallway. She tapped her nose and pointed at herself. "One who *stands* in a *sitting* room is defying the name of the room!"

"Exactly," Reynie said, glancing back. "Kind of like being in the dining room and not dining, right?"

"Right!" Tai exclaimed. He was walking behind Constance with his arms wrapped around the bucket and his bowl of oatmeal balanced on its flip-top. "Oh no, I forgot my spoon." He started to turn back, but Kate scooped him up, bucket and bowl and all, and when she had deposited him in the sitting room, she produced a shiny spoon, as if by magic.

"Orion," Reynie said, crossing the room to take one of the paintings from the wall. "Do you remember Sticky telling you the name of this constellation, Tai? Well, guess what? In Greek mythology, Orion is known as the Hunter!"

Tai, his mouth full of sugary oatmeal, nodded vigorously.

"'Dare hunt the hunter in his frame,'" Kate said. "Of course! The picture frame! But why does he say 'dare,' do you think? Is there something dangerous about taking down the painting?"

"Poetic license," Constance said with a shrug.

Tai was fascinated. "There's a license for *poetry*?"

"What? No," Constance said. "Poetic license means having the freedom to bend the rules to create whatever kind of effect you want. I just meant that Dad wrote it that way for the rhyme. 'Dare hunt' has the same sound as 'Where one' from the first line."

"It sure does!" said Tai agreeably. He directed another spoonful of oatmeal into his mouth, which, for no apparent reason, he was opening far wider than necessary.

Reynie carefully leaned the painting against the wall with its back facing them. The frame behind the canvas had been covered with heavy brown paper, held in place by small metal fasteners. "'Strike the clenches from their floor,'" he murmured. "More poetic license. I think he just means remove the fasteners."

Kate took out her Swiss Army knife. "A 'clench' can refer

to a nail or other kinds of fasteners," she said to Tai. She began removing the fasteners at high speed.

"I know that, of course," Tai replied.

"Oh, really?" said Kate with an arched eyebrow. "When did you learn that?"

"Just now!"

"It doesn't quite work that way, sport," Kate said, carefully peeling the brown paper away from the frame.

There, in the hollow space behind the painting canvas, was a sealed plastic pouch. It appeared to contain folded papers, and a message had been taped to the outside. "This is written in Tamil," said Kate, who had learned some Tamil from Reynie and his mother Miss Perumal over the years but could read only a little, and with difficulty. Kate handed the pouch to Reynie. "Obviously, Mr. Benedict was counting on you to be here."

Reynie read the message at a glance. "Not just me. This says, 'REMEMBER THE DUSKWORT? WHAT A STICKY PROBLEM!'"

"Hey, duskwort!" Tai exclaimed. "That was the plant that makes you fall asleep."

"Yep," Kate said. "But what does this have to do with Sticky? That's the question."

"Sticky was the only one to see the duskwort under a microscope," Constance said. "Maybe that matters somehow."

Reynie pursed his lips. He turned the pouch around two or three times in his hands. "The thing is," he said slowly, "if whatever is in here needs to be read by Sticky, Mr. Benedict could have just counted on us to figure that out. So why did he place this message on the outside of the pouch?"

"Because he wants Sticky to be here when we open it," Constance suggested. "But why would that matter so much?"

"This pouch is airtight," Reynie observed. "Maybe its contents will be affected when they're exposed to fresh air."

Tai, who had been busily tapping his nose and pointing his finger every time someone spoke, piped up: "The dusk-wort got de-cinerated really fast!"

"Disintegrated," Kate said. "It's true. If it wasn't in the perfect conditions, it just crumbled to dust. So what do you think, Reynie? Maybe Sticky is the only one who can read these papers fast enough?"

"And memorize them," Reynie said, nodding. "Yes, I think so. I think these are all security measures. Whatever's inside this pouch, Mr. Benedict meant it for us and only us. But listen," he added just as Kate, he could tell, was heading for the intercom. "Let's take the pressure off as much as possible. We can just ask Sticky to read the papers because Mr. Benedict wants him to, which is true."

"You're suggesting we don't tell him everything?" Kate furrowed her brow. "Not sure I'm crazy about that idea, Reynie."

Reynie grimaced. His conscience had been bothering him enough already. But this was a critical moment—wouldn't it be wrong *not* to avoid risks if possible? "I'm only suggesting," he said, "that we don't have to mention that there might be a time limit. Sticky's so fast it shouldn't matter, right? I'm just trying to spare him the pressure—which would be, you know, considerable."

"Maybe you're right," Kate conceded reluctantly. "I don't

like it. But it's true that absolutely everything could depend on whether he succeeds."

Constance gave Kate a bleak look. "I was actually trying not to think of it like that."

"Think of what like what?" asked Tai, who was furiously scraping the last of his oatmeal out of the bowl and seemed not to have been paying attention.

"She's worried you're going to eat all the sugar in the house," Kate said.

"No, she isn't!" Tai cried with a laugh.

"I am a little bit," Constance muttered.

Down in the Blab, Sticky Washington was checking the supply cabinets, making notes, checking the computers (there were several), making more notes, checking the workbenches (no notes)—all in perfect silence, for he had activated the Husher. Sticky had come here to clear his mind, which for him meant shoving worrisome information aside, if only for a few minutes, by focusing on other information. It was like eating a roll while waiting for hot soup to cool; soon he'd be able to handle the soup. As for the Husher, he'd discovered long ago that silence helped. Silence reduced distractions.

Silence also allowed Sticky to yell with frustration and not be heard—something he suddenly felt a powerful need to do. He set down his clipboard, carefully removed his spectacles, threw back his head, and yelled at the top of his lungs: "Why didn't I think of that! Why, why, why? Come on, brain! Come *on*!" He jumped up and down a few times, stomping the concrete floor as hard as he could. All in perfect silence. Breathing hard, he dug a cloth out of his pocket and gave his spectacle lenses a thorough polishing. Then he resettled them on his nose. *Okay*, he thought, feeling calmer. *Okay.*

Sticky's mind returned to the nightmare he'd awakened from this morning. All those scorpions on the floor. Contrary to what others might expect, he didn't imagine they represented Ten Men.

"You're dwelling on your mistakes again," his mother had said to him not long ago, and not for the first time. "It's good to acknowledge them, but I do wish you'd not forget everything you get right."

They'd been having breakfast in their home across the street. Sticky had just awakened from a similar dream.

Sticky's father had nodded his agreement, which for such a profoundly quiet man was a significant contribution to the discussion.

"I know," Sticky had said, taking up a glass of grape juice, then setting it down again. "You're right, Mom. I know that. I just get so frustrated! I never see Reynie make the mistakes I do."

His mother regarded him with hooded eyes. "Can Reynie do all the things you can do?"

Sticky sighed and rubbed his scalp. "No, I know. I just don't like making mistakes."

"Reynie makes his own share of mistakes, love," said Sticky's mom. "*You* just don't dwell on those. Do you know who probably does?"

Sticky pursed his lips. "No idea. Constance?"

They all chuckled at this.

"Well, *she* probably does, too," Sticky's mom admitted. "And on everyone else's. But there's a reason, you know, that your father and I are comfortable with you making your own decisions. You're doing a wonderful job leading your life. We only hope you'll come to us for love and support— and maybe, sometimes, even advice. Who knows?"

"I'll always come to you for all of those things," Sticky had said, rounding the table to hug his parents. "Advice included."

Now, in the Blab, Sticky took a deep breath and let it out. He tapped a pencil on the clipboard. Yes, he'd forgotten the chemicals on the rooftop patio, and it hadn't occurred to him to get a copy of Mr. Curtain's letter, and he hadn't thought to ask Tai about his reading abilities before scanning the letter. That was okay. He couldn't think of everything. He was who he was, and that was enough. He knew that. He believed it. And now it was time to rejoin his friends. Sticky went to the Husher and switched it off.

"—IN THE WORLD ARE YOU?" Constance's voice was screeching through the intercom speaker. "ARE YOU AT A *SPA* GETTING A *MASSAGE*, OR WHAT? DID IT EVER OCCUR TO YOU THAT WE MIGHT—"

"Intercom off," Sticky said quickly. The speaker went silent.

He took another deep breath and reached, once more, for his polishing cloth.

⚬⋅⚬

"Check this out," Reynie said as Sticky entered the sitting room. He handed over the plastic pouch, resisting a sudden urge to tell his friend everything. Was this a mistake, after all? Or did he just feel guilty, even though he was trying to do the right thing?

Everyone formed a semicircle around Sticky, who studied the plastic pouch. "'Remember the duskwort,'" he murmured (for he could read most languages, including Tamil). "I wonder what he means, exactly."

"I'm sure we'll find out," Reynie said. "Mr. Benedict clearly wants you to be the one to read those papers, though."

Sticky nodded. "It sure looks that way. Okay, let's see what we have here." He unsealed the pouch. A strong chemical odor filled the room, and all of them wrinkled their noses.

"We look like bunnies!" Tai exclaimed.

Sticky's brow was wrinkled in addition to his nose, for he was pondering the source of the odor. He paused, looking thoughtfully to the side and saying, mostly to himself, "What do you suppose *that's* about? I can name at least five chemical agents that smell like that."

"Any of them dangerous?" Reynie asked quickly.

Sticky shrugged. "No, but some have curious effects when combined—"

"Maybe the answer will be in those papers," Reynie interrupted.

A hint of annoyance appeared on Sticky's face. "Okay, that's true enough," he said, and removed the contents from the pouch. After a process of careful (and, to his friends, agonizingly slow) unfolding, those contents were revealed to be blueprints: three very large sheets of paper covered with diagrams of buildings, some of the drawings obviously incomplete, others represented in great detail. The margins were filled with a variety of tiny sketches and notes written in three different colors of ink. The semicircle of onlookers craned their necks to get a glimpse of what Sticky was seeing. At least three of them felt a little sick—the amount of information on those pages was overwhelming.

"Let me take these to the dining room table," Sticky said as he perused the blueprints. "I'd like to spread them out."

"Let's just do it right here!" Kate said. "We can use the floor!"

Sticky gave her a puzzled look. "It would be easier on a table, but whatever." He placed the three pages side by side on the floor and knelt over them. He gave a low whistle. "This required a *lot* of work."

Reynie noticed Tai about to say something and put a finger to his lips. Tai nodded and dutifully covered his mouth. He had already been advised that they should keep as quiet as possible to allow Sticky to concentrate.

"The thing is," Sticky said, "there's a lot of contradictory information on here. There are three separate keys—red, gold, and blue. Do you see the different colors?" He looked up for confirmation, and everyone nodded quickly. "Okay, well, each key is consistent within itself, but not with either of the others. I think we can trust only one of the keys. But which one?" He leaned back on his haunches and looked thoughtfully to the side again. "I wonder if he expects me to figure it out just by studying the schematics. If so, I'm not sure how yet. Maybe there's some other kind of clue."

"We can all think about it together," Reynie said as casually as he could. "Right now you can just make sure you've looked carefully at everything, and then—"

Now Sticky was visibly frustrated, and with a sharp look at Reynie, he said, "So I can't even take five seconds to think about something? And do you think I'm *not* going to look carefully? For crying out loud, Reynie, everything doesn't have to be done exactly your way."

"I'm sorry, George," Reynie said, averting his eyes. "You're right." He put his hands behind his back and clenched his fists.

Sticky sighed. "Well, I certainly don't want to argue about it. I'm sorry, too." He turned back to the blueprints. After only a moment, however, he looked up again. "The odor has faded, hasn't it? Or is it just that I've gotten used to it?"

The odor had indeed faded, almost entirely, and the others hastened to agree that this was the case.

"Hmm," Sticky said. "That narrows the options. About the chemicals, I mean."

Tai shuffled close to Constance and tugged on her sleeve. She bent down so that he could whisper in her ear. "Shouldn't he be going faster?"

It was indeed a whisper, but not an especially soft one— and in that quiet room, at such close quarters, it might as well have been a shout.

Sticky stiffened. He jerked his gaze toward Tai and Constance, then at Kate and Reynie. "Wait a minute, is there some kind of time constraint I'm unaware of?" Their expressions, at once sheepish and anxious, spoke every bit as loudly as Tai's whisper had.

"Oh, *great*," he moaned, immediately returning to the blueprints.

Everyone leaned silently forward, and everyone saw, at the same time, the markings on the pages growing fainter. The papers themselves weren't disintegrating, but they were going blank. Everyone held their breath, including Sticky, who stared and stared. In less than a minute there was nothing left to stare at.

The silence held. No one spoke. Then Sticky released his breath and looked up. "Don't worry, I got it all," he said, and smiling at their sighs and relieved expressions, he added, "I actually had it almost immediately, you know. I've just been making sure I didn't miss anything."

"You could have *told* us!" Constance snapped. "That would have been nice."

"Yeah, and you could have told *me* the *ink* was going to disappear!"

"We didn't know it would!" Tai said cheerfully. "We thought the paper was going to disintegrate."

Sticky looked at Tai and bit his lip. After a moment he said, "Did you think that was interesting, Tai, seeing the ink disappear?"

"It was amazing!" Tai exclaimed.

Sticky smiled, nodded, and gathered up the empty pages. "Do you want to keep these?"

"I can *keep* them?" Tai whispered as Sticky handed them over. "Thank you so much! Kate, can I put them in your bucket?"

"Knock yourself out," replied Kate with a wink.

"THANK YOU SO MUCH!" Tai squealed, and with great reverence he folded the blank sheets of paper and placed them inside the bucket.

⌣∴⌣

As Tai busied himself with Kate's bucket under the dining room table, the others sat around it, discussing what Sticky had learned. Or rather, they were *going* to discuss it as soon as Sticky was ready. He'd felt so annoyed with his friends—especially with Reynie, whose idea he knew it had been to keep him in the dark—that he'd declared himself hungry again, though he wasn't really. He'd only wanted a minute to calm down, and he'd claimed it by going into the kitchen. By the time he returned with an entire stack of fresh toast, settled into his chair, and poured more tea for everyone, his friends were almost quaking with impatience. But all, even Constance, were careful not to show it.

"So, about these conflicting keys," Reynie said gently, passing Sticky the marmalade. "What kind of information do they relate to?"

"The location of entrances, the layouts of certain buildings, schematics for various alarm systems, several other things. If you were trying to infiltrate the multiple layers of security, your choices would depend entirely on which color key you trust." (Here Sticky interrupted himself with a grunt of frustration. In preparation for the marmalade, he was trying to spread butter on his first slice of toast, which he kept accidentally tearing with his table knife.) "That even includes your approach to the buildings. Which makes me think that two out of the three routes would lead you directly into traps."

"That's great," Constance muttered. "Really, really great. I'm loving this."

Kate was eyeing Sticky's clumsy efforts to spread the butter on his toast. She had to make herself look away.

"There are also lots of cryptic notes," Sticky went on. "Directions written like riddles. You could spend ages trying to figure them all out—which might not even be possible, since we have to consider that some of the notes could simply be gibberish, meant to engage your attention while offering zero hope of finding a solution—but even if you succeeded, how would you know which of them to heed and which to disregard?" He looked dejectedly at his mangled toast. "It's colossally tricky."

"It doesn't have to be, though," Kate said cheerily. She presented him with a perfectly intact slice of toast she had just buttered for him. "Once we know how to do it, right? We just have to figure out which key to use, and then rely on our different skill sets. Mr. Benedict obviously made those blueprints specifically for us, so he knows we can do it."

"Why do you think Dad hid the blueprints, anyway?" Constance asked. "If he expected us to need them for some reason, why not tell us ahead of time?"

"You said it yourself earlier," Reynie said. "Mr. Benedict always has multiple backup plans. He probably had a suspicion that we might need them someday, but he couldn't share them with us because we don't have the proper security clearances. I'm guessing there's a clause in his contract that allows him to share the information with trusted individuals, but only in the case of dire emergency."

"I would think this qualifies," Constance said.

"Imagine if the Ten Men had searched the house," Reynie went on. "Or anyone, for that matter. First of all, there's almost no chance they would find the blueprints. But even if they did, if they didn't happen to read Tamil, they would probably open the pouch without realizing they would have only a minute or two to study the blueprints."

"And even if they had a camera handy," said Sticky, "and took pictures of everything, the pictures would be useless without knowing which key to follow."

"Speaking of pictures," Kate said, "do you think you could reproduce the blueprints for us, George? We could study them with you. It might help."

Sticky shook his head noncommittally. "I can try it as a last resort. But it would take me hours, and, well, I don't have your artistic abilities, you know."

"Good point," Kate conceded. "You aren't exactly steady with a pencil."

At this Sticky narrowed his eyes, but he couldn't disagree. And in fact, he had a feeling that Kate had been trying to put it nicely.

"Maybe George can try to draft a few of the more important things later," Reynie said, "but I don't think that's how we'll figure out the right key to use. I think the answer is in the message Mr. Benedict sent to us yesterday. The first three lines helped us *find* the blueprints, right? My guess is that the last line will tell us how to *use* them."

Kate slugged the last of her tea and clapped the cup onto

its saucer. "Right! Let's get this figured out!" She turned to Constance, who was looking increasingly sullen, and said, "Do you think you could try again to remember exactly what Mr. Benedict said?"

"I told you," Constance mumbled. "Something about a door made out of clay. A kind of door that the French use. That's all I've got. I was fighting a war in my head at the time."

"We know," Reynie said gently. "And you're having to ward off the Listener even as we speak. We all know this is incredibly hard for you."

"And, frankly, amazing," Kate said. "It's amazing, what you're doing."

"Agreed," said Sticky.

"Agreed!" came Tai's voice from under the table.

"Agreed," said Reynie.

Constance looked as though she wasn't certain whether to cry or scream. Her face contorted, and she averted her eyes. "Thanks," she said. "I'm sure you maybe mean that a little, but I also know you're just trying to soften the blow. Because you want me to leave. I can't be here when you solve this."

It was true. Between Constance and Tai, there was too much risk of information leaking out. Sticky had the blueprints in his head, Tai couldn't control his abilities, and Constance was in ceaseless battle with the Listener, whose own abilities might increase at any time. They all knew it.

"We don't *want* you to leave," Reynie said. "And we all mean that more than a little. But we do have to be careful."

Constance gave a curt nod and rose from her chair. "Come on, Tai," she said, rapping on the table. "Let's go find something fun to do."

"Can we play with the Husher in the Blab?" they heard Tai ask.

"I think you just like saying those words," Constance said.

"I do!" Tai said, emerging from beneath the table.

"You can get the Husher," Sticky cautioned, "but you'll need to take it elsewhere, Tai. There's no playing in the... in the Blab."

Kate flickered her eyebrows, delighted to hear Sticky use her word.

Reynie caught Constance by the arm. "Before you go, can you tell us what the message looked like in your mind?"

Constance considered. "It didn't look like anything. It was just Dad's voice. He wasn't trying to send me images."

"That's what I figured," Reynie said. "Images would have been too risky. They would have given away too much. Okay, thank you, Constance. And listen," he said, squeezing her arm, "we won't be long. You've already helped me more than you realize."

Constance shot him a wry look. "Well, I'm glad your confidence is back. That should help. But you shouldn't say stuff like that. It's hard for me not to think about it, you know."

"You're right," Reynie said, frowning. "That was bad judgment. I only wanted—"

"To make me feel better. I know. But you're wasting your energy." Constance pulled away from him. "Just...just figure it out so we can move on." She looked down at Tai, who was butting his head against her hip like a goat, evidently trying to move her toward the door. "Okay, little goat, lead the way."

Tai bleated happily, and the two of them went out.

Reynie watched them go, then turned back to Kate and Sticky, who were watching him expectantly.

"Well?" Sticky asked.

"I don't know yet," Reynie replied. "I was trying not to think about it too hard while they were in the room."

Kate pointed at him. "But you think you're close. We heard what you asked her. You weren't just satisfying your curiosity. You think it matters that she could only hear his voice."

"We've known from the beginning that images are easier to communicate," Reynie said. "Mr. Benedict might simply have imagined a piece of paper with those words written clearly on it—that wouldn't have given away images of Orion, right? It would have been like Tai seeing Mr. Curtain's letter in George's head."

"That's plausible," Sticky said. "It could also be that he thought Constance would find his voice comforting."

"Both could be true," Kate said. "Doing several things at once is kind of the way Mr. Benedict operates. So, what do you think, Reynie? And by that I mean, *think*, Reynie."

Reynie did. He closed his eyes, took a deep breath, and thought.

Poetic license. He did it for the sound.

Reynie opened his eyes. "Okay," he said. "I have it."

$\mathbf{W}$hat took you so long?" asked Kate.

She was joking, of course, but Reynie thought it a good question. Strange that something he hit upon so easily today had felt so impenetrable yesterday. Sleep and food had made a difference, he knew. But he also knew there was more to it than that.

"What's most surprising to me," Reynie said, "is that Constance didn't solve this herself. She's the one with the perfect sense of rhyme and meter, and we know how she identifies patterns without even trying. For her not to be able to reconstruct the last line of Mr. Benedict's message—well, I think it shows us better than anything what she's really dealing with. We can't see that battle raging in her head, but it's obviously a fierce one."

For a moment they all considered this, all felt a pang of sympathy and protectiveness. Nobody was a greater test of their patience than Constance, it was true, but neither was there any person in their lives more remarkable.

"So, what's the secret, Reynie?" Sticky asked, keeping his voice neutral. He still felt mildly resentful but was determined not to show it. "What do rhyme and meter have to do with this?"

"Okay, think of the pattern of the message," Reynie said. "He gave it to us in the form of a poem:

> *Where one who stands defies the name,*
> *Dare hunt the hunter in his frame*
> *And strike the clenches from their floor . . .*

"We didn't get the exact wording of the last line," Reynie continued, "because Constance was distracted, but we can figure it out based on the rhyme and meter."

"Rhyming couplets," Sticky said, nodding, "in iambic tetrameter. Da DUH da DUH da DUH da DUH. And the last word of the last line rhymes with 'floor.'"

"Door!" Kate cried. "Constance said there's a door made out of clay!"

Reynie tapped his nose. "She also said it was the kind that the French use."

"Which made no sense," Kate said, frowning.

"Right," Reynie said, "but think about what we know Constance heard—she absolutely heard the words 'French' and 'door,' and based on rhyme and meter, we can guess where those words would appear in the last line."

"There's a rhyme connection between 'French' and 'clench,'" Sticky observed, "and 'floor' and 'door'!"

"How about this?" Reynie said. *"And like the French, use the clay door."*

Kate tried it out:

> *"And strike the clenches from their floor*
> *And like the French, use the clay door.*

"I like it, Reynie," she said. "It seems right. But how is this the answer?"

"Because it's all about the sound!" exclaimed Sticky, almost leaping from his chair. "Mr. Benedict wasn't talking about a door made out of clay! In French, it *sounds* like 'clay door'—"

"Oh!" Kate cried, slapping her forehead. (For although neither she nor Reynie could compete with Sticky in the language department, they both had studied several and knew a good deal of French.) "'And like the French, use the *clé d'or*'!"

"Exactly!" Reynie said. "It sounds like the English 'clay door,' but it's actually the French *'clé d'or'*—the gold key!"

The three friends couldn't help grinning, laughing, and congratulating one another, for even in emergencies—*especially* in emergencies—it's no small thing to solve a puzzle upon which so much depends, and here was one whose solution had determined their course. True, that course was dangerous, but this they had already known. What mattered most was that they had significant information McCracken didn't have. They had an advantage. They had their start. They were on their way.

Soon enough, however, celebration turned to deliberation. Sticky perused the blueprints in his mind's eye, focusing only on the diagrams and notes in gold ink. "It all holds together," he murmured. "The path is fairly clear even if the obstacles along the way aren't. I think some of the notes aren't going to make sense until we're actually there—like the last line about the *clé d'or*. Before we found the blueprints, we never could have figured out what that means."

"Well, that's great news!" Kate said.

Sticky looked at her askance. "How is it great news that we're heading into a dangerous situation with a ticking clock counting down to potential disaster *without* knowing ahead of time how to get through these different layers of security?"

Kate was already, and very speedily, clearing the table. "Because it means we can get moving!"

Reynie and Sticky jumped to help her. (And by working as fast as they could, they even *did* help her, a little.) Soon everything was squared away to Kate's satisfaction, and in the meantime the three of them had discussed what their next steps would be. With Sticky monitoring from his computer workstation, Reynie spent some minutes on the radio, obtaining and distributing necessary information. And then it was done. The arrangements had been made. They had their plan.

A quick use of the intercom system brought Tai Li bursting

into the dining room, where he found Kate and Reynie waiting. Trudging in behind him came a still decidedly grumpy-looking Constance Contraire.

"We used the Husher to sneak up on Captain Plugg!" Tai announced with a burst of giggles. "She sprayed coffee out of her mouth like a fountain!"

Kate gave him a stern look. "I told you we had rules about that, remember?"

"But you don't even *like* the rules!"

"True," Kate said. She snatched her bucket from Tai, placed it on the floor, and pointed to it. "Nevertheless, have a seat on the red stool, young man."

Tai's eyes widened. He looked as if he were about to be given a marvelous present. He dropped onto the bucket and sat very still, his hands on his knees. "Am I being punished?" he asked with a hopeful look.

"Severely," Kate replied.

Tai covered his mouth to suppress a giggle, then composed himself and made an obvious effort to look unhappy.

Constance, meanwhile, had slouched into the easy chair in the corner and drawn her feet up under her. "So you three got it all figured out," she said gloomily. "That's so great."

"You did say you wanted us to, after all," Reynie said. He hoped that his light tone might make a difference in her mood, but Constance only looked coldly at him from behind a veil of scarlet hair. He cleared his throat. "You also said you wanted to move on, and it's time to do that. We all need to pack a small overnight bag. No matter how things go, there's a good chance we won't be back here for a day or two, maybe longer."

Tai, who was still enjoying his punishment, raised his hand. Kate gave him a nod of permission, and he asked brightly, "Where are we going? I don't have any other clothes. Or a bag. Or a toothbrush." He thought for a moment. "Or toothpaste."

"We're going to help Mr. Benedict," Kate said. "Sticky's going down to the Blab right now to make a serum he needs—"

"We saw George on the stairs!" Tai interjected.

Kate gave him another stern look, and he clapped his hands over his mouth. "Anyway, we're bringing that serum to Mr. Benedict, and we're going to stop the Ten Men from breaking out Mr. Curtain."

Tai whispered, "Wow!" behind his hands.

"But to do that we have to go out of town first. We'll explain that part later. Right now, you can change into the clothes you were wearing yesterday—I've already taken them from the fumigator and washed and dried them. And ironed them. And replaced your broken shoelaces."

Tai's eyes grew enormous. He raised his hand.

"I was up early," Kate said, and he lowered his hand.

Reynie turned to Constance. "Will you please help him pack a bag? You're the only one with old clothes here that are small enough to fit him."

Constance gave a grudging nod and climbed out of the chair. Despite her unhappy look of reluctance, she was actually moving quickly. It was only by a constant force of will that she was managing her anxieties about Mr. Benedict. No matter what required doing right now, Constance would not be a source of delay. Not this time.

"Let's go, Tai," she snapped as she headed for the door.

Tai looked at Kate, who signaled that he could get up.

He leaped to his feet. "That was terrible!" he exclaimed. He drew the back of a hand across his forehead as if in relief. "Can I bring your bucket on our trip?"

"Are you kidding? You *have* to bring the bucket," Kate replied. "What if you misbehave again?"

∵∴

Ten minutes later, Reynie stood in the dining room once more. The lights were off, but morning sunlight streamed pleasantly through the windows. He was wearing his backpack, ready to go. The room was very quiet, very still. He wondered how many times he had seen it like this. Not many. For it was not just empty. There are empty rooms, and then there are rooms that feel crowded, corner to corner, with absence.

Not long ago, in this very room, Reynie and Mr. Benedict had talked about the exact thing Reynie was feeling now. It was after lunch, the dishes had been cleared away, and the others had all excused themselves. Mr. Benedict had decided to enjoy an extra cup of tea before returning to his study and, no doubt having sensed the hesitation in Reynie's goodbye, invited him to sit and have an extra cup himself.

"I know I've spoken to you often about my artist friend Violet," said Mr. Benedict, passing Reynie the honey. "And I know you're familiar with her work. You've told me you admire her paintings in the sitting room, of course, but if I recall correctly, you also spent some time with the catalog of her work that I keep in my study."

Reynie was stirring honey into his tea. He smiled. "If you've ever failed to recall something correctly, Mr. Benedict,

I certainly can't recall the occasion. Yes, that was just before we built the platform. I remember hearing Constance yelling about the leak in the ceiling—how the plaster was peeling, how annoyed she was feeling—just as I finished looking through the catalog."

Mr. Benedict tapped his nose. "I recall that we intended to discuss Violet's work further, yet we were understandably sidetracked and never returned to the subject."

"That's true," Reynie said, sipping his tea. This was not news to him. There were many subjects that they had agreed to discuss at some point, and the list was always growing. They both kept mental track of these bookmarked conversations and often returned to topics months after they'd first been mentioned. "I admired everything I saw in the catalog."

"So you said at the time, and I was pleased to hear it. Some of her work does not appear in that catalog, however, and I thought now might be an appropriate time to mention it." Mr. Benedict set down his teacup and laced his fingers together. "When Violet was a child, she lost her brother, and her early artwork reflected her grief in a striking way. She rendered familiar scenes in which one would typically expect to see people, yet the people themselves were missing."

"I imagine that made for unsettling effects," Reynie observed.

"Indeed," said Mr. Benedict. "And appropriate. Nothing is more unsettling than losing those we've loved. Yet I would propose for your consideration, Reynie, that there is something powerful, even important, in missing them. Missing our loved ones is in itself a connection with them, is it not? Painful, perhaps, but special."

Reynie nodded, a little embarrassed. He assumed Mr. Benedict was hinting at Reynie's own worries about missing his friends and family—indeed, everyone in Mr. Benedict's circle, not least Mr. Benedict himself—if he went away to a university. Reynie had talked about it with Miss Perumal, but only a bit. More than once he'd come close to knocking on Mr. Benedict's study door, only to change his mind and creep away. Now it occurred to him that Mr. Benedict had been aware of those almost-knocks. In fact, Mr. Benedict's decision to "have an extra cup of tea" had likely been meant to make it easier for Reynie to approach him. No need for knocking. Mr. Benedict had removed the door.

"When the time comes for you to go away, Reynie," Mr. Benedict said after a pause, "whether that be soon or far down the road, and whether it be for a temporary sojourn elsewhere or a more permanent relocation..." Mr. Benedict's voice faltered slightly. He cleared his throat, and with a small shock Reynie realized that Mr. Benedict's bright green eyes had tears in them. "When that time comes, my friend, I shall miss you dearly. Just as I miss Rhonda; just as I shall miss all the others whose cherished faces I'm so accustomed to seeing around this table, yet who may find it best, at some point, to leave the table for good."

Mr. Benedict took a handkerchief from his pocket and blew his large, lumpy nose. "But special people tend to go and do special things," he continued, "and one must accept it as best one can. Whenever I miss old friends, I remind myself that this very act makes them a part of my life. We may be separated by time and distance, and very often by the lack of hours to write each other proper letters, but we remain friends, and I remain grateful. Violet, for instance, I haven't seen in years, but I think of her every day, and I take pleasure in knowing she's in the world."

Something occurred to Reynie. He was surprised that he had never thought of it before. "The violet you keep on your desk..."

Mr. Benedict tapped his nose and smiled.

Reynie thought of Kate's bucket and spyglass in his chest. He also had a pair of Sticky's old spectacles on his dresser, and he knew that Sticky had given Kate a different pair. (She and Reynie had preferred different ones, so it had worked out neatly.) What would they remember *him* by? he wondered. He needed to think about something to give them. Constance, too, of course. Nothing sprang to mind, though, and for some reason Reynie found this troubling. Was it really because he couldn't think of a specific memento? No, he decided, it was that he had never thought of these items as mementos before. Thinking of them in that way made everything all too real.

Reynie realized that he had been staring into his teacup. Mr. Benedict was sipping his own tea, politely giving Reynie time with his thoughts. When their eyes met again, Mr. Benedict's expression had shifted slightly. There was a reluctance in it that made Reynie uneasy. What was he about to say?

"I've shared these perspectives of mine," Mr. Benedict began, "simply in the hope that you may find some of them useful in the days ahead. Perhaps you will, perhaps you won't. My own perspectives are admittedly sometimes strange. But there is one related matter, a bit closer to home, that I would urge you to address."

Suddenly Reynie understood. Having anticipated Reynie's embarrassment, Mr. Benedict had been trying to help Reynie by talking about *himself.* But now he was going to offer direct advice, without having been asked, and it made him uncomfortable to do so.

Mr. Benedict cleared his throat again. "In short, Reynie, if you find yourself missing someone long before you have even decided to part, you should consider the possibility that you are suffering unnecessarily. Sometimes when you've lost something, it won't come back on its own. Sometimes you must attempt to retrieve it. That can be a frightening endeavor, for of course there is always the prospect of failure."

Reynie's throat felt tight, and he was having to make an effort not to avert his eyes. He was glad that he did; otherwise he would have missed the sudden twinkle in Mr. Benedict's own eyes. He would have missed the wink.

"Of course," Mr. Benedict had said, rising, "there's also the prospect of success, and you have rather a good record of succeeding, have you not?"

◡:◞

Standing alone in the dining room, Reynie found that his eyes had naturally drifted to the chairs in which he and Mr. Benedict had sat that day. He'd been imagining the scene. There had been so *many* scenes in this room, he thought, from the mundane to the frightening to the wonderful.

Through those currently sunlit windows he had looked out upon windy days and snowy days, sunshine and storms. They all had.

Reynie heard Sticky's familiar footstep in the doorway. Reynie started to turn, but something checked him, and he remained as he was, thumbs hooked in the straps of his backpack, regarding the empty room. After a moment he heard Sticky walking quietly up beside him. He hadn't needed to turn. Sticky knew that Reynie knew he was there. And he knew that if Reynie had wanted to be left alone, he would have done something different. They had been friends a long time. Still, Reynie found that he wished he had turned, had gestured for Sticky to join him.

"It *is* a really interesting room," Sticky murmured. He adjusted a strap on his own backpack. "I can see why you're so fascinated."

Reynie smiled and glanced over at him. "We've always come back to this table. Every time we've gone and done something dangerous together, we've come back here and sat around this table."

"And talked about everything that happened," Sticky said, nodding. "And enjoyed feeling safe."

They stood in silence for a time, taking in the room together.

"Let's make sure we do that again," Reynie said.

The cameras placed by the Scaredy Katz meant that leaving Mr. Benedict's house by the front or back door was out of the question. Thus, in accordance with their plan, Sticky and

Reynie found Kate standing near the third-floor platform, saying goodbye to Madge. The beautiful falcon was perched on Kate's leather-glove-protected arm, and Kate was stroking her feathers. Kate was wearing her parachute, the better to carry it while also toting the large duffel bag she had packed, which rested on the floor nearby.

Hiding behind Kate was Tai Li, holding the red bucket up in front of his face like a shield.

"It's nonsense," Kate was saying to him. "You can't listen to what Constance says."

"But Constance can read her mind!" Tai squeaked.

Kate turned to Sticky and Reynie with a look of exasperation. "Constance is in a fine mood. She told Tai that Madge wants to eat his toes."

"Maybe she does!" Tai cried. He seemed genuinely nervous but also appeared to be enjoying the dramatic possibilities of being hunted by a falcon.

"Don't be silly," Reynie said. "Madge doesn't want to hurt you." Even as he said this, however, he shared a private look with Sticky. Neither of them had ever been entirely certain that Madge didn't want to hurt *them*.

"Why would Constance say something like that?" Sticky asked.

"Because I didn't want to wear my shoes, and she said I had to, and I said I didn't want to, and she said I didn't get to choose—" Tai took a breath.

"You do have to wear your shoes," Sticky said simply, and Tai nodded. Maintaining his balance with some difficulty, he lifted one foot to show that he had already complied.

Constance came stalking down the hallway with her

backpack on. Reynie started to ask where Tai's bag was, then thought better of it. Probably she had packed his things in the backpack with hers. And if she hadn't? One glance at her face suggested that the wise course was to let the matter drop.

Kate tossed a treat down the long hallway and sent Madge after it. Meanwhile, Captain Plugg had come up to say goodbye. She hugged them each in turn (despite the sullen look on Constance's face, she squeezed the beloved guard rather fiercely); implored them to be as careful as they possibly could; then took the protective glove from Kate, for she had promised to care for Madge until Kate's return.

"Now, don't you worry," Captain Plugg said, adjusting the strings of the glove to account for her thick forearms. "You know I've taken good care of that sweetheart in the past, and you can be sure I'll do it again. We'll have a lovely time together, won't we, Your Majesty?" This last she called down the hallway, then blew Kate's whistle to summon the falcon to her arm.

"Oh, Madge, we're all sorry you can't come with us," Kate said as Sticky and Reynie made polite noises of agreement. "But that nasty old McCracken remembers you too well. You stay here and be a good girl, okay? You mind Captain Plugg!"

With that, Kate snatched up her duffel bag and joined the others on the platform. They all waved at Captain Plugg and Madge (all except Constance, who was glowering at her shoes), and Kate said, "Let's do this the proper way, shall we?"

"Let's not," Constance muttered.

"Doesn't someone have to stomp on the floor?" Tai asked.

"Come on, Connie girl," Kate prodded. "When was the last time we did it together?"

Constance blew hair out of her eyes. "Fine," she said. She glanced down at Tai. She took his hand. "Hold on, you."

Constance stomped.

Reynie stomped.

Kate stomped.

Sticky stomped.

The trapdoor in the ceiling fell open, and up they went.

It had been a while since the Society had used what Kate liked to refer to as the Zipper. The first reason they had stopped using it was because Number Two (once she'd found out about it) had inspected it and deemed it too dangerous. After that happened, the Society had secretly made adjustments to address Number Two's safety concerns. The second reason they had stopped using the Zipper was because Number Two had found out again and inspected it again and had again declared that the Zipper was not safe enough. Unfortunately, their families had all agreed with Number Two. ("Take only necessary risks, Kate," Milligan had reminded her.) And so promises were solicited from the Society members not to use the Zipper again.

"Except in case of emergency," Reynie had made sure to say.

Number Two had narrowed her eyes. "Except in the case of a *genuine* emergency."

And to this they had all reluctantly agreed.

Now here they were, accompanied by a little boy firmly secured to Kate's belt by a tether, making use of carefully placed handholds and footholds to climb the roof's north-westernmost gable. Before long the rooftop patio was a distance below them, they were peering out over the tree-lined street, and all except Kate felt a nervous fluttering in their bellies. Directly across from them was the Washingtons' house, a cozy abode that Sticky had for some years now called his "home across the street" (for Mr. Benedict's house was also his home), whose rooftop lay well below their current position. Rising vertically from the peak of the Washingtons' roof was what once had been a decades-old television antenna — the sort that looked like a skinny metal tree stripped of its leaves and lower branches — but currently functioned as the Society's drop-off point.

After confirming that the street was clear and quiet, Kate opened her duffel bag and removed an oversized crossbow, followed by a grappling hook attached to a coiled length of cable. After securing the free end of the cable to a metal bracket in the roof, Kate moved the heavy coil to her opposite side, well out of Tai's reach. She loaded the grappling hook into the crossbow.

"Are you going to shoot that?" Tai whispered. He started to edge sideways for a better look, but three pairs of hands had a firm grip on him, and he found he couldn't move an inch. He held still.

Kate gave him a nod. She shifted her position, raised the crossbow to her shoulder, and took a slow, deep breath. As she exhaled, she squeezed the trigger. There was a sharp *twang!* The grappling hook vanished, the coil of cable beside Kate made a metallic sizzling sound (it seemed to melt away as if by magic before Tai's astonished eyes), and then Kate was yanking back on the crossbow as if she were wielding a fishing pole and had just landed a big one. Across the street, the grappling hook wound round and round one of the metal projections of the antenna, catching and holding with a distant *clink!* that set the now-taut cable quivering. Kate worked a small crank attached to the bracket in the rooftop, tightening the cable even further. Then she put away the crossbow, took out a rather complicated-looking harness-and-pulley contraption, and, adjusting the harness to accommodate the parachute on her back, buckled herself in.

"Is Kate going to zip across the street?" Tai breathed when he saw her attaching the pulley to the cable.

"Kate always goes first," Sticky whispered in reply. "Just to be on the safe side, in case something goes wrong."

"But what would she do if something went wrong?"

Sticky shrugged. "We have no idea. We just know we'd have to see it to believe it."

Kate connected the end of a spool of almost invisible fishing line to the harness and handed the spool to Sticky, who explained to Tai that this was for bringing the harness back. The spool was attached to a reel to make the retrieval easier. Tai studied the reel, then looked at Sticky to signal that he understood. When he looked back, Kate was gone.

Past the highest branches of the elm tree she zipped, over the tops of the smaller trees along the sidewalk, over the street, over the Washingtons' front yard, and at last to the drop-off point, where she came to a stop not with a loud bang or clang (the pulley was equipped with special padding) but with more of a satisfying *thunk*. For a moment Kate dangled from the antenna (which had been reinforced with much stronger metal and heavy bolts to support the Zipper's true function), and they could all see her grinning even from across the street. Then she lowered herself onto the rooftop, put down her duffel bag, and removed the harness.

As Sticky reeled the harness back, he explained to Tai that Kate would now inspect and doubly secure the grappling-hook end of the cable. "So it really is very safe," he whispered. "There's no need for you to worry."

"I'm not worried!" Tai whispered. "Can I go next?"

Of course he could go next, Sticky said, and so Tai did, covering his mouth the entire way to keep himself from exclaiming in delight. Kate caught him at the other end, removed him from the harness, and tethered him to her belt again. Constance went next, then Reynie, and finally Sticky. They had always crossed the street in this exact order because Kate needed to go first, Constance hated waiting, and Sticky wanted as much time as possible to work up his nerve. Today, however, Sticky went last simply out of tradition.

"You did it!" Tai whispered when Sticky arrived. (He had whispered the same thing to Constance and Reynie.) "Let's all stick our tongues out at the camera on the fence! Because we tricked it!"

And so, from the peak of Sticky's home across the street, the five of them stuck their tongues out at the camera, which could not see them.

They had completed their first daring maneuver of the day.

There were many more — and much more dangerous ones — to come.

PLAZAS, PLAYGROUNDS, AND PARTS UNKNOWN

$\mathbf{F}$rom the roof of the Washingtons' back porch, Kate leaped into a tree and then to the ground, and presently she returned with a ladder for the others. Soon they were all bustling into the cellar, where Kate unlocked the heavy steel door that opened onto the secret passage to the Monk Building.

Everyone looked expectantly at Tai.

He gasped.

The improvement of lighting and the reduction of vermin in the secret passage had been one of the Society's many projects, and so it was into a rather pleasantly lit and only moderately dank and creepy tunnel that they now hurried. Kate removed her parachute and handed it to Reynie to carry; Tai handed Kate's bucket to Sticky (having first tried to hand it to Constance, who only looked at him); and then Kate took off with Tai riding piggyback, followed at a distance by the others, who knew better than to try to keep up.

"This is the tunnel!" Tai said into Kate's ear. "The one you took from the Monk Building to Mr. Benedict's house on the day you met!"

"Right you are," Kate said. "We'd just gotten through one batch of Mr. Benedict's tests and were on our way to more. It's so strange to think that we had no idea where we were heading then. Nowadays this tunnel is where we tend to go when we want some peace and quiet. Especially on rainy days. With so many people around, it never gets completely quiet indoors."

"You could use the Husher if you wanted things to be quiet."

"Well, it uses a lot of energy. Even with special batteries, it doesn't last long enough for you to really clear your head. No, the best thing is usually just to come here—see how quiet it is? The only trouble is that sometimes we all want to use it. We had to make a sign-up sheet. Isn't that funny? Everybody taking turns just to get into a boring old empty tunnel?"

"It isn't boring! It's a secret!"

"Excellent point. If you put it that way, what could be better?" Kate hitched Tai up a little higher.

"You don't come here together, though?" Tai asked a bit sadly.

"We used to every now and then, of course," Kate said. "But usually this is a spot for solitude. A place to escape to when everyone seems to be stepping on your feet and getting on your nerves. You want to know my secret name for it?"

"Oh, yes!" Tai whispered.

"Bill," Kate said.

Tai giggled. "Bill?"

"Why not? Bill is a good, solid name, Tai."

They had arrived now at the bottom of the stairs leading up to Mr. Benedict's office on the seventh floor of the Monk Building. Kate glanced back to ensure that her straggling friends were fine (and so they were, though she could hear their panting even from a distance), and she headed up the winding stairs with Tai on her back. By the time the others caught up, she and Tai had already reached the office's secret anteroom, looked through hidden peepholes to ensure that the office was empty, and selected from a rack some clothing that would form Kate's disguise.

Constance, Reynie, and Sticky arrived gasping and perspiring. As they stood with hands on hips, regaining their breath, Kate put on her parachute again. Over it she slipped a pair of coveralls that normally fit the circus-strongman physique of Moocho Brazos. "I'll have to be a hulking figure with a hunched back," she told her friends. "Since it won't do to be seen in public with a parachute."

"We discussed it!" Tai declared proudly. "Also, we have to hide Kate's bucket in her duffel bag because it's famous."

"I don't recall using that exact word," said Kate, pulling her hair up into a tight bun, over which she placed a greasy mechanic's cap.

"You said it's 'well known,'" Tai amended.

"And that much, I think, is safe to say," said Kate with a satisfied nod.

Soon they were all ready, the anteroom vacated, and the plain interior of office 7-B filled with an unlikely assemblage: a large, stooped mechanic; an average-looking young man in the blue uniform of a local high school; a handsome young dockworker with stylish glasses; an angry-looking kitchen employee with a flour-dusted apron and an ugly hairnet; and a delighted-looking little boy (undisguised). The backpacks made the disguises less than perfect, but as long as they weren't seen together as a group, they should attract little special attention.

Reynie looked at Constance. "Based on my information, we probably have a clear route to the parking deck, but what's your feeling about this building?"

"Nothing weird on this floor," Constance said at once. "Let me take a look outside." After listening at the door a moment, she slipped out of the office and down to the end of the hallway. A window there afforded a good view of the city streets around the building. She looked out for several seconds, then returned and said, "I think you're right."

They used the building's public stairwell, which was always empty, and descended together, stopping every so often for Constance to sniff the air with her mental bloodhound's nose. No, the building was safe, she was sure of it now, and at last they were gathered on the first floor. Everyone donned sunglasses. The mechanic went out first, holding hands with the little boy and carrying a duffel bag. Two minutes later, the kitchen worker and dockworker left together. And finally the high school student walked out of the doors of the Monk Building onto its sunlit front plaza.

Never particularly graceful, Reynie walked as casually as he could, his mind in a state of agitated confusion. The first time he'd crossed this plaza, years ago, he was walking into a new life. He could not help but wonder if he was doing the same thing yet again, this time walking in the opposite direction. His future had seemed so mysterious to him then. Now, after so much had changed, he found himself walking across the exact same plaza feeling almost exactly the same way. It seemed so strange. How many more plazas, Reynie wondered, would he cross in his life?

Meanwhile the city streets appeared no different than usual. Plenty of pedestrians, plenty of traffic, plenty of noise. Plenty of businessmen in nice suits, too, and at first Reynie walked slowly, his wary eyes darting this way and that. Then he spied, some blocks ahead of him, the kitchen worker and the dockworker disappearing around a corner. If any of the Baker's Dozen were around, Constance would know it. Reynie picked up his pace.

On the dimly lit underground level of a parking deck, a dilapidated old station wagon occupied one of the rental spaces. Only its tires looked to be in good condition; otherwise it gave the impression of having been abandoned, with dents, scrapes, rusty patches, two missing hubcaps, and an empty bird's nest in the radiator grille. As Reynie hastened to join the others already inside the car, Kate cranked the engine, which came to life with the roar of a hundred lions.

"Hop in!" she called brightly. Reynie hurriedly stowed his backpack in the rear of the car, with Kate's parachute and the other packs. The front passenger seat had been left unoccupied for him. He had to yank a few times on the door to get it to open, but finally he succeeded and climbed in. Sticky and Constance were seated in the back, flanking Tai Li, who was making a cheerful fuss about his booster seat.

"I've never been in a booster seat *or* a station wagon!" Tai informed Reynie.

"Today's your lucky day!" Kate laughed, and she threw the engine into reverse.

"Um, Kate," Reynie cautioned, hurriedly buckling his seat belt, "we need to avoid drawing attention to ourselves, remember?"

Kate's hand tapped the gearshift, a look of disappointment settling onto her face. "Right," she murmured. "Right, right, right." She backed out of the parking space — smoothly and expertly, but without the least bit of panache. She sighed and drove them up onto the street.

Kate, Reynie, and Sticky had already discussed their route out of Stonetown. Every train station, airport, and tollbooth in the city was compromised. The Ten Men had their old network of local spies up and running — sharp-eyed informants who, out of fear or greed or both, would immediately contact McCracken with any news of the information he sought. In this case, believing most of the Society to have fled the city, McCracken had positioned those spies at all the usual points of entry. If Mr. Benedict's young friends came back to help him, McCracken hoped to know it.

"But they aren't on the lookout for people *leaving* the city," Sticky was explaining now to Tai, "so as long as we're careful, we're not likely to be spotted."

"Oh, good!" Tai said. He was craning his neck left and right, curious to see out of as many of the station wagon windows as possible. "But how will we give Mr. Benedict what he needs if we're going away?"

"We're coming back soon," Sticky said. "First we just need to get a little help."

Constance removed her hairnet and threw it onto the floorboard with a look of disgust. She pulled her hair over her eyes. Outside the station wagon, the downtown streets gave way to those of quieter neighborhoods. Kate was taking a roundabout path to an old, lesser-used highway out of town.

Perhaps because everyone had been silent for several minutes, when another question occurred to Tai, he didn't blurt it out but rather raised his hand politely. Sticky smiled and asked him what his question was.

Tai lowered his hand. "Why were we worried about McCracken trying to get S.Q.? Didn't he work for Mr. Curtain, just like the others?"

Sticky hesitated. He saw Kate's eyes studying him in the rearview mirror. The fact was, he hadn't considered how to answer this complicated question—not to a five-year-old, not under the circumstances— and he felt a horror of messing something up. He cleared his throat. "Someone else want to take this one?"

"Why don't you, Reynie?" Kate suggested. "I'm so busy driving and everything."

Reynie shifted in his seat so that Tai could see his face. "You're right," he said. "S.Q. and the Ten Men used to be on the same team, kind of. But here's the situation, Tai. Mr. Curtain's letter said that S.Q. was getting something for him — that serum we mentioned. Well, if you were a bad guy like McCracken, and you weren't crazy about the idea of trying to break into a place that's supposed to be impossible to break into, and you realized that this serum, if you got your hands on it, might make you so powerful that you would never need Mr. Curtain's help for anything again… well, you might prefer to get it from S.Q. before he could bring it to Mr. Curtain. That way you wouldn't have to try to do the big break-in — you wouldn't have to take any risk at all. Does that make sense?"

Tai's eyes widened. "You mean McCracken was going to *portray* Mr. Curtain?"

"Do you mean *betray*? Then, yes."

"But that's terrible!"

"You can say that again," Kate put in. "They don't call them the Ten Men because they have ten ways of *helping* people, you know. *Hurting* people is what they do best. But S.Q. got away, thanks to Milligan. So now if McCracken wants to get more powerful, he either has to do what Mr. Curtain told him to do in the letter, which is risky for him, *or*—"

"*Or* he could try to catch *us*!" Tai said. "Because Sticky made the serum he wants!"

Three hands tapped three noses. Constance, for her part, said nothing. Behind her screen of scarlet hair, she might have been sleeping for all anyone could tell. (No one believed she was, however.)

"McCracken and his men might still try to break Mr. Curtain out," Reynie said, "even if he did catch us and get the serum. Mr. Curtain gave them a lot of reasons to try.

But, you know, we'd rather not get caught. I assume you feel the same way, Tai?"

"Oh, yes, I do!"

"Perfect. We'll make sure not to get caught, then."

Eventually the station wagon made its way through the outskirts of Stonetown, crossed an out-of-the-way old bridge, and finally turned onto a rural highway that passed through pleasant rolling farmland. The road was wide open, with excellent visibility, and would seem to invite—indeed, even beg for—driving at excessive speeds. And yet the station wagon proceeded at a sensible pace, observing the speed limit with remarkable precision.

Reynie looked over at Kate. "How are you holding up, champ?"

"Great," Kate replied, flashing him a strained smile. "This is great. Beautiful day for a drive."

Reynie noted her clenched jaw, the white-knuckled grip she had on the steering wheel. No one in the world suffered so much as Kate Wetherall from not moving as fast as humanly possible whenever the occasion allowed. Driving at this moderate speed was requiring a heroic effort on her part.

In the back seat, Sticky had taken out a couple of newspapers and was flipping through them, page after page. He had to keep apologizing to Tai for bumping him with his elbow, and Tai kept giggling and saying, "That's okay, just don't do it again!" Then giggling harder every time Sticky "accidentally" did it again.

"Here's an interesting news item," Sticky announced. "Tai, did Constance tell you about the Salamander?"

"She didn't have to," Tai said. "I already know what a salamander is. It's an insect!"

"Well, no. If you're thinking of the *animal*, a salamander is actually a lizard-like amphibian."

"Okay!" Tai said agreeably. "Now I know that!"

"Right. Good. But the Salamander I was referring to is an armored amphibious vehicle—sort of a big metal boat with tank treads, so that it can go on both water and land. I know," Sticky said, noting Tai's delighted expression, "it's fun to think about. Except this particular one belonged to Mr. Curtain and the Ten Men. It wasn't so great when *they* had it."

Tai frowned and shook his head.

"What's the news item, George?" Reynie called from the front seat. "I mean, I have a feeling."

"Me too," said Kate.

"It's pretty obvious," Constance said from behind her hair. Those were the first words she'd spoken in the car.

Sticky informed Tai that after Mr. Curtain and the Ten Men had been captured, the government had decided to install the Salamander in the playground area of Stonetown's largest park. Every day children climbed into it, pretended to drive it, hid beneath it during games of hide-and-seek, and attacked it with sticks.

"That sounds so fun!" Tai cried.

"Unfortunately," Sticky said, pointing at the newspaper article, "according to this, the Salamander was stolen from the playground yesterday by a couple of men in business suits. No one was hurt in the process, although a number of children were seen to be crying."

"Ten Men! They're so mean!"

There was a general murmur of agreement in the car.

"They must have had an extra set of keys and some spare parts in that vault Mr. Curtain mentioned," Kate mused.

"The Ten Men probably stole the Salamander," Sticky explained to Tai, "in order to get to the island if they try to break Mr. Curtain out. The shoals in the bay are treacherous, and the currents are tricky, but with the Salamander they could manage the crossing fairly easily."

"Roger that," Tai said. He scratched his head. "What island do you mean?"

Sticky raised his eyebrows. "Wait...you don't know?"

Tai shrugged. "How should I know?"

"Well, because—I guess I was thinking, since Constance told you about when we went to the Institute..."

"I didn't tell him about the prison part," Constance said with an exasperated sigh. "Why would I tell him that part, George?"

"Which part?" asked Tai, squirming in his seat. "Which part!"

"Should I not have mentioned...?" Sticky wondered aloud.

"Probably too late now," Kate said.

Tai began chanting, "Which part? Which part? Which part?"

"The part about where Mr. Curtain is imprisoned now," Reynie called back to him. "Where he and Mr. Benedict are. The place we're going to have to go to."

"Go *back* to," Constance muttered.

Tai gasped, for now he understood.

The Society was returning to Nomansan Island.

WHERE ONE
DRAWS
THE LINE

Much had happened in the years since the members of the Society made their fateful trip to Nomansan Island, where they had enrolled as students at the Learning Institute for the Very Enlightened (LIVE, for short) and, as secret agents for Mr. Benedict, foiled Mr. Curtain's plot to "improve" the world with the help of his horrifying mind-control invention, the Whisperer. In the aftermath of that desperate adventure, the island had been evacuated. Bewildered students were reunited with their families, and those *without* families—there were many of these—were found good homes. Mr. Benedict, of course, had devoted himself to helping the brainswept Helpers, while several of Mr. Curtain's former employees—those Executives and Recruiters who hadn't managed to escape with him—faced varying degrees of justice and therapy.

Nomansan, for its part, became the subject of governmental squabbles. The rocky, hilly, unapproachable island in Stonetown Harbor had belonged to Mr. Curtain, as had the massive stone buildings of the Institute. Thanks to Mr. Benedict and his associates, the Institute's tidal turbines—yet another of Curtain's inventions—had eventually been repurposed to provide much of Stonetown with inexpensive electricity. But for a long time the island had remained abandoned, for no one with any government authority could agree on what to do with it.

That is, until Mr. Benedict had begun to apply his considerable powers of persuasion. For many reasons, he argued, his genius brother should not be held in the Citadel along with the Ten Men. The Citadel in Brig City was the most secure facility in the region, and all extremely dangerous criminals were sentenced to incarceration there. Although a breakout had been deemed impossible by the authorities, Mr. Benedict nonetheless convinced them that to keep both the brains and the brawn of Mr. Curtain's wicked syndicate in the same location—to afford any chance of collaboration and plotting—would be to court disaster.

As it so happened, Mr. Benedict had a perfect solution to offer. Surrounded by water and treacherous shoals, connected to the mainland only by a single narrow bridge, Nomansan Island was already notoriously inaccessible. With certain renovations and additional layers of security—all designed and overseen by Mr. Benedict himself—the Institute could become the most high-security of high-security facilities, and at very little cost. The solution was accepted; the arrangements were made; the work was begun. The Institute was reborn as the Key Enclosure for Enemies of the Public—the KEEP, for short—and although one day it would house a significant number of criminals, its first inmate (and at present its *only* inmate) was Mr. Ledroptha Curtain.

So it was that Mr. Curtain had become, quite literally, a prisoner in a prison of his own making.

Renovations of the facility were ongoing, but Mr. Curtain's security suite had been completed right away, for Mr. Benedict had insisted that his brother be removed from the vicinity of the Ten Men as soon as possible. Thus for over a year now, Mr. Benedict's weekly routine had included many hours overseeing and directing the modifications being implemented at the KEEP—and, during breaks and at the end of his workdays there, visiting his surly twin, often in the agreeable company of S.Q. Pedalian.

"So Mr. Benedict was right!" Tai declared when all this had been explained. "If Mr. Curtain had still been at the Citadel when the Ten Men escaped, they could have taken him with them right then!"

"Fortunately, Mr. Benedict has a gift for predicting problems," Sticky said. "He may not have been able to prevent all of this mess we're in, but it certainly could have been worse."

Tai frowned. "But if the KEEP is so insuccess-able—"

"Inaccessible."

"—inaccessible," Tai continued, "then how are we going

to give Mr. Benedict the serum he needs? Is he just going to let us in?"

"As for that," said Reynie from the front, "Mr. Benedict's security contracts prevented him from telling us much about the facility, but we know he wouldn't be allowed to just wander around the place right now, not when the Baker's Dozen are threatening an assault. And Mr. Curtain's letter confirms that. To remain behind with Mr. Curtain, Mr. Benedict had to be locked into the security suite with his brother; there's a small protected visitors area with a sofa and a little pantry for Mr. Benedict, and a bathroom and such. Mr. Benedict can't get out of there unless someone *lets* him out. So, no, he can't just open the front door for us. Besides, McCracken will have men posted on the lookout. If we showed up at the bridge gate, we'd be snatched away before we could even announce ourselves."

"Then, how *are* we — ?"

"And that's enough questions for right now, Tai!" Kate said cheerfully. "It's better you don't know just yet."

"Well," said Tai with a shrug, "Constance knows, but she's trying to keep it from me."

"I'm trying not to think about it at *all*," Constance growled from behind her hair. "For a hundred reasons, but not least because I'm trying to keep *her* from getting a whiff of it. So stop trying to figure it out, Tai."

"I'm not *trying*. It's like your thoughts are pushing mine down. It makes me notice!"

"How about we give you something else to think about?" Reynie suggested.

Tai brightened. "Okay! Will you tell me stories about your adventures?"

Thus began a long stretch of storytelling, with Reynie, Kate, and Sticky taking turns, freely interrupting each other whenever the occasion suited. They spoke of their travels across the ocean, of their many narrow escapes, of all the clues, puzzles, and riddles they'd solved together. They spoke of their encounters with the Ten Men (downplaying the more frightening aspects and emphasizing their successes). And they spoke of the many projects they'd worked on together in less dangerous times — with special attention paid to the comical mishaps.

"I thought we'd *never* get the orangutan out of the kitchen!" Reynie was saying, when Tai, who had been giggling nonstop, abruptly lowered his head and fell asleep.

"That's my cue," said Constance, who had been silent for the last hour. She leaned her head against the door. "Wake me up when he wakes up. Feel free to keep enjoying story time," she muttered, and in a moment was fast asleep herself.

Kate, Sticky, and Reynie looked around at one another, all with the same wistful expressions. It had been great fun reminiscing about their times together, and they would have gone on quite a while longer if Tai had stayed awake. But now no one wished to wake him, and in silence they returned to their individual thoughts as the station wagon rolled on.

They drove past a number of small towns, as well as a few large towns that *used* to be small. In between the towns was endless farm country, field after field of young crops that would grow and grow, eventually be harvested, and finally be replaced with different crops the following season.

Reynie, without meaning to, kept thinking the same things. *A town is still a town even if it's a bigger town. A field is still a field even if the crop is different. Friends are still friends even if their circumstances change.* All of those things seemed true, yet at the same time all seemed mysterious. *No matter how much you know,* he thought, *there's always more that you don't.*

"We're almost there," Kate said. She pointed to a sign ahead, unreadable to Reynie until they had drawn a good deal closer: WELCOME TO PEBBLETON.

In the back seat, Tai had awakened and nudged Constance in time for her to read the sign.

"Where is this?" he whispered.

"My dad grew up here," Constance murmured. She yawned and rubbed her eyes. "Well, he moved here when he was around my age."

The day had turned breezy, and on either side of the road young green cornstalks shuddered and swayed. Cloud shadows raced across the fields. Kate drove slowly into the quiet town, turned right at the old train station, and drove slowly out of town again. They went down a winding country road, rounded some wooded hills, and at last came to a handsome old farmhouse. A few vehicles were parked in front of the house, but it was the vehicle behind the house, the one sitting in a cornfield (several rows of which appeared to have been plowed under to accommodate its presence there), that drew everyone's attention. For it isn't every day that one sees an airplane in a cornfield, even a modest single-engine airplane like this one. Even rarer, perhaps, is to know that one will soon be boarding that plane and flying off on a dangerous mission.

"Why here?" Constance asked as Kate parked the station wagon. "Why not an airport?"

"Too much communication between airports," Reynie said. "Too many records of the flights coming and going. Rhonda suggested that this would be the best place."

Tai squeaked. "Rhonda Kazembe's here?"

"And Number Two," said Constance, peering with narrowed eyes at the farmhouse.

Sure enough, just then the front door opened wide and out strode Rhonda and Number Two. They were a sight for sore eyes, and what a sight they were: The slim, tall figure of Number Two, with her yellowish complexion, yellow flight suit, and rusty-red hair, presented a striking contrast with Rhonda's coal-black skin, and her long, lustrous braids, and—to everyone's surprise—her bright blue blouse looking as if she'd hidden a cantaloupe beneath it. She laughed and nodded as they all swarmed out of the car and rushed upon her, full of exclamations.

"It's true, it's true," Rhonda said, hugging everyone in turn. "There's another little scientist on the way. I told you I was going to start a family, didn't I? Why are you so surprised?"

It was a wonderful discovery on a very trying day, and for a brief spell everyone felt almost as if this were simply a happy reunion and nothing more. Even Number Two, usually so brusque and nervous, kept glancing at Rhonda's belly, grinning, and kissing Rhonda on the cheek. She had quick hugs and kisses for everyone else, too, of course, except for Tai Li, to whom she cordially extended her hand.

"May I have a hug and a kiss?" Tai asked, looking sadly at her hand.

Number Two looked ready to cry at this. "Of course!"

she declared, pulling the little boy close and kissing him on the head.

"I was going to surprise you all with a visit next *week*, if you can believe it," Rhonda told them. "Talk about timing! This isn't exactly the way I was expecting to tell you that I was, well, expecting. Oh, I so wish the circumstances were different."

"But how is it that *you're* here?" Constance asked Number Two. "You were on the ship with everyone else."

"Oh, well, I thought you might need me, of course," Number Two said matter-of-factly. "And Milligan had radioed to let me know at which airport he'd landed the plane. So it was only a matter of Captain Noland arranging a rendezvous with a cargo ship, then having myself smuggled into Stonetown in a shipment of bananas (I blended in rather well, as it happened, although the big spiders were a nuisance) and, finally, proceeding in disguise to the airport, where I hot-wired Milligan's plane—having first engaged the noise-cancellation mechanism—and took off unnoticed in the darkness before dawn. I flew directly to Littleview to refuel, after which I simply sat and awaited word—which I received from Reynie within the hour—and now here I am!"

"That's all?" Constance said.

Number Two blushed. "Well, I didn't mean to make a big fuss about it."

"She's teasing you," Rhonda said, squeezing Number Two's arm.

The farmhouse door opened again, and this time a man emerged. He was advanced in years, probably Mr. Benedict's age or older, and walked a bit stiffly. It was easy to tell he was a farmer from his jeans and work shirt, tanned arms and face, and baseball cap that bore the words "I'M A FARMER." Most of his face was obscured by a thick gray beard, but he had kind and intelligent eyes, and a voice to match them.

"John Cole," he said, introducing himself with handshakes for everyone. "I'm an old friend of Nicholas's."

"Your hat says you're a farmer!" Tai declared.

"Does it now?" said Mr. Cole, whipping the cap off his head to look at it. "Why, so it does!" He scratched his head bemusedly—his hair was a short tangle of gray—then laughed a great, booming laugh and tugged the cap back on. "I actually almost never wear this, but this seemed the right occasion. It was a gift from Nicholas, years ago. His idea of a joke. Requires about three long stories and a leap of the imagination to find it as funny as he does. We'll save those for another time."

"Mr. Cole," said Reynie, "did you really have to destroy part of your crop to help us?"

"Now, listen to me, son," said Mr. Cole in a serious tone. "You needed an airstrip far away from prying eyes, and now you have one, and that's all you need to think about. I happen to know all about you, and it's an honor for me to stand here with young people such as yourselves. Just as it's going to be an honor to have you at my table—I'm sure you need some food in your bellies as soon as possible. As for Nicholas Benedict, well, what can I say? I would plow my *entire* crop under and sell the farm, too, if that's what it took to help him. And that would be an honor, too."

Mr. Cole was right—they were all hungry—and soon they were gathered at a long table, making a meal of fresh bread, cheese, and garden vegetables. The food was plentiful and delicious, but still Mr. Cole apologized for its simplicity. His wife was the superior cook, he informed them, but she had taken their old border collie to the veterinarian and wouldn't be back until evening.

"Time is a riddle, is it not?" the farmer mused, returning from the refrigerator with a jar of homemade raspberry jam. "The last time I saw Nicholas, that ancient dog of ours was a puppy. And you know what? I remember that the two of us felt old *then*! So, what does that make us now?" He laughed and shook his head. "And yet at the same time we both agreed that part of us still felt like the boys we once were—like we hadn't changed a bit.

"And do you know what Nicholas said? I remember it plainly. He said that he doesn't believe we become different people as we age. No, he says he believes that we become *more* people. We're still the kids we were, but we're also the people who've lived all the different ages since that time. A whole bunch of different people rolled up into one—that's how Nicholas sees it. And I can't say that I disagree. How else to explain that sometimes I want to run and jump the way I used to—but can't anymore—yet at the same time enjoy sitting with a cup of coffee and a newspaper in a way you couldn't have paid me to do as a boy? Well, it's a wonder."

Mr. Cole apologized then for rambling on, but everyone assured him no such apology was necessary. Indeed, his words could not have found more sympathetic ears. There were at least four people at his table who had only recently wondered at how very much like children they felt while also feeling very much *not* like children. Where did one draw the lines? Well, according to this new theory Mr. Cole had shared, perhaps one never had to draw lines at all. One simply became *more.*

"I'm five," announced Tai, who evidently was picking up on everyone's thoughts. "I think I'm still just one person," he said with a shrug. "But that's okay. Mr. Cole, what's your dog's name? And may I please have some jam?"

Mr. Cole smiled as the jar was passed down the table. "You may be amused to learn that my dog's name is Nicholas," he said. "That's another joke that only gets really funny if you know a few stories."

"I already think it's funny!" Tai declared, and he popped a spoonful of raspberry jam directly into his mouth.

At last the time had come to do a few walk-throughs, as Kate called them, and everyone headed out into the cornfield. They wouldn't be leaving until just before dark, which, according to Kate, gave them more than enough time to practice.

"Practice what?" Tai wanted to know.

Kate hesitated, but Constance rolled her eyes and said, "I've got it covered, Kate. She's not going to find out."

"Find out what?" Tai asked as Sticky gave him a lift to the plane's open doorway. "Hey," he called out, moving farther inside, "there are three more parachutes in here!"

"Well, how about that?" Kate said.

She started with Reynie, showing him how to climb out onto a metal step attached to the wing, where to place his hands on the wing strut, how to jump off and properly arch his back. The effort was minimal, but Reynie found himself sweating nonetheless. Sticky's experience was much the same. The idea of jumping backward not onto a bunch of flattened cornstalks but rather into empty space thousands of feet above the ground was, to say the least, disconcerting. But it was impossible to land a plane on Nomansan Island, and if they were to arrive there in secret, parachuting was their only option.

"Okay," Kate said to Reynie when Sticky had done his walk-through, "let's practice it again."

"What about me?" Constance asked with a frown—a frown that immediately transformed into a furious scowl as she realized the truth. "Wait, you're planning to go *without* me? No way! No, no, *no!*"

(Muttering softly about "seeing to the dishes," Mr. Cole discreetly withdrew to the farmhouse.)

"How can you possibly think you'll go without me?" Constance shouted. "How *can* you? You need me! You may not think you do, but you do!"

"Of course we could use you," Reynie said as calmly as he could. "Of course. But I promised Mr. Benedict to keep you safe, didn't I? And we're older than you are. We're responsible for you—"

"Why can't *I* be responsible for *you?*" Constance interrupted. "Who gets to say? Why do *you* get to say?"

"We're—we're *older*, Constance," Sticky tried. "A lot older, right? And the older you get, the more responsibility—"

"I was part of the team when I was *two!*" Constance shouted, crying now. "I helped save the world when I was *two!*"

"You did," Kate said soothingly. "Of course you did. But

we didn't have a choice then. The situation was different. This time—"

Now Tai was crying, too—wailing, actually—and clinging to Constance's arm.

Constance snarled, "This time you can do it without me? That's what you think?"

Reynie started to touch her shoulder, saw the look in her eyes, and withdrew his hand. "We just think that we should try," he said, speaking up to be heard over Tai's wailing. "Think about it: McCracken would love nothing better than to get his hands on you, Constance. The rest of us, sure, he'd be delighted to hurt us if it was convenient. But *you*? Who knows what lengths he would go to if he thought he could get at you?"

"He won't," Constance said, wiping at her eyes. She glared at Reynie. "I won't let him. Believe me."

"Believe her!" Tai sobbed.

Reynie grimaced. He gestured at Tai and said quietly, "But you have to keep him with you to keep him safe, right?"

"I can come, too!" Tai howled.

"He can come, too," Constance said, "and I will make sure to keep him safe. This is the way it has to be."

Rhonda and Number Two, who had been standing back, albeit with looks of great concern, started shaking their heads at the same time. Constance whirled on them.

"Don't even start!" she said. "I happen to *know* that there is a *much* better chance of saving Dad if I'm part of the mission, so here's how it's going to be: Either Tai and I come along—making promises to be extra-careful or whatever—or I will cling to the landing gear of this plane. If you try to pull me off, I will scream and bite and kick. If that doesn't work, I'll make you change your minds, even if it makes me sicker than I've ever been. Do you all understand? You are *not* going *without* me, and that is *final!*"

Everyone was quiet except for Tai, whose wails had subsided into loud sniffles. Constance was too angry to comfort him much, but she patted him a few times on the back and waited, looking around at everyone, meeting everyone's anxious eyes.

Kate sighed. "Well, come on, then, Connie girl. Let's do your first walk-through."

There was obviously no need for further discussion. Constance and Tai were going along.

As Kate went through the routine with Constance, Sticky drew Rhonda aside to ask her "a chemical question." The two stood apart from the rest of the group, talking with furrowed brows. Rhonda gave the occasional nod, and at length she clapped Sticky on the shoulder. He looked relieved and gratified.

"That means a lot coming from you," he was saying as they rejoined the group, to which Rhonda replied that if the shoes were on the other feet, she could say the same thing to him.

"Also," Rhonda said, "I must say I love your new spectacles. I don't want to embarrass you, but you look so stylish! You've really become quite handsome, haven't you?"

"Uh-oh, Rhonda, you *did* embarrass him!" Tai chirped. He had quickly recovered from the earlier upset and seemed thrilled that everyone was getting along again.

"Oh dear," said Rhonda. "My apologies…it's George now, right? My apologies, George. Now, Tai, why don't you come along and help me fetch the flight suits from my car? I have one for everybody—even you!"

"Yay!" said Tai. "But why would you have one for me if you didn't think I was going on the mission?"

"If there's one thing I learned from Mr. Benedict," Rhonda said, slipping her arm over his shoulders, "it's always to prepare for every possibility."

Indeed, Rhonda had arrived in such an astonishing state of preparation that she might have been planning for months rather than hours. The parachutes had been inspected and reinspected; the black flight suits were perfect fits for everyone; and the three walkie-talkies she gave them, in the event that they had to split up or they got separated, were sophisticated and completely secure.

"They automatically switch to different frequencies at the first hint of intrusion," Rhonda said, "so you don't have to worry about anyone listening in."

Constance rolled her eyes. "That's not exactly true for all of us, you know."

Rhonda went to Constance and wrapped her arms around her. "I do know that," she said softly. "And I know that you're a brave, brave girl." Constance stood glowering for a moment. Then she leaned into the hug.

By the time evening began to settle in, the Society had been through their routines multiple times. As Kate had explained it, some of them would be tandem jumping, which involved being buckled to another person and sharing the same parachute. Tai, naturally, would be buckled to Kate, and when Kate insisted that Constance also be buckled to someone, Constance insisted that it be Sticky.

"That way if he passes out or freezes up," Constance explained, "I can be there to pull the rip cord so he doesn't die."

"I'm *not* going to pass out or freeze *up*!" Sticky snapped indignantly. "I don't do that anymore, and you know it!"

"I hope not," Constance muttered, loudly enough for everyone to hear.

Reynie would be on his own, and the duffel bag full of supplies would get its own parachute, which Kate would arrange to deploy when she tossed it from the plane. Tai was particularly delighted about this for some reason and kept saying, "I'm the bag!" and then pretending to be the duffel bag by stretching out his arms, swaying back and forth, and saying nothing.

Just before they boarded the plane, Reynie took Constance aside. She came reluctantly, a resentful look on her face that she seemed determined not to lose. "I don't want to hear it," she said.

"Well, I'm going to say the words," Reynie said, "and you can choose to hear them or not."

Constance crossed her arms, averted her eyes, and waited.

"You're right that we have a better chance of succeeding with you along," Reynie said. "Every one of us believes that. And this was a scary thing that we were going to do without you, so please consider what that means."

"Why don't you tell me what it means?" Constance snipped. "I'm all out of considering."

"It just means that we care about you," Reynie said. He hesitated. He needed to be careful about what he revealed and didn't reveal to Constance. "I guess that's it," he said at length. "That's the only reason we were planning to go without you. For what it's worth."

"You think I didn't know that?" Constance said, giving him a cutting look. She shook her head and stalked away.

Reynie sighed. "It's all so easy," he muttered, and followed after her.

Number Two had already said goodbye to Rhonda and Mr. Cole and climbed into the cockpit of the plane. Now everyone else said their farewells, promising to be careful, promising they would all laugh together again on the other side of things—whatever and whenever that might be. One by one the Society members and Tai Li boarded the plane. Kate secured the door. They all waved. Rhonda, wiping tears from her eyes, raised one hand and held it aloft. Mr. Cole took off his cap and held it over his heart.

"Everyone ready back there?" Number Two called from the cockpit.

Everyone was.

"I'm engaging silent mode until we're clear of the area," Number Two said. "We can talk again at ten thousand feet." She flipped a switch, and the world went quiet.

Tai's mouth opened, but no sound came out.

In silence the plane's propeller began to turn, slowly at first, then faster and faster until it was a blurred circle. The wind from the propeller caused Rhonda's braids to fly about her face. She secured them with her hands—all in perfect silence. Mr. Cole's cap got away from him and sailed silently over the young corn. The plane began to move, turning silently around in the circle Mr. Cole had plowed for that purpose until it faced its corn-lined runway. They could feel a trembling in everything that grew stronger as Number Two accelerated and the plane bucked forward. They looked out the windows as the cornstalks moved silently past, faster and faster until they were a wave of green and gold. And just before the plane reached the end of the field, they felt themselves rising, up and up, over the silent farmhouse, over the silent hills, and up into the great silent sky.

RETURN TO NOMANSAN ISLAND

The Society, in its bubble of silence, was at six thousand feet and climbing. Tai kept poking Sticky and Kate and pointing out the window, then gesticulating to try to explain what had amazed him so much. His pantomimes were impossible to interpret, but it was easy to understand his wonder. He'd never been on a plane before, never seen the countryside from above, never seen its features grow smaller and smaller while, at the same time, the quilt-like pattern of farmland grew more and more apparent. Nor had he ever passed through a cloud, an experience that—gauging by his expression, his gestures, and his soundlessly moving mouth—made him positively giddy with delight.

Reynie.

Reynie took his eyes off Tai and looked at Constance, who was staring at him.

In case it matters, the entire Baker's Dozen is now hidden in the woods on the mainland across from the island. Exactly where Mr. Benedict and the others were hiding when we were at the Institute. They're watching the harbor, the roads, and the bridge gate. They're waiting for something.

Reynie nodded.

Is it us?

Reynie didn't actively reply, but of course Constance sensed the answer. *Please don't dig any deeper,* he thought. *You might jeopardize the mission.*

Constance looked peeved, but she nodded.

Not that it's a big deal, Reynie thought. *Thirteen of the most dangerous men in the world, plus a telepath. So what? It's a cakewalk, really.*

Constance smirked. *Whatever.* After a moment she thought, *I've tried to talk to her, you know. Tried to convince her she's on the wrong side. She doesn't respond. McCracken has warned her not to trust us. He's convinced her I'm so powerful that I can show her false things to make us seem like the good guys. He's convinced her that they were only trying to help Tai, that they've all been falsely accused. She should know better, but she's confused. She's afraid of him. But I think she's afraid of us, too.*

We'll try to help her if we can, Reynie thought. *When we get through this, we'll do everything we can.*

Constance nodded. *I've stopped hating her, anyway. That's a start.*

That's always a good start.

"—and you can see the lights coming on in all the buildings and the cars on the road—oh! And now we can hear again! Hooray!"

Tai's voice had returned, along with the roar of the plane, and now they heard Number Two calling back to them from the cockpit.

"We have about an hour until we go silent again," she said. "How is everyone?"

"We're great!" Tai shouted.

"Peachy," Number Two replied. She did not sound happy. Everyone knew that the thought of Mr. Benedict's being in danger was upsetting her, and the idea of sending the rest of them into harm's way was only making matters worse.

They would be flying over Nomansan Island low, quiet, and dark. Number Two had already studied the flight paths of all scheduled flights in the area, and she was monitoring the communications of Stonetown's air traffic controllers. There would be no accidental collisions in the sky—that much she could control. The rest would be up to them. Kate had shown Sticky and Reynie how to read their altimeters (a lesson that took all of two seconds), and they had agreed upon the altitude at which they should deploy their parachutes. Number Two was going to approach the island from the side opposite the mainland, and they would drop down on that side, hidden from the mainland by the island's hills. Based on the blueprints in Sticky's head, they would make their way to the

KEEP. If all went well, they would sneak inside without ever being spotted by McCracken and his crew.

If all went well.

"What about the guards?" Tai asked.

"It's all automated at the moment," Kate told him. "Just alarm systems and such. The only people on the whole island right now are Mr. Benedict and Mr. Curtain, locked into Mr. Curtain's security suite."

"That seems lonely," Tai said.

"Well," Kate said, "we'll be there soon."

They roared on through the night sky.

Tai had, of course, asked Sticky what they should expect when they arrived, but Sticky would say only that there was a specific line of approach, a specific place where they were supposed to enter the KEEP: a kind of back door. Nor was Sticky being especially cagey with the information. For this outer layer of security Mr. Benedict had offered simple directions and no clues. Clearly, he had believed they would know what to do. And so for now all they could do was get themselves to that particular spot.

"Remember—" Number Two began.

"You've already told us three times," Constance said.

"Remember," Number Two persisted, "after we drop Kate and Tai—"

"And the duffel bag!" Tai interjected.

"Yes, and the duffel bag. After that, I will circle around and drop Sticky and Constance at exactly the same spot, then make one final circle for Reynie. Nobody get ahead of yourselves."

They all promised, and the plane roared on. In the distance, the lights of Stonetown appeared. Like all cities, it was beautiful when seen from a distance at night. It was an infinity of lights. Number Two veered wide. Soon they were out over the dark water of the ocean, seeing the lights of Stonetown from the other side. Closer and closer they came, and now the silhouette of Nomansan Island became distinct, the hills behind the KEEP, the floodlights on the façades of the buildings and along the bridge reflecting off the harbor waters.

"Doesn't it seem smaller than it used to?" Kate asked.

The rest of the Society had the same impression. Whether it was a trick of distance or a trick of years, their memories of what used to be the Institute had to make a rapid adjustment. The former Institute Control Building, with its unmistakable tower; the dormitories, classroom building, cafeteria, gym, and Helpers' barracks—they were very large buildings forming a very large complex, it was true, but they were not the galactic behemoths they had seemed once upon a time. How was it that the Society members had all grown a matter of inches, but the Institute seemed to have shrunk to half its former size?

It was another riddle of ages, perhaps, to be solved another time, if ever.

In the meantime, the KEEP was certainly imposing enough. And no doubt it would seem even more daunting when they were on the ground looking up at the buildings, rather than in the sky looking down on them.

"Well, it's time for Tai and me to shove off," Kate said, slapping her thighs and rising to her feet. "You all remember how to do the buckling, I know. Any questions?"

They shook their heads. Reynie and Sticky wished Kate

and Tai luck, Constance made a face at Kate and gave Tai a hug (at his request), and Kate, with a devilish look on her face, opened her mouth to make a witty parting remark.

Everything went silent.

Kate frowned. Then she shrugged, put on her helmet, and proceeded to buckle Tai securely to her front as Tai, beaming, gave a thumbs-up to everyone on the plane. In his goggles he looked ridiculous and positively adorable. They could feel the plane slowing down. Kate opened the door, and the air pressure inside the plane changed, but no one heard a thing. She tossed out the duffel bag and let Tai watch until its parachute deployed. He turned to smile at everyone. He seemed not the least bit afraid.

Kate gave a quick wave and, with Tai's feet on her feet, stepped out into the silent, windy darkness, clinging to the wing strut.

A few seconds later, they were gone.

The plane banked and began its circle.

Sticky and Constance buckled themselves together, checking and double-checking to be sure they had done it right. Then they gestured for Reynie to confirm as well, and had him turn around so that they could make sure his own parachute was in proper order. Which, of course, it was. They all knew that everything was in order, but in the absence of Kate's natural confidence, it was rather easier to worry about something going wrong.

Soon they had come around again. Number Two was signaling from the cockpit, holding up two fingers to indicate two minutes. Then one finger for one minute. Sticky gave Reynie a "wish me luck" look and put on his goggles. He and

Constance shuffled to the door, moving in lockstep. Number Two slowed the plane down again. Reynie had a terrible, irrational feeling that he was about to see his friends make some grave error. He could barely stand to watch.

Slowly, smoothly, moving in unison, Sticky and Constance made their way out onto the step. Reynie saw Sticky nod, as if Constance had just spoken to him, and suddenly realized that she *had* spoken to him. Of course, they were communicating telepathically! In complete silence, they were coordinating their every movement. They were actually *graceful*.

Sticky nodded again and then, as casually as if they were flopping into a swimming pool, the two of them fell away into the darkness. Reynie tried to look after them, but the night had swallowed them up. He felt the plane accelerate and begin its turn. He took a few deep breaths, put on his goggles, and waited for the sign from Number Two. Before long she was holding up two fingers. Then one finger. Then she placed a hand over her heart and nodded at him. Reynie returned the gesture and went to the door.

The plane slowed, and when Reynie stepped through the door he found that the wind was not as strong as he had feared. Kate had told him what to expect, but it was a relief nonetheless. He had to move carefully, but he had no trouble maintaining his footing and his grip. Out onto the step he went, holding on to the wing strut. He looked down. The plane was still over water, but his momentum would carry him forward, and he would be over the shore when he pulled the rip cord. He couldn't wait any longer or he would end up in the hills.

Reynie jumped. He arched his back exactly as Kate had taught him, and he fell through the night sky. He extended his arms and legs. The wind resistance was powerful now, and suddenly it was loud, too, roaring in his ears, so loud that it startled him despite Kate's warnings. The hills of the island seemed to be swelling before his eyes. He realized that he was quite frightened.

Fortunately, the practice sessions kicked in. He was following the routine that Kate had drilled into them. Reynie checked his altimeter, then checked it again. His trembling hand found the rip cord, and at precisely the agreed-upon altitude, he deployed his parachute. The effect was like being yanked upward by a giant hand. Reynie felt his stomach swoop. Then he was floating, drifting in a sudden silence—a silence so profound in its contrast to the roaring of the wind moments before that it was as if someone had activated a Husher.

He began to calm down. Now he could hear the creaking of the parachute lines, the rustling of the nylon canopy as he shifted about, trying to spot the others on the shore far below. He could hear the harbor waters surging against rocks. Now he saw a blinking light—Kate's flashlight, signaling him—and after locating the two control toggles, Reynie did his best to guide the parachute in that direction. It was a simple system, and he seemed to be sufficiently on course, enough so that his relief grew deeper—until a gust of wind began to pull him seaward.

He gave a cry of surprise and pulled hard on the toggles. The wind subsided, and now he was getting closer to shore, close enough to make out the indistinct figures of the others looking up at him. Another gust of wind pulled at him, though, and he felt himself lurch backward. Reynie was overcome by a horrible dread. There seemed to be a real possibility that he might end up in cold, deep water, struggling in the darkness, far from shore.

Constance's voice entered Reynie's head. *You're in danger. Kate wants to know if you trust her with the grappling hook.*

Reynie didn't hesitate. *Yes, yes, yes!*

The wind died down again, and again Reynie tried to steer himself—indeed to *will* himself—to shore. Closer and closer, lower and lower he drifted. There came another gust of wind, but this time Reynie heard a *twang* sound below him. He closed his eyes, bracing himself. He had the briefest moment to wonder how badly it would hurt to be struck by the grappling hook, before he heard something whistle over his head. He opened his eyes and saw the cable, saw the grappling hook sliding down along one of the parachute lines. It came close enough for Reynie to grab it, and so he did, clinging to it as if it were the hand of a dear loved one.

Kate's going to guide you in, came Constance's voice in his head.

That would be great. Please tell her thank you.

You look ridiculous. You're like a human kite.

Good to know.

Moments later Reynie was standing with the others on the shore. Tai was jumping up and down and asking Reynie if he'd ever had more fun. He certainly hadn't himself, he said, and he said a great many other things, too, but Reynie could scarcely concentrate as Kate helped him out of the parachute.

"Yeah, that was a bit of an ugly breeze there, wasn't it?" Kate said to him. "The rest of us had trouble, too, but we weighed more, and it wasn't blowing as badly until you came down. Were you scared?"

"Of course not," Reynie said, fumbling at his goggles with trembling fingers.

Kate laughed and pulled them off for him. "That's the spirit," she said. She took Sticky's backpack from the duffel bag and gave it to him, then handed her bucket to Tai, who was clamoring for it.

As the others dragged their parachutes to a spot where they could be hidden among rocks and untouched at high tide, Kate carefully repacked her own and shoved it into the duffel bag. She removed her flight suit and packed it away, as well. She ran through her quick routine, checking her pockets and her utility belt. At last she felt she was ready.

"Sorry it took me so long," Kate said when she and Tai rejoined the others. "I had to get myself squared away."

"What are you talking about?" Sticky replied. "We've only just finished hiding the parachutes."

"Well, that's great," Kate said, casting a skeptical eye over the heaps of nylon and cords crammed into a little alcove of rock and sand. She quashed the urge to straighten it all out right then. "And you've done a fine job, too. Everyone ready?"

Tai temporarily surrendered the bucket in order to ride on Kate's back—Kate deftly secured the bucket with her belt—and with Sticky wearing his backpack and Reynie carrying the duffel bag (no one even attempted to suggest that Constance carry something), the little group set out for the KEEP. It was to be a short hike, mostly sticking to the low ground between the hills, moving over sand and gravel and through the occasional copse of stunted cedar trees. Before long they were in an area that looked familiar to Reynie, who had once trekked through the hills on this part of the island. It had been dark then, too, and misty, and he'd been afraid that he was about to be in severe trouble. Now, as then, his heart was beating hard. He was certainly afraid. But it was different this time. He'd been here before. He knew what he and his friends were capable of together. Yes, he was having to make a real effort to shore up his confidence, but at least the confidence was there.

Why do you keep thinking that? Constance asked him. They had come upon an old, faded path and were making their way up a hill. From the top, they knew, they would be able to see the KEEP.

Thinking what? Reynie asked, although he knew the answer and was hastily burying his thoughts under a heap of distractions.

You keep reminding yourself that when things seem at their worst, that's when you'll know we've won.

Just trying to keep my confidence up.

That's a weird way of doing it. What does it mean, anyway?

Constance, you're not supposed to be reading my mind.

Well, quit shouting, then. It's not exactly helping my confidence for you to keep concentrating so hard on yours.

Sorry, I'll do better.

I'm still mad at you, by the way.

Reynie sighed.

They reached the top of the hill. There, across a shallow

valley to the northwest, loomed the KEEP. It was surrounded by hills, but their own hill was of a higher elevation, and their vantage point offered a decent sight line. They could see parts of the familiar stone buildings, as well as the familiar front plaza—all brightly lit from the outside. Nothing stirred. Beyond the buildings the bridge stretched across the dark water, lit along the sides like an airport runway at night.

Kate reached up over her shoulder to hand Tai her mini-binoculars. Eagerly looking through them, he whispered, "Couldn't the Ten Men just use the bridge? Why do you think they'd have to use the Salamander?"

Kate helped him aim the binoculars. "Do you see that gate at the far end? Well, it's very heavy-duty, and most people couldn't get past it."

"The Ten Men could, though, right?"

"With their laser pointers and exploding calculators, yes. But they have a limited supply of those right now, and of course that would also set off a lot of alarms, which they wouldn't care to do. But on top of that, there's a special security system on the bridge now. Everybody knows about it—it was in all the papers. If anybody breaks through that gate or tries to climb around it or get across in any other way they're not supposed to, the whole bridge is rigged to sink into the water."

"Wow," Tai breathed.

"Yes, and see that guardhouse? It's automated now. The codes change every day, and they're set remotely, by people far away. The Listener can't just read a guard's mind and get the code. So the bridge is completely off-limits. McCracken is too smart to try it."

"That's good," Tai whispered. "Because I like the bridge. It's pretty."

"It really is, isn't it?"

The time had come for Sticky to take the lead. He pointed toward the nearest hill behind the KEEP, directly opposite them across the shallow valley. "We aren't going all the way to the buildings," he said. "We're heading to a spot at the base of that last hill, one hundred thirty meters southwest of the building that used to be our dormitory. There's supposed to be an entrance there."

"That's drapeweed territory," Constance said.

"You mean the traps?" Tai whispered. "The pits all covered up with drapeweed—like the one George almost fell into?"

Kate hitched Tai higher on her back. "Don't worry— they're easy to spot. We'll just keep well away from any part of the ground that's covered in vines."

But when they had descended the hill, a surprise awaited them. The entire terrain before them was completely covered in vines.

"Oh boy," Sticky muttered. "I should have thought of this. The drapeweed's had years to spread."

"That's, um, not good," said Constance.

Sticky wiped his brow. "I know what the line of approach is supposed to be. We just have to follow it exactly. I'll go first, and the rest of you walk in single file behind me." Consulting the schematics in his mind, he took a few steps to the left, swallowed hard, and prepared to walk.

"One sec," Kate said, looping a cord around Sticky's waist and connecting it to her belt. "Last time you fell through, we weren't prepared," she said. "What is it they say about learning from experience?"

Sticky looked over his shoulder at her. "That we're supposed to? I don't recall a specific saying, though there are related aphorisms in just about every language."

"That's all I meant," Kate said with a chuckle. "Okay, we're all set."

Sticky found it a tricky business crossing the vine-covered ground. He would have preferred to shuffle his feet—the better to sense whether the ground abruptly fell away beneath the vines—but because the drapeweed caught at his ankles, shuffling was impossible. With every step he had to lift his foot high, sometimes straining against entangled vines, which made it difficult to keep his balance. And every time his foot came down, often awkwardly and with greater force than he would have wished, he half expected to keep plunging forward, down through the vines and into a trap.

It made for a most uncomfortable journey, yet Sticky was not afraid in the way he might once have been. He trusted Mr. Benedict's schematics, and he trusted his own ability to follow them. Moreover, if somehow he did make a mistake, he trusted Kate to keep him safe. No, he wasn't worried for life or limb. He simply felt uneasy, as anyone might, at the prospect of falling unexpectedly into a hole.

"A few more steps and we're at a hundred thirty meters," Kate said. They could no longer see the dormitories, for the final hill, the bottom half of which was also covered in drapeweed, rose up directly before them. It was so steep as to be almost vertical, and it obscured all of the KEEP from view. But Kate had fixed the spot in her mind from the top of the last hill, and no one doubted it.

"Makes sense," Sticky said, taking his last step. He now stood inches from a veritable wall of drapeweed.

"Now what?" Constance said. "All I see is vines."

"I suspect the traps aren't the only things the vines have covered over the years," Reynie suggested from the back of the line.

"That's what I was thinking," Sticky said. He reached through the curtain of drapeweed before him. Sure enough, his fingers touched not rocky earth but metal.

With all of them working quickly, the space was soon cleared of vines to reveal a heavy grate set into the hillside.

"Let me get that," Kate said. With a tool in each hand and startling quickness, she removed several screws and bolts, then took hold of the grate and pulled. It came free with a sucking sound. Briefly staggering under its weight, she leaned it against the hill and poked her head through the empty space where it had been.

Kate found herself looking down through a short vertical tunnel—an open duct with no bottom grate—below which was an astonishing vastness of space. Far, far below, an unseen light source revealed part of an empty concrete floor. It was like looking down at a sidewalk from the roof of a tall skyscraper.

"Wow, okay," Kate said. "Looks to me like this was some kind of heat exhaust vent. But I don't think we're going to be crawling through it. You should all have a peek. Here, Tai, I'll lift you up."

Tai wasn't the only one who gasped when he saw what Kate had seen. Reynie and Constance were equally taken aback. Sticky, for his part, felt a little queasy imagining a fall to that distant floor, but he wasn't surprised.

"I knew we'd be standing above an incredibly big space," he said. "You can't see it all because of the duct, but it's like an enormous stadium down there. My guess is there was a naturally existing cavern that Mr. Curtain converted to use as an assembly area for his Sweepers."

"The brainsweeping machines!" Tai whispered.

"That's right," Sticky said. "When we were secret agents here, we saw a huge warehouse full of them—"

"Memory Terminal," Constance interjected.

"—but we never saw where they were built," Sticky continued. "It only makes sense that Mr. Curtain would have had his own secret assembly plant here on the island. He was all about control."

"This is so weird," Kate said. "It's like being backstage at a play we all saw together a long time ago. But does Mr. Benedict really think we can get in this way? I rather doubt it."

"It is confusing," Sticky agreed. "I expected some kind of security door with a long passage behind it. There should be an elevator a little distance along the passage—well, but that doesn't matter, because we don't need to go down. Our next step is a control room on the same level as the passage."

"If the passage even exists," Constance said. "This doesn't make sense. Why would Dad give us all that information but get this business about the door wrong?"

Everyone looked at Reynie, who was rocking on his toes and heels, resisting an urge to pace. (Pacing did not seem exactly wise when there might be drapeweed traps about.) "Right," he said. "My guess is Mr. Benedict was being tricky on purpose. Isn't he always? Either his security contract didn't allow him to reveal the specific location of an entrance, or else he just wanted to make it harder for anyone but us. He knows we'll think this through."

Everyone nodded. Everyone continued looking at Reynie.

"Um, so, okay," he said. "I don't think it's a coincidence that the gold key led us exactly to this exhaust vent. He wanted us to know that it's here. So it may be useful. But if everything else is correct except the location of the door —"

"Then we should just keep looking!" Kate said. "Sticky, in what direction did you expect the passage to be?"

"To the right," Sticky said, already moving that way.

Kate caught his arm. "Remember, wherever there used to be a secret entrance, there was always a trap nearby."

"Roger that," Sticky said. He proceeded along the base of the hill with great caution, probing with a foot before every step, probing behind the drapeweed curtain with his hand. He found rock with his hand, solid ground with his feet. He stepped again, with the same result. After his fifth such step, his hand tapped against metal. He'd found the door.

Before anyone else moved, Kate knelt near Sticky's feet to shine her flashlight at the ground all around. "There," she said, pointing at a spot a few paces out from the hillside. "See where the drapeweed is kind of sagging a bit? That has to be the trap."

The others had a hard time seeing exactly what Kate saw, but they had no reason to doubt her and every reason to avoid the sagging drapeweed. They edged along the base of the hill to join Kate and Sticky by the door, which was rapidly growing visible as those two worked together to clear away the vines. Only its size and rectangular shape identified it as a door, however. Made of a formidable-looking metal, it lacked seams, hinges, or a handle.

"Try kicking it!" suggested Tai, who had loved hearing about the secret entrances at the former Institute, especially how one opened them.

"Unfortunately, this isn't that kind of door," Sticky said, studying it closely. "It can't be opened from the outside. See how the metal sits in a groove? It has to be slid to the left or right, but there'll be some kind of locking system on the inside."

Kate couldn't resist trying to shove the door inward, then to the left and right, just in case. She might as well have been trying to budge a tank. "He's right. It has to be opened from the other side." She untethered herself from Sticky and edged past the others to get back to her duffel bag.

"Could I please kick it just to try?" Tai asked.

They let Tai kick the metal, which was so thick and heavy that it didn't rattle or resonate at all. But he was satisfied to have made the attempt.

"Let me think," Reynie said. "There has to be a way we can work this out using the vent." As he spoke, he turned to look at the vent—they all did, and they all saw Kate, now wearing her parachute, poking her head through the opening again. Everyone froze.

"Oh, Kate, surely not!" Sticky hissed.

"Surely yes!" Kate replied, pulling her head back out to smile at them. "Don't worry—I've done the calculations. I'll see you all again in a minute or two. The trip down will be quick, of course, but then I'll have to take the elevator back up."

"You're going to skydive under the *ground*?" Tai asked in disbelief. "You're going to...*ground*-dive?"

"I guess you could call it that," said Kate with a laugh. "Wish me luck!"

"Good—"

But Kate had already dived headfirst into the hillside.

Everyone scrambled to the opening. Kate had left her bucket behind for Tai, who used it as a step stool, and with their heads all bumping together, they peered down in time to see what looked like the top of a mushroom—but was actually the canopy of Kate's parachute—sinking to the floor far below them. Within moments the mushroom wrinkled, folded, and collapsed to the side, revealing the minuscule figure of Kate Wetherall, who waved up at them with a broad sweep of her arm.

"Well, that made me feel like throwing up," Constance remarked.

Sticky and Reynie had felt the same. There was no time to dwell on the fact, however. Even now Kate would be making her way to the elevator, and they decided they should replace the grate and see if they could pull enough drapeweed over it to hide it again. Sticky got on one side of the grate, Reynie got on the other, and together they lifted it several centimeters off the ground. They set it down again.

"Okay, this is really heavy," Reynie said.

"It really is," Sticky said. "Also, I think Kate has the screws and bolts in her pocket. Plus the tools. We might as well wait."

"I didn't think of that," said Reynie, with evident relief. "Of course we should."

"You won't have to wait long," Constance announced. "She's getting close."

Sticky gave a little jump. Something had occurred to him. "Those blueprints contained schematics for some alarm systems. What if there's an alarm she needs to deactivate? What if she doesn't realize it?"

"Can't we tell her when she gets to the door?" Tai asked.

"That door is so thick," said Reynie. Like Sticky, he was hurriedly digging for his walkie-talkie, which was zipped into a pocket of his flight suit. "She might not be able to hear what we're saying."

Sticky got to his own walkie-talkie before Reynie managed to extract his, but no sooner had he switched it on than a rumbling groan sounded from behind the door.

"Constance, warn her!" Reynie said, and Constance squeezed her eyes closed.

Too late. The metal door slid sideways to reveal a grinning Kate Wetherall.

A siren began to sound.

Kate's grin vanished.

Sticky flew past her, his eyes darting all around. Locating the alarm panel and deactivating the alarm took him a few seconds—but *only* a few seconds—and in the ensuing silence they all looked at one another with wide eyes, daring to hope. The silence stretched into a full minute. They began to breathe again.

"Sorry," Kate said. "I didn't see it. Walked right past it and didn't see it."

"I should have warned you ahead of time," Sticky said.

"I didn't give you much chance, did I?" Kate said.

"Hush," said Constance. She had closed her eyes.

Everyone looked at her.

Constance opened her eyes again, and the fear in them was plain. "They're coming," she said. "They're coming, and they won't be long."

Across the still night, beyond the hill, over the water, a powerful engine started up. It rumbled loudly for a few seconds, then went abruptly silent—not in the usual manner of an engine shutting down, but as if it had simply vanished. All was still again.

"That's the Salamander," Sticky said. "They activated the noise-cancellation device."

"Why didn't they turn it on *before* they started the engine?" Tai asked, clutching Kate's bucket as Reynie ushered him into the passage.

"Great question," Kate said. "If Crawlings was responsible, that would explain it. McCracken's always getting on him for being careless."

"I think it was McCracken himself," Reynie said grimly. "I think he wanted to send us a message."

Kate narrowed her eyes. "Toying with us? Mocking us for setting off the alarm?"

"And letting us know he's on his way," Reynie said.

"What a jerk," Kate grumbled, applying herself to a heavy crank near the door, which rapidly slid closed.

"Can you reactivate the alarm?" Reynie asked Sticky.

"Not this one. I had to permanently disable it with a universal shutdown code—a sort of digital skeleton key. Mr. Benedict included it in the schematic. I think the regular codes must change every day, like the one at the guardhouse."

"Why would he make it so easy to disable?" Constance asked.

Sticky started moving down the passage and gestured for them to follow. "I wouldn't say it was easy. I had to enter a string of twenty-three digits with no pauses between them."

Tai, lugging Kate's bucket with one hand, began punching numbers into an imaginary keypad with the other. He counted under his breath. After a dozen or so he shook his head, eyes wide.

The passage was cold, dimly lit, and featureless. After a short distance they passed the doors to the elevator, which Kate said was of the clackety-clack metal-cage variety.

"It rises up along the wall, giving you a view of everything," she said. "I've never seen such a big indoor space.

'Enormous' doesn't come close to describing it. But it's entirely empty. Very weird."

"I want to see it!" Tai said.

"Maybe later, sport," Kate said, for they were hurrying on.

At the end of the passage, they came to a closed door. This one was a regular door, built of wood, painted gray, and with a plain-looking doorknob.

"Great, now what?" Constance said.

"Let me work my magic," Sticky said, cracking his knuckles. Then he simply turned the knob and pushed the door open.

Constance rolled her eyes.

"There shouldn't be any more obstacles until we reach the control room," Sticky said, "only a rather long walk. Kate, do you want to give Tai a ride?"

They hurried down passage after passage, several of which gave on to other passages and closed doors. Just finding the way to the control room would have been a major obstacle itself if anyone other than Sticky had read those blueprints. As it was, Sticky had only to follow the map in his mind, and the others had only to follow him.

"If I'm right about that cavern being a secret assembly area," Sticky said as they hustled along, "my guess would be that we're passing through old storage spaces—all these rooms would have contained different parts that would get sent down to the assembly floor by way of the elevator."

"What's in the rooms now?" Tai wanted to know.

Kate opened a door at random. "Looks like dust and spiders," she said.

They hurried on.

"That one takes you to what used to be the Memory Terminal," Sticky said, indicating a door on their left. "We're getting close to familiar territory now."

"Right," said Kate, who had an unerring sense of distance and direction. "We're just east of what used to be the classroom building."

"And several meters below, of course," Sticky said.

"Of course," said Tai, just to be involved.

At last they came to a door with a sign over it: SECONDARY CONTROL ROOM. It, too, had a simple knob, and with a somewhat dramatic "Here we go!" Sticky turned the knob and shoved against the door, only to thump into it and bounce back. With a sheepish look he tried again, this time pulling on the knob instead of shoving, and the door opened toward him.

"Here we go," he mumbled.

The room was small and simple: a single desk, atop which stood a computer and some kind of control board; two security-camera monitors mounted on the wall above the desk; and a second door, currently closed. One of the monitors displayed a view of the front plaza and the bridge in the distance beyond it. Both were unoccupied. The other monitor showed the interior of the security door that Kate had opened to let them in. It was still in place. If the Ten Men had reached the island yet, there was no sign of it on the screens.

Sticky slid into a chair at the computer station. "Okay, according to the gold key, there's an obvious first step now."

"Which is what?" Constance demanded, although Sticky had clearly been about to explain.

Sticky bit his lip, took a breath, and recited:

"First learn all that you can learn.
Unlocking with the code
Will burn your chances of return
And blocked will be your road."

Constance made an angry noise. "Another code? What code? How many codes are there, anyway?"

"I don't know, Constance," Sticky said, making an effort to speak calmly. "The gold key presents a kind of riddle we have to solve here, and I'm assuming the answer is the code. I can share the riddle in a minute, but can we agree that first I should race through whatever I can on this computer—you know, 'learn all that I can learn'?"

"Fine," Constance said. "Just hurry up."

Sticky glanced at the others for confirmation. They all nodded, especially Tai, who did so with great enthusiasm.

"While you do that," Reynie said, "why don't I run through all the security-camera views? Whatever they have to show us is another thing we can learn, right?"

They all agreed, especially Tai, and Reynie took the chair next to Sticky. The control board operated the security cameras, as Reynie had correctly guessed, and in no time he had scanned the system and figured out how to work it. There were dozens of possible views to be displayed, and each camera could also be repositioned or made to zoom in on a particular frame. Reynie's first move was to redirect the camera overlooking the plaza, scanning left, right, and below for any sign of the Baker's Dozen. Finding none, he began switching to the views provided by other cameras.

"I'm in the system now," Sticky murmured, and Reynie

looked over to see him paging rapidly through screen after screen of information—schematics, computer code, and great blocks of text (some of it in different languages). "There's an awful lot here. It could take me an hour to get through everything. What's it looking like out there?"

"No sign of them yet," said Kate, who, like all the others, was studying the monitors. The screens were now revealing views of long, empty, almost identical corridors.

"It's the old classroom building," Constance said. "How depressing."

"So strange," Kate murmured.

"Yes," Sticky said, still paging through screens on the computer, "the classroom building now appears to be the administration area. It's being renovated for use by general staff, guards, medical personnel, and so on."

"They should have plenty of room," Reynie said as more empty corridors appeared on the monitors. "I remember thinking that there must be miles of tiles here."

"You weren't wrong," Kate said. "And some lead to the old Helpers' barracks behind the classroom building. Is that where the security suites are located, George?"

Sticky tapped his nose and pointed in her direction without taking his eyes from the computer. He paged quickly through a few more screens, then turned in his chair to face them. "Okay, time is short, so let me tell you what I know so far. It's enough to form a plan A. If we end up having more time, I can keep digging and maybe come up with a better one."

Reynie switched back to a view of the front plaza—still empty for the moment—and left it there. They all kept an eye on it as Sticky continued.

"Between the blueprints I saw in Mr. Benedict's house," he said, "and what I've just learned here, I have a sense of how the KEEP is laid out. There are several layers of security—think horizontal layers rather than vertical ones. The first is the water, of course. Then you have the exterior of the buildings."

"And the traps!" Tai reminded him.

"And the traps," Sticky acknowledged. "But the walls of the buildings themselves have been fortified, along with the windows and doors, and they're all rigged with an alarm system that will radio distress signals to the mainland if there's any attempt to break through them. So that's the second layer of security.

"The third is a system of barriers that are triggered in different ways," Sticky said, rising from his chair. He went to the door through which they had entered, pulled it closed, and pointed at the ceiling just above it. "See that little gap between the doorframe and the wall? One of the barriers is up there and will drop down like a guillotine if it's triggered. It's made of glastanium—as clear as glass, as strong as titanium—and it doesn't have a lock or a security code. In case of an attempted break-in or breakout, all the doors to the different sections of the KEEP get sealed off with barriers like this one, and they stay that way for twenty-four hours. That allows plenty of time for security forces from the mainland to arrive in sufficient numbers and assess the situation."

Reynie gestured at the monitor displaying the KEEP's front plaza. "So if the Ten Men break in through the front entrance..."

"Then this barrier falls," Sticky said, "as will the barriers over every other entrance into this section of the KEEP."

"So they won't be able to get to us?" Tai asked hopefully.

"The barriers will definitely slow them down," Sticky said. "I don't know how many calculator bombs they have — evidently, not many — and it might take more than one to blast through a barrier. Their laser pointers won't be of any use, because the barriers don't have locks or door handles to burn through. They could probably burn a few tiny holes, but what good would that do them?"

"What if they burned hundreds and hundreds of tiny holes?" Tai asked. "Then they could make a big hole!"

"Smart thinking, pal," Kate said. "But the laser pointers are only good for a single shot, and they don't have many of those, either."

"Whew!" Tai said, and it was suddenly apparent to the others that he'd actually been anxious about the answer. Kate stepped over and put an arm around him.

"So, what's the bad news?" Constance asked.

"The bad news," Reynie said, "is that Mr. Benedict is in a different section of the KEEP."

"Exactly," said Sticky. "The section we're in includes this secondary control room, the old classroom building, and the secret passages leading up to it. Mr. Curtain's security suite is in the old Helpers' barracks."

"You're saying that the moment McCracken tries to break in, we're going to be sealed off from Dad?" Constance cried. "What are we waiting for, then? We have to run!"

Sticky grimaced. "We can't just run. First of all, what if

we didn't make it? There's only one entrance to the barracks, it's not exactly close by, and it's a security door that requires a code. And just to get there we'd have to pass through three *other* security doors that require a code."

Constance threw her hands in the air. "So that's what the riddle is for! We solve it for the code! Let's get on it! McCracken's getting close—I can feel it!"

Everybody instinctively squinted at the monitors. Still nothing outside.

"Listen to me, Constance," Sticky said, fixing her with a steady gaze. "This code from the riddle will have to be an override code rather than the normal one, which changes every day. And using an override code will drop the barriers. It's another emergency measure."

Constance looked ready to scream, but she squeezed her lips tightly together, balled her hands into fists, and said nothing.

"Okay, then, what's plan A?" asked Kate.

Sticky turned to the monitor control board, scanned it, and flipped a switch. One of the monitor displays changed, showing a long, empty dead-end corridor. Sticky pressed a button that zoomed in toward the dead end. High up on the wall, painted the same neutral color as the wall (and therefore difficult to make out), was a small electrical panel.

"The security cameras aren't the only thing we can control from this room," Sticky said. "I can also drop the barriers myself. But I can't drop just one. If I enter the command, there's a ten-second warning, and then *all* the barriers fall. Here's our loophole, though. The barracks entrance—the security door with the barrier over it—is on the other side of the wall with that electrical panel, which just so happens to control the mechanism for that barrier."

"So we can disable it?" Constance asked.

"Not exactly. The barrier will fall if we try that. But we can rewire it to make it think it's already fallen. If we do that, it won't be triggered when McCracken breaks into the facility. We can also use the override codes to get through all the security doors between us and the barracks. The overrides won't drop the barrier, either—"

"Because it will think it's already down!" said Constance.

"Right," Sticky said. "I mean, it would be nice to have that barrier between us and the Ten Men once we get into the barracks, of course, but—"

"We can!" Reynie said. "Listen, after Kate rewires the barrier so it won't be triggered, the rest of us can figure out the code and use it to open all the security doors except the last one—the one into the barracks. Then we'll hold the doors open for Kate. There are enough of us, right? If we don't let the doors close, we won't have to reenter the codes. Kate rewires the barrier again so that it *can* be triggered, rejoins us by way of the doors we're holding open for her, and then, when we use the override code to get through the *final* security door—"

"That barrier will drop down behind us ten seconds later," Sticky said. "Yes!"

"Great, let's make this happen," Kate said, rubbing her hands together. "George, if you'll just show me where that electrical panel is, I'll get going."

Sticky pulled up a schematic on the computer. "Okay,

before you can even reach the corridors, you're going to have to run up all these ramps to the next level of secret passages, which is right below the old classroom building. Then you have to follow this passage all the way around the perimeter"—Sticky traced his finger around the edges of the computer screen—"until you reach these stairs *here*. That's the only way you can get to the corridors where the electrical panel is."

"Roger that," Kate said.

Sticky pulled up another schematic, this one showing the classroom building corridors. They resembled an extremely simple maze, rather like a rectangular version of a nautilus shell, with dozens of corridors running parallel to one another. "See this security door here?" he said, pointing at the bottom right of the screen. "Once you've rewired the panel, the rest of us can use the override code to get through this door, take this long straight shot, pass through two more security doors near the midway point, and then all the way to the final security door—the entrance to the barracks. But first *you're* going to have to go down every single one of the other corridors to get to the electrical panel, which is right *here*." He pointed to a spot near the top right of the screen.

Kate whistled. "This is turning into quite a little jaunt!"

"Yes, it adds up to about two and a half kilometers. You won't have to come all the way back to our starting point, though.. Reynie had the right idea, but we'll actually only have to hold open one door. This one *here*." Sticky moved his finger slightly lower on the screen. "See, it's close to the barracks entrance. That will be your shortcut. Once we open that one for you, you can rewire the panel and meet us there."

"Perfect," Kate said. "Now, what should I expect at the electrical panel?"

Sticky pulled up another schematic. "Need me to explain it to you?"

Kate peered intently at the screen. "Nope. This will hardly be the first time I've rewired a control mechanism, you know. Easy-peasy."

During this time, as Sticky and Kate were conferring, Constance had been staring with greater and greater intensity at the display of the barren front plaza. Something wasn't right, and she suddenly realized what it was. "They're going to the back door!"

"What? Are you sure?" Kate asked.

"Oh boy, that does make sense," Reynie said. He quickly switched a monitor to display the interior of the back door, still closed. "It's out of view of the mainland, after all. I guess they knew about it from their days at the Institute. The question is how they'll handle it." He switched to a view the group hadn't seen yet, that of the cavernous space Kate had jumped into. It truly was amazing, like the interior of the largest cathedral in the world, if only the largest cathedral in the world were ten times as big.

Reynie used the controls to zoom in on one corner of the ceiling, where the metal-cage elevator Kate had described was plainly visible. It looked, bizarrely, like a jail cell attached to the ceiling, with doors that opened on either side. A few meters away from it was the bottom of the duct through which Kate had dropped before deploying her parachute. Reynie felt queasy again just imagining it.

"At least it's empty for now," Kate said. She turned to Tai.

"Hey, you saw how high up on the wall that electrical panel is, didn't you? I have the tools I need, but I don't have a step-ladder. Do you have any ideas?"

Tai's eyes widened. "You need your bucket!"

"Now, that," said Kate, "is an excellent idea."

Tai eagerly handed her the bucket, and the sight of her strapping it to her hip with her utility belt was surprisingly comforting to everyone.

"Okay, I'm off!" Kate said, going to the door. She threw it open to reveal a long series of ramps leading up to the higher level. The sight of them gave her an unexpected shiver, for they triggered vivid memories of the way Mr. Curtain had rocketed along in his demonic wheelchair, how very fright-ening it had been to all of them back then. She turned to her friends and could tell from their faces that they were having the same unpleasant recollections.

"What's that?" asked Tai, who was looking not at the ramps but at the monitors.

Everyone's eyes followed his pointing finger. In the opening at the bottom of the duct, something was mov-ing. Reynie checked the controls. The camera couldn't be zoomed in further, but as it happened, there was no need.

A pale bald head emerged from within the duct. An upside-down face, followed by an upside-down body in an elegant suit. Soon the entire figure of Crawlings, right down to his shiny black shoes, hung suspended beneath the duct, twisting slowly left and right. A line—on the moni-tor it looked scarcely thicker than a thread—was tied about his ankles; he resembled an elongated spider hanging by a strand of web. As he dangled there over the abyss, Crawlings casually buttoned his suit coat and tucked his tie into it to prevent its falling over his face, which, because of its inverted state, appeared to be frowning.

In fact, Crawlings was smiling.

"What are they going to do?" Constance whispered. "No way they just happened to bring parachutes, right? Will they blast open the door?" She squeezed her eyes closed, trying to search her way to the answer.

"We don't have much time, Kate," Reynie said.

"I'm on it," Kate said, and she was gone.

The others watched as Crawlings made a signal and was drawn upward into the duct again.

"They have a different plan," Constance murmured, her eyes still closed. "The Listener was afraid of the explosion, but then McCracken said something that made her less afraid."

"Can you read McCracken's thoughts?" Reynie asked.

Constance shook her head. "Not from here. If I could see him, maybe, but..." She was silent a moment, then opened her eyes. "Sorry, no."

"That's okay," Reynie said, still looking at the monitor. "I think we have our answer."

Crawlings was lowering into view again. In his hands was Kate's crossbow.

"The grappling hook!" Constance cried. "Kate forgot her duffel bag!"

Sure enough, in the next moment Crawlings fired the grappling hook at the bottom of the metal-cage elevator. The security cameras were not wired for sound, so there was no telltale *twang* or *clang*, only the unhappy appearance of a taut cable now stretching from Crawlings to the elevator. With an almost careless gesture, he reached up and released his feet, then swung in a graceful arc to the wall beneath the elevator. He began to climb. Smoothly and swiftly he ascended, until he was clinging to the exterior of the elevator cage. He withdrew something from his pocket, a bright red light appeared on the elevator door, and then Crawlings was inside the elevator. A moment later he was out of sight.

"He's just going to let them in through the door," Sticky said. "Just like that."

Reynie switched the monitor to display the interior of the security door. Crawlings stood before it, speaking into a walkie-talkie.

Constance had closed her eyes again, focusing on the Listener. "McCracken's angry. He didn't want Crawlings to waste a laser pointer getting into the elevator. Now she's scared there's going to be violence."

"She definitely doesn't know them well enough yet," Sticky muttered.

"She's also not warding me off. She's scared and confused. Her defenses are down."

"Why isn't he opening the door?" Tai asked.

On the monitor, Crawlings checked his watches. He shook his head and crossed his arms. Then he simply stood there.

"They're worried about the sirens," Constance said.

"They don't realize the alarm's deactivated," Reynie said.

"Something else, too. They're setting something up," Constance said. "She doesn't quite understand it, but when it's ready, Crawlings is going to open the door. And they're going to come after us at top speed. She's really focusing on it because she's afraid of what will happen. McCracken is talking about the secondary control room. He's sure that this is where we'll be, and he knows the way here."

"Of course," Sticky said. "They've all been here before, including her."

Reynie, doing his best to seem calm and unworried, had put an arm around Tai's shoulders. "It took us a few minutes to get from that door to this room," he said. "And we were hurrying. But they'll be much faster than we were." He considered a moment. "I think once Crawlings lets them in, they'll be here in two minutes, tops."

"George," said Tai, looking very nervous now, "could you please use the computer to drop the barrier thing over the door? Before they get here?"

"I will, Tai, I promise," Sticky said as calmly as he could. "The trouble is that when I enter the command, the barrier over the barracks entrance will fall, too." He got out his walkie-talkie. "Kate, what's your status?"

A few seconds passed before Kate replied, her voice loud and tinny against a background of rapid footsteps. "Believe it or not, I'm just now reaching the level below the corridors. My bucket handle came loose at the top of the ramps, and my bucket went crashing all the way to the bottom again, so I had to go after it. I honestly can't believe this. Never happened once in my life! Has Tai been fiddling with the screws or something?"

A quick glance at Tai's face told everyone in the secondary control room that Tai had, indeed, been fiddling with the screws or something.

"It's okay, Tai," Reynie said, trying not to panic. He had his own walkie-talkie out now. "Stand by, Kate," he said. "I mean, keep running, but stand by."

"Roger that."

"Okay, let's think!" Reynie said. "If we have to drop the barriers before Kate rewires the panel, we're stuck in this section."

"Crawlings is going to open the door for them in exactly six minutes," said Constance, who was scowling with her eyes closed. Even as she spoke, they saw Crawlings check his watches again.

Reynie spoke into his walkie-talkie. "We have eight minutes, Kate. Maybe less."

A pause. Then: "Roger that. I can do this."

Reynie looked at Sticky, who was shaking his head and murmuring to himself.

"George doesn't think she can make it!" said Tai in a thin voice.

Sticky met Reynie's eye. "It's two and a half kilometers. I don't know of any official world records for that specific distance, but I know the ones for the two-thousand-meter and three-thousand-meter races, both indoors and outdoors, men's and women's—"

"Please hurry," Reynie prompted.

"Right. Sorry. The best I can do is take a kind of complex average. And that would be about eight minutes, Reynie. But keep in mind those are record times set by world-class athletes, running on tracks with track shoes. Kate's wearing boots—"

"And carrying a walkie-talkie and a bucket," said Constance with a look of despair.

"And when she gets there, she has to rewire the panel," Reynie said.

Sticky shook his head. "She can't do it. Nobody could. It can't be done."

For several seconds, they were all silent.

Tai tugged on Reynie's hand, and looking up at him with wide eyes, he whispered, "Is there a plan B?"

A PLAN BY ANY OTHER NAME

It took Reynie about three seconds to form a plan B. It was far from a perfect plan, but it was a start. He squeezed Tai's hand.

"Of course there's a plan B," he said. "Here's what we'll do: We're going to solve the riddle for the override code. We'll give it to Kate and tell her to forget about rewiring the panel. Instead, she'll take that shortcut George showed her. After she uses the code on the first security door, she'll have ten seconds to reach the barracks entrance and use the code to get through it, too—which for Kate will be easy. The barrier will fall, but at least she'll be on the other side."

"But she doesn't have the serum!" Constance protested.

"The main control room is in the barracks," Sticky said quickly. "If Kate can get to that, maybe she can figure out another way in for us. I can help her—we'll use the walkie-talkies. There's only so much I can see from this side."

"But McCracken—"

"We'll have that barrier between us," Reynie said, pointing to the gap above the door, "plus the codes to the security doors, which they don't have. We can get through those doors and—well, that will slow them down, anyway. We'll avoid them as best we can. In the meantime, we can at least save Kate—and then maybe she can save us."

Constance glared at him. "Why don't you say the rest of your plan?" she snapped. "The part where you're thinking Tai and I can hide and you and Sticky will try to trick McCracken into taking you hostage!"

Reynie closed his eyes. "You really need to stay out of my head, Constance."

"Also, Reynie's right," Sticky said. "Only you can protect Tai if it comes to that, Constance—only you can keep him hidden from the Listener, right? And you could nudge the Ten Men away if they got close."

Constance turned her glare on Sticky. But then it softened, and her eyes filled with tears. "I know you two just want to protect us, but..." She sniffed and wiped at her eyes.

"We *promised* to," Reynie said. "And it would be a way to get the serum to Mr. Benedict, Constance. Mr. Curtain's instructions called for McCracken to have a couple of us with him. If we can just get there with the serum, we can figure something out."

"Would that be a plan C?" Tai asked, nervously bouncing on his toes.

"We're down to five and a half minutes," Sticky said, with a significant glance at the others.

Constance covered her face with her hands. "You're still not telling me things!" she growled. "And I'm trying not to look! Okay, okay, fine! Let's get that code! What's the riddle, Sticky?"

Tai stopped bouncing. Indeed, everyone held still and looked at Sticky, who wasted not a moment. He began to recite:

> *"A rose by any other name is still a rose, it's said.*
> *One's favorite flower's much the same, although it isn't red.*
> *The Institute, now called the KEEP, once had an evil in it.*
> *(One's secret agents took a peek and saw that in a minute.)*
> *This the Institute once had in common with the flower.*
> *The truth remains: all names contain a clue or hidden power.*
>
> *One name has changed; it's still the same; it's not a place you miss.*
> *Another name, once rearranged, will help you to do this."*

"This is hard!" Tai exclaimed after a short pause. "Can you say it again?"

Sticky recited the riddle once more; then, noting Reynie's narrowed eyes, he quickly said, "Listen, I've spent all day trying not to think about it. I was afraid if I *did* solve it, certain people might, you know, pick up on the answer."

"Right!" Reynie said. "Thanks for the reminder. Constance and Tai, I'm sorry, but we need to be extra-careful. Can you two cover your ears and hum songs and think about ridiculous things for a minute?"

Constance scowled at the suggestion, and Tai giggled, but both immediately complied. It was unclear what song Constance chose to hum, for Tai's rendition of "Row, Row, Row Your Boat" was quite loud and enthusiastic.

Sticky stepped close to Reynie and said quietly, "You have it, don't you?"

Reynie nodded. "The flower is 'violet.' Rearranged, it will help us 'to live.' I assume the keypads are alphabetical."

"They are indeed," said Sticky. He raised his walkie-talkie to notify Kate.

"Wait a second," Reynie said. "We need to be careful what we say. If we tell her she can't make it—"

"Oh, right, she'll want to try even harder," Sticky said, lowering the walkie-talkie. "Well, what do you suggest? We're down to three minutes." He pointed at the monitor, where, sure enough, Crawlings was standing at the ready over the crank that would open the security door and admit the rest of the Ten Men. He was flexing his long fingers in eager anticipation.

Reynie lifted his own walkie-talkie. "Kate, listen, we have

a better plan now. We need you to skip the electrical panel and head straight to the barracks. Cut through that security door Sticky showed you. Remember, you'll have only ten seconds from the moment you enter the code, which is 'to live.'" He repeated the code and spelled it to make sure she had it clearly, then told her they would explain everything later.

"Roger that," came Kate's breathless reply.

Sticky and Reynie looked bleakly at each other. It had just occurred to both of them that Kate might not even reach the security door in time.

Tai, quite dramatically, took a huge breath and renewed his vigorous humming. Constance, her ears still covered, was watching the monitor on which Crawlings could now be seen opening the security door.

Reynie gestured toward the computer. "Do you think you could learn anything else that would help us?"

"In two minutes?" Sticky shook his head. "I think I should bring up the command screen and be ready to drop the barriers if Kate doesn't trigger them in time."

"Agreed," Reynie said.

"This humming is driving me crazy," Sticky said, "but before we make them stop, let me ask you about the riddle. Mr. Benedict is the 'one' who has a favorite flower, right? And the one 'whose secret agents took a peek'? That refers to us, when we were students here."

Reynie tapped his nose.

Watching the monitor, Constance shuddered. McCracken had stepped into the passage. He was followed by the familiar figures of Sharpe and Garrotte, and still more Ten Men started to stream in through the doorway behind them. Meanwhile, McCracken's keen eyes, scanning the passage, had spotted the security camera. He now seemed to be staring directly into the control room, directly at Constance. He smiled. A pencil appeared in his hand as if by magic, and with a flick of his wrist he whipped it toward the security camera. Constance flinched. Now the monitor displayed nothing more than the spiderweb pattern of the camera's shattered lens.

"Less than two minutes," Sticky said. "Last question: Do you think 'peek' was a clue, since it's 'keep' spelled backward?"

Reynie nodded. "The Institute's acronym was LIVE—which, spelled backward, is EVIL. I think he wanted to call our attention to the letters. The only way that 'violet' has an 'evil' in it is that it contains those four letters."

"That's what I thought," Sticky said. "All those things were dancing around in my head; I just couldn't put them together quickly enough." He cleared his throat. "By the way, I'm terrified right now. Am I doing a good job of hiding it from Tai?"

Reynie gave him a rueful smile. "I think so. Am I?"

They nodded at each other, then signaled to Tai and Constance that the humming could cease.

"I was thinking about S.Q.'s big feet!" Tai announced. "Guess what I was humming?"

"It's about time!" Constance snarled. She pointed at the closed door they'd come through. "Why hasn't the barrier dropped? Do you realize they're on their way?"

"We do," Sticky said gravely. "Evidently, Kate hasn't reached the security door yet." He sat in front of the computer and typed out a command. "Okay, it's ready to go. One push of the button and I can drop the barrier."

"Come on, Kate," Reynie murmured. "Get there."

"They're almost here," Constance said.

"Should Sticky push the button?" Tai asked.

Reynie lifted his walkie-talkie. "Confirm you're almost to the security door? Over."

There was no reply.

"She's probably too busy punching in the code," Sticky said, offering Tai a strained look of optimism. "We'll know in a second when the warning goes off."

But no warning sounded. And no reply came from Kate. Reynie hailed her again. Still no reply.

"They're at the end of the passageway!" Constance said. "They're coming!"

There was no help for it. Sticky pushed the button.

A hidden bell began to clang. From a speaker by the door came a recorded voice: "Warning! Step away from all doorways! Warning! Step away from all doorways!"

"That's so loud!" Tai yelled over the noise. He was looking uncertainly back and forth between the control room's two doors. "Do I need to step away?"

"You're fine," Reynie said, squeezing the boy's shoulder. He tried not to sound defeated. "You're fine, buddy."

From the gap over the door a sheet of crystal-clear material dropped with alarming speed. If Tai gasped, no one heard it over the clamor. Then the clamor halted, and all was silent.

"The barrier thing worked," Tai whispered. "That's good, right?"

The others nodded, but no one spoke. With all the strat-egizing and humming and riddle-solving, there had been no time to dwell on what might be about to happen. But now it had happened. They were stuck in this section with no way out, and McCracken was on his way. The barrier would keep them safe for the moment, but the Ten Men would get through it eventually. It was only a matter of time.

Reynie swallowed with some difficulty. "We need to find out what happened to Kate," he said. Yet no sooner had he said this than Kate's voice suddenly blared out of their walkie-talkies.

"You all...still there?" she said, speaking through gasps of breath. "Did the barriers...go down?"

"At least she's okay," Sticky muttered. He raised his walkie-talkie. "Roger that. Where are you, Kate?"

"I have...to be honest," came Kate's reply. "That panel was a lot...harder to rewire...than I..."

"You have got to be *kidding* me!" Reynie cried, leaping forward to change the monitor display.

The image flickered, then revealed a corridor at the end of which an open electrical panel was plainly visible, a bucket on the floor beneath it, and beside the bucket, sprawled on her back with a walkie-talkie in her hand, a visibly gasping Kate Wetherall.

"Hooray!" Tai said, throwing his hands into the air.

The others all felt like cheering, too. Just like that, they were back to plan A.

Sticky spoke into his walkie-talkie. "You're the miracle we needed, Kate. But why didn't you do what Reynie said? We're looking at you through the camera, by the way."

On the monitor they saw Kate wiggle the fingers of her free hand. Evidently, it was the best wave she could muster. Her other hand pressed the button of her walkie-talkie, and she said, "I've known...Reynie...a long time. You think... I didn't guess...what that was about?" She paused for a few breaths, then added, "I told you...I could do it...didn't I?"

They were all looking at one another, shaking their heads, still in awe.

Reynie lifted his walkie-talkie. "Roger that, Kate," he said. And then with a little laugh he pushed the button again. "Roger that."

THE WOLF
AT THE
DOOR

With a glance at the computer, Sticky confirmed that Kate had rewired the electrical panel properly. The barrier over the barracks entrance, "believing" it was already down, had not dropped. Nor would it when the four of them entered the override codes for the security doors between themselves and the barracks entrance. Once they were in position there and Kate had rewired the panel, they'd be able to trigger that barrier as they slipped into the barracks, leaving one more obstacle between them and the Baker's Dozen.

Reynie told Kate that they would notify her when they

were ready. Kate, still lying on the floor, presented a weak thumbs-up to the camera. Reynie switched the monitor to a view of an empty corridor.

"Time to move," Sticky said quietly. He rose and put on his backpack.

Constance, however, had crossed her arms and was glaring at the barrier. She gave every impression of staying exactly where she was.

Tai, for his part, was looking apologetically at Reynie. "I guess I shouldn't have cheered," he said in a meek voice. "I don't know why, but I'm sorry."

Reynie, taken aback, tried not to show it. He had been worrying about Tai's cheer; it was true. "You don't need to be sorry," he said. He jerked his thumb toward the barrier. "I would just rather those meanies not know you're here if we can help it. Same goes for you, Constance. Let's get you out of this room pronto."

In response, Constance merely intensified her glare.

"Constance?"

Sticky took Tai's hand. "Let's have a look at those ramps," he said in a cheerful voice. "We can wait for these two at the top."

"Okay!" said Tai, eagerly tugging Sticky to the door.

Sticky gave Reynie a look that said "good luck," then closed the door behind them.

"So I guess we're waiting to say hello?" Reynie said. When Constance didn't respond, he took a deep breath and moved to stand by her side. His mouth was dry, and he found he didn't know what to do with his hands. First he crossed his arms like Constance's, then he let them hang at his sides, and finally he clasped his hands behind him.

They didn't wait long.

A knock sounded at the door behind the barrier. "Little pig, little pig, let me in!" The doorknob turned, the door opened, and McCracken filled its frame. His shoulders almost touched the doorjambs on either side of him. His glistening, well-coiffed brown hair almost brushed the ceiling. It was impossible to see beyond him into the passage.

McCracken smiled, revealing a row of perfectly straight, perfectly white teeth. "Aren't you going to say something about your chinny-chin-chins? No?" He tapped the barrier with a fingernail, then leaned forward to sniff it, his huge nostrils flaring. "Glastanium," he said. "Well, well, that's top-notch. I suppose the idea is that when the special forces arrive, they want to be able to see what's waiting for them on the other side."

Reynie said nothing. He could feel his clasped hands trembling behind his back. He knew he and Constance were protected by the barrier, but in the looming presence of McCracken, he didn't feel the least bit safe.

"I have a little secret for you," McCracken said. "No one is going to be arriving. No special forces. No help. Just us." He put on a pitying look. "Are you hoping I'm wrong? Are you thinking that even now a distress signal is being sent out to the mainland, where officials are scrambling to respond? Do you think a whole army of special operatives is being dispatched to help you? Is that what you're counting on? Is that why you're standing here so defiantly? You think everything's going to be all right?" He clucked and shook his head. "Poor, sad little chickies."

Reynie had no answer for this. He waited to see if Constance would say something, but she only glared at McCracken. If she felt the fear he felt, she certainly didn't show it.

"Here is the truth," McCracken went on. He drummed his fingers on the barrier, a jaunty little *tap-tap-tap-TAP.* "We have our Disrupter up and running. We've plugged into the tidal turbine power grid, so it will function as long as we need. No signals from the island can reach the mainland, I'm afraid. And when we take *this* down"—he rapped the barrier so sharply with one knuckle that Reynie and Constance flinched at the sound—"we'll do it so quietly you won't even hear it yourselves."

"How exactly do you intend to do that?" Reynie said. He spoke casually, as if genuinely curious. "Doesn't the blast radius of your calculator bombs exceed the range of your noise-cancellation device? Wait, no, don't tell me. I suppose you've brought some sort of armor for the device. Or else you plan to shelter it in one of the rooms off the passage. That's risky, though. The walls between your section and ours have been reinforced, but I don't know about the walls of those rooms on your side."

McCracken looked amused. "Why, Reynie dear, are you actually trying to help me?" He put his hands on his massive chest. "I'm touched. You're very kind. Or perhaps you're hoping to slow us down by making us rethink our plans. Hmm? If you must know, we have armor for our device, *and* we intend to shelter it in the nearest room. It's being installed as we speak. Do you intend to wait around for the show, or shall we catch up with you later?"

"We'll be moving along," Reynie said. Constance didn't move, however, and so he remained where he was, hands behind his back, as if simply waiting for the appropriate moment.

"A wise decision," McCracken said. "Much better for your health in the short-term, at any rate. But, Reynie, as long as we're speaking candidly, allow me to make a proposal. This one," he said, flicking his fingers in Constance's direction without looking at her, "this little scowling songbird of yours, is of great interest to me. I can't tell you how delighted I am to discover she's here with you. Now, what if I were to tell you that I would actually *help* you make your precious delivery to your beloved Mr. Benedict? I understand you're finding it challenging—I have it on good authority that you've been in here racking your brains to solve some kind of riddle. Oh, does that surprise you? I know a great many things you might not expect.

"At any rate," McCracken continued, with a friendly smile, "I would gladly help you, and what's more, I would *guarantee* your safety. I would! Because, you see, I don't truly consider you a threat. We could work out an arrangement for your friends, as well. All you have to do is give us your little scowler here. Oh, see how she scowls!" He laughed and turned his gaze directly on Constance. "Does that frighten you, ducky? To know that you're important to us? To consider that your friends might give you up to save themselves?"

"That doesn't frighten her," Reynie said, his voice quavering with anger, "because she knows it isn't a possibility."

"Well, well," McCracken said, still gazing at Constance with amusement. "If a look could hurt me, I'd be in agony right now, wouldn't I?"

A voice from behind McCracken called out: "Almost ready, old sport!"

With an expression of mock regret, McCracken bowed. "I'm so sorry we'll have to interrupt our little chat for now. But, Reynie dear, do keep my proposal in mind. You may find it easy to reject now, with this barrier between us. Later, however, you may find it suits your purpose to give the offer more serious thought."

"Don't count on it," Reynie said coolly.

For the first time, Constance moved. Her arms still crossed, she stepped forward until she was inches from the barrier. McCracken raised his eyebrows. He cocked his head to the side and waited to see what she would do.

"Your pants are unzipped," Constance said simply. Then she turned on her heel and walked to the door. Reynie quickly followed her, but not before he saw McCracken give a start and check his zipper.

"Made you look!" Constance called without even glancing back. She threw open the door and went out.

Up the ramps they hurried, joining Sticky and Tai at the top, then up a stairway into the old classroom building, where they used the override code to pass through the first security door. They scurried down a remarkably long corridor, the appearance of which had a strange effect on the Society members, for although in their time at the Institute they'd never been down this particular one (which lacked the yellow tiles that indicated to students which corridors were permissible), in all other respects the tiles, stone walls, and ceilings were both intimately familiar and weirdly alien. It was a place from a dream—a bad dream, at that—and yet as their feet quickly covered ground, they all felt how far they had traveled in other ways since their last days here.

"Surely the ceilings aren't actually lower, are they?" Sticky puffed.

"I was wondering the same thing," said Reynie, puffing even harder because he was carrying Tai on his back. "I think our eyes are just a little closer to them now."

"I don't like them at *all!*" Tai declared in a tone that suggested he actually *did* like them but felt it polite to say otherwise.

Constance said nothing, only cast sidelong angry looks at Reynie, which he was trying to ignore.

They had just passed through the second security door when they felt, but did not hear, the first calculator blast. The walls shivered, and dust fell from the ceiling above them. The second blast came a minute later. They tried to quicken their steps, with only moderate success.

"They're in the secondary control room," Constance panted. Her eyes were open, but they had a dazed look about them, and she was running with her hand on Sticky's elbow, letting him guide her as she peered mentally elsewhere. "They have the schematics up on the computer. He's sending his fastest men ahead, giving them laser pointers to get through the security doors. They're trying to catch us before we reach the barracks."

"Too bad for them!" Tai declared. "Right?"

The others made unintelligible gasping replies.

"Reynie, why are you thinking about S.Q.'s feet again?" Tai said, laughing. "And why are you pretending to be afraid of them?"

"Here's the next security door," panted Reynie, whose fear was very real, though not actually related to S.Q. Pedalian's feet.

Sticky quickly punched in the code, and the four of them burst through the door. Straight ahead in the distance they saw the final security door—the entrance to the barracks. And halfway down the corridor on the left was the one that Kate would use as a shortcut.

Even as they spotted it, Kate's voice came over their walkie-talkies: "Any day now, people."

Sticky ran down to the door on the left, entered the code, and held the door open. "Wire away," he gasped into his walkie-talkie. "And I know it goes without saying, but, um…the faster the better."

"That did go without saying" was Kate's reply.

Constance, Reynie, and Tai hurried to the end of the corridor, where they waited by the barracks entrance. Tai tapped Reynie on the shoulder and pointed happily at the gap in the ceiling. Yes, up there was the barrier that would save them from their pursuers…but only if Sticky had properly understood the schematics, and Kate rewired the panel properly, and Kate managed to get from there to here before McCracken's fastest men caught up to them.

"Yep," Reynie said. He found he could say nothing more.

Something clicked inside the wall. From a distance came the sound of rapid, pounding footsteps. Reynie watched Sticky at the other door, eager for a sign of Kate's appearance.

"Uh-oh," said Constance. She was looking down the corridor at the security door through which they had just come. It was closed, and it looked just as it had before she spoke, but Reynie's stomach flopped.

He listened to Kate's footsteps growing louder by the second, made a quick mental calculation, and entered the code. A bell began to clang. The recorded voice issued its repetitive warning. Sticky let go of the door he was holding open and ran toward the others. An instant later Kate flew through the closing door, her bucket once again securely fastened at her hip.

An instant after that, a glowing red spot appeared near the handle of the security door at the other end of the corridor. The door handle clattered to the floor. The door opened.

Reynie was reaching for the door in front of him when suddenly Kate was beside him smashing it open, shoving him and Tai through it, reaching back to grab Sticky and Constance and yanking them forward, too, faster than they could have moved on their own, and finally leaping through the door herself just as the barrier came down.

No sooner had it dropped into place than two razor-sharp pencils cracked against it and fell in pieces to the floor. In the open doorway at the end of the corridor, the Katz brothers shrugged, exchanged looks of mutual regret, and retreated from view.

"Hooray!" Tai shouted as he climbed to his feet (for Kate's push had sent him and Reynie sprawling to the floor), and he skipped from person to person, giving hugs. The others, in various states of agitation and excitement from their close call, hugged him back fiercely.

They were in a large, dimly lit place with very high

ceilings, rather like a gymnasium missing its bleachers, at the center of which appeared to be a small garden of flowering plants. The gurgle of a fountain could be heard from the direction of the garden. Reynie, wondering about the plants' need for sunlight, looked up at the high ceiling and discovered three skylights—no doubt made of glastanium, and currently reflecting the soft artificial lights from below.

As the others stood taking it all in, Tai moved toward the garden. After two steps there was a clonking sound, and he staggered backward rubbing his face. He giggled. He had walked directly into a transparent wall.

"I think it's a kind of exercise space," Reynie said. He pointed toward the garden. "You can just make out our reflections there, see?" (Everyone stared, and sure enough, barely visible, ghostly versions of themselves were assembled among the plants.) "The garden's surrounded by glastanium, too. Between that wall and this one there's a lot of room for walking around. Did you see this on the blueprints, Sticky?"

"Yes, though they didn't identify the nature of the room. We're in a protected passage that runs around the perimeter." Sticky pointed to the far right corner of the huge room. "There's a door back there that leads to the main control room. And on the opposite side, to the left of the garden, is a hallway that leads to the security suites—the empty ones, that is. There's almost certainly a barrier blocking it off now."

Everyone squinted in that direction, and sure enough, they could all see the opening of the far-off hallway, but the dim light and distance prevented all but Kate from spotting the barrier.

"What can I tell you?" Kate said. "I have good eyes. So,

George, you said the *empty* security suites are down that hallway. What about Mr. Curtain's?"

"His is separated from all the others," Sticky replied. "It's on the right side, beyond the control room."

"Mr. Curtain gets his own special space?" Tai asked.

"It's the most secure," Sticky replied. "Not that it's likely anybody could break out of the other security suites, but Mr. Curtain's is that much harder. There's one more thing from the gold key that we'll have to figure out to reach Mr. Benedict. I'll share it when we get there."

"Why are they called security suites?" Tai asked. "That sounds really nice—like sweets that you eat—but if you're in one, aren't you a prisoner? Which *isn't* nice."

Sticky smiled and tapped his nose. "Exactly. It's kind of a joke. When this place was the Institute, there were lots of things that sounded nice but actually weren't."

"Everyone rested up?" said Kate, who didn't seem very well rested herself. In fact, she appeared to be trembling. Her race to the electrical panel had taken a toll on her. "We should get moving. Who knows how long we have?"

"I do," Constance said flatly. She was digging something out of a pocket in her flight suit. A granola bar. She handed it to Kate. "Here, eat this. I think you need it."

Kate accepted it gratefully. "Why in the world do you have a granola bar?"

Constance shrugged. "Number Two offered it to me back at Mr. Cole's house. I only accepted because I thought it was a candy bar."

"Constance, did you just say that you know how long we have?" Reynie asked.

"Yep," said Constance tersely. "And the reason I know is because I read McCracken's mind. They only had three laser pointers and two calculator bombs left. They've used them all up, which means they can't get through this barrier. It won't lift for twenty-four hours, right? So, yeah, I know how long we have."

Tai lifted his hands as if to cheer, but sensing that the mood was not quite right for cheering, he lowered his hands again and said nothing.

"Well done," said Reynie, though he could tell from Constance's look and tone that she would just as soon bite him as accept any compliment from him. "I thought you might be trying to find that out. That's one reason I mentioned the calculator bombs to him—to make him think specifically about them."

"Yeah, well, I didn't need your help," Constance snapped. "Any more than I needed you to tell me to get out of that room. I'm done with you deciding things for me without asking."

"What? Constance, of all times—"

"How about we move this conversation into the control room?" Sticky interrupted. He pointed through the barrier. "I'd rather not be standing here when they show up. I don't want to have to look at them looking at me."

They all knew what Sticky meant. Few things were as unnerving as having a Ten Man stare at you, so casually sure of his power over you, so certain that he could crush you under his heel—and so happy to do just that if the opportunity arose.

"Let's do," said Kate, leading the way. She took a small

canteen from inside her jacket, sipped from it, and handed it to Tai. "And how about everybody has a drink of water? Maybe that will help us calm down."

"It's full!" Tai declared. "Didn't you drink any after you ran?"

"I was too tired to unscrew the cap," Kate said.

By the time they entered the control room, everyone had had a drink of water. But not everyone had calmed down. Constance stalked to an empty bench against the rear wall (the bench was the only noticeable difference between the main control room and the secondary one), pulled her hair over her eyes, and sat down in a huff. Tai climbed onto the bench beside her, swinging his legs and watching with interest to see what the others would do.

"They aren't just going to give up," Reynie said.

"No," Sticky agreed, taking a seat at the computer. "I'll see if I can figure out what they might try."

The two monitors on the wall currently displayed the empty front plaza and the entrance to the barracks. Reynie went to the control board and began flipping switches. "The secondary control room only had access to the security cameras in the outer section. This one connects to all of them. We can see out there, but they can't see in here, so that's something, anyway."

"Can we see what they're up to?" Kate asked.

Reynie quickly ran through all the views of the classroom building corridors. All of them empty. "They must still be in that control room," he said. "Probably sitting at the computer, doing exactly what we're doing—trying to figure out how they might get in here."

"That would be a tight fit!" Tai said. "The whole Baker's Dozen?"

"Good point," Reynie said. "Some are probably still out in the passage."

He began flicking through displays of the barracks. There weren't a great many: There was the exercise space; a few long, curving corridors; an empty room of no obvious purpose; the open doorways of the dozen or so unoccupied security suites ("They look cozy!" Tai remarked); various maintenance closets, storage rooms, and a staff lounge; part of a long hallway whose walls, curiously enough, were painted in a green plaid pattern; and, finally, a large, mysterious-looking space with an extremely wide gap in the floor and, beyond the gap, another security door.

"George," said Reynie, "can you give us some explanations about what we're seeing here?" He flipped the views back to the empty room.

Sticky looked up from the computer. "That's a safe room," he said. "If there's a breakout or some other kind of threat, any guards or staff in this section can run in there and drop a barrier over the doorway. It can also be dropped from here in the control room. It isn't on the same system as the other barriers—it doesn't get triggered by override codes or anything like that—but it works the same way. If you drop the safe-room barrier, a distress signal goes out, and it won't open for twenty-four hours. Well, unless the people in the safe room push the button again, in which case the clock resets for another twenty-four hours. That way they can stay safe for as long as necessary."

"What if you had to go to the bathroom?" Tai asked.

"There's a toilet in there," Sticky said. "The camera just doesn't show it."

Tai wrinkled his nose.

"Could a person inside the safe room raise the barrier if everything seemed okay?" Reynie asked.

"Evidently not. I think it's to prevent a hostage situation. If you were in the safe room, but I wasn't, and a prisoner was threatening to hurt me if you didn't raise the barrier—well, you might raise it. But what if the prisoner was lying? I think the system was designed to avoid that kind of scenario."

"Okay, and what about the last two places?" Kate asked. "I'm curious about the green plaid hallway. I mean, I think I can guess where it leads."

Reynie changed the displays accordingly. Sticky glanced at the computer screen, then back at the displays. "You're right—the green plaid hallway leads back to Mr. Curtain's security suite. It takes you to that giant, weird-looking room with part of the floor missing. The door on the other side of the gap is the entrance to his security suite."

"Which is where my *dad* is!" Constance cried, leaping to her feet. "If it's that simple, we should go straight there! He needs the serum!"

"And so does Mr. Curtain!" Tai said, likewise leaping.

Constance shot him a look. "Like I care."

Tai shrugged. "It's true, though."

"There's a problem," Reynie said, pointing to the display of the green plaid hallway. "I didn't see it at first, but I knew something looked odd. See that small shiny spot in the air? That's light reflecting off something."

"A barrier?" Kate said.

"He's right," said Sticky, furiously typing at the computer again. "It dropped when we entered the override code."

"Are you kidding me?" Constance shouted. "That means we're cut off from my dad! Why didn't you think about that *before?*"

"Because I didn't *know* before!" Sticky snapped. "I haven't had complete information, Constance! I'm doing the best I can!"

Reynie cut in, speaking softly. "If you want to blame someone, Constance, blame me. I figured it would happen. This was the only way—"

"You *what?*" Constance snarled. She grabbed Reynie's arm and shook it. "You *what?*"

"Okay, okay," Kate interjected, making "calm down" gestures with her hands. "Let's all take deep breaths here. We—oh, very good, Tai, you can let it out now—we have time to work on the problem. Mr. Benedict's going to be okay. The rest of us know this, Constance, and if you concentrate, you'll see that. He's not suffering or sick or anything like that, all right? He's fine, and we have time to figure out how to reach him."

"Um," Sticky said. He pointed at the computer screen. "That actually might be...changing. Someone's in the system. He's altered something."

"Probably Sharpe," Kate said. "He's a computer expert."

"It *is* Sharpe," growled Constance, who had released Reynie's arm and covered her eyes.

"Give me a minute," Sticky said. He paged through a few screens of computer code. He lingered on the last screen for several seconds. "Okay, not good." He turned in his chair to face them. "He found a loophole."

"What is it with all these loopholes?" Constance cried. She crossed her arms and began to pace.

Sticky cleared his throat. "Here's the thing: Sharpe couldn't just give a command to raise the barriers. They don't work that way. It's impossible. But what he figured out he *could* do, with some clever reprogramming, was change the time interval."

"Can you override it?" Kate asked.

"Not until the cycle's complete. Once the barriers go up, I can change it back and fix the loophole. And I can enter the command to drop them again right away—but there's that ten-second delay."

"Right," said Reynie. "And we can be sure they'll be gathered at the entrance to this section, ready to hurry through the moment the barrier goes up. Okay, what sort of deadline are we looking at? How much time?"

Sticky rubbed his head. "He changed the interval from hours to minutes. So, well . . . twenty-four minutes."

"Twenty-four *minutes*?" Constance cried.

"Is that bad?" asked Tai, looking from face to face. "I feel like that's bad."

"Not necessarily," said Reynie.

Everyone turned to stare at him.

"In fact," Reynie said, "I think it's exactly what we need."

Of all times and places

They solved our problem for us," Reynie said, speaking quickly. "When that barrier at the entrance goes up, so will the ones over the doors that lead to the security suites—both the empty ones and Mr. Curtain's—and we'll be ready. Constance, you and Tai and Sticky will be waiting at the barrier that leads to Mr. Benedict. Kate, you'll be waiting at the one that leads to the other security suites. I know, I know, just give me a second," he said when everyone began to speak at once. The others fell silent.

"The reason you'll be over there, Kate," Reynie explained, "is because we need McCracken to see someone going in that direction. We need to lure them that way, and you're the obvious choice. If you can draw them deep into that section, you can seal yourself off from them in the safe room. And then from here *I* can seal *them* off by dropping the barriers again. George can show me the command sequences. The Ten Men will be stuck—they won't be able to get to anyone. We can have a whole army of law enforcement waiting here when the barriers go up in twenty-four hours.

"In the meantime," Reynie went on, "the rest of you will be safe on the other side of your own barrier, figuring out how to get to Mr. Benedict—and you'll have plenty of time, without McCracken breathing down your necks."

"I kind of like it," said Kate. "I also kind of hate it. What happens if I don't manage to get them to follow me? Or what if they split up? You'd be a sitting duck in here."

Reynie turned to Sticky. "Do you think Kate's bucket would hold up under a barrier?"

Sticky looked dubious. "It…might? You're thinking I could place it so that the barrier wouldn't go all the way to the floor."

"Right, and I could follow you and squeeze under the barrier if I had to make a run for it."

"First of all, it's risky," Sticky said. "Second of all, shouldn't you be the one going to Mr. Benedict? I already know what to do on the computer here, and you're our best problem solver. I told you there was one more thing to figure out by using the gold key."

"Yes, but we have walkie-talkies," Reynie argued. "I could still help you from here—"

Kate huffed with exasperation. "That works both ways, Reynie Muldoon! Why couldn't Sticky use the walkie-talkies to help *you*? You should be there. You might notice something the rest of us would miss."

"Well, but Sticky has the serum—"

"That's ridiculous!" Constance barked. "As if Sticky can't just give you his backpack? What in the world are you thinking?"

"Oh!" exclaimed Tai. "He's thinking that because he's suggesting a risky plan, he should be the one who takes the risk!"

Reynie grimaced.

"*Thank* you!" Kate said. "Finally something that makes sense! Also, Reynie, you have *got* to stop doing this."

"Doing what?" Reynie asked, though he knew the answer. He crossed his arms, feeling strangely upset. It was because the uncomfortable truth was all coming out, he realized. Of all times and places, here it came.

"Trying to do things your own way!" Kate cried. "I mean, it's fine to do things your own way, but not when we're working together as a team. Think about it—what would have happened if I'd done what you said, and skipped the electrical panel? What kind of mess would we be in then?"

"She's right," said Sticky, who felt upset in much the way Reynie did, though he was less certain of the reason. He only knew that he was afraid of the conversation, but here they were, having it. "I thought it made sense when you mentioned it, I admit. But we should have trusted her. Just like you should have trusted me with the full truth about those blueprints. You could have told me there was a time limit. I don't like being under pressure, true, but I could have handled it."

"These are the things you're complaining about?" Reynie replied. He felt hurt and angry and was struggling not to. "You all realize that I've been doing my best under extreme pressure, right? I'm supposed to be this great problem solver, but when I see what looks like the best solution, I'm not supposed to act on it? When there's so much at stake?"

"Not without asking us first!" Kate said. "Unless you have absolutely no choice, you have to bring us in! If we fail, we fail, but at least we do it together. We're still a team, right? You haven't gone off to be some star student at a university yet, you know."

Reynie was taken aback. "What's that supposed to mean? What does that have to do with any of this?"

"She means—" Sticky began, then cleared his throat when he found his voice trembling with emotion. "She means that we know you feel like we're holding you back, but as long as we're all still here, shouldn't we—" Here Sticky's voice cracked, and he didn't finish.

"Are you being serious?" Reynie asked. He looked back and forth between Kate and Sticky. "*That's* what you think? But it's the exact opposite! I've always felt like I'm at my best *because* of you. I just, I don't know—other people go to universities, and I had these opportunities and figured I should consider them and—" He shrugged. "The truth is that I don't know that I want to go right now. The idea scares me.

It would be much easier to stay home with all of you. But, you know, obviously that isn't going to last forever. You both have your own plans...." He trailed off, avoiding their gazes.

"Why are we talking about *this* right now?" Tai said in a hushed voice. "It's so weird!" He was looking anxiously from face to face.

"The question is why we haven't talked about it sooner," Kate said. "I guess, speaking for myself, it's that the whole thing's made me uncomfortable. I don't like the thought of us splitting up, even if I do want to become an agent, like Milligan. So I've just avoided the subject. Which I realize is dumb."

"Same here," Sticky said. "I've been afraid of feeling hurt. But I was feeling hurt anyway, so why not come right out and talk about it with my closest friends? I would trust you with everything else, but not this? It's ridiculous."

"It is ironic," Reynie said with a sheepish smile. "We've done an awful lot of dangerous things, but we've been afraid to have a conversation." He took a deep breath, let it out, and said, "I'm really sorry. I don't know why—"

"It's because he wants to protect you!" Tai announced. "Wow, Reynie, your thoughts are really loud right now! You feel like you make mistakes because you love them and want to protect them so much, but you don't always do it the right way!"

Reynie blinked. "Oh my goodness, Tai. Okay."

Kate laughed. "Tai, someone needs to tell Reynie that we all want to protect him, too. I think sometimes problem solvers just want to control things a little too much."

It was at this point that Constance broke. She had been following this conversation—in which she seemed not to be included at all—with a rising fury. All her feelings suddenly concentrated into a single emotion, and Constance screamed. So loudly and piercingly did she scream that all the others cried out and covered their ears and looked wildly about them for the source of her anguish. Then she stopped screaming and turned her red eyes on Reynie, Sticky, and Kate, who instantly understood that *they* were the source.

"What about *me*?" Constance demanded. "You all think you've done a bad job talking to one another? Do any of you remember that there used to be a *fourth* member of the Society? I know I'm a lot younger than the rest of you, and I didn't used to think about that very much. But I'm not a little kid anymore, and I'm still supposed to be part of the team, am I not? You all make your secret plans and have your secret discussions, and you've all been thinking about whether or not it was okay to go away and do your own things—but all you're worried about is each *other*. Have you ever considered what it will be like for *me* if you all go? I don't have any friends my own age. I don't have any friends at *all*."

"I'm your friend!" Tai said, raising his hand.

Constance ignored him. "Yes, I know that you've had to keep some things from me to be on the safe side, because of the Listener and Tai. Which, by the way, I'm telling you right now that I can handle. I know I can keep the Listener out of my head now, and out of Tai's, too, if he's with me. Just for your information, you know, in case anyone cares at all about what's going on with *me*. No, let me finish!"

The others, all of whom had begun to speak, closed their mouths.

"I get that part," Constance went on. "I really do. But the

rest of it is really unfair! And I guess I'm just going to say that right now, because I may never have the chance again. It just seems pretty clear to me that you're all more important to one another than I am to you, and it really hurts, and I really hate it. You especially, Reynie. You used to be the best at making me feel like I was a part of things, but not anymore. Thanks for forgetting about me. That's all." With that, Constance pulled her hair over her eyes and crossed her arms and dropped onto the bench.

"Oh, Connie girl," Kate said after a pause. "I'm so sorry."

"Me too," said Sticky.

"Me too, Constance," said Reynie.

(Tai whispered, "Me too," just to be included.)

The older three all looked at one another, alternately nodding and shaking their heads. At last Kate said, "I'm going to tell her."

Reynie said, "I don't think—"

But Kate, eyebrow arched, interrupted him. "Reynie, what did we just talk about?"

Reynie bit his lip.

Constance had parted her hair and was looking up at Kate with hooded eyes. "Tell me what?"

Kate stepped over to the bench and knelt down before Constance. "First of all, you shouldn't feel that way about Reynie. This whole thing was his idea."

"What...what whole thing?"

"Before I tell you, is it true what you just said to us? You're absolutely, positively sure you can keep the Listener out of your head? And out of Tai's, as well? And you will make absolutely certain to keep focusing on that, no matter what? Because there's a lot riding on this, you know. But whatever you tell me, I'm going to trust you. We're all going to trust her, right, boys?"

Reynie and Sticky nodded. Tai had waited to see what they would do, and now he nodded, too.

Constance rolled her eyes. "Yes, I'm absolutely, positively sure, and I will make absolutely certain."

"Okay, then. Well." Kate clapped her hands against her knees. "Constance, my dear, this whole thing is a trap. The KEEP is a trap. A trap for Ten Men."

Tai gasped.

"You see," Kate went on, "a long time ago Mr. Benedict mentioned to us that Mr. Curtain and the Ten Men had surely established a plan for breaking out if they were captured. It wasn't likely they could ever succeed, but as long as the Katz brothers were on the loose, there was always a chance. We didn't know what it was they were looking for, but we knew it was probably something that would help them free their comrades. And it was Reynie who said that there should be a trap waiting if that ever happened."

Constance was shaking her head in confusion. "Why...? How...?"

"Well, you can imagine that Mr. Benedict tapped his nose at this. He'd already been thinking along the same lines, of course. But it was Reynie who made the point—and Sticky and I backed him up on it—that if this ever happened, we were absolutely going to be involved. Certain things had to be kept secret from us, this was understood, but we insisted that Mr. Benedict keep us in mind as his plans developed. We made solemn vows that, no matter the time or place, whether it was soon or decades later, whether it seemed as safe as a bedtime story or as dangerous as we could imagine, the three of us were going to be involved. We talked about this with our parents, too. They weren't keen on the idea, of course, but in the end, they all agreed. After what we've been through together? After all we've done? They kind of had to."

"Even though it would be this dangerous?" Constance asked. "I don't understand. And how is this supposed to make me feel better? I can tell you're trying to, but it sounds like one more thing that you didn't include me in."

"It really does!" Tai chimed in unhelpfully.

"That's because it's all *about* you, Constance," Kate said, taking Constance's hand and squeezing it.

Constance stared. "It...what?"

Kate looked over her shoulder at Sticky and Reynie. "Shouldn't we all be telling this together?"

They nodded and came closer, and Sticky said, "We knew that if the Ten Men got loose, you would never be safe. Not for the rest of your life. There's no greater threat to a bunch of sneaky criminals' plans than a telepath, right?"

"And no greater tool for them," Kate added, "if they could capture you and use you for their own purposes."

"We also knew," Sticky continued, "that we would never let you face that threat alone. Reynie's idea was that if we were all going to end up in danger anyway, why not choose the circumstances? Why not *create* them—so that we would have the advantage?"

Constance sat in stunned silence, her eyes drifting from face to face.

"Privately we thought of this as our biggest project ever," Reynie said. He smiled. "We figured you could write a poem about it."

Constance started shaking her head. "I don't...I don't know what to say. Why were you keeping all this from me? You kept it a secret long before you knew about the Listener. Why not tell me?"

The others hesitated.

Searching their faces, Tai said, "Oh! They didn't tell you because they thought that if they tried this and somebody ended up getting hurt, you would blame yourself! They didn't want you to feel bad!"

Constance burst into tears.

"Well, I think it's good we had this little talk," Kate said, patting Constance's hand. "Now, how about we do a quick round of hugs, get these bad guys locked away, catch up with Mr. Benedict, and call it a night?"

Kate's plan was quickly initiated. There were hugs all around, with Constance crying freely the whole time, and promises of full explanations later, and, in Reynie's case, one last apology.

First came Constance's sobbing apology to him, which she murmured into his ear as she hugged him, dampening his shoulder with her tears and, unfortunately, a fair amount of snot. But when she pulled back, Reynie held on to her shoulders and looked her in the eye.

"You don't owe me an apology," he said. "Also, you're right, I haven't been doing a good job including you lately. Not just because of this big secret, but because I've been worried about myself too much. I'm really sorry."

Constance sniffled and wiped at her runny nose. "We just get used to things," she said. "I'm used to you helping me out. But I shouldn't complain about being treated like a little kid and then be mad because you aren't treating me like a little kid."

Reynie chuckled. "It's complicated. Especially when you're a genius telepath. I'll cut you some slack if you cut me some."

"It's a deal," Constance said.

"You're supposed to shake hands when you do deals," Tai said matter-of-factly, and so Reynie and Constance shook hands, which Tai found very satisfying.

"We're down to seven minutes," Sticky said. "We should get ready."

"This makes us nervous!" Tai declared, hopping from one foot to the other. Kate put an arm around him and gave him a squeeze.

"Yes, it does," Reynie said. He looked at Sticky, who was bent over the desk, hurriedly scribbling with pen and paper that Kate had given him from her bucket. "You sure about this? If it goes wrong—"

Sticky looked up at him. "I'm sure. I understand the risk. This is what we're doing, Reynie."

Reynie rubbed his furrowed brow. "But if it goes wrong..."

"Reynie. This is what we're doing." Sticky handed him the paper. "That's from the gold key. With luck I can join you, but if not, well, you'll do your thing."

Reynie stared at the paper. He gave a tight nod. "I'll do my best. But...um, George, do try to be there, won't you? I mean..."

Sticky laughed nervously. "You mean if I don't join you, it will be because I'm suffering untold horrors? Don't worry, Reynie, you can count on my trying to be there."

Reynie couldn't bring himself to laugh. "Promise me — I don't know, promise me whatever you can."

Sticky clapped his hands on Reynie's shoulders. "I promise. Let's do this."

The two embraced.

Kate slid her bucket from her belt and passed it to Tai. "You guys are going to need this," she said. "Thanks for letting me borrow it."

"But it's yours!" Tai said, giggling. "I think you should wear it all the time, the way you used to. I like it better."

Kate tousled his hair. "I think you may be right." She turned to Sticky. "I just had a little thought. I don't suppose you could disable the warning system for the barriers?"

"I would say that's a gigantic thought!" Sticky said. "And it might be possible. I'll see what I can do."

With five minutes left to go, they all wished one another luck. Kate went to the door leading back to the exercise room. Sticky gave Reynie his backpack and sat down at the computer. Beads of perspiration trembled on his scalp. He was taking slow, deep breaths. Constance, Reynie, and Tai went to the other door.

"On three?" Kate suggested.

Everyone nodded except Constance, who was looking at Reynie and frowning. "What's wrong?" she asked.

"Nothing, nothing," Reynie said, shaking his head. "I can tell you later. All right, Kate. On three."

"He's thinking about S.Q.'s feet," Tai whispered.

"Are we doing this countdown or not?" Kate asked, for if Reynie was trying to keep Tai out of his head for some reason, the distraction would certainly help. "Tai, do you want to start us off?"

"Okay!" said Tai, and he began: "One..."

The others all joined in: "Two..."

Then Reynie groaned and said, "Wait." He looked at Constance with a pained expression. "I don't want to suggest this."

Constance blinked. She stared at him. And then she said, "Oh! Of course!"

"I know you want to get to Mr. Benedict as soon as possible," Reynie said. "And this is much riskier. But..."

"No, of course, this makes the most sense! It's our best chance of succeeding!" Constance gave him a quick hug and hurried across the room to join Kate. "I'm coming with you," she said. "No offense, but I'm much better bait than you are. And I can nudge them when we go by to make them think we're joining up with the others. They'll follow us for sure—they'll have no reason to come this way."

Sticky let out a gush of air. "Oh, wow. I like this new plan. Oh my goodness." He took the cloth from his pocket and patted his damp scalp.

"Thank you, Reynie," Constance said.

Reynie nodded. "Stay safe, you two."

They all looked appreciatively at one another, and then expectantly at Tai, who caught the hint.

"Three!"

THE BAIT, THE BARRIER, AND THE BATTLE

They're waiting at the barrier," Constance said as she and Kate left the control room. "Every one of them."

"Perfect," said Kate. "We can give them a little wave as we pass by."

"I'll be doing more than that," Constance said in a low tone.

Moving at a brisk trot, the two followed the passageway along the wall of the exercise room. Sure enough, McCracken's enormous frame filled the entrance. It was rather disconcerting to be running toward him; from a distance there appeared to be nothing to prevent his lunging forward and seizing them as they went past. But they knew the barrier was there, and as they drew nearer they could see his eyes following them. He looked exceedingly amused.

"Well, well, well," McCracken began when they drew within earshot. "It seems—"

"Sorry, no time to chat!" Kate interrupted, and Constance gave him a contemptuous glance.

"Oh, surely—"

"Nope!" Kate interrupted again.

They hurried past, following the passageway toward the opposite corner of the room.

"That drove him crazy," Constance said with satisfaction. "He hates being interrupted. He didn't want to call after us, though, because it's hard to sound smug when you're doing that."

"Perfect again," said Kate. "That was my intention. And how about your special project?"

"We're all on the same page now. She's told them what I was thinking—which is that you and I had split from the boys but then came to a dead end, so now we're trying to get back to them."

They were nearing the far corner of the room, where the transparent barrier blocked the entrance to a short and rather plain-looking hallway. There was a closed door at the end of it—not a security door, but it made Kate nervous enough to reach for her utility belt.

"Be advised," she said, "if that door is locked, I'll have to pick it."

Constance's eyes widened. "Really?"

"Don't worry—I'll be quick about it. Just didn't want you to be surprised." Kate tapped the barrier with her knuckle. "I don't suppose you gave them some idea of how we happen to be on the other side of this from Reynie and Sticky?"

"They know I'm mad and confused about how it happened," Constance said. "That's all I could think of."

"I can't imagine anything better," Kate said. "And how do you feel?"

Constance grimaced. "Queasy. A little trembly. I really laid it on thick until I was sure they bought it. I could hear Garrotte and Sharpe, too—they were right behind McCracken. They're all convinced. But, yeah, I don't feel so hot."

"That's what I figured," Kate said. "You're the bee's knees, my dear. Just hang in there a bit longer, and then you'll have the marvelous reward of being cooped up in a safe room with me for twenty-four hours. And the pleasure of turning the tables on these jerks, of course."

"I just hope Reynie can get to Dad quickly," Constance said. "I'm confused about how all this is supposed to work. Is there—?"

Constance didn't finish her question, however, for just then something boomed in the ceiling above them, followed by a terrific squealing sound as the barrier began to slide slowly upward. As soon as there was room, Kate rolled under it and flew to the door at the end of the hallway. It was indeed locked.

"Teeny-tiny bit of a shame Sticky didn't know about this door," Kate muttered. But with her lock-picking tools she had the door open by the time Constance joined her, and after the two of them had hurried through, she closed the door and locked it behind them.

"How far is it to the safe room?" Constance asked as they took off along a well-lit, curving corridor.

"It's a fair distance," Kate said, not wishing to discourage her. "We have to go past all the security suites to get there," she said just as they were passing the first one. Its door stood open, revealing a glimpse of a bed and a chair. "Oh, they really *are* cozy."

The security suites were spaced four to a corridor. Constance and Kate were in the second corridor, and had just passed the sixth security suite, when a great, echoing, smashing noise sounded in the distance behind them.

"That was probably McCracken opening the door," Kate panted.

"It was," Constance gasped.

The two hurried on, both breathless and exhausted now. They could hear the sounds of many footsteps, but the Ten Men were walking, not running.

"They're being careful," Constance said. "They want to make sure we're not hiding in one of the security suites waiting for them to go past us. Sorry, I have to walk." She slowed down, clutching her side.

"This really isn't the moment for walking," Kate said. "Here, it will be just like old times." She stooped forward, and Constance climbed onto her back. "Oh, wow, you've grown a bit since then."

"Was I not supposed to?" Constance retorted.

Kate staggered a few steps, adjusted her grip on Constance's legs, and set out jogging. They reached the third corridor, the sound of footsteps still echoing behind them. But they had a good lead, the sound of the footsteps diminished, and Kate's confidence grew stronger with every step, even as her legs grew weaker. And soon enough they were past the last of the security suites, curving into a fourth and final corridor, at the end of which they could see, facing them, the open doorway of the safe room. They hurried past maintenance and storage closets until finally, with profound relief, they found themselves standing outside the safe room.

The room could hardly have appeared less welcoming — no furniture, a curtained-off toilet and sink in one corner, and a big red button on the wall. But the button promised safety, and that made it beautiful. The safe room might have been a ballroom, the button a chandelier.

Constance slid down from Kate's back. "Thanks," she said absently, for her mind was elsewhere. Suddenly she frowned. "Something's wrong. The Scaredy Katz are nervous — they think something's up. She can hear them whispering about it, and it's scaring her."

Kate ushered Constance into the safe room and whipped out her walkie-talkie. "Sticky, you need to drop the barriers immediately. Over."

"There's a problem with that," came Sticky's reply. "I haven't figured out how to disable the warning system yet, and a fair number of the Ten Men are within sprinting distance of the barrier. I'm looking at them on the monitors right now. They could reach it in ten seconds. Over."

Kate raised her walkie-talkie again. "Are any of them within a ten-second sprinting distance of *us*?"

"Negative. Not yet, and they've all slowed down. They stopped. They seem to be discussing something. Over."

Kate turned to Constance. "Promise me you'll stay in here. Right now, okay? Promise me, Constance."

Constance looked distraught. "What are you going to do?"

"I'm going to draw them farther in. As soon as I do, I'll tell Sticky to drop that barrier and hightail it back here. When you see me coming, you hit the button."

Constance was shaking her head in horror. "You're exhausted! What if you don't make it? You'll be trapped out there with them!"

"Constance," Kate said firmly, "I promise you I will do my absolute best not to let that happen. Trust me on that. But I can't manage anything if I take you with me. So you have to stay in this room, no matter what. Promise me, okay? And make it snappy."

Constance fought back tears. "I promise," she said in a strangled voice.

Kate kissed her on the head and charged from the room.

The third corridor was empty, but by the time she reached the end of it, Kate could hear McCracken's deep voice. He was politely issuing some kind of order, though she couldn't make out his words. She suspected he was trying to find out why some of the others were lagging.

"Get up, Constance!" Kate hissed into empty air. "Get *up*! Reynie found them! Come on!"

Dead silence now issued from the other corridor. Just as she'd intended, she'd been "overheard." She waited, steadying her breathing, preparing herself. She thought that Sticky might tell her if her plan was working—he could see on the monitors what was happening—but then she realized that if he spoke to her over the walkie-talkie, McCracken might hear what he said.

"Sticky," she hissed into her walkie-talkie. "Wait for us there. We're almost there. Constance is dragging. Don't reply. Over."

She waited. It was very possible, she knew, that McCracken was sneaking toward her, moving in practiced silence. She withdrew a few paces. How was she supposed to know if the rest of the Ten Men were also on the move? Had McCracken silently beckoned them farther in? Or had he signaled for them to stay put? She tried to think, but her mind was racing, and all she could hear was Constance's voice in her head saying... Wait, that really *was* Constance's voice in her head! Kate shoved her other thoughts aside.

Please start over, Kate thought, and Constance did.

McCracken issued orders for the others to either catch up or send an explanation forward. Everyone is hurrying to him except for the Scaredy Katz and Crawlings. The brothers are nervous, and she's scared, and Crawlings is staying with her. They're moving, but very slowly. They're extremely wary.

Can you nudge them?

From here? No. I'm getting all this through her.

Can you reach Sticky? You can picture where he is. He isn't far.

I'll try.

Kate waited, listening hard. She heard nothing. She could envision the other corridor, could imagine a long line of elegantly dressed men standing silently in it. Or creeping quietly in her direction. *Life is weird*, she thought. Then Constance was back.

*Sticky thinks they're all out of range of the barrier now. But . . .
wait. No! Kate, the Scaredy Katz and Crawlings have changed
their minds. They know it's a trap! They're turning back!*

Kate raised her walkie-talkie. "Drop them now, Sticky!
Now, now, now!"

A clanging bell sounded in the distance. The recorded
voice issued its warnings about standing clear of the doors.

"Well, that's a shame," Kate said to herself. Into her walkie-
talkie she said, "Don't feel bad. I know you tried. Over."

From the next corridor McCracken's voice thundered:
"Come back! Don't even try, fellows—you'll never make
it! Come with me! If they wish to trifle with us, we'll make
them pay dearly! Starting with *you*, darling Kate! I know you
can hear me!"

This speech was followed by the sound of several large
men breaking into a run, and Kate's stomach seemed to
squeeze to the size of a marble. She had already turned to
flee, but she had also done the math in her head. By the time
she reached the safe room, there would be no ten-second
gap between her and her pursuers, if there was any gap at all.

"Sticky," Kate said into her walkie-talkie, "drop the safe
room barrier, too. Right now."

"Roger that," came the reply. "You have ten seconds. Please
make it."

From the fourth corridor came the sounds of the warning system. And even as Kate ran toward it, before she had
taken three steps, she knew there was no way. Her legs were
spent. She couldn't run full speed, not even close.

But Kate, being Kate, would do her best, anyway.

As she neared the end of the third corridor, she heard McCracken's footsteps suddenly grow clearer, which meant that he had rounded into view. Instinctively she dropped into a tumble, and sure enough, a pencil whizzed through the air above her. Then she was on her feet again and stumbling into the final corridor.

"Hurry!" Constance screamed from inside the safe room. She was frantically beckoning Kate with both hands.

Dutifully, if not hopefully, Kate hurried.

She was halfway there when the barrier dropped.

"Nooo!" Constance wailed. "No no no!" She banged on the barrier with her fists.

Kate slowed to a walk. So that was that. She approached the barrier until she stood face-to-face with a crying Constance on the other side. "Sorry, Connie girl. I did try my best. I promise." She saw Constance's face change and knew that McCracken had appeared in the corridor behind her. She didn't bother taking evasive action just yet. She knew that upon seeing her trapped like this, McCracken would toy with her.

"You should close that interior door," Kate said to Constance. "Things could get messy out here. You don't need to see it."

Constance scowled at her. "I will *not*."

"Well, do me a favor, anyway. Use that special noggin of yours to tell Mr. Benedict the situation here, okay? And listen to me: He's going to be fine. I promise. Things may look dicey right now, but the important thing to remember is this: We've won."

"Is that supposed to be our new stupid slogan or something?" Constance said, still crying. "Reynie was thinking the same thing outside."

"Well, it's true if you think about it. We've trapped them! Now please tell—"

"Oh dear, Kate!" McCracken called out. "I see you have *plenty* of time for a chat now! Were you hoping to find yourself on the *other* side of that barrier, by any chance? You were running so slowly, I thought you were trying to lure me into yet another trap. Ha ha! I do believe you were just tired!"

"I'm tired of your voice, that's for sure," Kate said, turning to face him.

McCracken grinned. "Is that so? Well, enjoy your witty retorts while you may, Kate, my dear. I may not seem so, but I am exceedingly angry." He held up his briefcase and gave it a jiggle. "I intend to take it out on you, I'm afraid. You may have noticed that your daddy isn't here to protect you."

Sharpe, Garrotte, and a handful of other Ten Men came into the corridor behind McCracken. The corridor was just narrow enough, and McCracken was just huge enough, that Kate couldn't see them clearly, but it didn't matter. She had a difficult road ahead of her. She saw that clearly enough.

I'm with you.

Kate stiffened. She looked back at Constance, who nodded once. Her eyes were fierce.

"Well, okay," Kate said aloud. "You and me. But take it easy on yourself, Connie girl." She took out her tranquilizer gun and turned back to McCracken, who was shaking his head in amusement.

"Do you really wish to waste your darts?" McCracken

said. "I have a briefcase. You've seen how that works. Or are you planning on tranquilizing yourself? I have to say, that would be the wisest course."

Kate shrugged. "The darts aren't for you."

"No? Do tell me for whom they're intended."

"For whoever is left," Kate said. She frowned. "Or whomever. Whatever the case, in the meantime, before you say good night, allow me to tell you that this spectacle of a bunch of huge men threatening a couple of young women is really not the thing. It's time for us to change this narrative, McCracken, my dear."

McCracken's thick eyebrows went up. "Oh my, my, my." He guffawed. "So your idea is to..." He looked suddenly confused. "Wait. This is very strange. I have a powerful urge to take out my handkerchief, place it against my nostrils, and breathe deeply."

"Knock yourself out," Kate said.

McCracken promptly did.

With their enormous leader on the floor, Sharpe and Garrotte now stood fully exposed. It is a rare thing to see a Ten Man startled, but they looked quite startled. They saw Kate's tranquilizer gun pointed at them, and each instinctively lifted his briefcase, prepared to deflect incoming darts, but Kate didn't squeeze the trigger, and their startled expressions turned to puzzlement.

Kate heard Constance give a little moan of misery behind her. Without looking back, she said, "Okay, that's more than enough. You need to lie down."

"No," groaned Constance. "Not yet."

Sharpe and Garrotte tossed their briefcases onto the

floor near McCracken's. They looked thoroughly confused, and they flapped their hands violently as if they'd just been shocked. Then, as if the motion reminded them of their shock-watches, they extended their hands and shook them until the watches were clear of their shirt cuffs. An electrical whine filled the room. The men turned toward each other like sleepwalkers. There was a flurry of wires between them, and then they, too, were on the floor.

Kate heard Constance throwing up.

"Oh, you poor thing!" she cried without looking back. "Did you at least make it to the toilet?"

"The sink," came Constance's miserable reply.

"Gross," Kate said.

The other three Ten Men in the corridor, astonished by their comrades' inexplicable behavior, had stood frozen all this time. Now, however, they leveled their gazes at Kate. She had never met these particular men, but they were familiar enough with their expensive suits, their briefcases and shiny shoes, their friendly expressions and cruel eyes. She could tell they were poised to spring. She saw their hands sliding to the latches on their briefcases. Then she saw them remove their handkerchiefs from their suit pockets and knock themselves out.

Momentarily alone in the corridor, Kate risked a glance behind her. Constance was leaning against the barrier, her horribly pale face pressed to it so that her nose looked like a pig's snout, her eyes glassy and red, her mouth hanging open.

"Oh, you beautiful, beautiful girl," Kate said. She felt tears start to her eyes. "Please lie down, Connie girl. You've done more than enough. You've saved me."

"Uh-uh," Constance moaned. She appeared to be drooling. "You...saved...*me*."

"Okay, fine. We're both pretty amazing," Kate said with a laugh. "Now lie down!"

Constance tried to shake her head, but the effort caused her to lose her balance, and she sank to her knees. Then she sagged over onto her side and drew her knees to her chest. "Maybe...just for a minute," she mumbled.

"That's the ticket," Kate said soothingly. "You rest. I'll be back in a bit to check on you."

By the time Kate had walked all the way back to the first corridor, she had fired four tranquilizer darts, and four Ten Men now lay here and there, their neckties askew, their poses anything but elegant. She would have given them other options, but although the men had lacked briefcases, they had retained their usual inclination to attack when frightened, angry, or bored, and so Kate had put them down for their naps. Now, as she made her way over the shattered door that McCracken had smashed upon his entrance, she found the Scaredy Katz staring wistfully out through the barrier, like children trapped inside on a rainy day.

"I must say I'm surprised," Kate said as they turned to look gloomily at her. "You didn't make it out?"

They shook their heads in unison. One of them—was it Felix?—said, "That devil Crawlings knocked us down in order to get past us."

"He didn't have to do that," the other brother said.

"He really didn't. He tried to make it seem like it was the woman's fault, too. Just poor form."

"Poor form indeed," the other agreed.

So Crawlings was out there, Kate thought with a pang of worry. She hoped her beloved bucket had held up under the barrier. Otherwise Sticky was in a terrible spot right now.

"Well, I've dispatched McCracken and all the others," Kate informed them. "Shall we do this the easy way?"

The Katz brothers agreed that, under the circumstances, the easy way was indeed preferable. In a life full of headaches, they said, it's always best to avoid them when one can.

"Very wise," Kate said as she locked each brother into his own security suite. "Only take necessary risks, right?"

Then, although she was very tired, Kate set about her final task. It was no easy thing to remove all the Ten Men's weapons—shock-watches and neckties, mostly, but a few of them had dagger shoes, and of course there was McCracken's dangerous tooth—then drag each man down the long corridors and lock him up in his new home. But Kate could no sooner leave all those Ten Men lying about than she could leave a table covered in dirty dishes.

And just as she often did when clearing the table, Kate whistled while she worked.

NEVER ODD OR EVEN

When Sticky had seen Crawlings and the Listener escape before the barrier dropped, his first emotion was pity for the Listener. The small woman appeared to be terrified, running awkwardly with her hands covering her face, being dragged along by the wiry Ten Man, who looked rather like a skeleton in a suit. Sticky's second emotion was mortal fear, because he knew that Crawlings would be coming this way. And even before *these* emotions hit him, Sticky had been worried about Kate, for he'd just dropped the safe-room barrier while she was still far away. And on top of *that* he was racked with guilt for failing to disable the warning system, for if McCracken hadn't heard it go off, he might have ordered everyone to follow the Katz brothers, thinking there was still a chance to get out. That would have given Kate plenty of time to sneak back to the safe room and drop the barrier herself.

It was truly a lot for Sticky to be feeling all at once. But there was only one thing to do, and that was to run for his life.

First locking the door to the exercise room (it was just a regular door, unfortunately, and he knew that Crawlings could get through it quickly), Sticky dragged the bench over in front of it, followed by the two chairs, and then fled through the opposite door.

Soon he was in the green plaid hallway, where he found Reynie and Tai waiting for him. Reynie was tugging anxiously at the straps of his backpack, but at the sight of Tai jumping up and down and pointing at Kate's bucket on the floor, Sticky's heart soared. The bucket had worked! Oh, how he loved that bucket!

Sticky plunged onto his belly, wriggled beneath the barrier to the sound of Tai's excited cheers, then pulled mightily on the bucket, trying to wrench it free so that the barrier would fall the rest of the way. He pulled, and pulled, and pulled. Reynie grabbed the bucket and pulled, too. Tai reached through their legs, found a tenuous grip with the tips of his fingers, and tried to help. The bucket didn't budge. They tried to raise the barrier even an inch so that they might slide the bucket free, but even an inch proved impossible.

"It seems very well designed," Tai said, to the bemusement of both the young men.

"I suppose it is," Reynie acknowledged.

They turned and ran.

It was a very, very long hallway, down the length of which were several doors that Sticky and Reynie hurriedly threw open, hoping Crawlings would feel compelled to investigate what lay behind them. Meanwhile Tai, who unlike Sticky and Reynie wasn't worried about what Crawlings might do to them, chattered happily all the way. "Why, do you think, do the walls have this pattern like Mr. Benedict's old suits? Is it because Mr. Curtain and Mr. Benedict both find it soothing? That's what Constance said—that green plaid is soothing to them. It used to help keep Mr. Benedict calm, which helped him with his narpo... narlo..."

"Narcolepsy," Sticky panted.

"Right! And Mr. Benedict doesn't have that problem anymore because of Constance, but Mr. Curtain still does, and I guess it makes sense that they would want him to be as calm as possible so he wouldn't be falling asleep as much when they let him go to the exercise room. Does that make sense to you?"

"Uh-huh," Sticky panted.

"Sure," Reynie panted.

"But I wonder if it works on other people, too? Do you feel calm and soothed? I think I might! I think it might be working on me!"

"That's great, Tai," Reynie wheezed.

At last the hallway took a sharp turn and opened onto the large, mysterious room they had seen on the monitor.

With its high vaulted ceiling, its tile floors, and the sound of rushing water echoing off the stone walls, the room seemed to be some strange combination of secret grotto and shopping mall atrium. The gap in its floor, which ran from wall to wall and was several meters across, turned out to be a kind of flooded canal. The water, a couple of meters below floor level and of uncertain depth, gushed along with alarming speed and turbulence. A retractable metal bridge was set into the side of the canal just below them, folded up like an accordion, with no obvious way of extending it.

They looked behind them and spotted a control board on the wall. Sticky went straight to it.

"Right here," Reynie said to Tai, pointing to a spot on the floor well away from the edge of the canal. "You can't get any closer to the water than that, okay?"

Tai gave him a jaunty salute and sat down cross-legged in precisely the spot Reynie had indicated. The little boy was enthralled by the room. "Where do you think the water comes from?"

"Well, from the harbor. I suspect it's connected to the tidal turbine system somehow."

"Do you think I'd drown if I fell in?"

"Let's not risk it. My guess is it would whisk you away and deposit you in some secure location, where you would have to be retrieved. But I don't know where that location is, or even if I'm correct, so don't you move."

"Roger that!"

Reynie joined Sticky at the control board. It had a tiny display screen at the top and a large switch on one side. The rest of it was a grid of metal buttons, below each of which was a letter from the alphabet. "Any thoughts?"

"It's a simple code system," Sticky said. "You push a button, and the corresponding letter appears on this little screen. Six letters total. Then you can extend and retract that bridge with this switch. There should be"—he turned to peer across the room—"yes, there's another control board on the opposite wall, right next to the security door."

"So if we can get to the other side, we can retract the bridge to *that* side? Meaning Crawlings couldn't get across the water? Could he flip the switch and bring it back?"

Sticky shook his head. "It doesn't look like that kind of system to me. If you retract the bridge to your side, you're the only one who has control of it. Besides, he doesn't know the code."

"Neither do we, yet."

A small splash sounded behind them. They spun around in alarm. Tai was safely where Reynie had left him, however, standing as high as he could on his knees and craning his neck to see something in the water.

"Wow, it goes so fast!" he cried.

Reynie looked at Tai's feet. "Did you just throw one of your *shoes* into the water?"

Tai laughed. "You should have seen it go!"

"Well, but now you have only one shoe."

Tai sat back again. "Oh, that's true," he said mildly. Evidently, he hadn't thought the matter through.

"By the way," Reynie said, "I should have said so sooner, but we need to be very quiet."

Tai nodded, and upon a moment's reflection, he got up and hopped over to them, using only the shoeless foot because socks, after all, are quieter than shoes.

Sticky and Reynie were studying the control board. At

exactly the same time, they both pointed to the "D" and "E" buttons. Tai giggled at this—he couldn't help it—but immediately cut himself off and whispered, "Why did you both point at those buttons?"

"They're both a bit shinier than the others," Sticky whispered, and Tai, staring, saw what he meant. Most of the buttons were dusty and, in some cases, even slightly corroded from moisture. He nodded approvingly at their detective work, and by the time their scanning eyes had settled on the "R" button, Tai had spotted it, too, and was able to point at it right when they did.

"Nice job," Reynie whispered.

The trouble was that they couldn't find any other buttons that showed signs of use. They needed six total letters, but they had only three to choose from. Each letter obviously had to be used at least once, but some obviously had to be used *more* than once. Which ones, though? And how many times each? And in what order?

"Can't we just try different sequences until we find the right one?" Tai whispered. "It's only six letters. How many sequences can there possibly be?"

"Five hundred forty," replied Reynie and Sticky at the same time. They traded amused glances and crossed their eyes.

Tai gasped. "How did you both know that? And how could there be so many?"

Sticky tried to think of a quick way to explain to Tai about combinatorial mathematics, about using the inclusion-exclusion principle to enumerate the union of finite sets, but then Reynie simply whispered that they would explain the math to him later, and Sticky, immensely relieved, took the opportunity instead to go and peek into the green plaid hallway. Still no sign of Crawlings.

"This is where we use the gold key," Reynie was saying to Tai when Sticky rejoined them, and Tai eagerly dug into his pocket.

While the two of them had been waiting at the barrier, Reynie had memorized what Sticky had written down, and then—upon Tai's pleading—had given the piece of paper to Tai with strict instructions not to drop it. ("We don't want to risk anyone else finding it," he'd said.) For this reason, Reynie's heart skipped a beat when Tai said, in a panicked whisper, that the paper wasn't there.

Then Reynie saw that Tai was searching the wrong pocket, and with a sigh of relief he pointed this out. Tai echoed his sigh, adding greater emphasis, and pulled the paper out of the other pocket. Though he hardly understood it at all, this was what it said:

For feline perambulation:
Ponder your penultimate clue.
Prepare your postulation.
One's level best one wants to do
To reach one's destination.

(No more word clues for you now—no, not another peep.
You've shown your own full-blown know-how in mastering the KEEP.)

"There are three big words that start with a *P*," Tai observed. "What's a feline—?"

"A perambulation is a walk," Reynie replied, anticipating

the rest of Tai's question. He also anticipated all the other questions Tai would ask him if he didn't quickly explain what he could, and so in a hurried whisper Reynie said, "'Feline perambulation' clearly refers to the catwalk—"

"What's a catwalk?" Tai interrupted.

Reynie blinked. He had not anticipated every question, after all. "In this case it means a narrow metal bridge or walkway, like the one over there. And 'penultimate' means 'next to last,' so, since this clue is the last clue, evidently we need to think about—or ponder—the clue that came before it, which is the one Sticky and I solved to get the override code. By 'postulation,' I think Mr. Benedict means a possible explanation for something."

"So if you ponder the other clue, it will help you figure out this one?" Tai asked.

Reynie and Sticky tapped their noses.

"What do you think?" Sticky asked Reynie.

"I think the answer may have something to do with wordplay," Reynie said. "Did you notice how the last clue used the words 'one's' and 'wants' and 'once' a lot? Words that sound very much alike? At the time I thought it might mean that the code needed to include the number one—but then the code turned out to be purely alphabetical. Now I'm thinking he was just trying to call attention to the way words look and sound. He used 'one's' and 'wants' in this one, too—I'm guessing as a reminder."

Sticky, who had come to a similar conclusion, was nodding along as Reynie spoke. "And with this one he's used a few multisyllable words that start with *P*—"

"Three!" Tai said.

"Right, three. Oh, and in the last one he referred to words like 'LIVE' and 'EVIL,' 'KEEP' and 'PEEK,' which—"

"I have it!" Reynie said, and without wasting a moment he pressed the buttons in the following sequence: REDDER. A soft buzzer sounded inside the box. He threw the switch, and behind them the catwalk began to extend across the canal.

It did so, unfortunately, very loudly. Clacking and rattling and clanking as they unfolded, the metal sections slowly stretched over the water. With Sticky and Reynie each holding one of Tai's hands, the three of them ran to stand at the edge.

Never had anything seemed to move so slowly as the catwalk did now. Repeatedly glancing over their shoulders toward the hallway, Sticky and Reynie urged the catwalk onward in their minds.

"How did you know the answer?" asked Tai, speaking up to be heard over the noise.

Reynie supposed it didn't matter at this point. "You heard Sticky mention the words 'live' and 'evil' from the last clue, right? They have the same sequence of letters—they just run in opposite directions. It's the same thing with 'keep' and 'peek.' Now, what if you put each pair of words next to each other—'live evil' and 'keep peek'? If you take them together, each pair of words is exactly the same whether you read forward or backward."

"Hey, that's true!"

"Well, that was a hint. If you look at—wait, where is that piece of paper, Tai?"

Tai let go of their hands and looked into his own, decidedly empty ones. "Oops."

Reynie turned and saw the piece of paper on the floor. He ran back for it, rejoining them just as the catwalk, with a final clatter and bang, reached the opposite side of the canal. He took Tai's hand again, and together they dashed across, their feet booming on the metal. Sticky ran to the control box, entered the code, and threw the switch. Now the process was reversed—the catwalk detached from the opposite side and, making just as much racket as before, retracted toward them.

"The catwalk goes backward and forward just like those words!" Tai said. He gave a little jump, delighted to have thought of this.

"Excellent observation," Reynie said, glancing nervously toward the hallway. Just a few seconds longer and they should be safe. "And do you know what we call a word that's spelled the same both backward and forward? A palindrome."

Tai's jaw dropped. "That's another big word that starts with *P*!"

"It sure is," Reynie said. "That was another hint. Also, there's a reason Mr. Benedict told us to do our 'level' best— 'level' is a palindrome, too, isn't it? And his final hint came when he said 'No more word clues for you now—no, not another peep.' He was telling us that the word 'peep' is a word clue. Can you guess why?"

"Because it's a pandrilome!" Tai squeaked excitedly.

"A palindrome," Reynie corrected. "But yes. Just like 'redder' is."

With a last screeching, thunking sound, the catwalk completed its journey, now snugly folded up against their side of the canal. It was a wonderful thing to see. Less encouraging, however, was the fact that Sticky had been trying without luck to get the security door open. He had entered the override code on a keypad next to the door, but nothing had happened. Assuming he had entered it incorrectly, he had tried again—twice. The door remained locked.

Reynie, who had been keeping an anxious eye on this frustrating process, glanced quickly about for another solution. Now he spotted, on the other side of the door, a tiny speaker with an intercom button.

Sticky followed his gaze. "Oh!" he cried, and leaped to push the button. "Hello in there! Mr. Benedict?"

There was a pause, and then: "My dear George, is that you? How delightful to hear your voice! And Reynie and your charming new friend are both with you, is that correct?"

"That's correct!" Tai shouted. He was very excited to be meeting Mr. Benedict at last.

"We're expecting less-pleasant company any moment, though," Sticky said. "I don't suppose you could give us the code to the door?"

"Of course," came Mr. Benedict's reply. "I can't say it aloud—Ledroptha might overhear me—but I can point you to it easily enough. It's one of my favorite words, and I said as much over a particularly lovely dinner last fall, when you had all taken turns jumping into the spectacular pile of leaves that Kate had raked up."

"Were we eating roasted apples when you told us?" Sticky asked.

"Indeed!"

Reynie and Sticky looked at each other and nodded. They remembered quite well that most pleasant of autumn evenings, not least a discussion about a chess game that Mr. Benedict had recently played with Mr. Curtain. (The genius brothers made use of notation but not of a chessboard; they simply announced their moves to each other and kept track of the games in their heads.) In describing certain aspects of the game to the Society members, Mr. Benedict had revealed his fondness for the word 'zugzwang,' a chess term referring to a situation in which a player's only possible moves are to that player's own disadvantage.

"Never a happy position in which to find oneself," he'd said, chuckling, "but it's awfully fun to say, is it not?"

Sticky entered 'zugzwang' into the keypad. A sound of turning gears issued from inside the wall. The door slid open.

"Do wait for me!" shouted a familiar voice from behind them.

Reynie, Sticky, and Tai, each uttering his own personal sound of dismay, turned to see what they knew they would see.

Crawlings had entered the room. He was approaching the canal at a sauntering pace. In one hand he carried Kate's duffel bag. His other gripped the wrist of the Listener, whose back was to them all, for she was attempting, with her own soft cries of dismay, to run back into the hallway. Her efforts seemed to have no more physical effect on Crawlings, however, than a fluttering sparrow's might have had. He seemed almost not to notice her there.

"Hold the door for me, won't you, little ones?" Crawlings called, dropping the duffel bag at his feet. In one fluid motion he reached into the bag, came up with Kate's crossbow, and fired the grappling hook across the canal. With a reverberating *clang*, the hook found purchase on the folded catwalk, a cable stretched taut over the canal, and Crawlings backed up. Screeching in resistance, the catwalk began to extend over the water.

"Let's not hold the door for him," whispered Tai.

For once the little boy looked and sounded as scared as Sticky and Reynie felt.

"Let's not," Sticky said.

"Agreed," said Reynie.

The three of them hurried through the door, but even as it closed behind them, they heard Crawlings's voice ring out across the water.

"Oh dear, how very rude of you!" the Ten Man cried. "Also, I might add, how very pointless! I know the code, you see. Oh yes! That little boy of yours has a leaky mind, and my friend here has a very acquisitive one. I know the code. I know the code. I *happen*. To *know*. The *code*!"

I didn't mean to!" Tai looked ready to burst into tears. "I couldn't help hearing it when you were thinking about it, and so I was thinking about it, too, but I didn't know she was listening! I'm sorry!"

Sticky and Reynie did their best to comfort him, hugging him and patting him and telling him that it wasn't his fault and that everything would be fine. Tai badly wished to believe them, of course, and with an effort he held back his tears.

They found themselves, at long last, in Mr. Curtain's

security suite. They stood in a well-lit visitors area, separated from Mr. Curtain's residence by a wall of glastanium. To the right was a modestly appointed kitchenette, beyond which lay the entrance to a bathroom. To their left stood a couple of chairs, a small sofa, and a desk with a computer on it. Rising from this desk and striding happily toward them now was Mr. Benedict.

His white hair as rumpled as his suit, his bright green eyes as lively as his nose was large and lumpy, Mr. Benedict was a most welcome sight. He greeted Reynie and Sticky with arms outstretched, and he instantly cheered up Tai with a wink and a joke about the pleasures of single-shoe perambulation.

"I know that word now!" Tai said with a laugh of recognition. Then he grew serious again. "Crawlings is outside, and he knows the code because of me."

"Is that so?" Mr. Benedict rested a hand on Tai's shoulder. "All will be well, dear boy." He turned toward the wall of glastanium. "Ledroptha, you have visitors!"

"So I noticed," replied the man, in a gruff voice remarkably similar to Mr. Benedict's own, although with none of the warmth. "And here I've forgotten to set out tea and cookies."

Mr. Curtain's residence was, at present, far more dimly lit than the visitors area, and as a result the newcomers found themselves peering through their own reflections to find the source of that gruff voice. Indeed, the inner space was illuminated only by a night-light near the foot of a simple bed, upon which lay the shadowy figure of a man. (It *was* nighttime, after all. Nonetheless, the idea of resting on one's bed in the midst of all this excitement was perfectly amazing to the visitors.) As they watched, the figure sat up and reached for a bedside lamp. With the click of a switch, Mr. Curtain appeared, glaring out at them from his bed. Except for his close-cropped hair and disagreeable expression, he looked exactly like his brother. He wore a pair of green plaid pajamas.

"Are you Mr. Curtain?" asked Tai. He knew the answer, of course, but in his nervousness he found he couldn't resist asking.

"What do *you* think?" muttered Mr. Curtain, rising from his bed. He shoved his feet into a pair of green plaid slippers.

"I think you are! I'm Tai Li. I'm five years old."

Mr. Curtain eyed him coolly. "Yes. Well." He clasped his hands behind his back. "Good for you." His eyes traveled to the faces of Reynie and Sticky, who nodded politely for Mr. Benedict's sake. Mr. Curtain grunted softly and said, "Time is annoying." Then he looked past them, for even as he spoke, the security door was sliding open, and into the room came Crawlings.

The Ten Man had a curious and immensely creepy way of entering unfamiliar rooms: First his head eased into view—the bald pate, bone-white, and the face with a single eyebrow that twitched as his dark eyes roamed about—followed by his tall, slender figure in its black suit, which emerged in a stooped position, then seemed to unfold itself in the room. As he straightened to his full height and the fragrance of his expensive cologne filled the air, Crawlings drew through the doorway his long left arm, and with it the unfortunate woman known to them, so far, only as the Listener.

The woman was trying to shield her face with one hand,

and she still struggled to free the other from Crawlings's unbreakable grip. She was quite small—she seemed barely half Crawlings's height—and wore a simple gray dress with tattered sneakers. Her hair, fine and black, with streaks of gray, fell just above her shoulders. Her skin was of an olive complexion, and when at last she lowered her hand and looked fearfully about the room, her features were so familiar that Reynie and Sticky glanced at each other in confusion, and Tai's jaw dropped. Crawlings, his own glittering dark eyes drawn now to Tai's face, began to chuckle.

"Well, well, well," Crawlings said. "Do we see a family resemblance? How wonderful! It seems no surprise that certain things would run in the family, does it, Mr. Curtain? After all, isn't it true that two of the greatest geniuses on the planet turned out to be identical twins?"

Mr. Curtain had stepped forward to the clear partition, the better to see what the others were reacting to. Glancing back and forth between the face of the little boy, who seemed pleasantly baffled, and that of the woman, whose large eyes now brimmed with tears, Mr. Curtain raised a bristly eyebrow but offered no comment on Crawlings's observation. Instead he said, "Hello, Crawlings. Do remember your manners, won't you? Not even a proper greeting after years apart?"

"Forgive me, forgive me," Crawlings chuckled, shaking his head. "*Hello*, Mr. Curtain. Better? You must be pleased to see me, no? As for the rest of—TOUCH ANYTHING ON THAT COMPUTER KEYBOARD AND YOU WILL INSTANTLY REGRET IT!"

This last Crawlings had directed to Mr. Benedict, who

had returned to his seat at the computer desk and who, in response to Crawlings's shrieked command, leaned calmly back in his seat and laced his fingers together well away from the keyboard. He looked steadily at Crawlings and waited in silence. Indeed, they all waited in silence, for the Ten Man clearly believed himself to be in control of the situation and would abide no resistance.

"Now then," Crawlings said, once more in a casual, affable tone, "what was I saying? Oh, we were speaking of seeing one another after years apart. I must say, look at these two boys. You, George—how is it that you've come to be so handsome? Is it the spectacles, perhaps? Naturally, I've always admired your one good feature"—with this, Crawlings ran a hand over his own smooth head—"but otherwise, well, I never would have guessed you had it in you. And as for you, Reynard—oh well, we can't all be matinee idols, can we?"

"To answer your question," Mr. Curtain said with more than a hint of impatience, "I am indeed pleased to see you, Crawlings. I trust the others are well? Will they be along soon?"

Crawlings uttered a disagreeable snicker. "Are the others well? Unless by that you mean well *cooked*, I daresay not, Mr. Curtain. No, I'm afraid I'm the only one in any position to help you, my dear old employer. But fear not! I'm more than up to the task. Here, you, make yourself comfortable on that sofa," he said, directing the Listener to take a seat.

The poor woman did as she was told. She could not take her eyes off Tai, who returned her gaze with a look of sweet encouragement and, to her evident surprise, climbed onto the sofa and sat quietly beside her.

"I will allow that," Crawlings said to Tai. "But if you wish to avoid unpleasant consequences, do not move again without my permission. Blink three times if you understand me."

Tai, holding very still, blinked three times.

"Now then," Crawlings said. "Here is how we shall proceed, Mr. Curtain. First you'll explain to me how it is you intend for us to escape. I have the Salamander at my disposal, but between *me* and *it* stands an impenetrable barrier. Your letter suggested that you have your own way out, and I should love to hear about it.

"Next I'll wish to discover the location of the cache of weapons you referred to in your letter, as well as—I shall even say *especially*—the location and nature of that most intriguing and mysterious one you mentioned. Once these things have been established, you can advise me on how best to free you from your sadly cramped chamber. How diminished your circumstances appear, I must say! What do you have in there—a bed, a desk, a chair? I suppose that door behind you leads to a bathroom? And that's all? And to think that you used to consider yourself the future master of the earth!"

Mr. Curtain stared at Crawlings with hooded eyes. He was visibly clenching and unclenching his jaw. At length he said, "I was never one for luxurious accommodations, anyway, you'll recall. It's true I once enjoyed greater freedoms, however, and I should like to again. If you'll—"

"Yes, yes," Crawlings interrupted. "I know you wish to be freed, and I daresay you're keenly interested in not succumbing to the poison you so boldly imbibed. Reynard, my dear, I assume you have the desired serum in that backpack of yours?"

Reynie nodded. "I'd like to—"

Crawlings held up a bony white hand. "Do not speak. Do not. Simply produce the serum."

As Reynie slipped off the backpack and unzipped it, Crawlings turned again to Mr. Curtain. "How are you given things, anyway? Oh, I see, this clever drawer set into the wall. The metal flap opens and the drawer extends, as if I were making a deposit at a bank's drive-through window. But what's to keep you from reaching through and grabbing someone's hand? Or yanking the drawer and mashing a fellow's fingers?"

"It's designed so that I cannot open it if your side is open," Mr. Curtain said coolly. "And vice versa."

"Clever indeed!" Crawlings said, his lone eyebrow twitching with emphasis. "And now for the serum."

Sticky said, "It isn't—"

"I said, no speaking!" Crawlings barked, and spinning on Sticky, he extended his hands, shaking his suit cuffs to expose his shock-watches. Sticky flinched—indeed, everyone in the room flinched—but then Crawlings took on a puzzled expression. No electrical hum filled the air.

"If I may," Mr. Benedict volunteered, raising his eyebrows questioningly. When Crawlings looked at him, evidently willing to hear what he had to say, Mr. Benedict said, "When you entered this room, you passed through an electromagnetic field that temporarily disables any electrical devices on your person. I'm afraid your watches won't function for some time. Also, if I may add, it was Reynie whom you instructed to keep silent, not George."

Crawlings's eyebrow drew inward at a slant. He tapped

the crystal of one watch and held it to his ear, then repeated the action with the other. He sighed. "Another clever feature of the room," he admitted. "And very well, Mr. Benedict, I take your point. George, I apologize for frightening you unnecessarily. When it's time for you to be *necessarily* frightened, I'll let you know. It won't be long now."

Sticky glared at him but said nothing.

Crawlings held out a hand to Reynie, his long arm seeming to stretch halfway across the room, and into that hand Reynie placed two stoppered beakers filled with pink fluid. Crawlings held them up to the light. "It looks thickish, I must say, and not a pleasing thing to swallow. But I will most gladly drink it down. Oh yes! Don't look so surprised, everyone! You said yourself, Mr. Curtain, that if this serum worked its effects upon a supposedly 'average intelligence' like mine, why, then the floodgates of genius would be opened! Did you not?"

Mr. Curtain was stony-faced. "I don't believe I used those precise words."

"Well, we won't quibble," Crawlings said with a lopsided smile. "My point is, why should I bother negotiating terms with you? I have a telepath working for me whose abilities can and will be developed. In the meantime I can simply direct her to extract from you all the information I desire: your plan for escape, the matter of the weapons, and the formula of the serum itself. Ha! Do you not admire the brilliance of my plan? It's as if I've already drunk the serum, is it not?"

Reynie raised his hand.

Crawlings, rolling his eyes, gave him nodding permission to speak.

"I ask you to consider," Reynie said carefully, "that you could allow them to receive the antidote and still get everything you wish. Nothing else about your plan would need to change—you could still obtain all of that information and make your escape. You'd have the formula to the serum, right? So—"

"That's enough," snipped Crawlings, and Reynie fell silent. "I may not be a verifiable genius yet, but I don't need you to spell out every little detail, young man. And the fact is that I *have* already considered what you say. Considered and rejected it. There are always so many things that can go wrong between now and later, you know. I prefer not to wait.

"My question now is this: Did you really bring enough for both brothers? One beaker each? Or did you intend to save only your precious mentor, in which case you expected him to drink *both* of these beakers? The answer matters, you see, for depending on the dose required to become a certified genius, I might actually let Mr. Curtain have what he needs to survive—for old time's sake, you know."

"You're too kind," Mr. Curtain growled.

"Now, let's see," Crawlings said, stroking his chin and studying Reynie's and Sticky's faces, which they were clearly endeavoring to keep impassive. "I don't actually require any assistance in figuring out the answer to my first question. I've seen all of Benedict's crew in action often enough to know that they cannot resist helping even those whom they despise. It appears to be some sort of mania. Therefore, you're in luck so far, Mr. Curtain. As long as a single beaker is all I require for my own purposes, you'll be more than welcome to the other. So, tell me, what is the proper dose for me?"

"You shouldn't do this," Mr. Curtain replied tersely. "What if I'm wrong about the formula? You shouldn't risk making me your enemy in that case. You'll need me."

"Oh dear, I didn't ask for your opinion," Crawlings said. He pointed a finger directly at Mr. Curtain's face. "I *asked* you what the proper *dose* is for me, and you had better answer me now. You know what I'm capable of, and I am holding all the cards here. What is the proper *dose*?"

"A single beaker," Mr. Curtain said, narrowing his eyes. "Now do get on with it and pass me mine."

"With pleasure," Crawlings said, and with his teeth he ripped the stopper from one of the beakers.

"You're not really going to drink that, are you?" said a small voice. "Not when you know that Mr. Benedict needs one, too?"

Crawlings pivoted slowly to level his gaze at the owner of the voice. Tai Li's face looked up at him as if from the bottom of a well, so much smaller was he than Crawlings, and his big eyes were wide with innocent disbelief.

There are times when even the worst of men—the most selfish, the most vindictive, the cruelest of men—need only be confronted with the wisdom of small children to be reminded of the children they once were themselves; to be reminded, in short, of what it is to imagine a world of magic and kindness rather than a world of wickedness and violence.

This was not one of those times. Crawlings winked at Tai and drank the beaker down.

He shuddered, winced, gasped—and then laughed. For he had done it. He had become a genius. Except that Crawlings didn't *feel* like a genius just yet, and the idea that came to him next, he knew, was no better than the idea of any common mortal. Still, it was an important idea, and he felt very pleased to have been its source. His eyes swiveled to the timid woman on the sofa.

"Tell me what he's thinking," Crawlings intoned. "For it occurs to me that of *course* he would say I needed only one beaker, because he wants the other for himself! Let's just be sure about this, shall we? Tell me, and tell me quick—what is the proper dose?"

The sad woman, her face a mask of fear and confusion, did what the Ten Man instructed her to do. She stared intently at Mr. Curtain, who closed his eyes and shook his head as if in disgust, and then she said, very quietly, "Both beakers. I'm sorry, but both beakers. That's what he's thinking."

"I knew it!" Crawlings roared. He jerked the stopper from the other beaker and flung it carelessly at Reynie, striking him on the forehead. As Reynie rubbed the painful spot, and he and Sticky looked on with expressions of helplessness, Crawlings gulped down the last of the serum. He turned and flung the beaker triumphantly at the wall, where it exploded into a thousand tiny pieces. He shivered and shook his head, and then he straightened to his full height and stretched his arms out wide. "Yes! Let the new era begin!"

Mr. Benedict rose from his chair. "Congratulations," he said quietly to Reynie and Sticky. He shook their hands. "Very well done indeed."

Mr. Curtain, with a look of disdain at Crawlings, went and sat on the edge of his bed.

"You are a wonderful young man, aren't you?" Mr. Benedict was saying to Tai, and turning to the Listener, he said,

"I'm so sorry for all you've been through. We'll help you find your way, I promise."

"Excuse me?" Crawlings said. He bugged his eyes at the others in the room. "Hello? Are you aware of what just happened?" He concentrated, waiting for his genius to kick in, the better to understand these mystifying reactions.

Reynie and Sticky shook hands and hugged, clapping each other enthusiastically on the back. They hugged Tai, too, and in soft voices began to offer assurances to the Listener, whose face, for the first time, showed signs of hope.

"I'm still here!" Crawlings shouted. "Everyone be silent!"

They all turned to face him. His chest was heaving. His eyes darted back and forth. He felt extremely agitated and confused.

"Tell me," said Mr. Benedict, "can you lift your arms? I advise you to be seated at once."

"Of *course* I can—" Crawlings began, but then he looked at his left arm, and then at his right arm. Both dangled unmoving. And indeed, he only managed to look at them by directing his eyeballs, for his head seemed unwilling to move as well.

"Be quick, my friends," Mr. Benedict said, and Reynie and Sticky jumped forward to catch Crawlings before he collapsed. They eased him onto the floor, where he sat with his palms upturned, his knuckles near his knees, and his face a picture of bewilderment.

"But you said both beakers," Crawlings said, directing his eyeballs toward the Listener. His voice slurred. "Wass it ssupposed to be only one?"

"Oh, even one beaker was one too many, I'm afraid," said Mr. Benedict.

The front of Crawlings's suit pants grew very dark, and he tried to frown but found he could not.

Tai gasped. "Did Mr. Crawlings just wet himself?"

"Unfortunately," said Sticky with a shrug. "It's no surprise. Consumed in such quantities, the formula would certainly have that effect. It isn't meant to be drunk at all, in fact, but injected, and only in a fraction of that amount. I suppose we should help him lie back so that he doesn't strike his head on the floor."

Together he and Reynie did just that, leaving Crawlings to stare at the ceiling for a few moments longer, still wondering when his genius would come galloping in to save the day. But alas, his genius was delayed indefinitely, and what arrived instead was a long-lasting slumber, followed by a long-lasting residency in the KEEP.

It was a fine late morning to be on the roof. Clouds moved swiftly across a fair blue sky, streaming after one another as if called home and eager to arrive. Beneath them a falcon could be seen gliding in graceful arcs. The patio had been swept clean, the railing mended, and one of the previously mangled tables, likewise put to rights, had been positioned in the middle of the patio and covered with a lace-trimmed tablecloth. On the table stood a vase of fresh-cut roses, a smuggled teapot, four smuggled cups and saucers, and an assortment of smuggled necessaries such as teaspoons, honey, sugar, and milk. A light breeze ruffled the rose petals, a few of which drifted pleasantly down to settle on the tablecloth, and the pleasant clatter of cup and saucer accompanied the pleasant chatter of four fast friends.

An extravagant lunch was due to be served in the dining room in less than an hour, but the Society was enjoying a private, pre-lunchtime patio party, which Kate delighted in referring to as their PPPP. Nor could they stop laughing, for they all wore their finest clothes, and the very idea of their being so properly dressed while having a tea party on the roof was impossible to bear with straight faces. And indeed, that had been the point. Every time Sticky, in his houndstooth blazer, raised a teacup to his lips, a fresh round of snickering commenced. Reynie, in his tweed jacket, couldn't ask for honey or milk without prompting snorts and guffaws. The sight of Kate, in her elegant black dress with long sleeves and high collar, was more shocking than funny, but to be repeatedly shocked simply by glancing at one's friend was funny enough on its own to provoke endless merriment.

Constance, for her part, was in her usual green plaid suit. But the fact that she had refused to sit in one of the folding chairs, had insisted, rather, that the others haul—of all things—the *Whisperer* out of the attic and place that formerly terrifying mind-control machine at the table, so that she now sat daintily perched at the edge of an oversized metal chair with a red helmet affixed to its back, sipping her tea like royalty on a throne—well, it was too much. Her friends could hardly look at her without spewing their own tea or choking on it, and they soon learned to manage the timing of their sips.

"I can't shake the feeling," Sticky observed, "that we're pretending to wear nice clothes and have a tea party on the roof. Yet we actually *are*."

"If it felt natural to us, it wouldn't be nearly so entertaining," said Kate. She kept touching her hair, which she had pulled up and fixed in place with tiny decorative combs, and nervously touching it again now, she said, "This business is going to have to come down soon, though."

"I challenge you to make it all the way through lunch," Reynie said.

Kate narrowed her eyes. "You had to go and make it a challenge. Crafty of you, Muldoon."

The way the PPPP had come about was this: The Washingtons and the Perumals had felt that if they were going to meet Mr. Benedict's oldest friends, and Rhonda Kazembe and her husband were making a visit, too, then they ought to recognize the special nature of the occasion and wear suitable clothes. Neither Sticky nor Reynie had felt enthusiastic about the prospect, but when Milligan had referred to his three-piece suit as "one of his favorite disguises," Kate had snorted and clapped her hands and announced that she had it in mind to wear a dress. Upon hearing this and receiving Kate's preposterous party proposal, the young men caught the spirit, helped each other tie their neckties (which Kate later retied for them), and laughed all the while. Constance had found none of this as amusing as the others did, but even so, she had yet to properly complain. In fact, she had rarely been in a brighter mood.

"Speaking of challenges," Constance said now, "you do all realize how difficult it's been waiting for your explanations, don't you?" Returning her cup to its saucer, she scooted back in her seat, drew up her knees, and wrapped her arms around them.

"You have been impressively patient," Sticky said, and the others nodded.

The truth was that Constance had had little choice. Though she'd finally recovered from her sickness—which had taken a full day, even with the help of Sticky's fruity concoctions—they had all been constantly busy and (more to the point) never alone. Constance had been forced to settle for promises of full explanations to be given at the first official meeting of the Society. Yes, she had been tempted—more than once—to fish around in her friends' minds for details, but she had nobly resisted the temptation and saw no need to mention it to anyone.

"Let's start with the Scaredy Katz?" Kate suggested, and Reynie and Sticky signaled their agreement. "The weird way we went about things, Constance, was mostly because of those jokers. They were so good at sniffing out traps, you know. We had to do everything we possibly could to convince them that the KEEP *wasn't* a trap. Then Tai and the Listener came into the picture, and things got doubly hard."

"As you said, Constance," Reynie said, "it's a good thing we've had so much practice keeping our most secret thoughts to ourselves. The trick for us was to keep hidden what we already knew, but to let slip just enough for McCracken to feel convinced of the situation. Thanks to the Listener, he knew that Mr. Benedict was sending us clues and informing us of the supposedly poisoned tea he'd drunk—"

Constance's eyes widened. "That's why you had me tell

Dad that we weren't going to take any risks, even though you knew McCracken wouldn't believe me!"

Reynie tapped his nose. "McCracken would expect us to try to throw him off our trail. If we didn't at least try, he would have been suspicious."

"And later," Constance said, thinking back, "when you and I faced him at the barrier—he said he knew that we'd been trying to solve some kind of riddle. You were probably *glad!*"

Reynie grinned. "I was. One more convincing detail, right? The harder the situation looked for *us*, the less it would look like a trap to *them*. We needed to know as little as possible. But we trusted Mr. Benedict to have done everything he could to give us the advantage. He knew what we were capable of—and, well, he is a genius, after all."

"*We* knew what we were capable of, too," Kate said. "And that includes you. What you did back there at the safe room—we all imagined you could do something like that. So did Mr. Benedict, of course. We were trying to protect you by keeping you out of things, but believe me, it definitely boosted our confidence to have you there. It made the rest of us safer.

"Speaking of which," Kate went on, giving Constance a shrewd look, "I happen to know now what you really did for me—what you did for *all* of us."

Sticky turned to Reynie. "Do you know what she's talking about?"

Reynie shook his head. They both looked expectantly at Constance, who merely shrugged and rested her chin on her knees, and then at Kate, who was shaking her head with a look of admiration.

"When I was trapped with McCracken and company," Kate explained, "I asked Constance to inform Mr. Benedict of the situation. I thought there might be some chance he could help me out, you know." (Here Sticky and Reynie nodded knowingly.) "At the time, I just thought he wasn't able to, for whatever reason, or that Constance hadn't been able to get through to him.

"But I learned from Mr. Benedict just this morning that she *did* get through to him," Kate said, looking at Constance with an expression of mock disapproval, "and he told her that he could protect me, but that doing so would make me miserably sick for a while—and not just me, but also you boys and Tai—and he asked her if the situation was dire enough to warrant that. She told him never mind."

Now it was Reynie and Sticky's turn to look admiringly at Constance.

"Really?" Sticky said. "You did that for us, even knowing how sick it would make you?"

"You are something else, Constance," said Reynie. He put a hand over his heart.

"Something else and then some," Sticky said, echoing the gesture.

"Oh, for crying out loud," said Constance, who looked very pleased to be acknowledged in this way, "any of you would have done the same thing for me, and you know that you would. Also, I overestimated how much I could help Kate! I thought I could take them all out, but I only managed a few. What if something had happened to her after that?"

"Yes, it was a very shameful performance," Kate said, furrowing her brow. "You only disabled the most powerful

Ten Men with your mind." She laughed. "Maybe deep down you had a tiny speck of confidence in *my* abilities. What do you think about that?"

"Maybe," Constance said with a roll of her eyes. "But how was it that Dad could have helped you, anyway? He was stuck in that security suite. Could he have pushed a button and released some kind of gas, maybe?"

The other three all tapped their noses.

"Thanks to Sticky," Reynie said. "I mean George. Sorry."

Sticky cleared his throat. "You know what? I've been thinking about this. I would rather you three call me Sticky. I've never gotten comfortable with your calling me George."

"Well, *that's* a relief," Kate said, refilling everyone's cups from the teapot. "I've had the hardest time remembering."

Reynie looked uncomfortable. "To be honest, for me the challenge has been how it's been making me *feel*—like I'm talking about a different person instead of one of my best friends. I've wanted to do it for your sake, and I still will if you change your mind. I think it would be easier now. Before, I already felt like I was losing you in some way. Something in me kept wanting to blurt out the old name, maybe to resist what I feared was happening. I really didn't mean to, though. I'm sorry about that."

Far from being annoyed by this revelation, Sticky was touched, and he assured Reynie that there was nothing to be sorry about.

Constance, for her part, *did* feel annoyed. She was having a hard time keeping up with what to call Sticky when she wanted to provoke him.

"No," Sticky was saying, "I think when I meet new people,

I'll introduce myself as George, but you can all, you know, stick with Sticky. I don't have to be one or the other. I can be both."

"Oh, like Mr. Cole said," Kate observed. "You aren't becoming a different person. You're becoming *more* persons." She frowned. "More people? Is it persons or people?"

"Technically—" Sticky began, but Constance cut him off.

"Technically, it was my *dad* who said that," she said peevishly, "and Mr. Cole was just quoting him. Nothing against Mr. Cole. But also technically, *George*"—this she said with a satisfied smirk—"you haven't explained about this gas for which, evidently, we owe you our humble thanks."

Sticky sighed. The gas, he explained, was the result of one of their special projects: He had seen duskwort under a microscope. He had learned enough about it before it disintegrated to embark on a series of productive experiments. With the brilliant input of Mr. Benedict and Rhonda, Sticky had made significant progress in the development of formulas that would diminish the unfortunate effects of narcolepsy and other sleep disorders.

"And why did no one tell me about this?" Constance interrupted.

The others laughed and rolled their eyes.

"This was around the time," Reynie explained, "that you began saying that if you heard another single word about chemistry, you would scream an endless scream. You wrote a threatening poem about it. The title, if I remember correctly, was 'The Endless Scream.'"

"Oh, right!" Constance said, her expression turning fond as she recalled her poem.

"After that we discussed it rather less around you," Sticky said. "And then we found even more reason for secrecy, because when my research led me to the formula for a unique sleeping gas, Mr. Benedict requested that I share the formula with him and Rhonda and then never mention it again. Well…" He shrugged. "At that point we all knew he intended to use it at the KEEP."

"Since then," Kate said, "we've never discussed it. We knew it needed to be kept an ironclad secret. But we all understood that it was a potential part of the trap."

Constance narrowed her eyes. "So those emergency security measures Dad went to implement had to do with the sleeping gas. If he was the only one who knew about it, he was the only one who could use it against the Ten Men."

"Exactly," Kate said. "And first he had to mix up a fresh batch from the formula. The gas loses potency within a few days. Sticky, tell her what you named it."

"I do feel rather proud of that," Sticky said. "It's called KeepSleep, and—"

Constance groaned.

"It's called KeepSleep," Sticky repeated doggedly, "and Mr. Benedict, Rhonda, and I are the only ones in the world who know the formula. I've never written it down. We agreed that it was too dangerous to risk its falling into the wrong hands."

"It poses no mortal threat," Reynie explained, "but it will knock you out for at least a day or two, unless you're injected with the antidote. Either way, when you wake up, you will definitely feel terrible for a while. So we knew that Mr. Benedict would use it as a last resort, or only in specific

379

circumstances, to protect us. Once we had the Ten Men trapped inside the barriers with us, though, we also knew that we'd *won*, because if things went badly enough, Mr. Benedict could just disperse the KeepSleep, and everyone would be knocked out—including the Ten Men."

"But how would that make things better?" Constance said, her brow wrinkling. "Wouldn't everyone just wake up eventually and be in the same situation?"

"As for that," Sticky said, "*everyone* wouldn't be knocked out, actually. The safe room would be, well, safe as long as the barrier was down, and *I* wouldn't be knocked out, either, because I injected myself with a special formula ahead of time. Unfortunately, having that in my system meant that exposure to KeepSleep would make me incredibly sick, but at least I'd be conscious, which would allow me to revive *you* all with the antidote."

"The serum!" Constance cried.

"Right," said Kate. "That whole business about poison was a ruse, and we knew it as soon as we saw it in Mr. Curtain's letter. When you thought Sticky was down in the Blab mixing up the antidote to this fictional poison, he was actually preparing the antidote to KeepSleep—enough to revive all of us if things shook out that way—and injecting himself with his special counteractive formula. He'd already volunteered to be the one to do that."

"I thought you all didn't discuss it," Constance said.

"Not recently," Reynie said. "We discussed it back when we realized that the KeepSleep would be part of the trap. We made certain decisions and then did our best to hide it all away in the backs of our minds."

From Constance's expression it was unclear whether she was about to chide them or thank them, but before she could do either, a screeching sound interrupted their conversation, followed by the telltale rattle and clank of the platform. The trapdoor fell open, and presently the smiling face of Mr. Benedict rose into view, followed by the rest of his body, smartly attired in a lavender suit.

"Don't get up, don't get up!" he cried, throwing the lever and stepping nimbly from the platform. "Why, how dashing you all look!"

Despite his admonition, everyone but Constance rose to greet Mr. Benedict, and they all exchanged compliments with him and inquired about the state of lunch preparation below.

"Moocho's profound lasagna is almost ready," Mr. Benedict told them. "The table is set, our guests are soon to arrive, and your parents are all wondering where you are. I've been dispatched to alert you. But I also wished to thank you. I'm delighted enough that John and his wife will be here, but to learn that you also arranged for Violet to come? What an occasion!"

"We didn't do much ourselves," Reynie said. "It was Captain Noland who agreed to bring her from Paris."

"Indeed, and as a guest of honor on his wonderful ship! I certainly owe Phil a debt of gratitude as well," Mr. Benedict said. "But you all had the idea, and you made the invitations and the arrangements, and I will be forever grateful."

Reynie, Sticky, and Kate tried to return the expression of gratitude—after all, they insisted, they had so much to thank him for, too—but Mr. Benedict would not be swayed from his course.

"Do you know," he went on, his bright green eyes growing brighter still with tears, "I haven't had all of my closest friends and family in the same room since I was a boy, when, incidentally, I *had* no family, and my closest friends numbered exactly *two*. To have all of you together today, well, I can hardly begin to express how much it means to me. It's a once-in-a-lifetime gift. Once in a lifetime, my friends."

Mr. Benedict took out a lavender handkerchief, dabbed at his eyes, and blew his nose. Then, ducking beneath the Whisperer's red helmet to kiss Constance on the top of her head, he added, "And it's still a marvel to me that I can allow myself to experience a pure emotion without the risk of falling asleep. For that I thank you again, my dear."

Constance briefly patted his shoulder. "You're welcome again. Also, Dad, it's super awkward when you cry in front of people, you know."

At this, Mr. Benedict laughed his distinctive laugh, rather like the nickering of a horse, and Constance said, "That's only slightly better."

Before Mr. Benedict left them to finish their private party, Kate informed him that they were finally giving Constance all the details of their complicated Ten Man Trap Plan. "Or plans, I should say, since we did have backup plans, and we knew you'd have them, too."

Mr. Benedict smiled. "Oh, yes! Backup plans beyond backup plans—from plan A to plan Q!"

"Only to Q?" Constance said. "Not Z?"

Mr. Benedict shrugged. "Alas, no. The whole business was complicated enough, I must say. Arriving at my agreement with the government authorities was the only simple part, to be sure: They were perfectly happy to give me a chance to capture the Ten Men before the officials were compelled to intervene themselves. For any confrontation with McCracken and his crew—even if ultimately successful—would no doubt result in many casualties among law enforcement personnel, and very likely innocent civilians as well."

"Weren't all of Milligan's best agents out of commission?" Constance asked.

"Indeed they were. A large number of reinforcements were quietly being moved into place, however, forming a secret perimeter around Stonetown. But their orders were to tighten the net only if the Ten Men decided to leave the city instead of trying to infiltrate the KEEP—or if they did take the bait but our plans went awry.

"Now, my dear," Mr. Benedict continued, "you may be wondering what the plan was if the Ten Men had never escaped in the first place. That, admittedly, would have been the ideal situation. Milligan did feel certain that we were closing in on the Katz brothers. If things worked out well, all would eventually have been transferred to the KEEP, and the final renovations made. The facility would no longer need its various trap-like elements, and of course special measures have to be taken in the case of individuals as uniquely dangerous as the Ten Men. You can be assured, for instance, that the doors to the control rooms have already been replaced by ones impossible to breach."

"I wondered about that!" Constance said. "They were just regular doors!"

Mr. Benedict chuckled. "I've had to deal with all manner of absurdities. When the government granted me a 'free hand' in the design-and-renovation process, they truly did mean *a* free hand. The other they kept firmly tied behind my back. Fortunately, for our purposes, I was still able to make a workable design, if not a perfect one."

"Personally, I loved it," Kate said.

"Thank you, Kate," said Mr. Benedict, and his tone suggested that she could not have given him a greater compliment. "And to answer one more of your questions, Constance," he said just as Constance was opening her mouth to ask it, "I had almost no control of facility operations from within Ledroptha's security suite. I couldn't open any doors or drop any barriers. The only option available to me was to enter a computer command that would disperse the KeepSleep and, simultaneously, send a unique distress signal to key figures on the mainland, Rhonda among them. They all knew the response protocols for that particular signal and would have followed them accordingly."

Constance considered this. "But how was that supposed to work? McCracken said they had a signal Disrupter."

"Indeed," said Mr. Benedict. "But if I hadn't anticipated that and invented my own Disrupter *disrupter*—well, I daresay I would hardly have been worth my *keep*. My *keep*, Constance!" Here he erupted into a boisterous, whinnying laugh, and Constance groaned again. This time she hid her face, however, for although she found Mr. Benedict's joke ridiculous, she couldn't help laughing just a little.

The others were more open about their own amusement, and everyone was laughing freely again as Mr. Benedict took his leave, promising Constance he would answer any remaining questions later. He said not a single word about the fact that she was sitting in the Whisperer at a tea party, as if this were the most natural thing in the world. Soon he was sinking out of view on the platform, and the Society was alone again on the roof.

"So," Constance said when the others' laughter had died down, "since I don't want to wait forever to get more answers from Dad, how about you all explain to me Uncle Horrible's letter? I had a chance to read it yesterday, and I don't know what to make of it. Was it all a lie? Or only parts of it? And how did Dad get him to write it?"

"We asked them both the same things after Crawlings went down," Sticky told her. "That secret weapon Mr. Curtain said no one knew existed? With the potential to change the world? What *he* told us was that it was his willingness to believe that the Ten Men weren't eternally loyal to him—something McCracken proved when he went after S.Q. Anticipating such a betrayal made Mr. Curtain very inclined to cooperate with Mr. Benedict, he said."

"But when we had a chance to speak privately with Mr. Benedict later," Reynie put in, "*he* said that he believed there was more to it than that. Mr. Benedict thinks that Mr. Curtain's secret weapon was the realization, the very slow realization, that he might have been wrong about *other* things—including the way he'd gone about trying to 'improve' the world. Mr. Curtain wouldn't admit as much to him, but he did show that he was willing to change the world forever in a positive way—whatever his motives truly were—by doing his part to help capture the Baker's Dozen."

"It's really a lot to take in," Constance mused. "I mean, he's so *bad*."

"That's for sure," Kate said. "But, well, Mr. Curtain knew that there was absolutely no way he would ever escape the KEEP. Mr. Benedict was telling me about this earlier today. He said he'd explained to Mr. Curtain all the measures that would prevent it, and Mr. Curtain, despite his arrogance, was just too smart not to see that he'd been beaten. Plus, you know how badly he wants to control things. After all these years of being completely *out* of control? He was desperate to be able to accomplish something, even if it meant helping to capture his former employees."

"So there was no secret cache of weapons, right?" Constance said. "And he didn't have any secret way off the island?"

They all shook their heads, and Reynie said, "I did ask him if he'd ever considered having an escape tunnel under the harbor, and he acted like that was ridiculous. But when I pressed him and asked if he'd never even *considered* it—"

"He flew off the handle!" Sticky interjected, laughing. "He totally blew up!"

Reynie said, "He turned purple and shouted, 'Of *course* I considered it, you dolt! I wanted one! But do you have any idea how much a secret tunnel under the harbor would *cost*? Snakes and dogs! It simply couldn't be done!'"

"Fortunately, he managed to lie down before he lost consciousness," Sticky said. "And that was the end of the conversation."

From the street came the sound of car doors opening and closing. The guests were beginning to arrive. Exclamations of greeting issued from the courtyard, whose gate screeched and clanged, and the Society discussed whether to go straight down or wait a few minutes and make a dramatic entrance. They were eager to be with their friends and families, but they were also reluctant to end their private party.

They were still debating what to do when the platform machinery sounded again, and before long they were presented with the unexpected sight of Tai Li wearing a bow tie and suspenders. He leaped from the platform and dashed to their table, exclaiming, "Look at me! I'm so uncomfortable!"

"We all are!" Kate replied, laughing, and everyone, even Constance, complimented Tai on his splendid attire.

Beaming, he announced that S.Q. Pedalian had arrived, and that his feet were indeed the most impressive feet Tai had ever seen, and that he had been *so nice.*

"He shook my hand and said he was charmed to meet me!" Tai said, happily accepting the small spoonful of sugar Reynie handed him. He touched his tongue to it, smiled, and went on. "And he actually *bowed* to Aunt Claire! Like in a movie! Except he bumped his head on the table! This is so fun! Aunt Claire was very nice to him, too. She offered to get him some ice."

He was referring, of course, to the Listener, whose real name had turned out to be Claire Li, and whose identity had been determined soon after that surprise meeting in Mr. Curtain's security suite. She was the older sister of Tai's father, and a scientist herself—an expert in invisible-signal technology. Whether her research had led her to Mr. Curtain or vice versa was unclear, for Mr. Curtain refused to discuss the matter. (No doubt, Mr. Benedict speculated, his brother knew that an apology was in order and did not yet feel capable of making one. Everyone else was skeptical about this, but politely accepted it as a possibility.)

What *was* clear was that Dr. Li was the reason that Tai's parents had been trying to invent a long-distance tracking device. It might have been used to help any number of people, but Tai's parents had wanted very specifically to find *her*.

"Your aunt Claire *is* very nice," Sticky said. "She's already becoming good friends with my parents—my mom especially. My dad likes her, too, but it takes longer to become friends with my dad, since he only speaks about one word a day."

Tai giggled. "She says she really likes them, too! And Miss Perumal and her mother have been helping her fix up her room!"

"Amma and Pati are very fond of her," Reynie said. "I think she's doing well, all things considered, don't you? She doesn't seem especially sad anymore, even though she doesn't have her memory back yet."

"She *isn't* sad!" Tai exclaimed. He had finished off the sugar and was emphasizing his words with flourishes of the spoon. "And she's *going* to get her memory back! Mr. Benedict says he's working on it, and if Mr. Benedict says it, you know it's true!"

They all voiced their agreement and expressed their gladness that the situation with the Listener had taken such an unexpectedly happy turn. Constance, in particular, had felt profound relief in losing an adversary and gaining an ally. Indeed, when she and Dr. Li had finally met face-to-face, they found themselves spontaneously crying, clinging to each other like long-lost friends. Constance, in rare form, had insisted that there was nothing to forgive, and in fact had promised she would do everything she could to help Dr. Li. The two had been especially kind to each other ever since and had spent a great deal of time talking about their telepathic experiences.

"Do you want to know something I hope?" Tai asked the table in general.

They all said they would be very gratified to know.

"I hope," said Tai, "that when Aunt Claire gets her memory back, she may be able to guess what my middle initial stands for! Because maybe I'm named for some relative I don't know about!"

"Wait," Constance said. "You don't *know* what the M stands for? Why on earth did you keep asking us to guess it, then?"

"I thought maybe you could!" Tai said with a carefree shrug. "I thought I might know it if I heard it."

The others laughed and shook their heads. Kate leaned toward Tai and whispered conspiratorially, "Have a look beneath the table, why don't you?"

Tai instantly complied, ducking out of view under the tablecloth. He emerged with Kate's bucket in his arms and a huge grin on his face.

Kate tapped him playfully on the nose. "Will you keep track of that for me until after lunch, when I can change into some decent clothes?"

Tai agreed that he would, and promptly stepped up onto the bucket to be on the same level as the others, or very nearly. He had never lacked for cheer, but the discovery of his aunt, the successful entrapment of the Baker's Dozen, and his own role in the matter had lifted his spirits to even greater heights. In the final moments of their mission he truly had played an important part, for he had told his aunt telepathically that she didn't need to be confused anymore, that he was with the heroes, and that all she had to do was help them and everything would be fine.

"And it worked," Dr. Li had said later. "All my confusion fell away. I felt the truth of what he was saying, so clearly. When I sensed that Crawlings was meant to drink the serum, I found it easy to play along. I knew everything was about to get better at last. And so it has!"

So it had indeed.

The Society had agreed that they were all staying put indefinitely. Their other opportunities had certainly been appealing, but it had become clear that, at least for the time being, the most special opportunities were right here. They had far too many projects that needed tending to: It would take all of them to keep Tai out of trouble, they told him (much to his delight); they wanted to help Mr. Benedict help Dr. Li; and the older three intended to help Constance find some friends her own age (she grumbled about this, but only half-heartedly, since in fact the prospect pleased her). And there were many others besides.

Also, Mr. Benedict had made an interesting request: The Ten Men would need to be offered productive activities that did not involve anything that could be used as a weapon. With their ability to do harm taken away, McCracken and his comrades were destined to be the most polite and agreeable prisoners in the world, but they did need something to do. (Sticky already had an idea, based on duskwort's fragile molecular structure, for a watering can and garden implements that disintegrated into powder if used to strike anything with force.)

Yes, the Society was going to be very busy indeed. In the meantime, their private party was at an end, and as Kate whipped the tablecloth out from under the objects on the table, which remained where they were, and the others all rose from their seats, Tai stepped down from the bucket and asked Reynie why he was thinking about the funny word.

"Zugzwang?" Reynie said with a smile. "Oh, I'd just been thinking how fitting it was that it was the code for Mr. Curtain's security suite. Crawlings had to make a move, but unbeknownst to him, the only options available to him were bad ones."

"And that's what that word means in chess!" Tai said, scooping up the bucket. "Mr. Benedict taught me that. But just now *you* were thinking that there's a word that's the *opposite* of 'zugzwang,'" he said, pronouncing the chess term with some difficulty. "What is it?"

"I'll see if you can guess it," Reynie said with a wink.

For they were all headed downstairs now, where they were to be so warmly greeted: Reynie with hugs and kisses from Amma and Pati; Sticky from his parents; Kate from Milligan, who was getting around quite nimbly, despite the casts on his legs; and Tai from his aunt, who lit up every time he entered the room—and all of them by everyone, from Moocho to Captain Plugg to Rhonda to Number Two to dear old S.Q. Pedalian. They would happily greet Mr. Benedict's lifelong friends as well, and meanwhile the delicious smell of Moocho's famous lasagna would be wafting in from the kitchen, and they would take their familiar seats at the dining room table, where they would all feel, now and forever, at home.

Acknowledgments

I would like to thank Mary Ruth Marotte, Brock Clarke, Michael Griffith, and Eric Simonoff for *Counsel and Confirmation*; Mark Barr for *Le Clé et le Clair*; Joe Williams for *Combinations and Confabulations*; Megan Tingley, Anna Prendella, Bethany Strout, and Barbara Bakowski for *Considerations and Clarifications*; and all my coconspirators for *Coming Back for More*.

Continue reading for a sneak preview of
The Secret Keepers.

WALKING BACKWARD INTO THE SKY

That summer morning in the Lower Downs began as usual for Reuben Pedley. He rose early to have breakfast with his mom before she left for work, a quiet breakfast because they were both still sleepy. Afterward, also as usual, he cleaned up their tiny kitchen while his mom moved faster and faster in her race against the clock (whose numerals she seemed quite unable to read before she'd had coffee and a shower). Then his mom was hugging him goodbye at the apartment door, where Reuben told her he loved her, which was true—and that she had no reason to worry about him, which was not.

His mom had not even reached the bus stop before Reuben

had brushed his teeth, yanked on his sneakers (a fitting term, he thought, being a sneaker himself), and climbed onto the kitchen counter to retrieve his wallet. He kept it among the mousetraps on top of the cupboard. The traps were never sprung; Reuben never baited them, and so far no thieves had reached up there to see what they might find. Not that the wallet contained much, but for Reuben "not much" was still everything he had.

Next he went into his bedroom and removed the putty from the little hole in the wall behind his bed. He took his key from the hole and smooshed the putty back into place. Then, locking the apartment door behind him, he headed out in search of new places to hide.

Reuben lived in the city of New Umbra, a metropolis that was nonetheless as gloomy and run-down as a city could be. Though it had once enjoyed infinitely hopeful prospects (people used to say that it was born under a promising star), New Umbra had long since ceased to be prosperous, and was not generally well kept. Some might have said the same of Reuben Pedley, who used to have two fine and loving parents, but only briefly, when he was a baby, and who in elementary school had been considered an excellent student, but in middle school had faded into the walls.

Eleven years had passed since the factory accident that left Reuben without a father and his mother a young widow scrambling for work—eleven years, in other words, since his own promising star had begun to fall. And though in reality he was as loved and cared for as any child could hope to be, anyone who followed him through his days might well have believed otherwise. Especially on a day like today.

Reuben exited his shabby high-rise apartment building in the usual manner: he bypassed the elevator and stole down the rarely used stairwell, descending unseen all the way past the lobby to the basement, where he slipped out a storage-room window. The young building manager kept that window slightly ajar to accommodate the comings and goings of a certain alley cat she hoped to tame, enticing it with bowls of food and water. She wasn't supposed to be doing that, but no one knew about it except Reuben, and he certainly wasn't going to tell anyone. He wasn't supposed to be in the storage room in the first place. Besides, he liked the building manager and wished her luck with the cat, though only in his mind, for she didn't know that he knew about it. She barely even knew he existed.

From his hidden vantage point in the window well, which was slightly below street level and encircled by an iron railing, Reuben confirmed that the alley behind the building was empty. With practiced ease, he climbed out of the window well, monkeyed up the railing, grabbed the lower rungs of the building's rusty fire escape, and swung out over empty space. He hit the ground at a trot. Today he wanted to strike out into new territory, and there was no time to waste. When they'd lived in the northern part of the Lower Downs, Reuben had known the surrounding blocks as well as his own bedroom, but then they'd had to move south, and despite having lived here a year, his mental map remained incomplete.

Of all the city's depressed and depressing neighborhoods, the Lower Downs was considered the worst. Many of its old buildings were abandoned; others seemed permanently under repair. Its backstreets and alleys were marked by missing shutters, tilted light poles, broken gates and railings, fences with gaps in them. The Lower Downs, in other words, was perfect for any boy who wanted to explore and to hide.

Reuben was just such a boy. In fact, exploring and hiding were almost all he ever did. He shinned up the tilted light poles and dropped behind fences; he slipped behind the busted shutters and through the broken windows; he found his way into cramped spaces and high places, into spots where no one would ever think to look. This was how he spent his solitary days.

It never occurred to him to be afraid. Even here in the Lower Downs, there was very little crime on the streets of New Umbra, at least not the sort you could easily see. Vandals and pickpockets were rare, muggers and car thieves unheard of. Everyone knew that. The Directions took care of all that business. Nobody crossed the Directions, not even the police.

Because the Directions worked for The Smoke.

Reuben headed south, moving from alley to alley, keeping close to the buildings and ducking beneath windows. He paused at every corner, first listening, then peering around. He was only a few blocks off the neighborhood's main thoroughfare and could hear some early-morning traffic there, but the alleys and backstreets were dead.

About ten blocks south, Reuben ventured into new territory. He was already well beyond his bounds: his mom had given him permission to walk to the community center and the branch library—both within a few blocks of their apartment—but that was all. And so he kept these wanderings of his a secret.

Despite her excessive caution, his mom was something else, and Reuben knew it. He wouldn't have traded her for half a dozen moms with better jobs and more money, and in fact had told her exactly that just the week before.

"Oh my goodness, Reuben, that is so sweet," she'd said, pretending to wipe tears from her eyes. "I hope you know that I probably wouldn't trade you, either. Not for half a dozen boys, or even a whole dozen."

"*Probably?*"

"Almost certainly," she'd said, squeezing his hand as if to reassure him.

That was what his mom was like. Their conversations were usually the best part of his day.

Crossing an empty street, Reuben made his habitual, rapid inventory of potential hiding places: a shady corner between a

Nobody crossed the Directions, not even the police.
Because the Directions worked for The Smoke.

building's front steps and street-facing wall; a pile of broken furniture that someone had hauled to the curb; a window well with no protective railing. But none of these places was within easy reach when, just as he attained the far curb, a door opened in a building down the block.

Reuben abruptly sat on the curb and watched the door. He held perfectly still while an old man in pajamas stepped outside and checked the sky, sniffing with evident satisfaction and glancing up and down the street before going back in. The old man never saw the small brown-haired boy watching him from the curb.

Reuben rose and moved on, quietly triumphant. He preferred bona fide hiding places when he could find them, but there was nothing quite like hiding in plain sight. Sometimes people saw you and then instantly forgot you, because you were just a random kid, doing nothing. As long as you didn't look lost, anxious, or interesting, you might as well be a trash can or a stunted tree, part of the city landscape. Reuben considered such encounters successes, too. But to go completely unnoticed on an otherwise empty street was almost impossible, and therefore superior. He was reliving the moment in his mind, exulting in the memory of the old man's eyes passing right over him without registering his presence—not once but twice!—when he came upon the narrowest alley he'd ever seen, and made his big mistake.

It was the narrowness that tempted him. The brick walls of the abandoned buildings were so close to each other that Reuben saw at once how he might scale them. By leaning forward and pressing his palms against one, then lifting his feet behind him and pressing them against the other, he could hold himself up, suspended above the alley floor. Then by moving one hand higher, then the other, and then doing the same with his feet, he could work his way upward. It would be like walking backward into the sky.

No sooner had he imagined it than Reuben knew he had to

try it. Glancing around to ensure that he was unobserved, he moved deeper into the alley. He could see a ledge high above him—probably too high to reach, but it gave him something to shoot for, at any rate.

He started out slowly, then gained momentum as he found his rhythm. Hand over hand, foot over foot, smoothly and steadily. Now he was fifteen feet up, now twenty, and still he climbed. Craning his head around, Reuben saw the ledge not too far above him. Unfortunately, he also saw how difficult it would be to climb onto it—his position was all wrong. He frowned. What had he been thinking? He didn't dare try such a risky maneuver, not at that height. He'd be a fool to chance it.

That was when Reuben felt his arms begin to tremble and realized, with horror, that he had made a terrible mistake.

He hadn't anticipated how drastically his arms would tire, nor how abruptly. It seemed to happen all at once, without warning. Now, looking at the alley floor far below him, Reuben became sickeningly aware of how high he had actually climbed. At least thirty feet, maybe more. The way his arms felt, there was no way he'd make it back to the ground safely. He probably couldn't even get back down to twenty feet.

Thus the action he'd just rejected as being foolishly dangerous suddenly became the only choice left to him, the only hope he had. He had to make the ledge, and by some miracle he had to get himself onto it.

With a whimper of panic, Reuben resumed his climbing. The trembling in his arms grew worse. He could no longer see the grimy, broken pavement of the alley floor below. His vision was blurred by sweat, which had trickled into his eyes and couldn't be wiped away. He was burning up on the inside but weirdly cold on the outside, like a furnace encased in ice; the alley's quirky cross breezes were cooling his sweat-slick skin. Beads of perspiration dripped from his nose.

In desperate silence he pressed upward. He heard the wind fluttering in his ears, the scrape of his shoe soles against brick, his own labored breath, and that was all. He was so high up, and so quietly intent on climbing, that had any passersby glanced down that narrow alley, they'd have noticed nothing unusual. Certainly none would have guessed that an eleven-year-old boy was stretched out high above them, fearing for his life.

As it happened, there were no passersby to see Reuben finally come to the ledge, or to note the terrible moment when he made his fateful lunge, or to watch him struggle for an agonizingly long time to heave himself up, his shoes slipping and scraping, his face purple with strain. No one was around to hear Reuben's gasps of exhaustion and relief when at last he lay on that narrow ledge—heedless, for the moment, of his bruised arms and raw fingertips. If any passersby had been near enough to hear anything, it would have been only the clatter of startled pigeons rising away above the rooftops. But in the city this was no unusual sound, and without a thought they would have gone on with their lives, reflecting upon their own problems and wondering what to do.

Reuben lay with his face pressed against the concrete ledge as if kissing it, which indeed he felt like doing. He had such immense gratitude for its existence, for its solidity beneath him. After his pulse settled and his breath returned, he rose very cautiously to a sitting position, his back against brick, his legs dangling at the knees. With his shirt, he dried his eyes as best he could, wincing a little from the smarting of his scraped fingertips. His every movement was calculated and slow. He was still in a dangerous predicament.

The ledge was keeping Reuben safe for the time being, but it was only a ledge, spattered here and there with pigeon droppings.

When he tried to look up, the wind whipped his hair into his eyes; to keep them clear, he had to cup his hands like pretend binoculars. The rooftop seemed miles above him, and might as well have been. Beyond it the early-morning sky was blue as a robin's egg. A perfect summer morning to have gotten stuck on a ledge in a deserted alley.

"Well done, Reuben," he muttered. "Brilliant."

He knew he couldn't get back down the same way he'd come up. He would have to edge around to the back of the building and hope for a fire escape. Otherwise his only option was to follow the ledge around to the street side, try to get in through one of the windows there. If he was lucky, perhaps no one would spot him. But if he couldn't get in, he would have to shout for help. Reuben imagined the fire truck's siren, the fierce disapproval on the firefighters' faces, the gathering crowd—all of it terrible to contemplate, and none of it even half as bad as facing his mom would be.

His mom, who thought he was safe at home in their apartment, reading a book or watching TV or maybe even back in bed. His mom, who even now was on her way to slice and weigh fish at the market, her first and least favorite work shift of the day. His mom, who had never remarried, who had no family, no boyfriend, no time to make friends—meaning Reuben was all she had, Reuben the reason she worked two jobs, Reuben the person for whom she did everything in her life.

His mom, who would not be pleased.

"Oh, let there be a fire escape," Reuben breathed. "Oh, please." Swiveling his eyes to his left, he studied the precious, narrow strip of concrete keeping him aloft and alive. It appeared sound enough; there was no obvious deterioration. A brown crust of bread lay nearby (probably some pigeon's breakfast that he'd rudely interrupted), but that was all—no broken glass or other hazards. His path looked clear.

Reuben began shifting himself sideways, moving left, toward the back of the building. He kept his shoulder blades pressed against the brick wall behind him, his eyes fixed straight ahead on the featureless wall of the building opposite him, just a couple of yards away. He tried very hard not to imagine the dizzying drop below him.

He had progressed a few feet when his hand came down on the crust of bread. Without thinking, he attempted to brush it away. It seemed to be stuck. Glancing down now, Reuben discovered that the bread crust was actually a scrap of leather and that in fact it was not resting on the ledge but poking out of the bricks just above it. What in the world? Why would this scrap of leather have been mortared into the wall where no one would ever see it? Was it some kind of secret sign?

Reuben pinched the scrap awkwardly between two knuckles and tugged. It yielded slightly, revealing more leather, and through his fingers he felt an unseen shifting of stubborn dirt or debris, like when he pulled weeds from sidewalk cracks. He tugged again, and a few loose bits of broken brick fell onto the ledge, revealing a small hole in the wall. The brick pieces appeared to have been packed into it.

Reuben took a firmer grip on the leather and gave another tug. More bits of brick came loose. The scrap of leather turned out to be the end of a short strap, which in turn was connected to a dusty leather pouch. Carefully he drew the pouch from the hole and up into his lap.

Not a secret sign. A secret *thing*.

He should wait to open it, he knew. It would be far easier, far wiser to do it after he was safely on the ground.

*Why would this scrap of leather have been
mortared into the wall where no one would ever see it?
Was it some kind of secret sign?*

Reuben stared at the pouch in his lap. "Or you could just be extra careful," he whispered.

With slow, deliberate movements, Reuben brushed away some of the brick dust. The pouch was obviously old, its leather worn and scarred. It was fastened with a rusted buckle that came right off in his hand, along with a rotted bit of strap. He set these aside and opened the pouch. Inside was a small, surprisingly heavy object wrapped in a plastic bread sack. It was bundled up in yet another wrapping, this one of stiff canvas. Whatever it was, its owner had taken great pains to keep it safe and dry.

Reuben unbundled the wrappings to reveal a handsome wooden case, dark brown with streaks of black. Its hinged lid was held closed by a gray metal clasp, the sort that could be secured with a little padlock. There was no lock, though; all Reuben had to do was turn it. He hesitated, wondering what he was about to find. Then he turned the clasp and felt something give. The lid opened with a squeak.

Inside the case were two velvet-lined compartments, both shaped to fit exactly the objects they contained. One of the objects was a small, delicate key with an ornate bow; the other appeared to be a simple metal sphere. Both had the dark coppery color of an old penny and yet, at the same time, the bright sheen of a brand-new one. They were made of a metal Reuben had never seen before. Something like copper or brass, but not exactly either.

Reuben very carefully lifted the sphere from its velvet compartment. It felt as heavy as a billiard ball, though it was not quite as large as one. He turned it in his hands, gazing at it in wonder. What was it? He'd expected that the key would be needed to open it, but there was no keyhole. Looking more closely, he noticed a seam, scarcely wider than a thread, circling the middle of the sphere like the equator on a globe, dividing it into two hemispheres.

"So you *can* open it," he murmured.

Holding the sphere in his left hand, Reuben tried, gently, to open it with the other. He used the same gesture he had seen in countless silly old movies he'd watched with his mom, in which hopeful men drop to a knee and open tiny velvet-covered boxes, proposing marriage with a ring. He imagined he felt every bit as hopeful and excited as those men were supposed to be.

The two hemispheres parted easily, smoothly, without a sound, as if their hidden hinge had been carefully oiled not a minute before. The interior of one hemisphere was hollow, like an empty bowl. It served as the cover for the other hemisphere, which contained the face of a clock. What Reuben had found, evidently, was a pocket watch.

And yet it was a pocket watch of a kind he'd never seen, to say nothing of its quality. Its face was made of a lustrous white material, perhaps ivory, and the hour hand and the Roman numerals around the dial gleamed black. It was missing a minute hand, but otherwise the parts were all in such fine condition the watch might have been constructed that very morning, though Reuben felt sure it was an antique.

A wild fluttering started up in his belly. His pulse boomed in his ears. How much, Reuben wondered, might such an exquisite device be worth? Indeed, the watch seemed so perfect—so perfect, so unusual, so beautiful—that he almost expected it to show the correct time. But the hour hand was frozen at just before twelve, and when he held the watch to his ear, he heard no telltale ticking.

The key! he thought. Reuben's mom had a music box that his father had given her before Reuben was born. You had to wind it up with a key. It must be the same with this watch. A closer inspection revealed a tiny, star-shaped hole in the center of the watch face. Could that be a keyhole?

A glance confirmed his suspicion. The key lacked the large rectangular teeth of normal old keys, but rather tapered to a narrow, star-shaped end, small enough to insert into the hole. This was the watch's winding key, no question.

Reuben was tempted. He even laid a finger on the key in its snug compartment. But once again a warning voice was sounding in his head, and this time he listened to it. He might fumble the key, drop it, lose it. Better to wait until he was in a safe place. Better, for once, to resist his impulses. This was far too important.

Reluctantly he closed the watch cover and put the watch back inside the case. He was about to close the lid when he noticed an inscription on its interior: *Property of P. Wm. Light.*

"P. William Light," Reuben muttered, gazing at the name. "So this once belonged to you, whoever you were." He closed the lid, fastened the clasp. "*When*ever you were." For whoever P. William Light was, Reuben felt sure he'd stopped walking the earth long ago.

Reuben rebundled the case and tucked it back inside the pouch, then stuffed the pouch into the waist of his shorts—no small feat in such an awkward, precarious position. Now he was ready to move.

He took a last look at the hole in the wall, wondering how long the watch had been in there. It had been put there by someone like him, someone who found places that were secret to others. It could only have been *found* by someone like him, as well, which made its discovery feel very much like fate.

Just don't blow it by falling, Reuben thought. *Boy finds treasure, plummets to his death. Great story.*

It was with exceeding caution, therefore, that he began to inch sideways along the ledge. A wearisome half hour later he reached the back of the building, only to find that there was no fire escape. No windows, either, and no more ledge.

"Seriously?" Reuben muttered. He felt like banging his head against the brick.

His bottom and the backs of his thighs were aching and tingling. Another hour on this ledge and he'd be in agony. Yet it would take at least that long, and possibly longer, to reach the front of the building.

There was, however, a rusty old drainpipe plunging down along the building's corner. Reuben eyed it, then grabbed it with his left hand and tried to shake it. The pipe seemed firmly secured to the wall, and there was enough room between metal and brick for him to get his hands behind it. He peered down the length of the pipe; it seemed to be intact. He had climbed drainpipes before. Never at anywhere near this height, but if he didn't *think* about the height...

It was as if someone else made the decision for him. Suddenly gathering himself, Reuben reached across his body with his right hand, grabbed the pipe, and swung off the ledge. His stomach wanted to stay behind; he felt it climbing up inside him. Now that he'd acted, the fear was back in full force.

Clenching his jaw, breathing fiercely through his nose, Reuben ignored the lurching sensation and got his feet set. Then, hand under hand, step after step, he began his descent. He went as quickly as he could, knowing he would soon tire. The pipe uttered an initial groan of protest against his weight, then fell silent.

Flakes of rust broke off beneath his fingers and scattered in the wind. Sweat trickled into his eyes again, then into his mouth. He blew it from his nose. Every single part of him seemed to hurt. He didn't dare look down. He concentrated on his hands and his feet and nothing else.

And then the heel of his right foot struck something beneath him, and Reuben looked down to discover that it was the ground. Slowly, almost disbelieving, he set his other foot down. He let go of the pipe. His fingers automatically curled up like claws. He flexed them painfully, wiped his face with his shirt, and looked up at the ledge, so high above him. Had he actually climbed all the way up *there*? He felt dazed, as if in a dream.

Reuben withdrew the pouch from the waistband of his shorts and gazed at it. This was no dream. He began to walk stiffly along the narrow alley, heading for the street. One step, three steps, a dozen—and then he felt the thrill begin to surge through him. He'd made it! He was alive! He'd taken a terrible risk, but he'd come back with treasure. It seemed like the end of an adventure, and yet somehow Reuben knew—he just *knew*—it was only the beginning.